BY KAREN MARIE MONING

THE FEVER SERIES

Darkfever

Bloodfever

Faefever

Dreamfever

Shadowfever

Iced

Burned

Feverborn

Feversong

High Voltage

Kingdom of Shadow and Light

GRAPHIC NOVEL

Fever Moon

NOVELLA

Into the Dreaming

THE HIGHLANDER SERIES

Beyond the Highland Mist

To Tame a Highland Warrior

The Highlander's Touch

Kiss of the Highlander

The Dark Highlander

The Immortal Highlander

Spell of the Highlander

KINGDOM
OF SHADOW
AND LIGHT

KAREN MARIE MONING

KINGDOM OF SHADOW AND LIGHT

A Fever Novel

DELACORTE PRESS

NEW YORK

Published in the United States by Delacorte Press, an imprint of Random House, a division of Penguin Random House LLC, New York.

DELACORTE PRESS and the HOUSE colophon are registered trademarks of Penguin Random House LLC.

LIBRARY OF CONGRESS CATALOGING-IN-PUBLICATION DATA
Names: Moning, Karen Marie, author.
Title: Kingdom of shadow and light / Karen Marie Moning.
Description: New York: Delacorte Press, [2021] | Series: A fever novel
Identifiers: LCCN 2020042381 (print) | LCCN 2020042382 (ebook) |
ISBN 9780399593697 (hardcover; acid-free paper) | ISBN 9780399593703 (ebook)
Subjects: GSAFD: Fantasy fiction. | Paranormal fiction.
Classification: LCC PS3613.O527 K56 2021 (print) | LCC PS3613.O527 (ebook) |
DDC 813/.6—dc23
LC record available at https://lccn.loc.gov/2020042381
LC ebook record available at https://lccn.loc.gov/2020042382

Printed in the United States of America on acid-free paper

randomhousebooks.com

246897531

First Edition

Book design by Caroline Cunningham

Once more, with feeling,
for the irrepressible M . . .

A NOTE TO THE READER

———— • • ————

GIVEN THE COMPLEXITY OF the Fever World, I've included a lengthy glossary at the end of the book, offering definitions of people, places, and things, with reminders of past events.

However, before you begin reading *Kingdom of Shadow and Light,* I think you'll find the following notes helpful.

PRONUNCIATIONS

Ixcythe: ix-SIGH

Aoibheal: ah-VEEL

Ryodan: RYE-uh-din

Lyryka: LEER-ick-uh

Azar: uh-ZAR

Severina: sev-er-EEN-uh

Masdann: maz-DAHN

Y'rill: yuh-RILL

Draoidheacht: DROWD-hay-oct

Spyrssidhe: SPUR-shee

Sidhe-seer: SHEE-seer

Damhan-allaidh: dah-vin-OLLY

Gh'luk-sya drea: Guh-LOOK-swuh-dray

Sidhba-jai: shee-vuh-JYE

FAE

There are two courts of Fae: the Light Court/Seelie and the Shadow Court/Unseelie.

THE HIGH QUEEN OF THE FAE/LIGHT COURT

MacKayla Lane-O'Connor, mortal *sidhe*-seer who was altered by Cruce's Elixir of Life and is now extremely difficult to kill and nearly immortal. Although not fully Fae, she presides over the Light Court, comprised of four royal houses.

Each royal house usually has both princes and princesses, but many are dead and have not been replaced.

THE LIGHT COURT ROYAL HOUSES

The Princess of Winter: Ixcythe (full-blood Fae) (no known prince)
The Princess of Summer: Severina (full-blood Fae) (no known prince)
The Prince of Autumn: Azar (full-blood Fae) (no known princess)
The Prince of Spring: Inspector Jayne (human turned Light Court prince) (no known princess)

THE UNSEELIE KING/SHADOW COURT

The original Unseelie king abdicated power and stepped down (*Feversong*) but has not yet chosen a successor. He watches multiple contenders for his throne including Cruce, Barrons, and Christian MacKeltar.

There are two Shadow Courts. The original Shadow Court was created by the Unseelie king during his efforts to divine the recipe for the Song of Making, which the first queen refused to share. That court was destroyed when Mac sang the Song of Making to save the Earth from destruction (*Feversong*) by black holes gouged into the fabric of reality when the Hoar Frost king roamed Dublin (*Iced*). The current Shadow Court was created by Cruce.

Three of the king's four original princes escaped destruction. Cruce survived by magical means. The two humans that transformed into Unseelie princes, Christian and Sean, were unharmed by the Song of Making.

Original Shadow Court/Unseelie Royal Houses*

(The Four Horsemen of the Apocalypse)

The Prince of War: Cruce (the only original Court, pure-blood Unseelie left in existence)

The Prince of Death: Christian MacKeltar (human turned Unseelie prince)

The Prince of Famine: Sean O'Bannion (human turned Unseelie prince)

The Prince of Pestilence: deceased and not replaced.

*There are no living princesses from the original court.

New Shadow Court/Unseelie Royal Houses*

The Prince of Dreams: Masdann

The Prince of Fire: not yet seen

The Prince of Water: not yet seen

The Prince of Air: not yet seen

*There are no princesses in Cruce's court.

FAERY

The realm of Faery includes all of the Light Court, all of the Shadow Court, the Unseelie prison, the king's castle that adjoins that prison, the Hall of All Days, all the Silvers but not the worlds to which they connect, the White Mansion, the IFPs, which are fragments of Faery created when the walls between realms fell on Halloween (*Faefever*), and the queen's private aerie. Originally there was no Shadow Court. There was a single Faery Court until the Seelie king left, declared himself the Unseelie king, and created the Shadow Court. From that moment on, Faery not only continued to expand and grow but also to fracture in countless ways.

KINGDOM
OF SHADOW
AND LIGHT

PROLOGUE

───── • • ─────

ONCE UPON A TIME in a sun-kissed kingdom across the sea, there lived a fair princess whose life was an enchanted summer's dream. Her parents, the king and queen, were kind, generous, and wise, and there were no uprisings in the land.

The sunny-natured princess loved every acre of her demesne, from silvery lake to forested glen, from the quaint, cobbled streets of her provincial town to the sophisticated city beyond, and she knew precisely how her future would unfold. She would fall in love with a prince, marry and raise children, and live happily ever after in their halcyon demesne.

In that splendid, magnolia-drenched kingdom across the ceaseless blue, no one warred for the throne. No one thought about the throne. The royals sat it so well and justly, all hoped the king and queen would live forever.

That's not this story.

The princess of this story will never have children.

She fell in love with the beast.

The human part of me—I'm not sure how much of that remains—feels a poignant regret for babies that will never be born. But a life with Jericho Barrons is worth the price.

If I did have a daughter, I know what I would tell her, and it's not what the blithe pastoral princess across the cerulean divide would have said. That princess would have raised her offspring to be cheerful, kind, enjoy life. She would have told them small lives hold great rewards and gazed through the castle window, smiling at her children as they sunned with friends by the pool.

That princess would have taken her daughters shopping for prom dresses then wedding dresses as she aged gracefully, lavishing love upon her grandchildren and greats, and, after a long, happy life, she'd have been tucked gently beside the headstones of her beloved king and queen.

That princess is dead.

I'm Mac Lane-O'Connor, High Queen of the Fae, and the path to my throne was paved with grief, lies, betrayal, war, and murder, much of it committed by me.

My kingdom isn't sunny. Nor is it completely known to me. Dark, rain-drenched, cold, often iced, it encompasses multiple realms: the Mortal lands; both the Light and Shadow Courts of Faery, including the abandoned Unseelie prison; the White Mansion; the Hall of All Days; the corrupted Silvers, and who knows how far beyond.

My castle is a temporally and spatially challenged bookstore I conceal from the world, as there are many that hunt me.

My entire court—with the exception of the banished, fertile Spyrssidhe—wants me dead and will stop at nothing to strip me of power and remove me from the coveted throne.

As this woman, I would tell the daughter I'll never have: You are elemental, essential, connected to all things in the universe. You are a creature of alchemy, transmuting all you touch, for better or for worse. Choose wisely both what and how you touch.

I would raise her to stand for her beliefs no matter the cost, because at the end of the day, shadows come lean, mean, and hungry to devour those of uncertain principle. A divided will cripples. You must know what you want, what you believe in, and be willing to live and die for it.

I would tell her hope is priceless and fear brings death—not mercifully swift on an enemy's sharp blade, but slowly and far more painfully, rotting you from within.

I would charge her with the protection of the many who can't defend themselves, because some are born with great strength, resilience, and ability to endure, while others are not.

I would empower her to be the thunder. Be the storm. Be the lightning that crashes. Be the hurricane that whips the ocean into crashing waves, become the wild tsunami that reshapes the shoreline.

Because if you aren't the thunder and you aren't the storm, someone else is, leaving you a fragile leaf caught on the biting, chilling, killing wind of another's making.

I would share with her the wisdom and grief of a brutal yet immutable truth. For some of us life is not an enchanted summer's dream.

It's deadly.

You must be deadlier.

PART I

The fog comes on little cat feet, Carl Sandburg said.

When I was young, I loved foggy mornings in Ashford, Georgia. Peering deep into the mist in our backyard, I'd imagine all kinds of fantastical creatures: unicorns, dragons, perhaps even the great Aslan bursting forth from those billowy, low-hanging clouds, as friends from beloved childhood tales slipped into my day via a mystical, smoky portal.

The Fae have more than a hundred names for ice, which I used to think was overkill, but now that I live in Ireland, I've found I need nearly as many names for the nuances of fog that are as much a permanent fixture in my life as those infernal Dublin roundabouts I never manage to exit properly without looping around a half dozen times, muttering curses beneath my breath.

Shika, a lacy, delicate mist that frosts the streets with whimsical beauty; Barog, a depressing, oppressive, grayish vapor that clings damply to your skin; Playa, dry, ground-level, ribbon-thin smoky tendrils that kick about your ankles in gusts before vanishing; Macab, a sullen, bruised, bone-chilling effluvium commonly found in cemeteries that doesn't drift in on a brine-kissed breeze but oozes with palpable menace from the soil; Oblivia, a sense-distorting, sinister cloud of opaque white that settles abruptly and seemingly from nowhere, to send you tearing off in the worst possible direction, certain sanctuary is directly ahead.

But, here, it's not just the fog that creeps up on you on little cat's feet and sits back on silent haunches, watching you with slitted predator eyes.

Here, it's betrayal that stalks stealthily, inaudibly nearer, watching with eyes that are a hundred-shades-of-Fae-ice, for the perfect moment to stab you in the back.

FROM THE JOURNALS OF MACKAYLA LANE-O'CONNOR

HIGH QUEEN OF THE FAE

DARKDREAM

* • *

You were my town

now I'm in exile seeing you out

DUBLIN, IRELAND.

After the war to end all wars, my city is perfection.

Flanked by princes, the full complement of the Light Court marching behind me, I glide through the streets of Temple Bar.

Looming beyond the rooftops of shops and pubs, a blood-rimmed moon hangs so round and low it nearly obliterates the night sky, reminding me of another planet where—a thousand life-times ago—I stood between Cruce and the Unseelie king and felt I might ascend to the edge of night, hop a pine-board fence and bridge planet to moon in a single leap.

Earth continues to change, becoming more like Faery with each passing day, growing lusher, more opulent and fantastical, befitting a species of jaded palates and hungers extreme. We who rule this planet alter the very fabric of the universe. Mortal physics do not apply. We shape reality; it cedes to our will.

Hunters fly overhead, gonging deep in their chests. I glance up as they glide past the moon, and their obsidian wings against the scarlet-ringed orb causes an unwelcome lightning flash of memory to explode, briefly illuminating my mind—a gaze of midnight stained with crimson, a man's hard, challenging, measuring stare: *Who the fuck are you?*

Demented laughter might bubble up inside me, but there is ash where once embers burned, and laughter doesn't bubble.

Nothing does. I am a bottomless, still abyss.

The clarity granted by the memory fragment fades. I turn from the sky and back to the street.

Phosphorescent fog, driven by an azure ocean lapping at Ireland's shore, drifts in lacy skeins across cobblestones shiny from yet another rain, draping streetlamps and storefronts in pearlescent webs. As we continue our parade through the district, canopies of velvety blooms explode in our wake, tumbling from window boxes, erupting from rooftop gardens, while a thick carpet of sea-foam and cerulean grasses push up through stones.

Cobbled streets will soon vanish, reclaimed by rich mocha soil. Buildings will be enfolded in the embrace of vines and dragged down until entombed in the earth. This world will be as it should be again.

Pristine. Natural. Fae.

Fog soothes me; concealing, distorting, making all things seem possible. Creates a frame for illusion, brushing the world softer, more malleable. Narrowing my eyes to blur my vision, I fill that frame with things that once mattered to me, hold the images suspended about me, try to insert myself into the frame but . . .

There is nothing for me there.

Dublin will never again be what I remember.

Nor will I.

There is a final act to which I will attend tonight before turning my attention to matters of Court. The soil cannot reclaim a certain bookstore fast enough for me. I don't trust that the Cauldron of Forgetting will completely eradicate Barrons Books & Baubles from the deepest catacombs of my memory should the earth fail to swallow it and should I, one day, encounter it.

This city, this planet is void of human life.

I am the only trace of humanity left, and I am but a memory of a vestige of a shadow of that complex, elusive quality. Less than a whisper. I cannot hear it and would not know what it means.

Mankind has been scourged from the planet. The old gods are dead, leaving the Fae sole owners of a coveted magic-rich world. The Nine are— I terminate that thought.

A distant part of my mind engages a struggle to understand how I got here, how this came to pass, but I cannot put the pieces together. They exist beyond, in a place I sort of remember though not really, where, once, I was a very different being.

A daughter. Sister. Friend. Lover to a dark and ravenous beast.

But I can't feel what I can't feel.

There lurk only distant, vague shapes, nebulous things that chafe at my mind, oddly familiar yet void of meaningful substance.

I lack context. A complete and utter dearth of it exists within me.

I apprehend existence in terms of stasis and change.

Beyond that, there is only today.

There is a single way this type of today can be endured.

If it amuses.

As I near the entrance to Temple Bar and approach the stone archway draped in blossoms that scent the air with exquisite, poisonous-to-all-but-Fae, night-blooming jasmine, a sharp-edged frost that refracts a thousand shades of sapphire slips down alabaster petals, rushes along vines to the street.

Ice encases the pavement and explodes toward me, licking at my feet. I invoke a carpet of crimson snow blossoms to shatter his ice as the ghost of a mirthless smile curves my lips. A ghost because the possibilities for us, once so ripe with limitless, thrilling possibility, are something I will be forever haunted by, yet never know.

"Mac." The greeting floats from the impenetrable shadows the Unseelie king has donned as a cloak. He walks the night as the night. Not even I can pry elements from Fae to reveal his true nature. He will remain unseen unless he wishes to be otherwise. His power is staggering.

"Your queen now," I parry.

"Never my queen. You chose," the darkness thrusts.

I didn't, I don't say. Let him think I did. Preferable to the truth. There was a time I demanded truth, no matter the price. Now I pursue the mercy of illusion with the fervency of a terminal sinner seeking absolution.

He doffs his shadow cloak and reveals himself in a pool of cobalt light that streaks his black wings indigo as they ruffle, shift, and settle. I shiver and draw my cloak more snugly about me. Though I am immune to the *Sidhba-jai,* I am not immune to the Unseelie king's allure. He's lust incarnate. Sexual in a set-your-teeth-on-edge kind of way that can make a woman who needs nothing comprehend the meaning of primitive, mind-consuming, addictive desire. Every nuance of darkness heaped upon every fist and blade of power, he is magnificent, nearly omnipotent and eternal. Explosive carnality saturates the air around him, charging the atoms between us with a wordless, erotic, irresistible compulsion that I yield to him in any manner he seeks. I wonder, with a catch in my breath: Am I still his weakness? Is he still unable to say no to me?

He possesses all those things the Light Court should have had. Might he bequeath those gifts upon us? Would he be willing? Could I, Queen of Illusion, Queen of Fire, seduce him into it? Even were I to fail, at least I'd share his bed. A shared bed is oft parlayed into concessions.

"Never." The words are soft. His gaze is not.

The king, who should have been my greatest ally, my lover, my consort, is my greatest enemy. But "should" means nothing to the Unseelie king.

"Should" is a false god that skews your aim before you even act, someone once said to me. *"Should have" is a devil that devours your soul once you've acted. Desire, Ms. Lane, is the only acceptable motivation. What do you want?*

I *want* my king.

And he will never be mine.

He will never forgive the things I've done.

Were I capable of caring, it would explode my heart. We were—are—the twin faces of a Janus head. Born to rule, side by side, day by night, sun beside black star.

When his dark court sifts in to assume position behind him, the ice of his nocturnal kingdom surges forward again, crashing into the flame of my day court. Tiny, fiery volcanoes meet geysers of glittering ice in the street between us, blazing radioactive, freezing, blazing again, as our powers battle without involvement from either of us. A hairline fracture splinters the ground between us and might widen into a planet-shattering chasm if we are fools.

Our very existence is at odds.

To merely stand facing each other is to war.

It should not have been this way.

I scan his army. Not with the assessing gaze of an opponent, rather, covetously. There—in the back, draped in a doorway—is one of the gossamer caste I didn't see until it was too late or, rather, didn't understand what I was seeing. Behind the king are two of his princes, massive black wings concealing a structure far stronger and more lethal than barbed titanium, capable of enfolding tenderly or crushing in an Iron Maiden embrace.

His Dark Court is a night symphony sung into existence from notes of satin, dreamy midnight, motifs of surreal slumber and dark stars. They are seductive and beautiful with no abominations among them. Focused and fiercely intelligent, they make many of my court seem simpletons. Even the most inventively lethal of the Unseelie are exquisite, commanding the eye to linger as they approach. And all the more deadly for it. Humans were unable to turn away. Compelled to look while Death stalked ever nearer, yet it was not his army—

I terminate that thought, too. "Recall your ice," I hiss.

"I am not the one that needs to get a grip on that element."

"My court is fire, heat, life."

"MacKayla Lane was fire. You are colder than ice. Emptier than a void, you birth only illusion. Blossoms may spring forth as you walk, but in your wake you leave destruction."

I suffer a moment of disconcerting duality where I'm myself yet I'm also an ancient queen, hearing precisely the same accusation from a different king and I wonder why it keeps ending this way. We had the added bonus of knowing the potential mistakes.

Still, we made them.

"Have you come to gloat? I will never grovel before you. None of us will." It's a lie and we both know it. His power vastly exceeds mine. If he demands, we will comply. We have no choice.

Perhaps I never did. Perhaps it was all chiseled in stone, long before my birth, painted on the ceiling of a bookstore that was erected as a bastion, to keep the monsters at bay.

Instead it birthed one.

His gaze shifts and flickers, filled with nuances beyond my understanding. He makes to speak, once, twice, yet says nothing. Starry shadows rush in his eyes, a muscle flexes in his jaw. For a time, I think we might stand and stare at each other in silence for all eternity. I wonder what he sees in my eyes. I wonder if there's anything in them at all.

I spin and walk away.

Or try to.

My feet remain rooted to the ground.

I wait, gaze locked with his, spine infused with an inexplicable tension, inhabited by a prayer I don't understand and have no idea how to voice.

He exhales heavily and extends a hand toward me. Slowly, aware the tiniest wrong move might incite battle. His hand is open, palm up, framed by long, strong, elegant fingers. Once, I dropped kisses in it. Felt it cradling my head, my jaw, spanning my waist, resting in the small of my back. "Take it. Let me show you the way back."

I don't say back where. The implication is "all the way."

As if I would trust him.

Could he really do that? Return me to where this all began? Before it went so terribly wrong? Envy is a razor poisoning me as it cuts—that he has such power to move us through time and possibles. I don't possess it. Suspicion poisons me further. His offer is illogical. I would not make such an offer in his position. He's goading me to trust.

What is trust but expectation one will behave in keeping with one's past actions?

God knows I didn't. Why would he?

I wonder, with what tatters of bitterness and pale shreds of emotion yet remain, why hope springs eternal; that stubborn element that exists within us—despite being carved and mutilated, twisted and maimed, brutalized and stripped of all we hold dear—some shred of our being that insists on clinging to the belief that there's a way back, or a redemptive way forward, or that it will all have been worth it somehow, even when we know full well we're clinging to nothing more substantial than a hope of a memory of a dream we can no longer feel and that may not have ever even been real.

How do we get so lost?

One infinitesimal misstep here.

One seemingly inconsequential decision there.

Often so simple as: If only I'd lingered to brush my hair, gone to the bathroom, delayed to make a phone call. If I'd chosen to walk forward instead of turning left that day in the foggy Dark Zone. If I'd not met with the enemy, accepted a glass of tainted wine, believing peace between us possible.

Staggering that the fate of worlds can hang upon such incremental, seemingly innocuous moments!

Staggering that one's very soul can be stripped away by such moments, leaving the pain (which will all too soon be dulled beyond recalling) of the loss of a way of being I will never know again.

I gaze at him in frosty silence.

He searches my eyes for a taut, suspended spell of time, and, when finally he speaks, emotion infuses his words with complexity I no longer fathom yet feel the vibration of—a nearly forgotten bass in my gut, a resonance where once my heart beat red-hot and true.

I endeavor to disdain it as the weakness it is, but some part of me suspects I'm fooling no one, not even myself. He has all the power.

And kept himself, too.

Jericho Barrons is, as ever, indomitable.

"Ah, Mac," he says roughly, "you've forgotten everything."

Not everything, I don't say.

I remember enough to wish I'd never been born.

1

I had a dream
I got everything I wanted

CHRISTIAN

THERE'S A BAT IN my belfry.

It darts erratically in the cramped timber housing four stories above me, swooping between bells, offending me on a figurative level because there was a time the phrase "bats in the belfry" suited me, and literally because I've been chasing the bloody bugger through my castle for the past twenty minutes.

The few maids willing to work on my blustery, forbidding estate consent to do so only if I keep the fortress free of the furry winged fellows that invade Draoidheacht as if it's connected by some mystic portal to a densely populated bat cave they're avid to escape. It's entirely possible—given my uncles' many raids on the king's unpredictable library in the White Mansion—we've introduced a number of disguised ingresses into the stronghold. The sprawling keep began as a peculiar place and has become only more eccentric of late. It's changing, restoring parts of itself, expanding others.

Personally, I don't mind the little guys. They're liminal creatures like me, mammals that can fly, existing on the fringes, living in the darkest, hidden reaches, feared and mistrusted, and, as I was soaring through the vaulted rooms chasing it, I had to laugh, considering the situation from the creature's perspective, which surely believes itself hunted by some enormous mythical god/demon of vampire bats.

Black wings unfurled to a majestic wingspan, then tucked swiftly to spiral behind the flying mammal through narrow, winding stone corridors, that's rather what I look like.

I nearly nabbed it twice, but as it flaps circles above me in quarters too tight for my width, I concede, it's outmaneuvered me. For the moment.

I drop down on a pile of the Unseelie king's mammoth books, prop my chin on a fist, and stare irritably up at it, aware of the portrait I paint; a savage, winged Unseelie prince thwarted by a tiny flying rodent. One would think, as Fae royalty—notably the prince known as Death, for fuck's sake—I might point a finger in a general upward direction and delete it from existence or, at the very least make it have a heart attack and topple to my feet.

One would be wrong.

I've spent most of my tenure as the lethal prince struggling to keep myself from inadvertently using the power I possess. I've no idea what I'm capable of until the dark magic erupts from me in some horrifying way.

The bat finally settles, clinging to a timber upside down, membranous forelimbs folded about its body, swaying gently. I've gone motionless. As long as I remain still, the creature may decide the malevolent god/demon has flown the coop and venture into the open so our ludicrous chase might begin anew: *What does Death do all day? Chase bats.* Christ. Hardly the life one envisions for such an entity.

As I wait, I glance about the ancient domed chapel. Like the rest of the castle, it's stuffed to overflowing with goods purloined from the Unseelie king's true library, and still we've barely made a dent in transporting the collection from within the White Mansion's halls. Jars and chests, artifacts, tomes, and scrolls litter the pews of the long-unused oratory and are strewn haphazardly across the flagstone floor. Larger relics are propped against the walls. I've learned a great deal about the Fae, yet precious little about the part I play in it. I need a card catalog for the king's eclectic collection. Not that it would help at this point. Assuming the library was ever arranged in some semblance of order upon those physics-defying shelves that careened vertically, horizontally, and diagonally, and soared to heights even I hadn't reached with my wings, those items we've removed certainly aren't now. It's chaos.

The problem, I fume, is that I really don't want to kill the bat. Each creature has its place in the balance of things. Bats pollinate, eat insects, consume roach dung; they're a necessary part of the cycle.

I frown, realizing I may have been going about it wrong. Perhaps it's not Death that needs to contend with the bat. I summoned the necessary elements to extinguish the ice-fire at the abbey without negative repercussions. Granted, that was before the Song of Making was sung and the Fae restored to our inimical, ancient power.

I tip my head back and stare up, open my senses, try to access the furry, winged life above me, sink into it, become it. Ah . . . there it is. Tiny heart hammering, a dangerously overworked drum accelerated by fear. And yes, it does think me a demon. I taste the fog of panic in its brain. It hovers on the verge of cardiac arrest from terror and frantic flight. I did that to it. It mortifies the Highlander-druid in me, raised to protect. It's but a wee bat doing wee bat things. Having a fine life.

Until. Me.

I withdraw, sink into my heart, and waft a tendril of the love I hold for my land and kin upward, envision it cocooning the creature, soaking into its sleek body. The mammal's heartbeat instantly slows, and the fog lifts from its alien, simple mind.

Relinquishing my constant, tiring grip on the *Sidhba-jai*—the lethal sexuality exuded by royals, both dark and light—I open my druid senses and tunnel down through the floor of the chapel, past the dungeon, sink beyond the stone slab foundation of the castle, to the fertile soil and deeper, penetrating layers of rock to touch the bountiful, magnificent energy of the—

Stop, my gut roars, *there's danger here!*

I abort the connection and slam my walls back up.

What the bloody hell was I thinking? I know better. The last time I permitted myself to absorb the power of the earth as it seeped up through the soles of my boots, I walked into the Cock and Crown and killed every man, woman, and child within. One hundred forty-two people died that day, exploding into clouds of black dust. Had I gone home, I'd have murdered my entire clan instead.

I banished the druid part of myself that afternoon, locked him away and never reached outward with my Keltar senses again, concluding the druid part of me had absorbed the earth-power without realizing it, and the uncontrollable Unseelie part of me had seized it, using it to lash out with massive, destructive force. A grand "fuck you, can't touch me" reminding me just who's in control. And not.

Still . . . what if I'd concluded wrong?

I narrow my eyes, rolling the subtleties of what I just tasted in the earth over my tongue, forcing myself to analyze it void of emotion. I'd long tried to divine how Cruce managed to subdue the *Sidhba-jai* and glamour himself so effortlessly. How he'd done *everything* so easily. Having just felt the enormity of power available to me, I'm willing to bet he was never using his own will but siphoning the elemental energy of nature, which is boundless and eternally replenishing. Willing to bet it was the source of power for all he did.

Which means it's the source of mine as well—and I cut myself off from it after one accidental misuse of power. Granted, one with terrible consequences, but there might never be a better time to try again.

The maids are absent.

Sean's an unkillable prince.

If I summon power today and fail, only bats will suffer. I can't continue living as a fractured entity, drenched in darkness, cut off from human contact, eternally at war with myself, searching books for mystical answers that may not even exist.

I quiet my mind and open my druid senses, warily at first then wider. Such a profusion of power blazes at the core of the planet; it's staggering, dazzling, humbling, and I'm part of it! We all are, but few have such a direct connection.

As I invite the abundance to enter me, it slams into my body with such force I nearly go flying backward off the pile of books. Regaining my balance, I relish the sensation of being blazingly, intensely alive, intimately bound to the planet. I missed this, the boons of my druid heritage. I vibrate with energy, bristle electric with it. I fear I might explode from so much pent—

Bloody hell, I know what I did wrong that day in the pub. It's so bloody simple I can't believe I didn't see it before.

Pent. Meaning trapped. When I'd subconsciously drawn energy that day, I'd done nothing with it. I'd not even really understood that I'd absorbed it. Then I'd strolled into a pub, with every atom of my being saturated with volatile power.

It had to *go* somewhere.

I hadn't chosen what to do with it. I'd offered it no outlet, no purpose. Nor had I returned it to the earth. Invited yet undirected, it did what any power would do, what it will do again, if I fail a second time.

Explode from me in my purest form—Death.

Gritting my teeth, rigid with the effort of containing the primal force that knows no bounds and obeys no laws once summoned but for those imposed upon it, I tip back my head and gaze upward.

The bat is calm, settled on a timber near a broken pane of stained glass.

Meticulously, I shape the earth-power, aim a tightly channeled gust of frigid air upward while simultaneously inviting a rush of warm wind in through the shattered window, giving the little guy purpose and direction. Bats don't like extreme cold. As the icy current encroaches from below, it does precisely what any heat-seeking creature would, flaps through the aperture into the warmth I've created beyond.

I touch its mind as it leaves. *Tell your kind to avoid my castle. Make it legend.*

Castledemonbadbadbad.

Yes, I murmur in its mind.

I break contact and instantly shunt the bulk of excess power back to the soil.

As it fades from my body and settles seamlessly into the earth, I laugh out loud—och, bloody hell, what a rush! Finally, I understand what I am and how to control my terrible potency.

Fae and druid are not so different as I thought. Both draw power from nature. Now I must learn to summon only the amount of power necessary for whatever I choose to do. Guileless as a child tasting ice cream for the first time, I'd gorged that day in the Highlands before I'd walked into the pub. I'd nearly gorged again now. Lesson learned.

I push up from the stack of books and stalk across the room to a mirror draped in dark cloth that's covered with cobwebs. Like the bats, spiders have overtaken my castle, draping their sticky webs everywhere. The maids give me an earful about them, too.

I rip away the covering and stare at my reflection. A towering, dark skinned, raven-haired Unseelie prince with ancient, cold eyes, black wings that unfurl to an eighteen-foot span and trail majestically to the floor stares back at me, torso bare, clad in faded, torn jeans and combat boots.

I've wearied of slicing shirts and sweaters, wear little in the privacy of my keep. Tattoos slither restlessly beneath my skin, a torque writhes like a living snake around my throat, and eyes that once flashed iridescent fire settled some time ago into a distant, wintry gaze that glitters in shards of black, blue, and crystalline ice, a cruelly arctic landscape beneath a frosted, sapphire dusk. My eyes don't match my heart. I ken why people fear me.

This time, instead of trying to summon internal energy to cast glamour, I beckon a dash of power from the soil to restore me to the man I once was. Gently. An invitation, as I was druid-trained. We work together, the earth and druids. We don't seize or steal.

The young Scot, Christian MacKeltar, is reflected in the glass.

I glance down at my body, marveling—both in the mirror and without, I'm me again! It was that simple. There's that killer smile the lasses used to love, void of actual death, the eternal five-o'clock shadow on my jaw unless I shave twice a day, the dark hair gathered in a thong at my nape. No longer inhumanly tall, I'm six foot three, lean, muscled, sporting a six-pack and amber tiger-eyes. Christ, I haven't seen this man in years. No one has.

I reach back to touch my glamoured wings. They aren't there.

You still haven't figured out how to cast a glamour that temporarily displaces your wings, allowing you to sit comfortably, have you? Mac said to me not long ago.

"I have now." I can't stop smiling. It took me years to figure this out. Knowledge is power. For the first time since I transformed into an Unseelie prince, I feel strong, alive, centered and radiate none of the lethal sexuality of a Fae prince.

I blink at my reflection, dazed. *None of the lethal sexuality of a Fae prince.* Glamoured like this, I'm a normal man—at least, as normal as a walking, lie-detecting druid can be—with a man's normal impact on women. A long forbidden fruit is no longer poisoned for me—I can *fuck* again! No longer will I kill any woman I touch. I can unleash a raging hell of celibacy on a woman. Or ten. I'd begun to think I'd never live to see this day. My mind races, as I try to decide where I might find the nearest warm, willing—

Och, Christ, what is *that*?

I narrow my eyes, staring into the mirror, opening my senses, but I can only see it, not feel it. It exists . . . *beyond* . . . inaccessible to both the Fae and druid parts of me.

Behind my reflection, a dense black cloud hovers, begins to ooze slowly near. As wide as my wingspan, roughly four or five feet tall, it's not a Shade; they were all destroyed when the Song was sung. Nor is it a Fae; my wards are powerful and none can enter my kingdom.

I whirl to confront it, but the amorphous, inky cloud rears back and up, retreating to the ceiling. Though it possesses neither form nor face, I feel oddly as if it's . . . assessing me. Taking my measure.

As suddenly as it appeared, it vanishes.

I wait for it to reappear. When it doesn't, I dismiss it. Present problems are problems. I refuse to entertain absent ones. Today is a banner day. I'm no longer at war with myself. No longer must I hide in my dark and stormy castle. I can have sex again. The agony of immortal life without intimacy had been making me feel far less human than turning Unseelie ever did. Dark prince I could deal with. Never taking a woman to my bed would have eventually turned me into the monster I resemble. Isolation dehumanizes. All of us, hero and villain alike, crave intimacy, connection.

I shrug off thoughts of the brief apparition. Draoidheacht is an odd place. Perhaps something I brought here from the king's capricious library contained this entity, and, if so, it will come again. I'll discover its nature and deal with it.

At the moment, there's a single thing on my mind. As I turn hastily for the door to find the nearest willing woman, I catch a stack of books and relics with the toe of my boot; tomes go sliding, artifacts topple, I hear the tinkle of breaking glass and freeze.

Glancing down to confirm my suspicions, I snarl.

I've shattered a flask, one that shouldn't have even been there. I'm careful to store the pernicious beakers on high shelves, well out of the way. But there it is, and I've splintered the narrow neck, yet not the voluminous carafe, within which rainbow-hued gems glitter and flit about like thousands of tiny luminous fireflies, as if suddenly agitated.

Or excited by the prospect of freedom.

I stoop and quickly clap my hand to the jagged, broken neck of the flask, but brilliantly colored mist leaks through my fingers, seeps around my palm, as my blood mixes with sparkling smudges of pink and green, orange, violet, yellow, and blue.

Cursing, I drop it, cracking the bell-shaped carafe as well, and back warily away. I just added Unseelie prince blood to the damned thing. Lovely. I wipe my hand on my jeans as if to dispel all trace of whatever mystical creature is about to appear.

The day Dani O'Malley unstoppered a flask in the Unseelie king's treacherous library she released Crimson Hag, the entrails-collecting, ghoulishly knitting Unseelie. In that rabid bitch's venomous hands I died a thousand deaths, lashed to the side of a cliff, disemboweled over and over. I've no love for the king's unholy beakers.

Tendrils of kaleidoscopic mist spiral up from the shattered flask, hover in the air, solidifying and dissipating, darting to and fro, assembling and reassembling in a manner that seems to imply whatever was contained within spent so long in non-corporeal form, it can't quite puzzle out its original shape.

As if we didn't already have enough problems. Old gods walking the earth; the Fae more powerful than ever before; the High Queen in absentia; the acrid, unmistakable stench of sulfur and brimstone growing ever more pungent on the wind, heralding the dawn of a terrible war.

Just then, my perimeter alarm booms: *Katarina McLaughlin has entered your kingdom.*

Great. I altered my wards to permit her passage so she might visit Sean when I wasn't about. So continues the fuckage of my plans to get laid.

No longer buoyed by my recent discoveries, chafed by the on-slaught of unexpected events, I drop glamour and become Death in all my towering darkness and savagery, wings wide, teeth bared, as I wait to discover just what the bloody hell I've unleashed on our world.

2

Killing me softly with his song

Ixcythe, Princess of Winter, manifested in the sacred Grove of Creation where no living being could die an unnatural death, where not even a High Queen could kill a Fae with one of the two Seelie hallows. Both of which, she brooded, as she pushed back the hood of her ermine cloak and rearranged her iced, silvery hair, were in the hands of mortals.

As was the True Magic of their race, sequestered within Mac-Kayla Lane's breast by the human-turned-queen, Aoibheal, who'd been secretly planted among them by the Unseelie prince Cruce while masquerading as V'lane.

The Seelie had been deceived and betrayed over and again.

Once, the lush, eternally blooming Grove of Creation had teemed with Fae nestled beneath gnarled roots, frolicking in the sky, roosting in a vast aerie of limbs, even dwelling symbiotically within the ancient towering trees planted at the dawn of time by the sacred goddess herself.

The grove was an enchanted paradise shaped by She Who Sang the Song that beckoned all things into existence—eons before the Tuatha De Danann had been born—and upon choosing to depart from this realm to planes unknown had bequeathed the divine melody of creation to the First Queen of the Tuatha De.

The First Queen had infrequently used parts of the Song, but there had never been a need to release the entire melody again.

Until recently.

Though the grove was not part of Faery, the Seelie recently regained their long-erased knowledge of it, along with countless other memories. They'd lived here once, during an all too brief golden hour in their existence. During the between of what they'd been and what they'd become.

Ixcythe tipped back her head, staring up at colossal trees ten times the size of the largest sequoias on earth, lush and green, vine-draped and rustling with jewel-toned birds and plush-pelted creatures, wishing memory of that peaceful era had never been restored.

When she sensed the disturbance of Azar, Prince of the Autumn Court, sifting in, followed by Severina, Princess of Summer, she stiffened. The two royals had answered her summons. If they, like her, were suffering similar debilitating effects, these next moments were fraught with peril.

Inspector Jayne, a human–turned–Spring Court prince, was one she would never summon. She wanted him dead and the rightful power of the royal line restored to a full-blooded Seelie. The other princes and princesses had been slain and not yet replaced. Now they might never be, given the curse afflicting their race.

It was but the three of them. It would have to be enough.

Digging sharp nails into her palms to distract from the cacophony of emotions raging in her frozen breast, Ixcythe bared her teeth in a glacial smile, noting, despite the fact that no Fae could be killed within the hallowed grove, the others had chosen to sift in at a considerable distance from her, forming a cautious royal triangle within the clearing beneath the vast canopy of branches.

We trust no one. Not even ourselves.

But they were going to have to, or they were doomed.

The Song of Making had been sung on the world to which the

seat of their power was bound. Unforgivably, Aoibheal had *tethered* the Fae to a planet. And never in the history of time had they been in such proximity to the entirety of the powerful melody as it was released.

It changed them.

Slowly at first and welcomed by all, restoring powers, reinvigorating their essence. Enhancing pleasure, a thing Ixcythe should have pondered more deeply, intuiting what the resurgence of satisfaction implied.

In Aoibheal's absence, the Seelie had quickly dispersed from the High Court where the queen had forced them to reside for too long and ruled them too tightly. They'd reclaimed their singular kingdoms and ways of life, indulging their desires, roaming freely between Fae and mortal realms.

For a time, existence was all they might have wished. She'd sculpted her castle a thousand glittering shades of shadow and pain, returning her demesne to its long-lost grandeur, lavishing her lakes and streams with exquisitely frosted patterns, adorning the silvery labyrinth with the iced sculptures of her enemies. The Autumn and Summer kingdoms had also been restored to their unique elemental majesty. Not the Spring kingdom, though. Jayne wasn't fool or capable enough to try to seize it.

But the changes to their race continued. Slowly at first.

Then escalating.

Enacting a hellish transformation.

The Unseelie king's Song had undone what the Cauldron of Forgetting had accomplished.

Restored their memories.

All of them. Including their origin, this grove, and She Who Sang the Song.

It had restored something else as well, thus the need to pierce flesh through to bone to maintain composure.

At least, that's what had happened within the Winter Court's boundaries. Ixcythe sought to know if all of Faery had suffered the same or if it was her kingdom alone. Yet she feared—yes *feared*—to leave her castle and walk out in the open to discover it for herself.

Hence this clandestine meeting.

She glanced first at Azar, his skin the color of autumn sun glancing off chestnuts, eyes glittering with the saffron and mandarin of twin Samhain fires, then at her summery antithesis, the voluptuous, gilt-skinned Severina, with her ankle-length golden hair and molten gaze.

She would never be able to glean truth from their faces, nor they from hers. Royalty were the most obdurate of the Sidhe, capable of concealing and withstanding much. Unless—Ixcythe shuddered imperceptibly at the thought—their condition continued to deteriorate.

"Why have you summoned us here?" Azar demanded imperiously.

"How," Ixcythe countered icily, waving a hand to banish her long white ermine cloak, too warm for the sultry grove, "did you know where *here* was?"

Memories erased by the Cauldron, they'd long ago forgotten they'd once lived in the empyrean orchard. That they'd been able to find it told her much of what she wanted to know, and she felt a flash of spiteful satisfaction that their memories, too, were restored. Suffering was *so* much more bearable when it was done with company.

Her query was met with silence.

"It happened to you as well. Your memories have returned." Memories too long, too burdensome to tolerate. Ixcythe had stolen the Cauldron from Aoibheal's kingdom and tested it on several of her subjects, hoping it might restore order from calamity. It hadn't worked. It was broken, useless. Old feuds had reawakened, and there were countless ancient quarrels among the race of immortals, endless grudges, eternal grievances. "As has emotion," she added flatly.

Azar said coolly, "I have no idea what—"

"I've shown you my hand," Ixcythe snapped. "Dare you disrespect the honor?" Royalty observed rigid formalities. They were too powerful to behave otherwise. To eschew courtesies was to incite war.

After a long moment, he inclined his head and said stiffly, "It is as you claim, both memory and emotion have returned."

Following suit, Severina nodded. "The Summer Court is . . ." She trailed off, compressing her lips to a thin metallic line.

"Chaos," Ixcythe finished coldly. "They can't kill, so they indulge in other amusements, using their powers against each other in horrific ways." The inhabitants of the Winter Court had become abominations, better suited to the Unseelie prison. If either memory or emotion alone had been restored, the effects wouldn't have been so catastrophic. And if only memory had returned, they'd have learned to deal with it. It was the emotion fueling their actions that was so deadly. The two combined were toxic to beings that had suffered neither for an eternity.

Azar was silent a moment then said tightly, "I've had to seal my castle against them. My own court refuses to hear, much less obey, me."

It was a damning admission for him to make, that he feared his subjects; an olive branch offered by a desperate prince. No less desperate, Ixcythe accepted it. "I've done the same." She could raise no army against humans, rally no troops, enforce no orders. Her court had devolved into mindless, emotional savages that she could no longer bear to hear or watch. If not for the strength innate to those who ruled the royal houses, she'd be in that dreadful courtyard herself, at this very moment, as gruesome as her subjects.

After a moment, Severina joined the delicate truce. "As have I. My court is vile as Unseelie, all of them!"

Not quite all. The lesser castes were younger, possessing shorter memories. Some had even been conceived in this Elysian grove, before the Elixir rendered the Seelie barren. The last born caste, the Spyrssidhe were unaffected by the insanity afflicting the Tuatha

De. Ixcythe despised and envied them for it. When the changes had first begun to escalate, her court had hunted them, driving the tiny Fae into hiding. "You speak as if it's only your court suffering. You feel it, too. The same desires. The hunger. The *need*." Obsessive. Consuming. Mind dulling. Painful for beings who'd not suffered pain for time eternal.

Azar's face tightened. "Unlike those fools, I control it."

Void of emotion, the Fae had long toyed with impassioned beings, to feel some shallow sensation. But they hadn't always been empty husks.

Severina shrugged. "We will learn to manage our passions again, and once we do, our existence will be richer for it. The Song hasn't undone our immortality."

Ixcythe seethed, "*Yet*. It has not undone our immortality yet. Are you fool enough to believe these changes will abruptly stop for no reason?"

The species from which they'd stolen the Elixir warned them they would regret it, as the price for immortality was the destruction of the soul. They'd deemed it a fair exchange. Why gamble on reincarnation or an elusive, illusory, never-once-glimpsed deity, when they might guarantee eternity with a sip?

Belatedly, they'd discovered the body was the house of passion, not the source of it. Souls slowly scorched to ash on a forbidden pyre, they'd traded a vibrant, impassioned, up to five-century-long lifespan for an eternity of shallow sensation. Still, they'd considered it a worthwhile trade.

Ixcythe knew now that they were feeling emotions again, mortality couldn't be far behind. The Song wasn't restoring them to the height of their power.

It was taking them back.

All the way back.

To what they'd originally been.

Mortal.

Despicably, vulnerably *killable*.

KINGDOM OF SHADOW AND LIGHT · 33

Soft-bellied and pathetically weak as mortals.

The Song had destroyed the Unseelie.

It was remaking the Seelie.

Both the Light and Shadow Courts had been deemed imperfect to varying degrees.

None knew where Aoibheal had concealed the Elixir of Life. Or how much was left. Whatever remained, Ixcythe vowed to have the first drops. She would *not* become mortal again. She despised these memories, these *feelings*. She'd torn apart the queen's bower, searched every glade, brook, and glen around it, every inch of the High Queen's castle seeking it. She'd dispatched scouts far and wide, to search. None had returned.

If the Goddess who'd seeded this grove had encountered the Tuatha De Danann at any other point in their history, she'd have destroyed them. But they'd met when the Fae had recently imbibed the Elixir, were celebratory, joyful, still fertile, not yet starved for sensation, and were benevolent, nurturing the land upon which they dwelled.

"How are we to take back what is ours from the human that holds it, if we cannot control our courts?" Ixcythe hissed.

Her royal counterparts said nothing.

Was no one thinking clearly but her? "The three of us must use the Elixir, force it on our subjects!"

Azar shot a look of such incendiary rage the meticulously sculpted icicles adorning her gown began melting, dripping to her slippered feet. "Do you have it?" he snarled, hands fisting.

"Am I behaving as if I have it?" she snarled back. "Use your power against me again, Azar—if only upon my gown—and I'll finish the war you start!"

"Had I the faintest idea where the Elixir was I would have drunk it instantly then rained it down upon my kingdom! And fuck your ugly gown! You think you can finish a war against me, princess?" he sneered. "Try."

By D'Anu, they were behaving little better than their lust-enraged courts. Ixcythe pressed a hand to her breast, beckoning the ice of her kingdom, restoring the frozen accoutrements of her dress, cooling her temper.

Eyes blazing, shuddering with the effort of subduing his rage, Azar said tightly, "Send a bit of that this way. If you would be so kind."

She wanted to ice the bastard, case him entirely in a glacial block. Slice the slab into tiny frozen pieces and feed him to her court. But she needed allies. Piercing her palms with her nails, she gusted a chilling breeze in his direction then did him the honor of graciously swirling it around him.

After a few moments, the heat Azar was throwing off abated and his burning gaze dimmed to banked embers. "My apologies, Ixcythe. The gowns of Winter are the epitome of loveliness."

"And the grandeur of your Autumn lands beyond compare," she rejoined, not meaning a word of it. Then she turned to glare at Severina, who snapped, "Well, I don't have the blasted Elixir. Have you searched the royal bower?"

Ixcythe snapped back, "Yes, and clearly I wasn't the first to do so." She'd feared one of them had found it first. But their volatile tempers were proof enough they hadn't. "The chest is nowhere to be found. Aoibheal must have moved it before she was interred in the Unseelie prison by Cruce, divining some inkling of her fate." Prophecy, a gift possessed by the queen alone, the limited ability to foresee events as they might unfold, now belonged to MacKayla Lane. Assuming the mortal ever discovered and learned to use it.

Severina shrugged dismissively. "What's the use? Even if we find it, the Song has been sung. It will nullify the effects of the Elixir again."

Azar snorted contemptuously. "Have the suns of summer cooked your brains? The Song destroys what it deems imperfect only while being sung. It doesn't continuously eradicate imperfections. If it did, nothing imperfect could ever exist. It would have been impossible for the king to create the Shadow Court!"

Ixcythe said, "Azar is correct. Though the effects settle into the planet's core, restoring ancient magic, the Song balances the scales a single time." Leaving sentient beings the free will to do as they wished—which was precisely as it should be. Gods such as the Fae answered to no gods. And gods were another of their problems—the Song had reawakened their old enemies. Should they learn the Fae were handicapped, becoming mortal . . . She shuddered, unable to complete the thought.

Azar said, "Which means the Elixir will mute emotion, restore immortality, yet do nothing to diminish the power we've regained."

Ixcythe inclined her head. "Precisely. MacKayla Lane possesses Aoibheal's knowledge and will know where the Elixir is."

Severina rolled her eyes. "What good does that do? We tried to kill her repeatedly and failed. That beast stands in our way, and she has the spear!"

"We sought her demise rashly. Before our memories were regained," Ixcythe said coolly. "Before we recalled this place."

"And we have a powerful advantage," Azar purred, with a smile. "Our memories have been restored, but she has only the knowledge of a queen who abdicated power before the Song was sung; a queen far younger than we are. We know more about our history and the powers we possess than she does, recall magic she never learned."

"But she's vanished," Severina argued. "None know where to find her."

"We send a message and make her come to us. Here. Where our lifeblood can't be shed by her or the beast with whom she consorts."

Comprehension dawned in Severina's eyes. "And we tell her if she gives us the Elixir, we'll stop trying to kill her. A splendid plan!" She added with a sneer, "Mortals always hunger for an end to war." While the Fae hungered for the exquisite pleasures of it, so long as they weren't in the fray.

For a moment, Ixcythe couldn't even speak, she was so stupefied by Summer's idiocy. "We tell her *nothing*, you bloody fool! An end to war for our 'queen' would best be achieved by watching us all die. She blames us for the death of billions of mortals! She despises us."

Severina huffed, "A queen isn't supposed to despise her own people!"

"Oh, by the blessed D'Anu, we're *not her people*! She's mortal! She doesn't want us any more than we want her. She wants to use our power for her people, not ours!" Ixcythe practically screamed. "Yet you think we should say, 'Oh, great queen, please help us because we're regressing and becoming mortal again and if you don't give us the Elixir, we're all going to die, leaving your world in peace, granting you the ultimate vengeance against us!' What is *wrong* with you?"

"It wasn't even us. It was the bloody Unseelie!" Azar said, his eyes blazing with fire and fury. "We scarce killed any humans at all compared to the Shadow Court! Who knows to what heights we might have risen by now had we not been twice deceived, twice enslaved to a human queen!"

"Precisely," Ixcythe spat savagely. "Hundreds of thousands of years wasted, obeying a queen we believed was one of us, only to have that traitorous bitch pass our power to another *human* who was born and bred to hunt and kill us. If MacKayla Lane catches even the faintest whiff that we are becoming mortal again—" Ixcythe couldn't bring herself to finish the sentence. Their own queen would destroy them. The idea of Fae being hunted by *humans*, helpless foxes scattering, terrified, on a reverse Wild Hunt, to be slaughtered like lesser beasts—how their "queen" would enjoy that! Never! "She must never know what's happening to us. That we've regained our memories, and we're reverting. *No* one can."

"If we do become—" Severina broke off, shivering, before managing to grind out the detested word. "—*mortal*, we could always move our courts to this sacred place."

Ixcythe fisted her hands so tightly the sharp tips of her nails slid through her flesh, puncturing the backs of her hands. That was it. At the appointed hour, when they met with the queen, the princess of Summer would no longer be speaking. "So that in our madness, rendered unkillable by the Grove, we could torture each other until we finally died of natural causes? Have you forgotten how many centuries that would be?" She soothed herself a moment, envisioning the sunny warmth leaching from Severina's skin, as she iced her blue and pale, forever frozen yet fully aware of her imprisonment, erecting her as yet another statue in one of her many glacial gardens where she was wont to store those she despised. "And that's assuming countless stolen eons don't instantly catch up with us once we reach a critical point in devolution, and we crumble into piles of ash!"

Azar went still, rendered immobile by the abhorrent thought. After a moment he growled so savagely the ground trembled beneath their feet, "That will never happen! You summoned us. That means you have a plan. What is it?"

Ixcythe smiled. "We want something back," she purred venomously. "We make that thieving human bitch want something back, too."

3

Anybody want a drink before the war?

MAC

CRUCE LIED.

No surprise there.

Technically, he counters mockingly in my mind, although he no longer exists, *I didn't.*

Technically, he's correct. The seductive master of deception was also a master of precision. Loopholes, details, omissions, and evasions were his forte.

After confirming the key to using the High Queen's power lay in forging a connection to the planet itself, Cruce also told me new queens were weak queens and required anywhere from fifty to five hundred years to attain their full strength and powers.

What he failed to share is fifty to five hundred years is the approximate length of time required to be able to wield the full powers of the High Queen *only if the queen is already Fae* and, although the True Magic can be passed to another species, the passage of it alone isn't enough to turn that species Fae. Which I recently discovered in the tenth or eleventh millionth file I've reviewed during my incarceration in this chamber wherein time moves differently than in the mortal realm.

I assumed the transfer of Aoibheal's power would transform me completely. My hair changed. Last time I saw myself in a glass, my eyes were eerily backlit, banked with luminous fire. I possess considerable Fae magic, from sifting to transforming elements to rebuilding things that once existed, to affecting the weather with my mood. I assumed *all* of me would change. Like Christian. Sean O'Bannion. Inspector Jayne.

I assumed wrong.

There are only two ways for a mortal to become truly, fully Fae: be transformed by a fully Fae High Queen, or reside for a lengthy period of time at the Light Court without ever leaving (bet the First Queen never shared *that* with the Unseelie king!).

Five thousand years at the Light Court, to be precise. I don't have that much time. I suspect I've already burned through months, mortal time, sequestered here.

After I sang the Song of Making and destroyed the black holes, Barrons and I went to Faery to meet the courts I was to rule. At first, the Light Court had rolled out the red carpet and made a great show of willingly embracing me as High Queen.

Their feigned acceptance had lasted exactly four days. Then the attacks had begun, forty-two of them in twelve hours, each more cunning and treacherous than the last. They'd tried to trap us with wards, separate us, spell us, imprison us, so they could steal my spear and use it against me. They were so determined to kill me in order to put a pure-blooded Seelie on the throne, they were willing to die to accomplish it. Barrons and I had been forced to slay countless Fae, primarily Winter Court, who proved my most savage, relentless enemy.

We'd sifted back to the bookstore, to find a way to buy time so I could learn to use my power. It wasn't as if it came with a convenient instruction booklet, or, if it did, that booklet had been buried somewhere within a gazillion chaotic files inside me.

When Barrons told me about the chamber the king created for his concubine before he finished the White Mansion, wherein time moved differently than the mortal realm, I realized it was exactly what we needed.

There, I would sequester, study, and learn to use the Song of Making so I could restore the walls between the realms of Mortal and Fae. If I couldn't rule the Fae—and they'd made it clear they would never accept me—at the very least, I needed to contain them.

Barrons had no idea how time moved in the suspended chamber, only that it was much more slowly. I might spend a few centuries within, while only a few months passed in Dublin. Or, he warned, it might be longer.

We deemed the lost time a risk worth taking. If I attempted to stay in Faery or the mortal realm, the Fae attacks would only keep coming, and I'd never learn to use my power. That was the Light Court's plan; so long as they kept me on the defensive, I could never go on the offensive.

Once I was inside the chamber, Barrons would stand guard beyond it, in the corridor of the White Mansion, until I exited. At some point during my confinement, I figured out how to attach the chamber to the bookstore and moved them both, better concealing us from our enemies.

I have no idea how long I've been in here, but it feels like centuries to me, and I've just discovered what I need isn't within my reach. I intended to walk out only when I was adamantine; a lethal High Queen capable of doing whatever must be done. But unless I move to Faery and manage to survive five thousand years in the thick of a court that wants me dead, I'll remain a partially endowed queen, unequal to my predecessors, forever.

Although I now know the true names of the Seelie, with a mortal tongue I'm no more capable of summoning my subjects than I was V'lane/Cruce. That alone will give me away to my court. *She is not fully queen,* they will hiss. *She cannot even command our attendance,* they will laugh. And do their best to kill me for eternity.

The problem is I hold power that, if taken from me by a Fae, will be used to enslave and, likely, eventually eradicate all humans. I must succeed at seizing my rule and governing the Fae. If I fail, I fail the entire world.

A little pressure there for a bartender from Georgia.

I'd sigh, but I seem to have forgotten how. Time in this place has left me feeling as disembodied as the *Sinsar Dubh* when it scraped me from my skin. I've suffered no physical demands. No urge to eat or drink, relieve myself, or stretch stiff limbs. I've sat, staring inward, sorting through a deluge of files and, although I've found much of use, I've uncovered nothing about the Song of Making other than legends, myths, and tall tales.

Still, it hasn't been a complete waste. I've learned how to do disturbingly horrific things. I've acquired an assortment of ancient, revolting spells. I rediscovered my lethal crimson runes, along with a cruel assortment of other weapons within the queen's arsenal. I know how to create wards and barriers, have memorized names and places, Fae history, possess an understanding of the Light Court I didn't before. I feel the burn of magic in the earth, can amplify and direct it in stunningly cruel ways.

Unfortunately, I still confront the same two choices I had the day I entered: find a Fae to whom I can transfer the burden of power, trusting them to leave our world forever and never return (never going to happen—our planet is steeped more richly in magic than ever before, and the seat of their power is bound to it—they will never relinquish it willingly) or get out there and try to govern the deadly Fae with what tools I possess.

If only Cruce had lived. I never thought I'd think that.

We'd made a Compact, he and I. I pledged to give him the queen's power once we saved our world, and he pledged in return to remove the Fae from our planet and never disturb us again.

If only.

Initially, I'd hungered to divest myself of the reign. It hadn't taken me long to realize ruling the Fae would be a never-ending, dangerous job and, as with any job I tackle, if I *had* to do it, I'd become obsessed with doing it well. Goodbye, humanity. I'd have no time for it.

What I've discovered leaves me no reason to remain sequestered here.

I'm all I can be without being Fae. Admittedly, I could spend another few thousand years in here reading files, but they may or may not teach me anything of use, while more time will pass in the human realm.

Disengaging from my internal study, I direct my gaze outward and push up from the sofa, stretch and twist, bend and turn, reacquainting myself with my body. God, it feels good to move, to be a living, breathing, hot-blooded woman again.

Speaking of hot-blooded.

Barrons.

The quiet burn of his nearby presence kept me sane. I recently felt Ryodan's and Dani's as well. Dani'd been troubled, so I'd projected a quick text onto the screen of her phone. Having suspended Barrons Books & Baubles in the clouds, I've felt little else. This chamber mutes what lies beyond.

Abruptly, I can't wait to grasp the knob of the door, feel it with my hand, yank it open, rush out of here, be corporeal, be part of Dublin again. I hope I haven't missed too much. I have no idea how long I've been in here in mortal time and that concerns me deeply.

I stand, readying myself. I must never let anyone discern what I've learned about my limits or that I have no idea how to use the Song. I must convincingly feign that I have access to all of the True Magic and make the Seelie believe I am their deadly-to-displease High Queen. Ruling with kindness, fairness is not an option. Mine is a cruel, avaricious, jaded species. How is one to command savages without savagery?

There's only one thing capable of keeping the Light Court in check: fear. If they catch the faintest whiff of weakness, they'll descend on me like a pack of anorexic Shades.

I must be cruel. Monstrous. Merciless.

Do the things I've learned to do, that will make them cringe like whipped dogs at my feet. Things that will make *me* want to cringe, although I dare not.

MAC.

The word explodes in my skull, roared by Barrons with urgency in his voice I've heard on precious few occasions.

Those times he believed I was dying.

I'm not.

For Barrons to roar in such a voice—to risk interrupting what he thinks I'm still doing here—that means someone else is in mortal danger.

And whoever it is matters deeply to me.

4

I am immortal

I have inside me blood of kings

CRUCE

"IT IS DONE, MY liege," the prince said as he entered the laboratory.

"You did as I requested?"

"Of course."

"Did you encounter any difficulties with your task?"

"None."

"And how was your first solo journey into the realm of mortals?"

Masdann smiled, dark eyes glittering in a face MacKayla Lane would recognize should it visit her in dreams—and it certainly would, but only in nightmarish romps through her subconscious. It amused Cruce to employ this particular genetic stamp for his Morpheus prince, and it would prove a powerful weapon. Humans and Fae alike always responded favorably to the face and form—with both desire and fear—and Cruce wanted the best the world had to offer his children.

"Far more intriguing than Faery, when I switched the Cauldron with your replica. More daring even than releasing the *damhan-allaidh* into their world. The mortal realm is more abundant and exotic than I imagined," Masdann said. "So many slumbering, so many doors from which to choose."

Doors into their subconscious minds. Cruce envied the ability he'd given his prince, command of a realm none had ever mastered, few could even walk within without succumbing to madness. He himself had successfully navigated only the outer perimeter of it for a short time, long enough to bed a certain *sidhe*-seer. He considered Masdann his finest creation, a prince capable of slipping in and out of the Dreaming, of altering the underlying currents of another's psyche in that unpredictable no-man's-land of ever-shifting terrain.

The Dreaming was fashioned of cosmic matter even more mysterious than the Song of Making. Logic and physics flowed differently there. What took place in the Dreaming—if tampered with properly, in what mortals called "lucid dreams"—could have lasting physical and emotional impact on the dreamer in the Waking, undermining convictions, confusing the heart, even ending a mortal's life.

He'd given each of his princes powers that were inordinately useful to him, his to if not possess, at least command. "And you enjoyed Chester's?"

Masdann's eyes glittered. "It was a veritable feast. Drunk, they succumb swiftly to slumber; their minds are malleable and weak."

"You saw Ryodan?"

"I did."

"And he believed you were Jericho Barrons?"

The prince inclined his head. "He did."

Cruce laughed softly. The devil was in the details, and he'd captured the nuances of personality unique to the owner of the arrogant, savage face he'd purloined to perfection in the simple yet defining inclination of his head; the tight slice of negation, always to the left, the way he stood and moved, the precise nuances of his eyes and voice. Dressing him was simple: the prototype favored expensive Italian suits, crisp shirts, and ties.

The original was his enemy, which made being served by a copy that obeyed his every wish and called him king even more enjoyable. One day, they would meet, face-to-face, original and copy, and, on that day, Barrons would know he'd been beaten by Cruce, all spoils to the victor.

Including the woman.

Cruce was feeling celebratory. His plans hinged upon Masdann's ability to pass as Barrons to those in MacKayla's inner circle; today had been a crucial test. "That is all for now. You may go."

"As you wish, my liege." Masdann turned, melting with inhuman grace from table to wall to door, nearly unseen.

As he closed the door, Cruce smiled, but it vanished swiftly as pleasure at Masdann's delight in the world above turned to rage at his own creator. King to a court of his making, Cruce had found the act of creation illuminating, understood more about his ex-liege than ever before.

He despised him all the more for it.

Creation was a kingly right, but it was accompanied by responsibility for what one created. The ex-king's Unseelie were lab rats first, children only much later, by default. He'd created ugliness when he might have spawned beauty. He'd made hundreds of thousands of horrific Unseelie, knowing they would be abhorred by the world. He'd made them rapacious, insatiable, and incapable of ever being sated. To live in such a fashion wasn't life at all. The Song of Making had been a mercy for the Unseelie destroyed, laid at long last to rest.

Toward the last, the ex-king had fashioned his four princes: Famine, Pestilence, Death, and War, and, while he'd made them superior to the rest of his castes in countless ways, possessing both emotion and the intellectual capability to govern it, Cruce's three brothers had been barren-minded fools governing barren domains. Death alone held a realm Cruce coveted, and he had no intention of letting the Highlander pup survive long enough to learn the true extent of his power.

Unlike his ex-liege, Cruce had chosen to elevate his royalty, gifted them powers to create, not destroy (although they could destroy, in inventive and horrific ways if they chose—point being: they had a choice), fashioning the princes of Dreams, Fire, Water, and Air; each lording power over a unique realm and, while he'd granted them staggering sensuality, he'd not hobbled their potential for evolution with the lethal Eros of the Fae. He'd taken the best of all he'd beheld in three quarters of a million years and blended it into forms capable of withstanding the tests of time, resilient, adaptive, ferociously intelligent, majestic. He'd not made princesses for his Royal Houses, deemed them unnecessary, liabilities, vying for power against his princes. His royal caste would have the right to select their own consorts.

He'd birthed a Shadow Court of fierce survivors, as brilliant as the stars, as elegant and imaginative as the cosmos, as potentially deadly as the vacuum of space. He'd succeeded in all the areas his king had failed. He'd created a court of entities that could thrive on any world, walk in the warmth and sunlight, in the open day, welcomed. At least those who were visible. Some of his children were too clever for the eye to spy.

The king had abdicated his throne years ago yet still hadn't chosen a successor. Occasionally the great dark cloud of kingly power would come and hover above Cruce, watching as he worked.

Then simply vanish. Leave, as if unconvinced, as if the choice of his correct successor wasn't as fucking obvious as the fucking sun in the sky.

He'd proven himself the superior king. What the bloody hell was the old fool's problem?

Although his court addressed him as their ruler, it wasn't enough. It would never be enough until the bastard ex-king acknowledged that Cruce was the better king and conferred all his power upon him.

He never betrayed you, Cruce, one of the king's many skins had said. *He betrayed none of his children. He gave up what he held most dear for them.*

Meaning that, although the king had, unbeknownst to all, completed the Song of Making, once he'd realized using it to make his concubine Fae would destroy the Court of Shadows, he'd chosen not to use it.

Cruce snorted. "Too little, too late, old man." One benevolent act did not an immortal lifetime of torment unmake.

Here, in this arena beyond time, where he'd labored for nearly as long as MacKayla had quarantined herself in a similar place, sorting through her new power—he knew because his laboratory afforded a private view of hers—he'd birthed a dark court beyond reproach, and bestowed upon them a gift of immortality far superior to that which the prior court had been given.

So many things the old half-mad king might have done, but he'd created his court only to find a way to save his concubine. Cruce had created his court for the pleasure of creation.

Motive defined results. Flawed motive, flawed results.

A sudden, unexpected motion in his periphery jarred him from his thoughts.

Cruce turned his head and watched through the shadowy, burnished glass that joined their chambers as, at long last, MacKayla Lane moved for the first time in several centuries, if one counted the way time moved in their suspended arenas. Slowly, she rose from the sofa, raised her arms above her head and stretched, long, lean, and lovely. In her dimly lit chamber, she shimmered with Fae radiance as she turned, twisted, and bent. Platinum hair swept the backs of her thighs. Green eyes shimmered with otherworldly luminescence. Deep within them glittered the fire of her Summer Court, the ice of her wintry realm. Like him, she was thesis and antithesis, fire and ice, equal capacity for beauty and horror. The high temper and passion of a mortal in the body of a Fae queen, nearly immortal herself, thanks to the elixir he'd given her at an intimate, uncomprehending moment. The concubine had drunk the queen's elixir, which eventually scorched her soul to ash. The elixir Cruce gave MacKayla had no such side effect. It left her soul—and immense passion—intact. Just one more way Shadow Court ways were superior to the Light Court.

Once, he'd had her beneath him. He had buried himself inside her, felt her essence to his core. Her power and potential were intoxicating; she was his equal in nearly every way. She'd been unaware of him then, despised him for taking her against her will. In his book, that time didn't count. He would erase it from hers.

If I'd met you first, she'd once offered.

You might have loved me, he'd finished for her. *And if you'd loved me*, he'd stopped and waited.

You might have changed, she'd said softly.

He'd seen truth in her eyes. He'd gifted her his half of the Song of Making, he—Prince Cruce of the Tuatha De Danann—had saved the world for a single kiss, a kiss that evoked the finest in him, that told him, had events played out differently, she might have chosen him over Barrons. Of course she would have. The playing field between him and Barrons had never been level. That would change.

I am not your Barrons and will never be, he'd told her. *Nor would I wish to. I am Cruce of the Tuatha De Danann, High Prince of the Court of Shadows. And you are MacKayla Lane-O'Connor, Queen of the Court of Light. Convince me on another day you would have chosen me as your consort.*

She'd convinced him—and kept her word to grant him four hours before she released the melody. Four hours to inter himself far beyond the Song's lethal reach, with aid of the bracelet he'd demanded in exchange for the contract they'd signed.

As she moved for the door, he narrowed his eyes, studying, measuring her. The power she'd channeled had increased tenfold, as majestically restrained and graceful as her lovely body.

Eyes alight with amusement, he wondered if she'd finally discovered his omission, ergo her departure from the chamber. She would never be full queen. Not without living in Faery for an extended period of time. And she would never survive five thousand years in Faery without him at her side, protecting her. He alone could glamour her, make her seem full queen even to the Seelie. He alone could summon her court, making it seem *she* was the one capable. Not even Barrons could keep her alive amid such deadly enemies for as long as was necessary to transform her. With Cruce at her side, the Light Court would heel like whipped dogs. Together, they would be unstoppable.

He wondered how long it would take, how much she would have to lose before she finally saw him for who he was. And who he wasn't.

Never her enemy.

Had events played out differently.

Wings arcing high, black feathers ruffling and resettling, he stood and moved for his own door.

Both had sequestered in places where time moved differently, testing their power, refining it, becoming more.

She believed him dead. Many were the times he'd envisioned her face when she discovered he wasn't, and that a new, vastly improved Court of Shadows had been born and was ready to claim its rightful place.

"So it begins," he murmured, as they stepped simultaneously from their chambers and into the world again.

5

---•◦•---

Truth is seldom found when a woman is around

CHRISTIAN

AS THE RAINBOW-HUED MIST morphs into a whirling tornado of color, I wait to see what it becomes, ready to duel to the death. I will suffer no disemboweling, dismembering, dis-anything-ing ever again.

When it finally solidifies and stills, fully manifested, I stare, baffled. "Mac?" I explode. Followed by an incensed, "For Christ's sake, put some clothes on."

"Who is Christ?" Mac asks.

"What?"

"I do not know that name," Mac says, with uncharacteristic formality.

I frown. How did Mac end up in that flask? What are the odds it would be the precise one I kicked? Coincidences raise every suspicious hackle on my spine, and I've got a lot of them. When insane things start lining up in sane patterns, someone's manipulating you and having a grand laugh while doing it. "What are you doing here?"

"You released me."

"Yes, but how did you end up in that beaker in the first place?" It's a struggle to keep my eyes on her face. I can have sex again. My body hungers. She's a beautiful woman and, although I've been disgusted with Mac at various points in my life (all of which I've gotten over; she's as much a pawn on this ever-tilting stage as I am), I've always found her attractive. From perky, determined pink Mac, to blood-and-gore-covered black Mac, she's the faint whiff of chlorine in a sparkling pool on a summer's day, hot, sun-kissed skin, wed to something deliciously, dangerously darker and complex. I like complicated women. They smell like sex to me. To hell with stiletto heels and cleavage. Give me a woman with the dichotomy of ice in her eyes, fire in her body, honor in her heart, and the oft-necessary dishonor of thieves in her soul. I find duality irresistible.

"Put some clothes on," I order, scowling. She's queen of the Fae; she can will them into existence. Why the bloody hell is she naked?

"I possess no attire."

"Glamour yourself."

She gives me a blank look.

I turn, stalk to the mirror, grab the dark cloth puddled on the floor, whirl and fling it at her. "Drape that around you."

"Is my form not pleasing to you?"

"Cover yourself." The body is frequently drawn to places it shouldn't go. Perversely, the more forbidden and unpredictable the partner, the more erotically combustible in bed. Mac is both forbidden and unpredictable. After years of enforced celibacy, I'm indisputably combustible.

She stoops, collects the cloth, and drapes it about her shoulders. Covering nothing.

"Clutch it closed."

She does.

I relax infinitesimally. At least parts of me do. "Why are you here? And what were you doing in that flask?"

"I'm here because you released me. I was in that flask because that's where I was until released." She glances down at the shattered beaker. "You broke my flask."

I'm struck by a sudden suspicion. "Your name *is* Mac, right?"

"That is not my name."

"Who are you?"

"You may call me the librarian."

"What?" I say blankly.

"Do I speak a language with which you are unfamiliar, or are you unusually dense?" she purrs coolly.

I roll my eyes. She does snark as proficiently as the woman she resembles. I shoot her a glacial glare, but she only shoots it right back at me. "What is your query?" she snaps.

"Query?"

Speaking slowly and scathingly, as if to a complete idiot, she says, "What portion of the Library are you having difficulty accessing?"

I blink, surprised. "You can tell me where to find things in this mess?"

"That is the function of a librarian." As she turns to scan the jumble of oddities gathered from the White Mansion, the piece of fabric slips from her shoulders, and she's once again nude, I'm once again uncomfortable, and apparently she's deeply offended as she hisses, "This is not my Library. What have you done with it? It's but a small portion. You've destroyed my filing system!"

Seething, I grit, "Have you a different form you can wear?"

"I knew precisely where everything was. Do you have any idea how long it took to arrange the contents with such meticulous precision?" she seethes right back.

"Don't make me repeat myself," I growl.

"Yes," she snarls. "I do."

"Assume it."

She shimmers, shifts, and suddenly Dani is standing in front of me. Nude. Snarling, I pivot sharply. Christ, this just keeps getting worse. Back when I was half mad from the horrifying process of turning Unseelie, I'd clung to the ideal of innocent young Dani as desperately as I'd clung to the tatters of my eroding humanity. Thoughts of her gamine, effervescent charm had driven back the soul-distorting darkness. Seeing her naked makes me feel vile. "Put the bloody cloth back on. Do you have another form besides that one?"

"You are difficult to please."

"Are you covered?"

"I am," she says tightly.

I turn back and suggest just as tightly, "Perhaps you could get smoky and indistinct again."

"Perhaps you aren't the only being that requires a mouth to communicate. If you prefer me smoky, do not expect replies to your queries."

A niggling thought takes root in the back of my mind. "How long ago did the Unseelie king create you to manage his library?"

She cocks her head, her eyes go eerily distant, then, "I have been in existence for seven hundred seventeen thousand three hundred and twenty two years, four months, and seventeen days."

"How do you even know that? What are you, a walking cosmic clock?"

"Perhaps I possess an internal device that records the passage of time."

The potential ramification of her lengthy existence sinks into my brain. If the king created these two forms for his librarian three quarters of a million years ago, how then does one explain Mac and Dani? Precisely how deviously—and intimately—did the Unseelie king tinker with his caste of *sidhe*-seers? Mac and Dani's birth mothers are known *sidhe*-seers, but no one has any idea who sired them. Is this why the *Sinsar Dubh* was able to settle so comfortably within Mac as an unborn fetus? Why Dani possesses such a diverse array of powers, unlike most of her kind? Why, perhaps one of the Hunters, the king's preferred steeds, selected her to transform into one of their species?

Was the bloody Unseelie king Mac and Dani's father? Had he

predetermined both their eventual birth and forms eons ago? Cruce was a master planner. The king was Cruce on steroids from hell.

I voice my suspicion about Mac and Dani's parentage aloud, to which the draped Dani replies, "There are no references to a 'Mac' or 'Dani' of which I am aware in the king's Library. I'm unable to answer your query."

"Did the Unseelie king have any children?"

She sweeps a derisive gaze over me from head to toe, end to end of my still extended black wings and arches a brow.

"I meant through the actual act of procreation," I clarify coolly.

"I have little familiarity with that word."

Because Fae don't procreate. Well, allegedly they don't. And to think this day had begun swimmingly well. At least, once I'd gotten rid of the bat.

"Shift back to Mac." I find her more bearable, although neither form is comfortable to me, especially nude. One woman is intimately bound to Barrons, the other to Ryodan. And although I thoroughly enjoy pissing off the Nine on occasion, this is not one of the ways I'd select to do it.

She complies, but the moment she shifts to her other form, the dark fabric slips from her shoulders.

She's Mac again.

And naked again.

As luck would have it, that's when Kat walks in.

6

・ ● ・

I am immortal
I have inside me blood of kings

JERICHO BARRONS

MACKAYLA LANE, HER GIVEN name.
    Just-Mac, as she stood nose to nose with me, in the flesh, in my bookstore for the first time, demanding information about the *Sinsar Dubh.* I'd relive that day ten thousand times. The woman from my mural had finally walked in; a formidable darkness feathered in deceptively bright plumage, radioactive with vengeance, passion, and hunger.

She couldn't see herself then. But I could.

Rainbow Girl, ah . . . that one gets me every time.

Beautiful monster, beast to my beast, capable of doffing every last vestige of her humanity to do what must be done.

Queen of the Fae, unwilling successor but no less committed for it.

The woman who sifts into Barrons Books & Baubles is all of those things to me, and more. I see her in every shade of who she is, has been, and will ever be.

Patterns have begun to shift. Our future is uncertain.

Not whether we will remain together.

I will destroy civilizations, raze worlds, turn back time, shatter the very fabric of existence to assure that.

But how we will remain.

7

Nothing compares to you

MAC

"WHO'S IN DANGER?" I demand as I materialize in the bookstore.

Barrons surges up from the chesterfield and stalks toward me, a ripple of dark, tattooed muscle, midnight eyes glittering bloodred as he rakes a feral gaze from my face to my feet and back again. Primitive energy charges the air between us; his beast is close to the surface. Dangerously close. There are times I adore him this way, especially in bed.

But not like this. Never like this. His beast is devouring him from the inside out, with cruel fangs of starvation. The trousers of his impeccable Armani suit are rumpled and hang loose on his hips, his jacket is wadded on the floor, shirt unbuttoned, sleeves rolled up, tie lying in a shredded heap. An ancient silver cuff is slack on his wrist.

Whatever he is—Basque, Mediterranean, an ancient unknown race of immortal beings—his skin is pale, stretched taut, and I know, if I press my ear to his chest, I'll hear no heartbeat. His cheekbones are blades in his chiseled face, and when he speaks, I glimpse fangs. He needs to eat. Now.

"Travails occur. And will be dealt with," he growls. "What is this moment?"

Time, space, problems disappear as I savor the joy of seeing him again, of being alive one more day, at his side. *The first time I've laid eyes on you in God knows how long.* Time, during which, he'd patiently, devotedly stood guard, my eternal bastion, starving to death. What the man wants from me, the man can have.

Act like it, flashes in his savage face, *if only for a moment.*

Between the difficult past and the uncertain future resides the only moment we have any power over: now. We can make that moment ugly or beautiful. We can lose it to fear, or strengthen it with hope. And sometimes, we can only shore ourselves with bracing moments to strengthen ourselves for the brutal ones to come.

I lunge for him, taking him down to the chesterfield beneath me. We meet in a kiss of such ferocity and hunger that his fangs pierce my lower lip, filling both our mouths with the coppery taste of blood.

"Not Fae yet," he murmurs. "You bleed human. Mostly."

"Others must never know." He can employ spells to help me conceal it. I understand his hungers and deepen our kiss, spilling more blood into his mouth. When at last we separate, there's a hint of color in his face.

"How long was I in the chamber?"

"How long did it feel to you?"

"Centuries."

"Mortal time, you were gone two years, one month, and seven days. It's currently five years, three months, and nine days since the Song of Making was sung."

I stare at him, horrified. I thought I'd been gone months, not years. "And you stayed here the entire time? How did you survive without food?"

"Lor was of assistance on occasion."

"What did I miss? How are my parents? Dani? Dublin, the world?" I ask, trying to wrap my brain around such an enormous lost chunk of time.

"Until recently, things were quite calm. Once you vanished, aside from opening a club in Dublin, the Fae were unusually quiet."

I notice he didn't address my question about my parents or Dani. "And now?" I ask warily.

"Your mother is missing."

My heart slams violently in my chest a single time, skips several beats, and for a moment my lungs are locked down so tight I can't breathe. I right myself on the chesterfield and clench my hands, resisting the mushroom cloud of fear and fury that's trying to explode behind my sternum. Although I once joked that my worst nightmare would be a kingdom of immortal Seelie with a full range of human emotions, it's their very dearth of emotion that makes them a lethal foe. They think and act; patient, detached sociopaths, and, after my battle with the *Sinsar Dubh*, I understand the monumental advantage of laser-focused thought, unencumbered by feelings. I will be no less remote and controlled. I unclench my hands and inhale slowly. "How long?"

"Since this morning."

"A short time. How is that cause for alarm? She often goes off on her own to—"

"Her presence can no longer be felt in the mortal realm."

"You branded my mother?" Fury blazes in my blood, not because of the brand but because if my mother isn't in the mortal realm, that means she's in Faery. Taken there by a *Fae*. One of *my* Fae. I'm High Queen. I'll crush them all. Turn them inside out. Leave them writhing in immortal agony. I have a veritable armory of soul-destroying (not that they have souls) spells to use against the fools. What Fae dare attack my family?

"Thank me later. And it's not precisely a brand. Rather a GPS tracker, void of emotional bond. I did the same with your father."

"When?"

"When you were the *Sinsar Dubh*."

Barrons thinks of everything that matters to me. I used to find his heavy-handed tactics irritating. I sometimes still do, but they're difficult to dispute when they keep saving my life and the lives of those I love. "Can you feel anything else about my mother? Is she frightened? Have they harmed her?"

He slices his head in negation, and the man who never repeats himself says gently, "Tracker only."

"Where is my father now?"

"At Chester's with Ryodan."

"Safe?"

"As long as he doesn't step outside the club."

"Have you told him that? Impressed it upon him vigorously?"

"We haven't told him your mother's missing."

Because he knows I want to be the one to tell him. And only *after* I've gotten her back. I sink back into the sofa, pressing a hand to my thundering heart. My court just said: *Fuck you, MacKayla Lane. We're coming for you and we're going to mow down those you love most*. "Ryodan better keep him safe," I hiss.

"He will."

My mother. Gentle, kind, loving, good-to-the-bone Rainey Lane is somewhere in Faery with the monsters I'm ill equipped to rule. Bile rises in the back of my throat. I quell it swiftly. Useless emotion. I can't hunt her alone. I need Barrons at full strength, and that means he needs to eat. "Go. Eat. I'll sift to Dani for the latest news—"

He's already halfway to the tall black mirror leaning against the wall near the fireplace that leads from our aerie bookstore via stacked Silvers to the White Room, and finally to Dublin below, moving in that fluid, nearly imperceptible way of his. "Dani isn't available."

I freeze, my heart skipping a beat again. "But she's okay?"

"She turned into a Hunter. Kat's your source for information. I'll meet you back here in one hour."

A Hunter? I gape. Lithe as a cat, flame-haired Dani is now an enormous, icy, black, dragon-like thing with fiery eyes and leathery sails of wings? How? Why?

He pauses and glances over his shoulder, an atavistic rattle stirring deep in his chest. *I don't like leaving you alone*, glittering blood-on-black eyes say.

I smile faintly and raise my fists, opening them to reveal handfuls of crimson runes, dripping blood, inflating and deflating like disembodied hearts, the cores of the Fae I will rip out and shred to ribbons. The only other time I was able to produce such dangerous, powerful runes was with the *Sinsar Dubh*'s help. I've learned, however, that the Seelie queen's powers and the Unseelie king's were once not so different, and I, too, can saunter through Dublin as fearlessly as my psychotic nemesis. At the moment, I feel nearly as psychotic. *I've learned much, Barrons. Let them try.*

The corner of his mouth ticks up in a blend of humor wed to insatiable lust beneath ancient, cold eyes—Barrons gets my beast, thinks she's beautiful—before he steps into the tall, cobweb-dusted mirror and is gone.

——— • ———

I sift to my father first. I have no intention of telling him Mom's missing, but I have an unshakable need to ascertain his safety with my own eyes.

When I arrive at Chester's, I lose a few moments, staring upward, mouth softly ajar. Dani's a Hunter, Chester's has been rebuilt; I wonder what else changed while I was away.

When I first tracked down 939 Rêvemal Street, looking for the mysterious Ryodan, owner of Chester's, the nightclub was a heap of collapsed brick and concrete, streetlamps, broken glass, and shattered signage, and I nearly walked away until Dani, with her super-senses, led me to the underground entrance to the dangerous, sordid, fantasy-fulfilling nightclub.

Chester's aboveground now soars six stories high, wrought of pale limestone and endless sheets of glass, a brilliantly lit, gleaming citadel that nearly rivals Barrons Books & Baubles as a landmark shattering the darkness of Dublin.

A set of wide, curved stairs leads to heavily warded titan doors that appear to be steel but are likely forged from the same unidentifiable alloy liberally employed throughout the vast underground sovereignty that holds countless clubs, the Nine's private residences, and dozens of other, unexplored levels and sub-clubs, including a notorious sex club and a damp, rock-hewn dungeon.

Although part of me longs to dash up those stairs and walk into the club, absorbing the changes, time is of the essence, so I text Ryodan a quick, "I'm sifting in, don't freak out," to which he replies a testy "try," to which I reply "watch me, jackass" then, holding thoughts of my father, blast through his wards without even feeling them, smirking a silent "take that, Ryodan." It's good to be queen.

I manifest within a suite of rooms on the fifth floor, behind my father, who's staring out a wall of windows into the night, at a sea of rooftops. I make a soft sound of pleasure at seeing him, and he turns sharply to face me.

I catch my breath with a sudden chill, as I get that first bitter, poison-in-my-mouth taste of what immortality means.

My father has aged.

For a time, after my parents arrived in Dublin, he and my mother seemed to grow younger, more vigorous, energized by their new life. But between losing my sister, Alina, for the second time and me being gone for the past few years, there's a weariness I've never before glimpsed in my charismatic, robust, handsome father.

And I think: *He's going to die.*

Not a premonition, just a fact.

Jack Lane is in his late fifties. If I'm lucky, I have three, maybe four decades left with him, given so few doctors, no medical innovations on the horizon, and people scrambling just trying to survive. What once seemed a long time at twenty-two and mortal is a slap in the face to me now.

I lose a moment, then, realizing something I never thought about before. A year seems so long, especially when you're waiting for things like prom, high school graduation, college graduation, Thanksgiving, Christmas, or even just Friday so you can celebrate the weekend. We wish away so much of our time, rushing to get to the next good thing.

But the harsh reality is a year is 365 days, ten years a mere 3,650 days. One decade, an enormously defining period of your life, is less than 4,000 days. If we live to seventy-five, we get 27,375 days. No wonder, to the Fae, we're short-timers, our lives the mere blink of an eye.

I'll still look the same when I hold my father in my arms as he dies.

The Nine endure this repeatedly yet continue to care.

I finally understand why Ryodan and Barrons are so meticulous about those they choose as their own and immerse fully, intensely in the present moment. Death will come, grief will rain down again and again, and the only way to survive it and remain an alive, passionate being is to pay the price of pain every time, or you will become as barbarous and icy as the Fae. It's always going to hurt. But as long as you're still capable of suffering you're still capable of joy. Better the depths of hell and heights of heaven than the horror of feeling nothing.

Jack Lane's once sterling-tipped dark hair is now a mane of silver. There are reading glasses tucked in the pocket of his shirt beneath a wool cardigan. Wrinkles frame his eyes, furrow his forehead, and bracket his mouth. Although he stands several inches over six feet, he seems somehow . . . smaller to me.

"Mac!" he explodes, breaking into a smile, opening his arms wide.

I rush into the waiting bear hug that always smells of peppermint, aftershave, and home.

"God, how I've missed you," he says, dropping a kiss on the top of my head.

"Daddy," I murmur and tip my head back to kiss his cheek, smiling up at him. No matter what I become, or how much I change, our relationship never will. This man will always be the immutable force that towered strong and protective over me when I was a child, making me feel safe and cherished. "I love you." I don't miss an opportunity to say that to the mortals I care about.

"I love you, too, baby." He grasps me by my shoulders, staring down at me. "How you've changed."

I don't say "so have you." I never will. I'll grant him the grace of always seeing him as the strongest, best, most dashing father in the world. Eyes sparkling, I tease, "And you, every bit as handsome as ever."

"Come," he says, taking my hand to lead me to a deep armchair before a fire. "Tell me everything. But start with why Ryodan dragged me here. What's wrong that everyone's trying to conceal from me?"

My legal-eagle father with the penetrating eyesight; it's always been impossible to hide things from him.

Refusing the chair, I glance away.

Flatly, he demands, "Where is your mother, Mac?"

Sighing, I glance back.

"Ryodan brought me here, alone. That means she's missing or worse, and they fear something will happen to me, too. Then you show up for the first time in two long years. Tell me everything."

I do, admitting it's not much, but she can no longer be sensed in the mortal realm. I tell him he's not to worry because the Fae won't harm her. They're dispassionate and patient and understand her worth to me—unharmed.

He listens grimly then says, "What can I do to help?"

Sadly, I shake my head. Not a thing and he knows it. That's why his hands are balled into fists and his eyes are rushing with thunderclouds. My dad isn't the type of man to sit back and do nothing. Yet where the Fae are concerned that's all most humans can do, which makes my responsibility even greater. I'm the one that has to tame the Seelie that would, without a care, devour our world. I have to find the way to make both species live in peace.

Or destroy one of them.

We gaze at each other a wordless moment then he crushes me into another of his bear hugs and I'm just-Mac again, absorbing the heat and strength of the man who is always my rock, my champion, bestower of Band-Aids and kisses, and, when necessary, my toughest critic, all too aware that one day—even if I'm lucky enough to get decades—losing him will still come much too soon and damn near destroy me.

"I'll get her back, Dad. I promise. We'll be a family and life will be normal again. I love you," I say, again.

"You, too, baby. To the moon and back."

As I sift out, I shake off the uneasy feeling those might be the last words we ever say to each other.

I know better. I'm just feeling vulnerable because the Seelie have my mom.

Nothing more.

8

There's truth in your lies, doubt in your faith

CHRISTIAN

"BARRONS IS GOING TO bloody well kill you," Kat finally manages to say, after an interminable silence during which her gaze darts from me to imposter-Mac and back again. "Repeatedly and slowly, making what you suffered at the Crimson Hag's hands seem a holiday in comparison."

I bristle. "But he wouldn't kill Mac? Don't you think when a woman cheats she's every bit as much to blame as the man she cheats with?" I wonder why I'm arguing the idiotic moot point, given it isn't Mac standing there naked, and we weren't having sex, but double standards offend me, and my mood grows increasingly foul with each new obstacle that arises between me and getting laid. "Besides, this isn't what you think it is," I say, even more irked that Kat hasn't noticed she's meeting my gaze without blood trickling from her eyes, or how effortlessly I muted the dangerous aspects of my Unseelie form the instant she walked in, summoning a smidge of earth-power, locking my Highlander glamour in place, to remain until I release it.

Shadows flicker in her gray eyes. "Did she use the *Sidhba-jai* on you, Christian?" she asks quietly then frowns. "Is that even possible—for the queen to overpower and use an Unseelie prince for sex against his will?"

"It would never be against his will," naked not-Mac says. "Sex is sex. All beings seek to mate."

"It would, too, be against my will," I growl, glad I'm the only lie detector in the room.

"Sex is not just sex," Kat says in a low voice. "Sometimes it's rape."

Naked not-Mac says, "Among mortals, perhaps."

"She's not Mac," I tell Kat.

Kat cuts me a look of bafflement. "Then who is she?"

I sense a disturbingly powerful displacement of time and space a split second before someone sifts in behind Kat, and I curse vehemently, as Mac—the real one—manifests in the chapel. "You've *got* to bloody be kidding me," I explode. What did I do to deserve such a lousy continuation of my so auspiciously begun day? Clearly, there's a sadistic force at work in the universe that delights in saying, *Gee, look down there, Christian MacKeltar's finally having a decent day. Let's shit all over it.*

Mac gapes at her nude self. "No, you've got to bloody be kidding—" She breaks off, skirting Kat, approaching her duplicate, and looks her up and down.

The librarian stares back, regarding her with an equal blend of wariness and fascination.

"That's not what I look like," Mac says finally.

"We strongly resemble each other," naked not-Mac disagrees.

"I haven't been native down there in years. And the rest of her is what I looked like when I first arrived in Dublin." Mac scans the duplicate's hair, her hands and feet. "She's natural everywhere. I can't believe you got me so wrong." She appraises me a moment, hard, then nods and says, "You've changed. Well done, Christian."

I was so discombobulated by seeing first Mac nude, then Dani, that I hadn't registered that it was pre-royalty Mac who'd drifted from the bottle. Queen Mac has platinum hair that hangs past her hips, and power crackles electric in the air around her. The librarian has shorter, sunnier hair and not a hint of royalty sizzling about her form. "I didn't make this woman, Mac. She came from one of the king's flasks. What do you mean 'well done'?" I probe. I know I've changed, but is she sensing something more with her queenly powers?

"Later. Still opening them, eh? What is she? And why does she look like me?"

"I have no idea, and I didn't open it on purpose. The bloody flask broke."

"All by itself?" Kat says dryly.

I shoot her a dark look. "I tripped on it, but it shouldn't have been there in—" I break off and snap, "Yes I broke the bloody thing, okay? But it wasn't there this morning. I have no clue how it ended up on the floor. I always keep the beakers put away." To Mac, I say, "Is she Seelie or Unseelie?"

"She can't be Unseelie," Kat says. "They were all destroyed by the Song."

Was that a fleeting look of shock on the librarian's face?

"It's possible, sealed in a bottle, she might have escaped destruction. We don't know exactly how the Song worked," Mac muses and frowns, studying her. "It eludes me," she says finally.

"How is that possible? You're queen. If she's Fae, you must know whether she's Shadow or Light Court."

"I've not encountered the melody she emits. It's . . ." Her eyes drift closed. When she opens them again, she says, "Confounding."

"Beautiful? Ugly?" I press.

"Different than anything I've heard. Yet . . . familiar."

"A singularity?" Kat offers. "But don't only the Unseelie have those?"

Mac paces a circle around the woman, examining her. "Perhaps a Seelie contained so long in the White Mansion, she changed. Which still doesn't explain why she looks like me."

"But wouldn't time in the Unseelie kingdom have killed her, as Cruce intended with Aoibheal?" Kat says.

"The White Mansion isn't the Unseelie kingdom," Mac replies.

I frown. Mac's eyes don't look good. Beneath lucent green, shards of ice glitter. Something is wrong. And whatever it is has nothing to do with the unknown entity in my castle. I decide to wait until later to tell her that the bottle-dweller has two forms, and Dani is the other.

The librarian is no longer looking at Mac but standing perfectly still, staring past her into the distance, as if trying to be invisible. Unfortunately she isn't, and she's still disturbingly naked. I growl, "For fuck's sake, whatever you are, put some blasted clothes on."

Instantly, the creature from the flask is no longer naked.

Kat is.

The lean, muscled *sidhe*-seer shrieks, ducks, and wraps her arms around her body, trying to shield her sudden nudity.

I summon earth-power to clothe her at the precise moment Mac does, and Kat ends up bundled in multiple layers, snug enough for the iciest of winters.

Mac and Kat both glare daggers at me.

"What?" I snarl, exasperated, glowering at the librarian. Though her eyes are demurely downcast, she's smirking faintly.

"Why didn't you just clothe the naked-me to begin with? You've mastered your power," Mac snaps.

"Why," I counter furiously, "didn't the naked-you just dress herself in the first place if she was able to snatch Kat's clothing? How was I to know she'd do that?"

"You mastered the power to rearrange small elements some time ago," Kat grits, as she yanks off the sweater Mac layered over the turtleneck I fashioned for her, then sits down on the floor to jerk at one of a redundant set of boots. I consider telling her not to bother.

Mac and I created things so simultaneously I suspect the shoes are fused. Tugging at the boot, Kat continues irritably, "If you'd dressed her, I wouldn't have ended up naked."

"It's been a complicated morning, and I get distracted by nudity," I roar. I don't know what's worrying me more, the ramifications of the inexplicable librarian, her blatant insouciance and deliberate button pushing, or the barely banked storm in Mac's eerie Fae eyes. "I'm a man. Shoot me for it or get over it. I *did* keep draping the cloth around her. She refused to keep it on."

"Volume!" Kat exclaims, clamping her hands to her ears. "And remove a pair of these boots." She begins wrenching at a boot too merged to doff. "And I only need *one* pair of jeans."

Mac—the real one—begins to laugh. I eye her warily. There's a touch of . . . not quite madness but definitely an undercurrent of . . . unhinged in it. "What's wrong, Mac?"

"Not now."

Kat cuts her a dark look. "How can you possibly think this is funny?"

"I needed a dose of absurdity, and I can always count on life in Ireland for that."

"Technically," I tell her, "we're in Scotland."

Mac glances around the chapel, crammed with the Unseelie king's books and baubles. "Where in Scotland?"

I clarify tersely, "So we don't further compound things, Mac, will you be removing Kat's boots and jeans or should I?" If we both do it, we'll be back to square one, and they'll both be pissed at me again. I'm pissed enough myself. People I care about getting pissed at me when I'm already pissed makes me pissier.

"I will," Mac says, and Kat's duplicate attire vanishes with the words.

Kat sighs with relief. "Thanks. I was hot."

"The Highlands. Draoidheacht Keep," I answer Mac's question. "How did you manage to sift here when you've never been here before?" It's difficult for me to sift to locations I've never been, unless I have additional means at my disposal, like a lock of Mac's hair.

"I was trying to sift to Kat at the abbey but got rerouted here." Her gaze moves back to the librarian, who's standing, eyes downcast. "Who are you?"

Gaze fixed on the floor, she replies, "You may call me the librarian."

"Of what?"

"What used to be the Unseelie king's Library until that inept one"—she stabs a finger at me with an accusing glare—"transported me and part of my collection elsewhere, and destroyed my method for locating things." She'll look my way, without discomfort, I note with interest, just not at Mac anymore.

"Are you Seelie or Unseelie?"

"I can't answer that one way or another."

Mac cuts me a look. "Lie-detect."

"Ringing true somehow but with an undercurrent I can't pinpoint," I say.

"You *are* Fae," Mac says.

The librarian shrugs.

"I asked you a question," Mac growls.

"I didn't hear a question mark," the librarian says coolly. "Sounded like a statement to me."

Mac's eyes narrow and she grits, "Are you Fae?"

Not-Mac sneers with palpable hostility, "How am I to know anything about myself? I live in a bottle, *O great queen*. Unlike you, I don't have the freedom to saunter about, indulging my royal desires."

"Address me like that again and you'll die in the bottle."

"It's the answer I have to offer."

"You know what I can do to you."

"Torture me. In many and varied ways. When one lives forever within a prison of glass, pain *is* something with which to occupy oneself."

"Why do you resemble me?"

"I could as easily ask why you resemble me. Who was made first?"

"I wasn't made. I was born."

"Made. Born. Same result. We are."

"How did you come to be here?"

Gaze centered on my sternum, the librarian replies, "That oaf broke my flask."

My wings lift, rustling with irritation. Who is this creature that thinks to address an Unseelie prince as an oaf?

Mac glances at me. "Seal her in another flask. We have more important matters to discuss. We'll sort her out later. Perhaps. Perhaps we'll never uncork her again." She cuts a hard look back at the librarian. "Unless you'd care to be more forthcoming."

"I have answered all your questions to the best of my ability."

"Clarify what you are and why you look like me."

The librarian remains silent.

"Cork her," Mac snaps.

"I could remain free," the librarian offers hastily, "and begin sorting the mess the dullard created. I can be useful in many ways."

Dullard. That's it. Glowering, I grab a bottle of Guinness with a few swigs left at the bottom, wipe sticky cobwebs from the mouth of the bottle, and thrust it at her, commanding the librarian, or whatever the hell she is, to get in.

"I can tell you how to find things in the Library." There's an edge of desperation in her voice.

"I said, get in," I snarl.

She approaches, bends to peer in the bottle, wrinkles her nose with distaste, and glares defiantly up at me. "It reeks! My prior flask did not."

"Now," I growl, trusting she is as compelled to obey as a genie in a bottle. If not, I'll use Voice.

Nostrils flaring, eyes narrowed, the librarian evaporates into a rainbow-colored mist and drifts with dramatic, insolent leisure into the bottle.

The moment she's contained, I cram a cork in the neck, seal it, and place it carefully on a high shelf. Then I level a hard stare at Mac. "Out with it. What happened? What's wrong?"

Her eyes flicker with silvery lightning. "The Seelie abducted my mother."

"Bloody hell," I curse. The Fae just declared all-out war.

Against their queen.

Which meant against the entire human race. No longer was the apocalypse a distant promise on a dark wind.

It was here.

9

Tuck those ribbons under your helmet

MAC

A FTER CATCHING UP WITH Kat and Christian, I sift back to Barrons Books & Baubles, arriving ten minutes before the appointed hour.

Sifting is one power of which I'll never tire. Gone are the days of twenty-hour plane trips with three layovers from Ashford, Georgia, to Dublin, only to arrive jet-lagged, starving, and exhausted. I won't miss the drudgery of human locomotion one bit. As one fierce redhead-turned-Hunter I know would say: feck slow-mo Joe-ing.

Now a mere thought can put me . . . say . . . out back, on our patio by the pool in Ashford.

Wait, what?

Barrons Books & Baubles is gone. I'm out back, on our patio by the pool in Ashford, deep in the land of sugar: sweet tea, sugar pines, sugared pecans, sugar ants, and that uniquely southern sugar in our voices when we skewer outsiders with a platitude-coated insult like "bless your heart," which usually means we find you far too ignorant to bother correcting.

I gape at my surroundings, horrified.

My childhood home, which my folks always maintained with loving care, landscaping the yard with magnolias and Annabelle hydrangeas, lilac bushes, azaleas, daffodils, and jasmine, even a growth of meticulously tended mountain laurel, is nearly unrecognizable.

Somehow, when Mom and Dad decamped to Dublin years ago, I never got around to wondering what they did with our house. I certainly never thought they might have sold it—sacrilege! In my mind, the historic Lane manor remained untouched by time, sitting there, ready and waiting for the day we decided to go back for a visit. And of course, we would, at some point, right? Things would return to normal, and we'd want to take a walk down memory Lane—pun intended.

They hadn't sold it. They'd done worse. If they'd sold it, at least someone else would have been taking care of it. As it was, Nature was owner and occupant and, in the Deep South, she's a voracious bitch.

My folks battened the hatches and walked away. Abandoned Casa Lane. Closed the pool, shuttered the windows, locked the doors, and left.

Kudzu—known as the vine that ate the south for good reason; it grows as much as a foot a day—encapsulates the sugar pines, creating a forty-foot wall of cloaked green blobs that spans the entire perimeter of our two-acre yard. What neighbors? I can't see a thing beyond the towering hedge.

Impenetrable curtains of wisteria drape the pool house, turning the one-bed, one-bath studio into a purple-and-green hump that lurks menacingly on the south side of the pool. Shingles are missing from our roof, and paint is peeling from our lovely corniced trim. Green algae, from the eternal high humidity in Georgia, stains the white frames of our windows, railings, and doors. The place looks positively derelict. Waist-high thistle and milkweeds fill the yard. I can't even see the pool.

I press a hand to my heart, dismayed.

This is my beloved home. My sunny kingdom across the sea where nothing ever changes and, despite the pervasive, lushly decaying southern clime, we Lanes always beat back the elements with panache, vigor, and a smile.

This is my happy place—obliterated by the relentless march of time. Forgotten. Fallen to disrepair. Never to be mine again. One more thing taken from me. Now when I reflect on my childhood home, *this* is what I'll see. Abandonment and neglect.

It's an affront to my senses, an insult to my history, a slight against the good Lane name. What do the neighbors think of us for letting our home decay to such an egregious degree? We're right off Main Street, for heaven's sake! Our yard is featured in the annual Christmas Tour. I form a vision in my mind and erase the offensive one, restoring the house and lawn to its glory, even going so far as to fill the pool and turn on the fountains, because Mom is always the happiest when the pool is sparkling in the sun, and Alina and I are home with friends and she's baking one of her—

Mom. Abducted by the Fae. Alina. Dead. Again. What the hell am I doing?

I scan the lovely view, disgusted with myself. I can't believe I actually wondered what the neighbors might think. Being in Ashford regressed me. How swiftly I capitulated to longing for a past that was gone and would never be again, casually, selfishly using the power of a Fae queen to re-create it.

And for what?

To make myself feel better.

Which is precisely what the Fae are infamous for: escaping into illusion to make their existence more tolerable.

No longer will I decorate my world, accessorizing the rotten parts, the better to conceal them. Things are what they are. And aren't what they aren't. Illusion will define neither my rule nor my legacy.

Squaring my shoulders, I restore my home to its appalling, dilapidated state (I even knock off a few more shingles and make the kudzu several feet thicker just to emphasize my point) then stand several long moments, drinking deeply of reality, before sifting back to the bookstore.

— • • • —

When I materialize in the rear of Barrons Books & Baubles, Barrons is reclining on the chesterfield in front of a softly hissing gas fire. He saturates every atom of air in the seating cozy, from polished hardwood floor to eighteen-foot ceiling with carnal, electrifying presence, which tells me he fed, and well. We stare at each other a charged moment, wordlessly acknowledging there's no time for us, but when there is, we'll definitely be taking advantage of it. Feeling his arms around me, his body against mine, takes me to a sacred place. In the meantime, just looking at him again is drug enough for me. Some see him as barbaric, stamped by genes too primitive to ever be handsome, possessed of a decidedly autocratic, even despotic demeanor, but to me he's grace in motion, the finest of beasts and men.

"What were you doing in Ashford?"

"How do you know I was?" Although I wear his brand, I'm fairly certain the Nine haven't managed to eradicate the IFPs, or interdimensional Faery potholes, while I was absent, and their presence on our world skews his ability to precisely pinpoint me.

"Pollen, sunshine, wisteria. A whiff of algae and chlorine."

Of course. He can probably smell the stench of nostalgia on me, too, as keen as his beastly senses are. "I was thinking about home and ended up there by accident."

"Work on that."

"Agreed." Vanishing inadvertently in the midst of a showdown with the Fae could prove disastrous. He'd changed clothes while he was out. Customarily clad in impeccable, expensive Italian suits, Barrons is slumming in faded jeans, a black T-shirt, and black boots. "Are we going down into the sewers again?" I can count on one hand the number of times I've seen him in anything but expensive suits (skin excepted), and each time, we'd ended up doing something disgusting or disturbingly dangerous, usually both.

"Fae court. Sewers." His shrug makes it plain he sees no difference. "What's your plan, Ms. Lane?" He uses the same aloof, challenging tone he employed during our earliest weeks together, a rebuffing of intimacy, a resurrection of distance and formality.

There's a time it would have rankled, but I've come to understand his methods and appreciate them. He does nothing without reason. Calling me Ms. Lane instead of Mac instantly jammed a steel rod up my spine, squared my shoulders, and hardened my attitude. It kicked me back to those days when I'd been determined to prove him wrong about everything he thought of me, and, right now, I needed to do the same with the Fae. They thought they could take from me? They thought they could openly declare war?

It was time for them to pay the piper. I would kick them so hard in the teeth they would never bare them at me again. "Kat filled me in on what happened at the Fae club, Elyreum, and how viciously the Winter Court preyed on our city while I was gone. They're also the ones that tried the hardest and most inventively to kill us while we were in Faery. I have no doubt Winter took my mother to force me to return so they can try to kill me again."

He stretches his arms along the back of the sofa, muscle and tattoo rippling. "Assumption."

"Got something better?"

"Ryodan said the woman leading Winter had nearly completed her transformation into a princess the night Dani killed a recently transformed Fae prince. That was months ago."

His point: She'd be fully a princess by now. And unlike me, fully Fae. "Dani was still racking up Fae kills, despite my edict, eh?" Kat hadn't told me that part.

"It was necessary."

I bite my lip and smile. Kat protected Dani through omission. Barrons just openly defended her. I'm not sure I've ever heard him defend anyone. Like Lor, he has a soft spot for the fiery, fearless, loyal-to-the-grave-and-beyond hellion. Good. Though not my blood sister, she's my heart-sister, my family, and everyone in my life should have a soft spot for her.

Barrons studies me through narrowed eyes. "He would have killed her otherwise."

"Uh-huh." I'm still smiling. And it's pissing him off. He's lived millennia untold in the midst of humanity, holding himself rigidly apart, never connecting, remaining a blank, emotionless enigma to everyone around him for eons, yet now there's a woman who knows him well enough to spot the nuances of emotion he meticulously conceals. Ah, yes, it chafes, and I'm not above enjoying it. It takes a lot to get under Barrons's skin. I'm good at it.

Midnight eyes narrow further, and crimson sparks flicker to life. "Your plan, Ms. Lane?"

My smile turns glacial as I let rage chill my blood to ice. "We burn Winter the fuck down." If they've harmed her, I'll burn the entirety of Faery the fuck down. But I strongly doubt they have. Fae aren't stupid. Abducting my mother is a play for power. They want me to come to them while they hold a trump card, and they know if they harm one hair on her head, and I arrive to see it, I'll use every queenly power I have to obliterate their species, which means Mom is safe for now. Once they send word of what they've done and demand I meet them, her clock will begin to run, encouraging me not to delay. Until their message comes in whatever form it does, we have time.

"And if you're wrong and the Winter Court didn't take your mother?"

"Then it's payback for attacking Dani and preying on Dublin while I was gone, and a message to whichever court did take her," I say without hesitation. "They're either on my side, by my side, or in my fucking way. It's time to make that clear."

Barrons says nothing. There's no faint lift at the corner of his mouth, no gleam in his eye that tells me he concurs with my plan.

"What?" I say irritably. Why isn't he backing me? Why aren't his dark eyes alight with anticipation at the thought of a war long overdue? "I can tell you want to say something. Just bloody say it."

"You're their queen."

"Precisely my point. It's time they accept that."

Another long silence.

"Elucidate," I grit.

"You're behaving as if you're queen of the humans."

I toss myself down on the chesterfield across from him and drum my fingers on the tufted arm, punctuating my words. "They. Took. My. Mother."

He leans forward, elbows on his knees, templing his fingers. "You say. Maybe. Maybe not. Regardless, they're your subjects now. The True Magic was passed to you. You pledged to guide them. If you want them to accept you as their queen, you must act like their queen." A weighted pause lends emphasis to his next words, "Not your mother's."

"You expect me to choose the Fae over my *mother*?" I explode.

Again, he says nothing.

I fist my hands and stare daggers at him and contemplate testing a few of my newfound runes on him. Why isn't he saddling up to ride hell-bent-for-leather at my side? He'll rise to Dani's defense in a heartbeat but betray me when all I'm after is justifiable revenge for—

I sigh, close my eyes and rub them. "Justifiable" and "revenge" are two dangerous words to fuse into a single bomb. Not that there's never such a thing, but those cases are exceedingly rare. I'd vowed to wield logic over emotion, yet I'd returned from Ashford with a single priority: protect my family. I'd returned in the grip of a rage fever, ready to reduce Winter to a wasteland.

My heart wants war.

My head knows better, as Barrons just reminded me.

There's so much more at stake here than my mother, than either of my parents, than any one or two or even three dozen people I love. No less than the future of both Fae and Mortal worlds rests in my hands. I have to persuade them to peacefully co-exist, or figure out how to wield the Song of Making and keep them permanently apart. I'd been thinking like a human, a daughter, not queen of the Fae at all.

So . . . back to my original conundrum: How to govern savages without savagery?

"I have learned that neither kindness nor cruelty, by themselves, independent of each other, creates any effect beyond themselves, and I have learned that the two combined, together, are the teaching emotion," Barrons murmurs.

I open my eyes, startled. That pretty much sums up our Voice lessons. And my humiliating, lunch-spewing introduction to pages torn from the *Sinsar Dubh*. And our first "hunting trip" together, when he left me hanging by my hair, suspended by the Gray Man's talons, while pedantically—and at great length—lecturing me on the techniques of a proper kill. "Did you just explain how you trained me? You never explain anything."

"*Zoo Story*. Edward Albee."

Kindness and cruelty. He'll get that in bed next time.

Dark laughter rolls. "Bring it on."

I snort. The day Aoibheal passed the True Magic of the Fae to me is scarred into the flesh of my brain, seared with painful permanence into my bones. It's the day I finally escaped my psychotic hitchhiker, the day I curled on the floor of my shower and wept myself to a dry husk, gutted by the horrific things I'd done in the clutches of the *Sinsar Dubh*.

It's also the day I sought the source of my power and ended up on another world, with an ancient, alien presence that felt so vast and wise, gentle and pure, I decided the Fae couldn't possibly have always been monsters while still managing to attract the support of such a sage, benevolent being. I'd searched my files for clues about their origin, who they'd been before they'd become soulless immortals, with no luck.

What have you come for? the bodiless voice had demanded.

The True Magic of the Fae, I said strongly.

What will you do with it?

My answer was instant and effortless. *Protect and guide.*

How will you achieve it?

With wisdom and grace.

I sigh. "They might be savages, but they're *my* savages. I accepted them."

He lifts a brow. "As I recall, argued for them. Permitted an ancient being to slip inside your soul and analyze the purity of your motives. Proved you meant it. But you could always renege on that," he says mildly.

Mildly from Barrons is never a good thing. It means I'm being such an ass he isn't even motivated enough to bother rubbing my face in it. He might as well say "bless your heart."

The Fae killed my sister, Alina. Nearly destroyed my beloved Dublin, time and again. Wiped out two thirds of the world's human population and preyed cruelly on millions more. Now they've taken my mom.

And I'm the queen pledged to rule them, prevent their extinction, and guide them with wisdom and grace.

Those things don't fit together at all.

I have to find a way to make them fit.

I lock gazes with him. *Thank you.*

For what? Dark eyes gleam as he milks the moment. He can count on one hand the number of times I've thanked him and, believe you me, I made him work for it.

For pushing me to do better. Try harder. See things more clearly. Jericho.

He catches his lower lip in his teeth then flashes me one of those rare, full-on smiles that always feel to me as if a white-hot sun just exploded unexpectedly, dazzlingly in a black velvet sky, warming my heart in the darkest of hours. It's sexy as hell and slays me every time.

Always. Mac.

10

---• • •---

All I really want is deliverance

LYRYKA

MORTALS HAD A SAYING—ACTUALLY, from what she'd read, mortals had many sayings, most of which were inane—but "you attract more flies with honey than vinegar" was one she might do well to employ the next time the Unseelie prince–hybrid thingie/whatever-the-blue-ice-hell-he-was released her from the hideous, smelly bottle.

The issue that signified was that he *could* release her.

Another issue she wasn't quite ready to think about, now that her original flask was broken, was that she had two pressing problems. One was merely a living condition—although, admittedly when one lived inside a flask, one's living conditions were everything—while the other was simultaneously too chilling and oddly thrilling to dwell upon, so she filed those matters away for later.

For the first time in her life, something had actually *happened*.

To *her*. She'd had an *event*.

She'd met an actual being from one of her books.

Several.

They existed!

And if anything that had recently transpired was real, she'd just encountered the High Queen of the Seelie herself. (Although Lyryka had worried she might be able to penetrate her glamour and see what she *really* was, she'd not found the queen nearly as impressive or half as horrid as she was in books. The Unseelie prince, on the other hand, not only met but exceeded her expectations for masculine sexuality and attractiveness, making her a bit light-headed and perhaps more tart than usual. She was, as far as she knew, the universe's oldest living virgin.)

There were beings in existence besides her and her father!

Although this Unseelie prince was a new thing in her life, her situation was old all the same for, once again, a male had ironclad control of her existence. He'd broken her flask and released her, then, before she'd even had enough time to begin thinking clearly (like about being honey instead of vinegar), he'd stuffed her back into a disgusting replacement.

She wondered if perhaps that was the only reason she existed—to serve at a male's beck and call—or if there was once some other reason, perhaps a critical choice that had been hers at birth, stolen from her before she'd even known it was her power to wield. The mere idea that all the stories she'd read were true—and what that implied about the story of *her* life—was almost too dreadful to contemplate.

The problem with being honey, not vinegar, was that she was profoundly irritable. She'd been irritable for as long as she could recall. Irritable might be her nature for all she knew. She knew very little about herself. And being in this smelly, sloshy-at-the bottom bottle was making her even more irritable.

Everything she knew about the world, she'd learned from the Library. Yet she didn't know if the stories she'd studied to pass the millennia were true or made-up fictions about a made-up reality. She'd only ever seen one person, periodically over three quarters of a million years. Eventually, she'd started to doubt even her father's existence, wondered if he was a hallucination, a bit of self-deceptive conjuring she'd done to leaven the monotony.

Her father claimed, even though there wasn't a single story about him in the Library, all the stories were true. But if they were true—she *did* understand procreation, even remembered, back in the mists of time, being rather smallish and filled with wonder—it implied that she had a mother, and that was a treacherous rabbit hole in which she might lose centuries brooding about why a mother might let a father put a daughter in a flask and seal her away forever.

Okay, she *had* lost centuries doing that.

Ergo, at any given point in time, she vacillated between believing the stories were true, based on a world "out there" (and that, as her father claimed, he'd sequestered her away only to keep her safe and, since she was in there anyway, he needed her to be the librarian so she could unearth and provide necessary information that might one day help him free her), and being utterly convinced none of it was true, and the Library was a passel of wildly imagined lies. (Or worse. Much worse. She could slide down the slippery slope of paranoia straight into the abyss of madness with the best of them.)

For, if all the tales in the Library were true, that strongly suggested her father was a selfish, possibly sadistic monster living a thrilling life in a vibrant, astonishing world, while forcing her to live, by herself, in a bottle with only the Library for companionship. (Which implied he'd probably killed her mother. Or stuck her in a flask somewhere, too.) And now that she had been stuffed into a wholly unfamiliar smelly bottle, she'd lost the meticulously replicated Library that had formed her prior flask, leaving her nothing whatsoever to do, which made her far, far more irritable.

Despite her suspicions, she lived for those rare moments her father came to see her; when he stood, radiant as a black sun, bearing new requests for information, for this potion or that, this spell or that ward, or, more recently, confusing orders for her that might, one day, he promised, make it possible for him to release her, a promise she used to believe but, of late, had begun to doubt he ever meant to keep.

She exploded with joy on the infrequent occasions he came. She fumed with a seething, silent fury she never let him see. If she wasn't nice to him, she feared he might never come again.

But today something changed. Now there was another being who could release her. Other beings, in addition to him. Perhaps females could release her as well. Perhaps a woman would be a kinder jailer, affording increased liberties. Perhaps everyone could release her. Perhaps there was a way to release herself. Perhaps no one should be kept in a bottle.

When her father told her recently that she would soon meet someone new (and precisely how to manage him when she did, which she'd essentially obeyed, at least the highlights; he hadn't specified her demeanor, only her actions), she hadn't fully believed him. His command, that she adopt two specific forms and never reveal her true self the next time she was released from her flask, chafed. She had pictures to compare herself to and, having a keen appreciation for the unique, knew she was spectacular. Of all the beings in all the books in the Library, out of all the Fae, she was not one of many in a caste—but a stunning singularity. After eons alone, she hungered to be seen.

She frowned, wondering why he'd wanted her to use a variation of the queen's form, and who the woman named Dani was. What was her father up to? Who were these people she'd met, and what did they mean to him?

Might they be persuaded to help her?

Her deepest longing was to go to the Hall of All Days and stand before the Sifting Silvers (in her true form) possessing the right to choose any of infinite destinies. At long last, she would be free to write her own story. And one day, perhaps *her* book would end up in the Library, and someone else would read it and be thrilled and inspired as she'd been so many times, poring over a book. Perhaps they would weep over her long, hellish confinement, seethe at whatever origin story had shaped it, share her triumph when she escaped, remain glued to the pages as she traversed worlds, having long-denied adventures.

The Hall of All Days was the greatest freedom she could imagine. She'd read and reread every story about it, countless times, even going so far as to place all those tomes on the highest of shelves, conferring upon them special status, far from the dirty, dog-earring fingers of patrons that never came. She hungered to chart her own course in the world. No matter that many Silvers, corrupted by an inimical curse, were dangerous. She was fairly certain she, too, could be dangerous. She wanted the chance to try. She wasn't afraid.

She feared only one thing.

Remaining trapped, alone, forever, released only at the ever-decreasing whim of her father.

Yes, the existence of this new male that looked as if he'd stepped straight from the pages of one of her many tomes strongly suggested—perhaps even irrefutably supported—that all of the stories in the Library were true.

Which meant her father was, indeed, a selfish, probably sadistic monster. How could the world out there not be safe for her after three quarters of a million years? Was he such a clod, so inept—he, the one so bloody powerful, allegedly all and sundry trembled before him—that he'd been unable to create a haven of some sort for her? Unfathomable!

It all meant one thing: she'd damned well better figure out how to get past her irritation and pour some honey on herself the next time the new male opened her flask because, perhaps if she weren't so irritable, prone to truculence and defiance, perhaps if she harnessed her temper, and made the Unseelie prince like her, he might take her to the Hall of All Days and set her free.

Then her father would never find her again. And there would never be another flask or smelly bottle. Life would finally begin.

She whirled to toss herself onto her bed, but recalled, mid-toss, that she no longer had a bed. Or a pillow. Or the vast expanse of the

Unseelie king's replica Library in which to live. Or a single thing to eat or drink. Not even one book. How was she to pass the time in any sort of bearable fashion without books?

Sighing, she sank down into the foul-smelling liquid and sat cross-legged, glancing about her murky confines. She possessed the ability to weave illusion, could create a false pocket of wonders in here for herself, but she'd long ago stopped wielding that power, already too confused about what was real and what wasn't.

She'd been so lost in thought she'd not examined her new abode. The bottle was roughly five times her width, giving her just enough room to lie down if she wished (as if she felt like sprawling out in that sour-smelling stuff). The walls appeared to be—oh!

She leaped to her feet and plastered her nose to the glass.

Dimly, she could see the shapes of things beyond.

She might have lost the comforts of her flask, the wonders and solace of the vast, miniaturized Library, its enormity tucked into an expanded pocket of reality and spun into her flask, but by D'Anu—if she pressed her face to the damp, odiferous glass—she could see *out there*! Her prior flask had afforded no such window, no proof of reality beyond her cage.

If the stories were to be believed, she was seeing the world in which her father lived—the mortal world, which connected to the Fae world, which connected to the Hall of All Days.

Shivering with excitement, she tapped her nails against the surface, ducking to peer beneath the label the simpleton had plastered to the side (it took her a second to mentally reverse it, but it was something called GUINNESS; apparently he couldn't be bothered to recall what he stored in various flasks—inconceivable). She labeled only the most dangerous, debilitating ones, not because she couldn't remember what was in every single thing, but in case her father picked up something he shouldn't.

Might she manage to do as the prince had done, and break the glass? Granted, he'd been outside it and considerably larger, but . . .

Squinting through the hazy bottle, she studied the room where her collections teetered and sprawled in such disarray and offense that it made her fingers itch to restore order, and concluded she'd been placed on a high shelf.

According to the hierarchy of her own filing system, that made her very special. He may have disheveled her meticulous Library, but at least the (devastatingly attractive) oaf had gotten her placement right.

The floor below was formed of very large, very hard flagstones.

She retreated to the other side of the bottle.

Channeling her pint-size strength, she launched herself forward with all the velocity she could muster in her stunted confines and rammed her body into the smooth glass wall.

Over.

And over again.

11

The cold never bothered me anyway

MAC

LOATH THOUGH I WAS to waste more time before heading out to find my mother, the many physical urges from which I'd been miraculously freed in the chamber beyond time were revisited upon my body with a vengeance.

I had to pee so bloody bad I almost couldn't even make myself start going. Then I caught a glimpse of myself in the mirror and realized I didn't dare go blasting off for my first encounter with my hostile, murderous subjects without tending to a few things first. Image matters with beings as vain as the Fae. Hastily, I brushed my teeth, smudged a damp cloth across my face, ran a brush through my infernal Rapunzel hair while making a quick, nonnegotiable decision about it then changed into black from head to toe. Rainbow Mac had died a long time ago.

"Did you know my bedroom is now on the seventh floor, and there's an elevator in the hallway outside your study? It's one of those elegant affairs with tufted leather, polished wood, an antique mirror, even one of those fancy intercoms in case you get stuck," I say, as I finish descending the stairs and enter the anteroom at the rear of the bookstore. I'd had to wipe surprisingly resistant cobwebs from the corners of the new conveyance, but other than that it was straight out of a millionaire's penthouse.

"I would have torn out a cheap one," Barrons says from the other room. "Although I do wonder where the intercom goes. Haven't seen any additional speakers about."

I suspect I installed one in our subterranean lair beneath the garage, still thinking like Mac who couldn't sift, afraid I'd get trapped in it while he was holed up in his beast-cave. "Are there other changes I haven't seen?" I ask as I enter the main room.

Barrons is standing near the fire, phone in his hand, texting. "There's a conspiracy of lemurs living on the third floor," he replies absently. "The fifth floor is crammed with Christmas trees."

"You *are* feeding them, right?"

"They're artificial."

"The lemurs. They'll starve in the bookstore."

That gets his attention, and he looks up with a scowl. "In what fucking reality am I responsible for feeding fucking lemurs? They kept shitting on my rugs until I trapped them up there."

I bite my lip to keep from laughing. He's picky about the bookstore, and the rugs have definitely taken a beating since I moved in, between me dropping burning matches on them, my heels spiking into the ancient, delicate weave, the Garda's attack with crimson spray paint, and now lemur droppings. "They'll smell when they rot," I say, as I hand him a pair of shears. "You won't like that."

"Then you'd better feed them." He slides his phone back into his pocket and says, "Why do I have scissors?"

I turn around and give him my back. "Because I have four feet of hair and you're going to cut it off. Take it to about five inches past the nape of my neck." I can still stick it in a high ponytail at that length and I'll no longer be drowning in it. "*This* is my nape," I say, pointing to the right spot. "Five inches longer than that." I don't want to end up scalped. Once, in the infancy of our relationship, Barrons painted my nails. I hope he's more proficient at cutting hair.

"I did a fine job with your nails," he growls.

"Passable, at best."

Then his hands are on the bare skin of my neck, and I shiver with desire. I love his hands. I love the man. He fists a handful of my insanely copious amounts of hair, tugs my head back, presses his lips to my ear and says softly, "You could always braid it and tuck it into your shirt." Teeth nip my ear, and I shiver again.

"Into my jeans, too? You try braiding four feet of hair every day," I grouse. Never going to happen. To say nothing of how absurdly thick it is. Even my eyelashes are longer and fuller.

I have a sudden vision of us, in bed, with my masses of platinum hair spilling across his dark-skinned, naked body and know he's seeing it, too. Us, tangled in crimson sheets, dripping with sweat, saying, "I need you like air and never fucking leave me" with our bodies, which is how we do it—those of us to whom words don't come easy, and we don't trust them anyway.

"I like your hair."

"Fine. You can have it after you cut it off. It's a liability in combat. Cut it. And make it straight."

Sighing, he unclenches his fist, smooths my hair, and begins to snip, warily at first then with increasing commitment and, hopefully, precision. How I long for the days I used to go to a hairdresser. I think that was about a few hundred and four years ago.

Snip. Snip. Snip.

I stand perfectly still while he works (chin tucked down so the ends will blend better), then braid my much shorter hair and weapon up. I never know what I might need in this city: Unseelie flesh, diced and crammed into a baby food bottle in a jacket pocket, Glock in my waistband, spear at my hip, switchblades in my boots. I no longer bother with a MacHalo. I haven't seen a Shade in just about forever, and besides, I can make myself glow like a small sun with a mere thought. I'd like to keep that power, too, should I find a way to not be queen of the Fae.

"Have you tried sifting to Rainey?" Barrons asks, as he tosses my shorn locks on the fire.

I nearly smack myself in the forehead. What is wrong with my brain? I haven't sifted much since I inherited the power. Once, I went to Lor (the night I had to kill him to make the point: Do. Not. Mess. With. Me. Ever. Again.), but I knew what graveyard he was in. More recently, however, I thought of Kat at the abbey and ended up going to Scotland where she actually was, which meant my queenly GPS—unlike Christian's—targeted people in addition to locations. Could I sift to an unknown location in Faery that I'd never been before, merely by thinking of Mom? I have no doubt they'll hide her well.

I stare into space, summoning a vision of my mother, bustling around her airy Dublin kitchen that's a baker's dream with the all-white counters and tall, mullioned windows, preparing a peach and pecan pie, flour-dusted and happy. The sound of her laughter, the delicious mom-scent of her that fills up a room with a perfume that has nothing to do with chemicals and everything to do with love and knowing the woman always has your back, even when you've screwed up.

Sifting feels like dying.

You're there one instant. The next, you're not.

Then you are again.

Once, I'd materialized partly in a wall. Another time I'd bounced Alina and me off Barrons's absurdly powerful wards that protected the bookstore, blackening her eye and bruising myself from head to toe. Barrons is a consummate warder. He can make anything impenetrable. And make it hurt like hell if you're foolish enough to try getting in.

Barrons's wards are *nothing* compared to what I hit this time.

I am.

Then I'm not.

Then I'm a fly on the highway, slamming into the windshield of a car going a hundred miles an hour.

Then I'm splatting into a messy puddle of guts and goo with not one single bone left intact.

Everything goes black.

I mean, black-hole black. Nothingness in the truest sense of the word. Sensory deprivation that is horrifically reminiscent of being stuffed into a box by the *Sinsar Dubh*.

Pain is the only way I know I still exist and I'm damned sorry I do.

Oh, God, the *pain!*

"Fuck, Mac." Barrons explodes from a far, far distance down a very long, very dark tunnel.

Then I'm lying on my back on the floor and above me is the coffered ceiling of Barrons Books & Baubles and I can't feel the various parts of my body for several long, terrifying moments.

Then Barrons is bending over me, pressing fingers to my jugular, checking my pulse, and I gather from his expression that I look like I feel: roadkill.

Abruptly, sensation beyond pain returns, and I'm stunned to realize I'm intact. I still have a body. The residual agony in every cell, however, is stupefying. I can't breathe or speak, it's so huge and all encompassing.

He opens my jacket, shoves up my shirt, and splays his palm over my heart. I stare into his dark eyes and watch them flicker and spark as he murmurs in a language I've never heard before, and the pain begins to recede by slow degrees. He grimaces a time or two, once even inhales sharply and slits crimson-sparking eyes nearly closed.

Stop taking my pain, I finally insist. *I'm well enough.*

The ward left a powerful residual in your body. It's dark, hungry, as if incomplete.

I know. And you've taken enough of it. I'll disperse the rest.

I say when enough is enough.

Funny, that makes two of us, and I said it first.

I push up to sitting—I have limbs, not puddles of destroyed flesh!—aching deep in my bones, but the breath-stealing pain is gone. "Am I bruised? Do I have black eyes?"

"You're not physically damaged."

"Then why did you look so horrified?"

"You flickered out then you were back, flat on the floor, white, stiff, and still as death. You *felt* dead to me for a brief moment," he says grimly. "I could no longer sense you."

A chill slithers up my spine. The brand that connects us springs from dark, blood magic, the most potent kind. It allows us to feel the constant, quiet burn of each other's existence—and it was completely shorted out by the ward for a split second. That's deeply alarming. "Good God, what did I hit? Who has so much power?"

"Me. Old gods. Some Fae."

"Sorry, but in comparison to what I just encountered, your wards are mere suggestions. That was a perfectly impenetrable barrier."

His nostrils flare and his eyes narrow. "I employ necessary force. Key word there being 'necessary.' Not one iota more. The Fae are egotistical, megalomaniac show-offs. Restraint, Ms. Lane, is the true measure of power. The deadliest among us conceal it."

Uh-oh, I'm Ms. Lane again, and his diction is getting stuffy and precise. On the rare occasions Barrons's ego gets bent, I can't help but laugh, and I'd have snickered now but I'm too busy obsessing over which Fae of mine is capable of erecting such potent, destructive, immutable wards that leave an immobilizing residue.

I was incapacitated.

Roadkill in the truest sense of the word. Rendered helpless, lying flat on my back, unable to defend myself. If someone or something had followed me back—and I've heard sifting can be traced by a rare few—I was a sitting duck, easy prey. Who among my court has the power to do that to their queen?

I consider trying to assail the ward again. Now that I know it's there, I'm prepared. Perhaps I can feel my way around it, slip through it, blast it to smithereens.

Barrons intuits my thoughts and says flatly, "I forbid it. We don't know for sure who has her or exactly what you'll be smashing up against. Perhaps they felt you. Perhaps they set a second ward or trap of some kind."

Forbidding doesn't work any better on me than it works on him. However, one of the courtesies we learned to grant each other while dodging my many enemies in Faery is we pull together and employ the less risky idea (assuming it's not a significant time suck) and only if that fails attempt the riskier one. I concede attempting the ward again carries a higher degree of risk.

I know who's behind it. He's the only one unconvinced.

Pushing to my feet, I hold out my hand and, when he takes it, lace our fingers together in preparation to sift. "Fine. We'll start at the Winter Court." I'm certain she's the one who has my mother. From what Kat told me about Elyreum, and our fallen *sidhe*-seer sisters who'd sacrificed sanctity, sanity, and life to infiltrate their ranks, attending the club, even sleeping with the enemy, Winter is my most powerful adversary, the one most inclined to prey on humans and challenge my right to rule. I can feel her presence out there; her icy, bottomless hunger to seize my crown, almost as if one of the many perks of wearing the crown is that the scent of pending betrayal gets gusted straight to the Faerie queen on a magic-infused breeze.

Years ago, Barrons and I toured Faery, meeting the various castes, inspecting the courts (before they began trying to kill me, while they were still playing nice). I know exactly where the decrepit, fallen-to-ruin castle of Winter is, as well as Spring, Summer, and Autumn, the High Court, and the queen's bower. I also know where the queen's secret aerie is; which none of her court knows exists. Years ago, so much about Faery was foreign to me, but I've been studying files on it for a few hundred years, suspended in a timeless chamber, and now possess a powerful advantage: The Light Court drinks from the Cauldron repeatedly, which means I know more about the history and powers of the Fae than they do. The queen's files are passed from one to the next. I have the most complete history of the Fae that exists with the exception of the Unseelie king.

As we sift out, I deposit a small indoor conservancy in the center of the third floor, with young trees, grasses, and rocks draped with tender mosses and delicate berries to feed the lemurs while we are away. As a hasty afterthought, I add a circular, stone-ringed pool of water and remove all rugs. Poop is easier to clean off hardwood.

———o o o———

The Kingdom of Winter is no longer derelict.

The Lane antebellum in Ashford, Georgia, is still downtrodden as hell, but, by God, Winter is restored.

That's just bullshit.

You might want to turn that off. Barrons gestures to my feet.

I glance down. The ice-crusted snow has melted in a ten-foot circumference around my boots, leaving sodden earth dressed with a brilliant carpet of bloodred snow blossoms.

I resent losing my home. I resent that Winter reclaimed hers, so I began taking it without even thinking about it. Fae emotion affects the climate.

Stealth is an advantage. Leaving bread crumbs as you hunt is not.

Point made. Retracting my emotions, I stuff them in a box and, as the flowers vanish, snow reclaims the land.

The kingdom of Winter is a diamond-crusted study of beautiful cruelties, lovely and inimically dangerous, for each alluring facet contains a hidden weapon or terror.

It's brutally cold—we ice where we stand—so I adjust our body temperatures by erecting a slice of warmer climate around us, and ice sloughs off us in great, melting sheets.

I sifted us in about a half mile from the castle proper, partially hidden behind a frozen and sometimes horrifically animated hedge that is part of a shoulder-high, statue-studded labyrinth; the better to assess our surroundings as I have no idea how many courtiers she might have in attendance or whether she'll have posted guards.

Last I was here, Winter was a desolate, iced landscape with drift blasting across the terrain, fogging the air white, tumbles of stone and ice and statues barely visible. Today it's clear, if not sunny. Sun doesn't exist in Winter; there lurks only an intermittently glimpsed frost-bitten orb of wan blue.

Beyond the labyrinth, four spires explode up from the castle, alabaster ice splintering the leaden sky. Each tower sports a circular walk at the apex, but there are no guards manning them. The castle is enormous, a fair chunk of the White Mansion, but the bulk of it is concealed behind forty-foot-high walls of silvery, metal-laced ice. With the exception of the slopes of snow-drifted roofs, flying buttresses, and the currently empty promenade that crowns the main hall, I can see none of the enormous courtyard I've read about in my files which is capable of comfortably accommodating tens of thousands of Fae. Last time I was here, the walls had collapsed and the castle was a dripping, icicle-drenched ruin, abandoned for millennia; all of it little more than a misshapen sloe of ice.

Frosted, low-hanging clouds gust across the arctic terrain, driven by a metallic-scented breeze, hovering a few feet from the ground, and, as one of them passes, I glimpse razor-sharp edges on the minuscule snowflakes of which the cloud is comprised. Getting caught in one would tear me up far worse than being stuck in a southern burr-bush patch and leave me bloody and tainted by some delicate (short-lasting) poison. It wouldn't kill me, but would certainly be a painful, irritating distraction.

It's too quiet, Barrons growls.

I concur. The hush that accompanies a once-in-a-century snowstorm, when the world is so densely carpeted with feet and feet of drifts that it mutes all acoustics and makes you feel like you might be the only person alive, muzzles the land.

I frown, glancing at the ice-coated forest to the south. Though the wind is blowing and knife-edged boughs scrape against one another, there isn't a hint of the tortured groaning/chiming sound they were making the last time I was here. To the west, the frozen river that gurgles and leaps beneath two feet of ice and shrieks with the voices of countless tortured humans who were abducted over millennia and sealed beneath the surface, their all-too-aware frozen souls permanently entombed, is as silent as the dead should be.

It's almost as if all sound has been forbidden, Barrons muses.

I glance at him sharply.

Yes, I say and abruptly realize what I was too distracted to notice before. Since we've arrived, Barrons hasn't spoken a single word aloud. Every bit of our conversation was passed between us in silence along the private communication channels of our brand.

I open my mouth to state the obvious, but no sound comes out. Eyes flashing, I growl, *Something is very wrong in Winter, Barrons.*

Nodding grimly, he takes my hand, and we begin the trek across the treacherous terrain to the frozen fortress ahead.

12

--- • • ---

You can have my isolation
you can have the hate that it brings

CHRISTIAN

BEFORE I BEGAN TURNING into an Unseelie prince, I was an ordinary Highlander with a healthy sex drive, you know, that kind of constant male background music of sex-sex-sex, find-it-have-it-drown-in-it-before-more-perfectly-good-sperm-die playing to an easy, sensuous beat in my head.

While every now and then a woman came along that made that music ratchet up to a hard-core version of NIN's "Closer," rendering me a bit dense when it came to the finer nuances of our relationship (those women were usually whacked; don't ask me why nut jobs are so much hotter in bed), nothing in my life prepared me for falling victim to the sexual appetites of an Unseelie prince, burdened with a killing lust.

I slake my lust, the woman dies.

Who even dreams up that kind of shit? What the bloody hell was the Unseelie king thinking when he created his royal caste? Did Death really have to be the death of anyone he fucked? Did the half-mad king sit around and cackle about that particular bit of nastiness? Did he even care?

I suppose the original Death must have instinctively known how to mute his killing *Sidhba-jai*, or learned in time to control it, or simply hadn't cared that he killed while slaking his needs.

Then again, confined to the Unseelie prison, perhaps he never got to slake his needs, which would go a long way toward explaining how rabid the Unseelie princes were when the walls finally came tumbling down. I know I'd be mad as a hatter after three quarters of a million years of celibacy, whether hobbled by a Fae sex drive or an average dose of male testosterone.

I wasted the rest of the day after Mac left, tamping down my raging desire to find the nearest willing woman and passing it, instead, with Kat and Sean, trying to teach the black Irish nephew of Dublin's most notorious, deceased crime mobster, Rocky O'Bannion, what I'd learned about how to control our power.

Sean and I walked the final paltry acres of grass in my kingdom, over and over, and bloody well over again, as I endeavored to instruct him on how to sense the earth beneath his boots and draw power from it without scorching the ground to charred ruin.

Over and over again, growing increasingly hostile as he went, he blackened the earth, drawing with the magnet of his rage the storm of the bloody century to my demesne. Worms screamed in anguish as they burned. Moles, disturbed from slumber, whimpered once then crumbled to ash. I suffered the soft implosion of larvae not yet formed enough to rue the beauty they were losing; subterranean life in all its dark, earthy grandeur. The occasional burrowing snake hissed defiance as it was seared to death.

Sean O'Bannion walks—the earth turns black, barren, and everything in it dies, a dozen feet down. Hell of a princely power. Again, what the fuck was the Unseelie king thinking? *Was* he?

Incensed by failure, Sean insisted hotly, as we stood in the bloody deluge—it wasn't raining, that scarce-restrained ocean that parked itself above Ireland at the dawn of time and proceeded to leak incessantly, lured by the siren-song of Sean's broodiness decamped to Scotland and split wide open—that I was either lying or it didn't work the same for each prince. Patiently (okay, downright pissily, but, for fuck's sake, I could be having sex again and gave that up to help him), I explained it *did* work the same for each of us but, because he wasn't druid-trained, it might take time for him to understand how to tap into it. Like learning to meditate. Such focus doesn't come easy, nor does it come all at once. Practice is key.

He refused to believe me. He stormed thunderously and suddenly off, great ebon wings dripping rivers of water, lightning bolts biting into the earth at his heels, Kat trailing sadly at a safe distance behind.

I was raised from birth to be in harmony with the natural world. Humans are the unnatural part of it. Animals lack the passel of idiotic emotions we suffer. I've never seen an animal feel sorry for itself. While other children played indoors with games or toys, my da led me deep into the forest and taught me to become part of the infinite web of beating hearts that fill the universe, from the birds in the trees to the insects buzzing about my head, to the fox chasing her cubs up a hillside and into a cool, splashing stream, to the earthworms tunneling blissfully through the vibrant soil. By the age of five, it was hard for me to understand anyone who didn't feel such things as a part of everyday life. As I matured, when a great horned owl perched nightly in a tree beyond my window, Uncle Dageus taught me to cast myself within it (gently, never usurping) to peer out from its eyes. Life was everywhere, and it was beautiful.

Animals, unlike humans, can't lie.

We humans are pros at it, especially when it comes to lying to ourselves.

I counseled myself to patient, repeated attempts despite Sean's pissy attitude. I had the advantage of being druid-trained; still, it took me years to figure out that the earth is the seat of my power, and how to nuance and finesse it.

Sean's lost in an inner darkness of his own creation and can see nothing—*wants* to see nothing—beyond it. He believes on some level he deserves to be lost in despair. I was in that desperate, bleak hell for a long time, too. I hated everyone and everything, blamed everyone and everything.

And as long as I felt that way, I made no progress.

We're fools to think injury or bad luck occurs from a single happenstance, or can ever truly be blamed on anyone or thing. We own our fates, we *choose* to get up in the morning, we *choose* to go out into the world and live, so we're always at least one part complicit. That doesn't mean we're at fault for what befalls us, merely that we must own what's befallen us, in order to continue forward in a meaningful way. Regardless of what hand life deals us, we are what we are, and railing against it makes not one bloody iota of difference and only keeps us trapped where we don't want to be and, honestly, don't belong.

You must be meticulous about the thoughts you send out into the universe. It's listening. Argue for your limits and, sure enough, they're yours. You have to argue for your dreams.

Speaking of dreams . . . I fold my arms behind my head and luxuriate in the bliss of sprawling flat on my back in bed for the first time in years, without the encumbrance of wings. I've always been a back sleeper, and since I didn't get to fuck today and it's now too late for me to find a woman that wouldn't require coin in exchange (that chivalrous Keltar romantic still beats powerfully in my heart), I've no doubt I'll be dreaming about sex for the paltry few hours I drift. I don't need to sleep anymore, but the human part of me enjoys it and keeps trying. My window of slumber, however, continues to shrink and grow more elusive.

Mac says princes don't sleep at all. If that's true, I'm not looking forward to completing the transformation. What is life without dreams?

———— • • • ————

I suspect since my last thought before falling asleep was about Mac's comment that princes don't sleep at all, I end up dreaming about her, which makes me paranoid Barrons might catch wind of it in the dreaming, and somehow black-magic his way into my subconscious and kill me—he's a prickly, territorial bastard. If anyone can pull off such a stunt, it's him.

Mac is sexy in ways I can't put into words. A fascinating darkness lurks beneath all that bubblegum pinkness she exudes that makes a man wonder just how flat-out ferocious and kinked she is in bed. Like I said, duality is my poison.

So I'm dreaming she's standing at the foot of my four-poster, spectacularly naked, and I'm so bloody aroused looking at her that it hurts so bad in all the good places, when she begins moving toward me, catching her lower lip in her teeth before flashing me a killer-hot smile that somehow manages to be equal parts innocence wed to a total lack of inhibition and tells me I'm in for one hell of a ride.

She's the stuff of dreams, lean and strong with a terrific ass. Her hair is—wait, why am I dreaming about the pre-royalty version of Mac, the one with shorter, sunnier hair?

An alarm goes off in my sex-befuddled brain as I dimly process that she has other hair, too, in places most women don't. Mac made it clear today she's a trimmer.

Fuck.

I'm dreaming about the sarcastic, flippant, irritating librarian.

Seriously? Why not someone else? Anyone else. Like Enyo Luna, with her dark, flashing eyes, dusky skin, and swaggering warrior's walk, who's scorching hot and been dying to make a battlefield out of my bed—or a convenient spot on the ground, or behind any semiprivate corner in the abbey, or in the middle of the street if I'd just agree—for the past few years.

But, no, I chose, for some unfathomable reason, to dream about a snarky genie in a bottle who insulted me repeatedly today and refused to cooperate with the queen, openly hostile, no doubt secretly traitorous.

"By the Goddess, you're everything the books said and more. So much more beautiful than the pictures," the librarian/Mac gushes, as she climbs onto my bed, straddles my thighs, and closes both of her hands around my—

"Stop that." I knock her hands away, biting back a rough growl because I really want her hands there but her sudden attack is disconcerting, and it's really weird and uncomfortable that she looks exactly like Mac. I might find her incredibly attractive but, well, it's Mac, and it doesn't feel right. Besides, I like to take my time, not just hit it and be done.

"What am I doing wrong? Teach me everything," she exclaims.

This isn't the dream I want. When I push her off me, she sprawls on the bed, legs askew, breasts jiggling, eminently fuckable.

I drag my gaze away and fix it on the wall. Deep in my gut, an alarm is sounding, red flags popping up everywhere. No idea why, but I've learned to listen to it. I roll out of bed and stand at the edge of it, studying her, trying to decide what I'm sensing that I can't put my finger on. Eventually, when no answer presents itself, I decide to terminate the dream and start over. "Begone. I don't want you here." I wave a dismissive hand.

"Lie," she says flatly.

I bristle. "I'm the lie-detector, and I said—"

"Complete rubbish," she cuts me off. "I may be a virgin, but I know what *that* means." She points at my hard dick. Then she pushes up to her knees, breasts bobbling beautifully, and reaches for it again. "It means you want to give me sex."

Irritably, I swat her hands away. "It means I need to piss," I lie. "Men often get a hard-on when they need to piss. Get out of my dream. You look like Mac, and I don't want you."

She opens her mouth to say something but then just kind of sits there, mouth hanging ajar, looking confused. Then she presses a hand to her chest, closes her mouth, swallows, opens it again, and a suspiciously yeasty-smelling belch erupts that goes on and on for like, five seconds while I gape in astonishment.

This is my idea of a sex dream? Clearly, I need more practice.

Scrambling to the edge of the bed, she claps a hand to her mouth, and laughs. "I belched!" she proclaims delightedly. "I always wondered what it would feel like." She frowns. "Ugh. Like a wee *ga-heena* was trying to crawl up my throat. Not a pleasant sensation at all. But once it started coming out, it felt *wonderful*."

She's perching, long, sexy legs dangling over the edge of the bed (butt-ass naked and hot as fuck) and gazing admiringly up at me.

I lean in and sniff.

Christ, my subconscious is warped. I'm not only dreaming of the defiant, bitchy librarian, but I've made her drunk on Guinness before coming to my bed. The things my slumbering brain chooses to link together stupefy me sometimes. "You're sloshed," I inform the figment of my warped imagination testily.

She belches again and laughs again, clearly ecstatic about her drunken state. "I am! I'm having another event. This is the best day. I was exhausted from crashing into the side of the bottle and I got thirsty so I drank some of the stuff in the bottle then stretched out to rest but I must have fallen asleep and—" Her face darkens abruptly and she hisses, "When I fell asleep, you great, big, fat blundering oaf," she stabs a finger at me, and her (Mac's) breasts jiggle so erotically that I barely even register what she'd just called me, "I nearly drowned in that nasty, smelly stuff. What kind of person does that to another person? Seals them in a stinking bottle they could drown in without a single thing to occupy themselves with."

"You're not a person and you can't drown."

"I'm every bit as much a person as you are. And I can, too, drown."

"Lie."

"It *feels* like dying."

That much was true. I knew it intimately from suffering at the Hag's hands. Though we can't actually die, we do, sort of. Then we come back around after healing while we're unconscious. "Fae don't sleep either."

"Do, too. Some of us."

My gut hears the ring of truth in her words. "This is not happening," I mutter, mostly to myself, yet, even to myself, I sound unconvinced. I refuse to believe the librarian somehow managed to break free of her bottle and came seeking my bed, ten sheets to the wind. "This is a dream and it needs to end. Now." I glower at her, waiting for her to pop out of existence.

She doesn't.

"It *is* happening." Another belch. A silvery tinkle of a laugh. "And I think it's divine," she bubbles happily. "I'd like sex now."

"I'm asleep and dreaming."

"No, you're not."

"There's no way you escaped your bottle. It's an unwritten rule. Genies can't break their bottles. If they could, there'd be no genies in existence."

"I see. You've met one?" Saccharine snark laces her words.

"No," I snap. "But everyone knows the rules."

"I," she says drunkenly and smugly, "am not a genie. I'm a librarian. And I'd like sex. Now, please." She gazes expectantly up at me.

"Enough!" I whirl and stalk naked, summoning clothing with my newly controlled power as I go. I need answers and know where to find them. Am I dreaming or am I awake? If I'm awake, one thing is for certain: The librarian will be finding a new home inside a solid silver whisky flask with an inch of *usquebaugh* at the bottom. If she's truly escaped and pulled a stunt like this, she deserves another drowning.

"Wait," she cries. "I want sex. Get back here." Another belch. Another delighted laugh.

Okay, that just downright offends me. A drunken woman, without a smidge of seduction, offering not one ounce of romance, is demanding I have sex with her, minus all foreplay. I whirl on her and snap, "You can't just perch naked in front of a man, demand sex, and expect to get it. It doesn't work like that."

"Of course it does."

"Does not."

She says blankly, "In what kingdom in what universe doesn't it work like that?"

"The only one that matters: mine!" I thunder. Whirling, I storm from the room and slam the door so hard the castle shakes and paintings rattle against the walls. A few doors down, in one of the unoccupied bedrooms, I hear the bolts of a great hanging mirror groan as they give way, followed by a resounding crash and the tinkling of glass.

Lovely.

Knowing my luck, it's an enchanted mirror, and something appalling is going to escape from that, too.

Like the Crimson Hag 2.0, determined to collect both guts *and* sex this time. And probably marry me. And keep me forever.

I really need to wake the fuck up.

13

· ● ·

She has the blood of reptile just underneath her skin

MAC

IN GEORGIA, THE LIGHT is brilliant, warm, and confident—even cocky on occasion—flooding every nook and cranny, elevating the mood and baring skin.

In Ireland, the light is secretive. Textured, uncertain, and cool, it falls short of corners, conspiring with shadows to fill every room and alley with an air of foreboding. Compound that baleful light with fog and a near-constant drizzle, and you've the perfect recipe for staying indoors, layering up, brooding into your cups before a fire and producing some of the world's finest literature. James Joyce, Oscar Wilde, W. B. Yeats, and even C. S. Lewis, born in Belfast, are but a few of Ireland's sons.

In Faery, the qualities of light, like everything else about the Fae, are intensified.

The light in the Winter kingdom is sullen, sinister, and sly, paling when you'd like more of it, brightening to a painful degree when you'd rather not see something quite so clearly, like the countless frozen statues of mortals and Fae that litter Winter's labyrinth, each immobilized and glazed in the midst of some horror being visited upon them, mouths wrenched wide in screams, and eyes that follow us as we go.

Creepy. I feel the weight of their gazes on me, imploring as I pass. *Free us!* shriek tormented eyes. *You're the queen, you can.*

When I was young, Dad took me to the beach on Tybee Island at low tide. I hate low tide. The ocean's retreat strands countless sea creatures, their tiny mobile homes flung far from the water where they're easy prey until the tide returns, by which time most of them are dead. I get the cycle of life. I know their demise has purpose.

What offended me that particular day were the humans walking the beach who, desiring a pretty trinket—or more likely something they'd casually throw away in a few hours after they showed friends—ruthlessly stripped the delicate beings from their shells and cast their vulnerable, naked bodies to the scorching sand, often directly in front of a seagull or heron's spear.

All for a shell.

Murderers! I wanted to scream.

Such was the kingdom of Winter at low tide, strewn with the suffering, and only I was capable of commuting their sentences. I could free the tortured souls and return them to the sea of life.

You don't know why she froze them, Barrons growled. *You don't know who they are or what they're capable of. You might end up releasing a Crimson Hag or worse. Perhaps it's a trap, they're Winter's frozen army, reporting all they see, and freeing them would put us in the midst of battle. Anticipate duplicity in Faery. Always.*

I stare out at the sea of statues. *Is my mother iced in here somewhere?*

If she were, I'd know. In Faery, I can feel her if she's in close proximity. I sense nothing.

I release a breath I didn't know I was holding. *That means if she's in the castle you'll know?*

If we walk all the wings, yes.

How the tables have turned: I'm no longer his OOP-detector;

he's my Mom-magnet. I cease looking left or right, resolutely ignoring the pleas for salvation and resume marching, gaze fixed
ahead, as the castle walls loom ever higher and more forbidding as
we draw near.

I narrow my eyes. *Am I seeing what I think I am?*

Barrons cuts me a dark look. *Every aperture on the castle is sealed
and spelled. Powerful stuff.*

So that's what I bounced off and ended up incapacitated by.
Winter warded me out of her castle. Successfully. Inconceivable.
Shields of glittering silver, etched with intricate runes, bar all in-
gresses to the demesne.

I drift inward and search my files for any instance of one of the
courts sealing their castle off.

My search yields zip, zilch, nada.

Which means she sealed her castle because she has my mother
inside, and this is her attempt—heavy emphasis on the word
"attempt"—to ward me out. *Told you she took her,* I fire at Barrons
with flashing eyes.

*Again, Ms. Lane, A S S out of U and M E. Stop it. Void of expecta-
tion you're never surprised. Unsurprised, you're ready for anything, not
merely the single option you've decided is true without a shred of evidence.*

Blah, blah, blah, I say irritably. *Take my hand. We're sifting in.*

*And hit the same ward you encountered before? Not a chance. We
proceed on foot.*

I arch a brow. *You said you didn't think Winter took her. Expecting
the same barrier implies—*

I don't expect. I concede all possibilities and chart the wisest course.

I roll my eyes but grudgingly concede.

We clear the labyrinth and approach the towering gate. My files
hold the passkeys to every kingdom, which is why Winter sealed
the castle. She knew she couldn't bar the gates against me. I sketch
symbols in the air before the towering double doors, conjure a rune,

and slap it onto the icy surface. The doors shudder for a long moment, as if trying to resist, then swing slowly open.

I take a step forward and stop abruptly, staring.

It takes a few moments to process what I'm seeing. To remind myself all the Unseelie are dead and they are, indeed Seelie, not Unseelie inside those walls. Or, at least, they used to be Seelie. I'm not sure what they are now.

Barrons says, *What the bloody hell is going on?*

I have no idea. But I've revised my opinion about why the castle is sealed. Winter barred it—not only to keep me out, but also to keep many somethings from getting in, and she eradicated all sound because she couldn't bear to hear what was going on in her courtyard below.

Which tells me something I would have thought impossible: Winter has lost control of her court.

Assuming she isn't somewhere in the vicious savagery before us, wearing a grotesquely mutilated form.

For, inside the walls of her kingdom, in hideous, eerie silence, all moans soundless, all screams inaudible, the Winter court is at war.

With itself.

14

It seems no one can help me now, I'm in too deep

CHRISTIAN

BLOODY HELL, I'M NOT dreaming.

The Guinness bottle crunches beneath my boots, shards of glass strewn across the floor of the chapel.

The librarian did as she claimed—flung herself against the inside of it until it toppled from the shelf, crashed to the flagstones below, and broke, freeing her.

No wonder my gut was screaming. I sensed what was happening was real, not a dream, and I was about to have sex with a genus of Fae not even the queen can identify. Knowing my luck, probably some form of succubus who'd greedily devour the tatters of my soul, leaving me a psychotic monster, along with the rest of the Fae.

"I don't understand why you won't give me sex," a plaintive voice says behind me.

I whirl on the broken glass, glowering. Of *course* she followed me. "Who are you? And don't bullshit me. You bullshit me, I'll put you in a full bottle of beer and you'll drown, over and over again. Forever."

"Are all males sadistic?"

"Are all Fae twisted? What's your game? Actually, what's your name? And put some bloody clothes on." I thunder the last.

I'm surprised and only slightly mollified when she instantly obeys, dressing herself in a short, sheer shift that's almost worse than nudity, the way it clings to every curve, clearly reveals nipples and mound, and leaves Mac's lovely legs bare to midthigh. "My name is Lyryka," she says quietly. "I'm trying to be nice, so stop making it so hard."

I blink. I'm being castigated by a succubus-Fae for being irritable when she's always irritable first. "*What* are you?"

"I can't tell you that."

"Why not?"

She belches again, but this time she doesn't giggle. "I've never been drunk before. I'm beginning to think I don't like it. When will it end?"

"About five minutes. We don't stay drunk long. I get roughly ten minutes of happy from a full fifth of whisky then a pounding head."

"Already with the pounding head part." Whimpering, she sinks down, cross-legged on the floor, dropping her head in her hands and clutching it.

Right. Now I'm supposed to feel sorry for her. I refuse. "Why can't you tell me what you are?" I demand.

Into her hands, she mutters, "Because I don't know. I'm Fae. But that's all I know."

"You don't even know if you're Seelie or Unseelie?"

She raised her head and shakes it, then flinches. "Ow."

"Answer me aloud." I repeat my question so I can subject her answer to my lie-detecting test. "Do you know if you're Seelie or Unseelie?"

"I lack a full body of evidence. I have doubts and questions that have never been answered."

Truth. And if she's Unseelie, she's the last Unseelie in existence. Well, besides me and Sean, and I don't categorize us as such.

She groans and massages her temples. "How long does a headache last?"

"About half an hour."

She says incredulously, "Longer than the drunk? That's not fair!"

I heartily concur.

After a pause during which she rubs her head and groans softly, she offers, "I know I'm the only one of my kind. A singularity."

Truth again. "Neither Mac nor Dani is your true form, is it?"

She starts to shake her head, winces and says, "No."

"Show me your true form," I demand.

"It is forbidden."

"I command you to show me your true form," I thunder, in full Druid Voice, impossible to disobey.

"Ow! My head hurts. Stop shouting at me. I said 'it is forbidden.'"

Voice doesn't work on her. I'll be damned. "By who?"

"Whom," she corrects irritably.

"By the fuck whom?" I roar.

She presses her fingertips to her temples, winces, and says exasperatedly, "I can hear you perfectly well when you speak in a normal tone. Thundering at me doesn't make me more inclined to cooperate but less. It's illogical and counterintuitive to shout at people when you want them to cooperate. I expect better of you. And I can't tell you 'by the fuck whom.'"

Where does she get off telling me she expects better of me? She has no right to any expectations about me. "Because that's also forbidden," I growl. "Why did you come to my bed?"

She says simply, "I wanted to have sex. I never have. I read about it in books, and I want to know what it's like. I want to know what makes mortals and Fae do things that defy logic. I want to know what the heart's reasons are that reason knows nothing about. It all seems rather grotesque and weird to me, but it must be terribly wonderful. Mortals die for it. Fae, well, I'm sure you've heard the story of the Unseelie king and his concubine." She shrugs. "You have all the right parts."

Gee, how flattering. I have the "right parts."

"And they're very nice parts," she adds hastily. "This is me trying to be nice again, in case you didn't notice. But I mean it, too. You have *exceptionally* nice parts. Just lovely ones. I know. I saw them all."

I've been listening with my gut the entire time I've been questioning her. She hasn't uttered a single lie. Of course, she hasn't told me a damn thing of use, either. I decide to take a different approach, ask peripheral questions and see if I get anywhere. I want to know if someone lets her out, and if so, who. "How do you organize the library when it's outside the bottle and you're inside it? Why didn't you know I was moving your things?"

"The organizing I do inside my bottle, in the replica Library, rearranges the real one. Apparently moving the real one doesn't rearrange my replica." Her eyes narrow and she bristles. "But you broke my bottle and destroyed my replica Library, so now the only way I can restore order to the collection is if you allow me to work with the real one. And clearly my original bottle had a significant design flaw," she seethes. "I resent that someone can be disheveling my Library and I have no way of knowing. Why even put me in charge of it? Apparently, I have no control over anything. Not even my Library."

"Who put you in charge of it?"

She shoots me a mutinous look and says nothing.

"Let me guess, that's also forbidden to speak of," I say dryly.

"Yes."

"You obey an unknown Fae."

She says nothing.

"You can't even tell me what species you obey? Fae, old earth god, maybe the Unseelie king himself?"

"I don't know if I could if I wanted to, and I don't. You're not nice and don't motivate me to cooperate. Something might prevent me from saying things I'm not allowed to say. Or maybe it *is* preventing me and just making me think it's my decision. Or maybe something awful would happen to me if I tried. More awful than living in a bottle for eternity and never having a single choice about anything at all."

Again, I read nothing but truth in her words, and suddenly I'm feeling sorry for her. I'd be irritable, too, were I trapped in a flask and so completely controlled. She's someone's imprisoned servant. And she's never had sex. Life indenture for a Fae is very, very long.

She glances at me sharply when I say nothing, and I look back, and an unexpected undercurrent passes between us; we both feel it.

She looks surprised then says wonderingly, "You feel compassion for me."

"You irritate the fuck out of me."

"Still, you understand that I'm in an impossible and terribly unpleasant situation."

Irritably, I nod. Fae are notorious for trying to put each other in unpleasant situations. With her, someone succeeded.

"I think empathy means you like me. Do you feel kindly toward me?" she says hopefully.

"I'm not giving you sex," I retort flatly.

She's quiet a moment then says, "I can accept that. For now. Perhaps, one day, you'll choose to give me sex. In the meantime, could we be friends? I've never had one. I'd like to. Friends watch out for you and help you and are *nice* to you."

I close my eyes and grit my teeth. My gut is screaming, *no, no, no,* yet my Highlander heart is bleeding for this woman. I read her as without guile, highly intelligent, self-possessed, socially inept, book-worldly yet life-innocent. If she's telling me the truth, and I'm ninety-nine point nine percent certain of my truth-telling skills, everything she knows about life she learned from books. She certainly behaves as if that's the case. Still, I need to know what her true form is. That's nonnegotiable. If she wants trust from me, she's going to have to fully reveal herself.

"Please don't put me back in a bottle. Not just yet. Let me live a little. Please," she pleads softly. "I'm begging you. I'd settle for just a tiny slice of life. I can't even imagine it. I've dreamed of it for so long."

I open my eyes and think, *I am so fucked because now I can't possibly make her go back into a bottle.* If I force her in and cork her off, returning her to her miserable existence without even the solace of her Library, I'll feel like the biggest shit in my kingdom, and I rather enjoy Sean owning that role. "Will you obey me if I let you stay out of it?"

Pure mutiny flashes across her features, and I nearly order her back into a bottle right then and there. I don't need any more problems on my hands, and, regardless of how downtrodden by fate she seems, she's a willful woman who's never had the right to exercise that will, a Cat-5 hurricane forming off my coast. The question isn't whether the storm will come hammer my kingdom, but when, and how catastrophic it will be. Knowing my luck, as catastrophic as is possible. I no longer even spend much time brooding about catastrophe. I plan for it. It's my life.

She says tartly, "If I must *always* obey a man, and *never* have any choice about my life, then yes, I'd rather obey one while outside the bottle than inside it. And perhaps if I'm an obedient little pet, I'll get a treat," she adds, eyes flashing.

I say defensively, "We don't know each other. I don't trust you. If the day comes that I trust you—"

"You'd listen to me? Like I'm a real person and everything?" she cuts me off excitedly.

"You're going to have to figure out how to show me your true form, to have a snowball's chance in hell of that."

She sighs forlornly.

Och, Christ. This woman. She gets to me. "Impress me with how well you obey the limits I give you. I'll endeavor to give you only the necessary ones." My gut is screaming again. This isn't going to go well, I just know it.

Still, I seem to be stuck on a runaway train, barreling down the track despite all warnings that I'm about to jump it and either crash into something horrific or end up in a no-man's-land without a compass. My damned Highlander heart. I'm an Unseelie prince with Keltar chivalry in my blood that will never cease governing my actions so long as my heart beats. No woman, no person should ever have to live without choices, without control over their life.

"What's your name?" she says then. "You know mine."

"Christian."

"No, I mean your Fae name," she clarifies. "Which Unseelie prince are you?"

I hate introducing myself this way. It makes me sound melodramatic and full of myself. "I'm Death."

She stares at me blankly a moment, then absence of expression morphs into pure terror.

Abruptly, she explodes into a cloud of kaleidoscopic mist, splintering into thousands of iridescent fireflies that swirl in frantic disarray above my head. After a few moments, she manages to reassemble herself into a cohesive mist that darts instantly into another of my empty beer bottles then sits quaking gently on top of one of the Unseelie King's metal-banded trunks I was using as a coffee table.

Sighing, I retrieve the bottle and speak into it, "I'm not going to hurt you, Lyryka."

"But you could, O great Death," floats up from inside the bottle with terror that holds a smidgen of a sneer in it.

Still irritable and defiant, despite her fear. She's a piece of work. "That's a risk we're both taking. We don't know each other. Do you really want to stay in the bottle?"

"For now," she says tightly, "I think so, yes."

"Fine. Have it your way. If you come out, you must come directly to me, and I will set the parameters you must obey. Deal?"

"Deal."

"If you disobey—"

"There's no need to threaten me, you overbearing brute," the bottle hisses, trembling with anger.

Whatever. I place her on a high shelf and leave the chapel, taking pains to close the door gently behind me. I've already broken two things in the past twenty-four hours and have no desire to release any more problems into my little corner of the world.

As I stalk down the damp stone corridor in a perfectly foul mood, still unlaid and raging with testosterone, fully aware that I probably just made a deal with some kind of devil or someone controlled by some kind of devil, Ryodan appears around the corner, stalking toward me, and I'm beyond offended because my perimeter alarms didn't go off, and I specifically warded against the Nine. He looks furious, which for him means a muscle twitches beneath his eye.

He's the bloody reason I have another of my problems: Thanks to him, Uncle Dageus is immortal and a beast while his wife is mortal and not a beast, which really crapped in all the Keltar Wheaties. We Keltar druids bond for life and beyond. Which means, for both my aunt and uncle, the "beyond" part is going to be—figuratively, at least—a long and lonely hell.

I tuck my chin and charge bullishly toward him, not about to yield an inch of *my* corridor in *my* castle in *my* kingdom. He has his own bloody kingdom. It's called Chester's, and he's a tyrant there. "What?" I growl. "If you're pissed at me, take a ticket and get into a very long line." Sean currently hates me, the librarian thinks I'm a controlling brute and is terrified of me; even Kat was casting me worried, doubtful glances after I failed so completely at trying to teach Sean to control his power. I've done nothing right all day with the exception of encouraging the bat to leave.

Ryodan continues stalking, looming large in the dimly lit corridor. The Nine don't give an inch either. "I'm not pissed at you. I don't know who I'm pissed at, and I need to know so I can skin the bastard and roast him alive. Dani and I were in bed—"

"No." I draw to an abrupt halt and cut him off, "Just fucking no. I don't want to hear anything about it. Not now. Not ever." I feel guilty every time "sex" and "Dani" happen together in a sentence. Does he know I saw her naked today, sort of? Is he reading my mind? Mentally, I mutter blah, blah, blah, over and over.

"Shut the hell up and listen to me. We were in bed and she vanished. There one instant, then gone. Taken from *inside* Chester's, which is impossible. I've got the club so heavily warded, even I have a difficult time getting past them, in beast form."

"Bloody hell, Dani's missing now, too?"

"That's not all. Lor just texted me that Jack Lane is gone as well. He left him alone for all of five minutes in one of the most heavily warded suites at Chester's," Ryodan says grimly as he stops and we stand facing each other. "The fuck did someone get past my security." It's not a question, but a statement of the impossible. I can smell the fury rolling off him. My own is rising. I feel like the librarian. Nothing is in my control.

Well, there's one thing that is . . .

Deliberately, I employ what was long one of Dani's favorite words, which I know irritates him. I'm spoiling for a fight to dump aggression, and we're both unbreakable. "Dude. Clearly, you need to work on your wards. Fail much?"

Silver eyes blaze.

I get the brawl I wanted.

15

All the good girls go to hell

MAC

WE EDGE WARILY AROUND the warring Fae—some fifty thousand of them—prepared to sift out in an instant, while I struggle to make sense of what I'm seeing.

What could drive immortals as egotistical, icy, and self-serving as the Seelie to turn against one another with such sadism? It isn't their nature. They're pleasure seekers who loathe even the mild discomfort of rain. Yes, they're also vicious, nasty, petty beings, but they turn that cruelty against other species, not their own.

The four Light Courts obey an elaborate hierarchy of internal courtesies; each caste knows its place, what it can and can't do without instigating a feud that might last centuries. Forever is a long time to have to watch your back. The Seelie prefer to watch other beings suffer.

This is all-out war. They've already hideously disfigured one another yet they continue to attack and maim, as if driven by some inexplicable external force to self-genocide.

Watch out! Barrons growls, as a heap of limbs with no discernible face breaks from battle, lurches within inches of me, and collapses to the ground where it lays, shuddering.

I bend and study the misshapen heap of parts—its melody is lower royalty, not a prince or princess but a courtier—and spy a yellow eye peering blearily from beneath a toenail, an upper lip with no gash for a mouth embedded in a shoulder that now resides where a knee might have been. The eye no longer shimmers with iridescent fire but is bleary, flat, and regarding me blankly. Unlike the statues in the labyrinth, it evidences no recognition of who I am. Understandably, for its brain is in quarters, embedded pulsating and bloody on the outside of its body.

It's almost as if we're invisible to them, even the ones with eyes intact, I murmur as I rise. The Winter Court tirelessly hunted us for a nightmarish eternity, yet here we are—and not one of them seems to care.

Don't count on it.

I stare at the raging chaos of Fae, eyes narrowed, fighting nausea. There's no such thing as an ugly Seelie. From the surreal, sense-distorting beauty of the highest castes to the lowliest among them, they are staggeringly, inhumanly beautiful.

Yet only abominations stalk, shamble, hulk, and scrabble through the Winter courtyard, most missing limbs, some split wide open like overripe, weeping plums, others turned inside out, wearing entrails for skin, blind eyes, deaf ears, and silenced mouths cocooned within, lying in raw, oozing heaps on the ground.

Some are deeply charred, skin bubbling with noxious blisters and erupting boils, others wizened with age, wrinkled as prunes and ugly as ancient crones.

All are afflicted.

All are horrific as Unseelie.

If not for my ability to hear the ancient melody of their individual castes, I would think the Unseelie have somehow returned from the dead.

As a horrifying thought slams into my brain, I stumble and

nearly go down on top of a badly burned Fae, but catch myself on Barrons's arm.

It's merely an amputated hand, he says, mistaking the cause for my alarm, as he kicks the oozing thing off my boot.

Not that. My mother.

I never had the luxury of time. I was never waiting on a message from Winter before mom's clock began to run.

If these monstrous, horrific, insane immortals have Rainey Lane, I'm too late.

She's already dead.

You don't know that, Barrons growls.

Or worse. Like one of them, she's been turned inside out but is still horrifically alive.

Fear kills, Ms. Lane. Pull it together.

Rage bubbles up inside me, cold, clear, and as psychotic as the carnage unfolding before my eyes.

Not cold, clear, and psychotic, Barrons says flatly. *You're hot, muddy, and enraged, and about to be completely out of control just like—*

He breaks off, and I gasp as, abruptly, what we're seeing makes perfect sense.

Just like them, he was about to say.

The Seelie aren't fighting like Fae.

They're fighting like *humans.*

As another severed limb scrabbles by, Barrons says, *Can you restore them? We need at least one of them with a functioning brain and mouth. Try one of the higher castes.*

He's right, we'll get no answers from these mutilated forms, and even if I'm successful at restoring one, we'll get answers only by lip-reading, given the unnatural silence blanketing the land and all inhabitants. I consider the things I've restored in the past: the bookstore, my yard in Ashford, Arlington Abbey. It's the last that makes me believe I can, and illuminates the path.

The abbey was massive, complicated, and detailed beyond anyone's ability to fully know and repair, particularly with the Underneath largely uncharted. That was the day I learned the planet holds a long and meticulous record of everything that has ever happened, and all that has ever existed.

I didn't re-create the abbey from my recollection, but from the earth's elephantine memory. I might just as easily have restored the abbey to the church that once stood there, or the shian that predated it. It wasn't my knowing that reconstructed the fortress but the timeless knowing of the cosmos, as if I merely invited a different time to exist again, replacing the current one. Not altering time, but elevating a moment to exist once more.

Gaze drifting out of focus, I clear my mind and commune with the power pulsing in Faery as strongly as it does in mortal soil, petitioning it to return the Winter Court to its former state and realize with a soft gasp that something fundamental to the universe *hungers* for order to be restored. It doesn't want disorder. It doesn't like destruction. It lists toward evolution, not devolution.

I couldn't possibly know—at least not yet, give me a few thousand more years—each and every Winter Court Fae, but the earth bore the intimate imprint of their beings, had resonated with their footsteps for millennia. I lift that memory, beckoning, adding my power to it, suggesting they be whole again.

Well done, Barrons says quietly.

Even though I felt the precise moment things shifted back into balance, I'm still astonished when I refocus and behold the beauty of the Winter Court, teeming by the thousands, whole and unharmed in the courtyard.

You can unfreeze them now, Barrons says.

I didn't freeze them. Yet they stand motionless.

For about five seconds. Staring as if stupefied.

Then they explode with rage and fall upon one another all over again, a battlefield of slathering, rabid dogs, casting curses, beating and slashing. In a matter of moments, they're disfigured and dismembered again.

It's lunacy.

I refocus, restore them again.

We get a four-second lull before they begin attacking.

Three more times I restore my court. By the third try, there's no lull at all between restoration and war. Fae are fast learners. Even insane ones. There's no point in trying to get answers. The Seelie are single-mindedly focused on destruction to their own self-destruction.

Is this happening at my other courts, too?

Sighing, I invite the earth to suspend them indefinitely, freezing them in battle, many once again mutilated and deformed, as solidly as Winter's iced statues littering the grounds.

Postulate, Barrons demands.

One: the old earth gods got revenge somehow and did something to make the Fae turn on themselves.

Good for the old earth gods, Barrons enthuses, dark eyes gleaming.

I cut him a look. *One, I'm their queen, remember. I'm responsible for them, and we still don't know where my mother is. Two, someone got the Unseelie king's power—*

Although the king abdicated power, he still has not chosen a successor. That power roams, undecided, watching.

You didn't tell me that. How do you know?

It lurks in the bookstore on occasion.

Watching him. Of course it would. The mural on the ceiling of Barrons Books & Baubles that I could never see clearly until a few years ago, mortal-time: Barrons as the Unseelie king, me as the queen and concubine.

Three, he presses.

I shrug. The Song was sung, reinvigorating the magic at the core of the planet. Anything might have happened. *I have no bloody idea, Barrons. You? Can you sense my mother?*

He slices his head to the left in typical Barrons economy-of-motion fashion. He's the most self-contained man I've ever known. *Not yet; we need to continue walking. But if she's in this mess, you've restored her.*

Assuming she was alive to begin with. Although I want my mother alive with every ounce of my being, I hope the queen's power isn't capable of reanimating the dead. For humans, death is the natural order of things. The universe will always exact a price if you defy that order.

You might get them back. They might even be resurrected in good condition, but I suspect those are the rare cases. Most myths hold some basis in reality, and there are countless zombie myths.

Still, you'd lose them again, one way or another, because they were meant to be dead.

My mother is *not* meant to be dead.

A cruel smile curves my lips.

If she's dead, I know exactly what I'll do.

I'll unfreeze the Seelie and leave them just like this, maiming and disfiguring one another for all eternity.

And I'll never look back.

16

---•◦•---

Who am I? Can I conceal myself forevermore?

LYRYKA

For the first time in my life, there's no cork in the neck of my bottle.

My father (assuming he has a way of finding me, even though I'm no longer where he put me) remains absent.

Choice is mine.

The world is *right there*.

The Hall of All Days, within reach.

I'm desperate to leave the bottle, plunge headfirst into all the experiences I've read about, meet people and not-people, have sex, and taste and touch and feel everything.

Yet, on my first foray into the world, with whom did I have my virgin encounter?

Death.

It's enough to give me pause.

There are countless of my species, billions of mortals, myriad mythical creatures. What are the odds I'd come face-to-face with the one and only Death on my first excursion beyond the bottle?

Astronomically and inconceivably small.

One in an infinity.

I know what that means.

Events of epic proportion, rife with internal and external conflict, are never wasted on secondary characters.

I'm one of the heroes.

As both librarian and reader, I'm steeped in metaphor and analogy, coincidence and fate, foreshadowing and red herrings, theme and motif, emotional currency and twist of plot.

And, like any astute reader, I'm deeply suspicious of the narrator.

I know the precise element that sets a hero on his or her most significant journey often leads to his or her untimely demise.

Few stories in the Library end happily ever after. I'm not certain who gathered them. I'd have assembled a collection harboring a bit more optimism.

I wasn't even graced with the subtlety of a metaphor.

Death was my liberator.

There's a stone upside the head for you that reeks of karmic mischievousness and implies a dreadful fate may well await me.

"I'm one of the heroes," I murmur wonderingly. Then I groan and drop my aching head in my hands, lightly massaging my temples. Death said the aftermath of drunk lasts about thirty minutes. It's time for my headache to be gone already.

"Lyryka."

My head whips up, and I gasp. "Father!" So much for thinking he could no longer find me.

"Omniscient, remember?" he murmurs with a playful smile.

I feel an answering smile tug at my lips. For so long, I lived for the times he would appear, planned conversations, verbal tidbits to charm him into staying longer, selected the forms that I would wear for him with great deliberation and care. His company was my greatest joy, the only change in a monotonously unchanging environment from which there was no escape.

I hate him for that.

I love him.

And I hate that.

"You did well," he says, starry eyes gleaming.

Wait, what? Blinking, I shake my head and instantly regret it. "You mean I was *supposed* to escape my bottle?"

"Of course."

Was *nothing* my choice?

"I might have placed the bottle before his boot. I did not, however, fling myself into the side of it until it fell and shattered. You did."

So that part was my choice. Or was it? I despise how easily he confuses me. Anything could be true. Anything could be a lie. He is my only source of information about the world. It's exceedingly dangerous to permit a single person to shape your reality.

Why did he choose these two specific forms for me? What mischief has he put me up to? "I'm not certain I understand what you want of me, father. Will you tell me more about what I'm to do?"

He shrugs. "Merely get to know him and his friends."

"Why?" I regret the word the moment it's out. My father arches a brow, regarding me too intently for my comfort. There's a palpable stress in his regard. I've never asked him why before.

"Consider it a test preceding your eventual freedom. Prove to me how well you will obey me, that my faith in you is not misplaced."

Nodding, I smile, careful to betray no other emotion.

Yet, I wonder why I have to prove anything to him.

He proves nothing to me. I demand nothing. Ever. I have no rights.

"I can't stay," he says then. "There are countless pieces in motion that require my attention. I came to tell you you're doing well. Carry on and stop second-guessing. The time nears when you will finally be free. When I will, at long last, bring you home. Have faith, obey, and all will become clear in time."

I study him as perhaps I have never studied him before. Who is this being to insist I lose my entire life waiting for what he deems the "right time"? Is he even really my father? Is anything I think I know about myself true? Why do I hear no knell of truth in his claim that he will set me free?

One thing I do know from reading billions of stories sprung from the myths of billions of worlds.

There is no right time.

There's only now.

"I'm free to leave the bottle?" I press. "Do as I wish?" As I await his reply, I wonder if anything is truly my wish. I wonder if he's so clever, king to my pawn, that he sweeps me about his chessboard, prepared all along to sacrifice me at a critical moment to achieve whatever endgame he seeks, if I'm one of thousands of pawns he's positioned during the eternity he's been free and I have not.

"So long as you obey the instructions I gave you, yes. But, Lyryka, if you show him your true form . . ."

He trails off, and I blanche, breath hitching in my throat, heart freezing in my breast. He didn't speak. He *showed* me what would happen to me inside my head. I never, *ever* want that to happen to me. There are worse fates than my bottle. An abyss of monsters, dark, dank, and terrifying, with no way out. Would he *really* do that to me?

My father is gone.

Leaving me to ponder the perfect conundrum he's created for me.

I can be free, but only if I never reveal my true form.

And Death, whom I find so attractive, and hope will be my friend and give me sex, will trust me only if I reveal to him my true form.

It's a vise of mutually conflicting and dependent conditions, a trap, a dilemma employed by an author of events to make or break a character.

I push to my feet, prepared to leave my bottle.

Oh, yes, I'm definitely one of the heroes. I will *not* be broken.

Then I drop right back down with another groan as a second, highly distasteful possibility occurs to me.

In all fairness, by such criteria, I might also be one of the villains.

17

— • ◦ • —

Run, you little bitch, I want your power

IXCYTHE

HIGH IN THE NORTH Tower, Ixcythe gazed down at the battle frozen below, lips drawn in a snarl, faceted eyes glittering with lust.

Rage and desire warred painfully in her breast, enough to rend flesh from bone. She hungered so intensely she *was* the hunger, a maddening, unquenchable craving for more of everything but most especially possession of the power that was meant to be hers, but had been thieved by a mortal.

The shields barring the ingresses to her castle were opaque from without, translucent from within, defying prying eyes, allowing her to spy.

The bitch queen was in her kingdom.

Headed straight for her door, escorted by the beast that served as her consort and guard.

Ixcythe coveted the beast, lusted for him with every atom of her being. He was a weapon as deadly as the spear of destiny and the sword of light, a living creature that could kill the Fae.

Were she to seduce him, he would be the dagger she'd thrust deep into the human queen's duplicitous heart. It would be dangerous to have him near; it would be thrilling to have him heel at her side; death on a leash, the end of any Fae that dared so much as whisper against her.

The beast of voracious appetites was legend. He'd lived among them for a time. He could be ruthless, he could be cruel; she could feel his hunger for all things simmering beneath his flesh, barely restrained. He was merely a dog that needed to be retrained, encouraged to once again savor his basest instincts and desires, rewarded each time he succumbed. Together, they would be unstoppable. With him, she would gain command of many such beasts, and her reign would never be overthrown.

Ixcythe had deliberately not yet summoned the queen; she meant for her to stew in debilitating emotions before commanding her presence at the Grove.

But the bitch had sauntered in, uninvited, unwelcome, with the beast heeling at *her* side, as if she had every right to be in Winter.

When the queen restored her subjects, Ixcythe held her breath, praying the mortal possessed the power to restore them completely, return their reason and immortality as well as their forms.

For a few moments, she'd thought the queen succeeded.

Then they'd fallen on one another again.

And again.

And again.

Now her entire kingdom was filled with nothing but statues.

She was princess of none.

Well, not quite . . .

There was another inside the castle with her, but that one was little better than the grotesque statues below.

With an icy smile, she turned to gaze at the human she'd abducted to coerce MacKayla Lane to obey her slightest whim.

It was still alive.

Barely.

She'd chosen to damage it in precise ways, and when she was done, she'd infected it with a slow-acting poison.

There was only one thing that could save it now.

The Elixir of Life.

18

· ● ·

You should see me in a crown

MAC

IN ORDER TO ASCERTAIN that my mother is not somewhere on this gruesome battlefield, we're forced to walk it. "Slow-mo-Joe it," as Dani would say. Trudgery—trudging drudgery—I would say. Sifting has spoiled me. There are things I prefer not to see, but a ruler can't afford that luxury, so I force myself to inspect the Fae we pass. No beings deserve the kind of brutality they've inflicted upon one another. I'm stymied, unable to fathom what could have driven them to it.

The moment we pass the final suspended mutation, I sift us up the absurdity of one thousand steps, framed by an elaborate pair of carved iced bannisters that lead to the towering door of the fortress.

As all things Fae, Winter's castle is an overblown creation. Numb to sensation, the Seelie believe the bigger and grander a thing, the better, ergo one thousand steps that no sifting Fae of a higher caste will ever place cosseted foot upon, and one thousand steps non-sifting lower castes will be forced to manually ascend, reminding them of their lesser status each time Winter commands their presence.

The door is wide, fifty times our height. Not because Fae are tall—they have a few feet on mortals—but because it's bigger and grander, therefore better. More waste. I live in a cozy, if spatially challenged, bookstore and, if I have anything to say about it, always will.

The surface of the door ripples with whatever fluid silver element Winter used to bar the entrances to her castle. Intricate runes rush up the door in hundreds of columns, reach the top and vanish. I realize they're looping, traversing the front, over the lip, and down the back of the door before reaching the bottom and rising up the front again, doubly securing the entrance against us. This is what I smashed into when I tried to sift to my mom. This is the magic capable of barring the Faery queen herself from one of her royal's castles.

Clever, Barrons murmurs. *I've not seen this before.*

That worries me. I drift inward, searching my files on wards, which I've organized and keep readily accessible. I spent a great deal of time studying all manner of protection while sequestered. Enemies abound, and I'll have to sleep sometime.

There's no mention in my files of a looping ward that encases an object, no tips on how to shatter it. I contemplate trying spells at random, starting with my all-powerful crimson runes, but random magic is dangerous. If you break a rune badly, you can turn it into something else. Adding blood to the wrong kind of rune can turn it into a living guardian. My crimson runes, once used to reinforce the prison walls, intensified them so the more violently an Unseelie struggled trying to escape, the stronger the walls grew. They were also recently used to cocoon two staggeringly powerful Unseelie Princes, operating on the same principle. The harder they fought the cocoon, the tighter it bound, and the more undefeatable it became. If I placed one on the door, it would likely only solidify the barrier.

How does she possess a method of warding that I know nothing about, that's capable of keeping even the Faery queen at bay? I hold all the files of the Fae, I say to Barrons.

Not quite. You hold files from the second queen onward, and it's possible there are eras of omission. The first queen died without passing the lore, leaving their origins secreted in the mists of time. We don't know if all subsequent queens chose to pass the power forward. Only that, on occasion, they did.

Still, the Fae drink from the Cauldron, repeatedly, shortening their memory to a lesser span of time.

Barrons goes motionless (a difficult feat for a man whose innate posture is still as death), and I can practically see him sorting through countless possibilities before alighting on what he deems the most probable one.

Fuck, he growls.

What? I demand.

Dark eyes narrow, nostrils flare as he scans the frozen Seelie. Again, I can see his mind whirring, chewing over whatever he's struck upon. He's lived so long, seen so much more than I, analyzed the nuances of events as power play after war spun out, and he often gets to the crux of things before me. It's irritating and incredibly useful.

The Seelie slowly grew more powerful, he finally murmurs, *after the Song was sung. The old earth gods were reinvigorated, substance restored, unique abilities amplified. What if those aren't the only things that changed? What if additional changes continued to occur in Faery, as they have in the mortal world?*

What continued to change in the mortal world?

Mirrors, for one. They might reflect you, they might not; some even serve as limited doorways. Toasters once returned toast. Now it's anyone's guess what you get back, if anything. Commodes consistently flushed down, not up. The laws of human physics have been growing increasingly unpredictable. Fae and mortal are bleeding together.

One more reason I needed to get the walls back up between realms. Toasters were keeping toast and toilets were flushing the wrong way? What else did I miss? *What are you saying?* I practically snarl. I don't need more problems. The Seelies' reinvigorated power is problem enough.

What if the Song began undoing and restoring other things as well?

Such as? I do snarl this time because I've begun to see where he's going and I don't like it one bit. It implies the advantage of long memory isn't mine at all—but theirs. *No,* I insist.

Denying with emotion what reason postulates is illogical. What if the Song restored their memories? My theory explains the ward you encountered earlier, as well as this one.

I turn to study the battlefield. What could more surely turn the Fae against one another than if they suddenly recalled countless feuds? If long-forgotten wars from forgotten times were abruptly fresh again? Though they possess only shallow emotion, grudges are something the Fae hold dear. Immense egos demand immense retaliation.

I sense the distortion of space sifted through another's hands at the same moment Barrons does. An aperture is being opened into Faery from a portal far away.

We whirl as one to face the intruder.

No one appears.

The aperture slits open, the size of a letter drop.

A scrap of paper flutters to the ground, and the slot closes.

I won't show myself at the Light Court.
  Fae attack every time I do.
  Dani vanished. Jack's gone, too.
  Both seized from inside Chester's.
  Ryodan says get your asses mortal-side now.

Christian

I inhale sharply, tip my head back, and stare up at the castle, blood icing in my veins.

Mac, Barrons says warningly.

I ignore him. They already had my mom. Now they have my father and Dani? Three people who mean the world to me, three who are kind and strong, brave and good, determined and valiant, who strive daily to make the world a better place.

The world needs them.

It doesn't need the vicious, petty Fae.

There's a tsunami building inside me fashioned of raw fury. I may lack knowledge of times gone by, but I'm the one and only vessel for the True Magic. It's time to see what it can do.

Rage focuses me like a laser. Rage is lovely that way. It obliterates obstacles, circumvents walls, targets the enemy like nothing else.

She thinks she's warded me out?

I'll shred her fucking door. Shred her castle. Shred her flesh from bone.

The Seelie may have their memory back, but emotion is *my* advantage. One they can never match.

An arctic wind kicks up, swirling around me, gusting the door, racing up the sides of the castle, swirling higher and higher, kicking snow and glittering shards of ice into the air as my rage alters the climate.

Barrons grabs me by the shoulders and shakes me violently. *You bloody fool, if you mishandle it, you'll kill them, too. I feel what's forming inside you. You think it's focused but it's not. You think it's light but it's not. Dark magic is far more dangerous, and you don't know how to control it. It takes decades to learn.*

The True Magic isn't dark, I tell him furiously. *Though capable of great destruction, it springs from a source gentle and kind.*

Bullshit. I feel what's in you, and there's nothing light about it. I know the dark side. I live there, for fuck's sake. Emotion shapes power. Terrible power comes at a terrible price. Shut it the fuck down and get your bloody emotions in check, Ms. Lane.

It's too late.

I can't.

I invited it.

It's here.

And it has to go somewhere. But he's right. I don't dare turn it on the castle because if Mom, Dad, and Dani are in there, it will destroy them, too. I must learn to wield this power with precision— quickly.

At the moment, I have to release it, or it will blast me apart at the seams, and that *so* isn't happening.

I whirl toward the tens of thousands of frozen statues in the courtyard, and, just when I think the power might tear me asunder, it erupts from me in a great, chilling, killing wind that blows down like an icy sirocco over the courtyard. The instant it leaves my body, I crumple to the ground, without bone, without muscle or tendon or ligament, for the second time in one day incapacitated and vulnerable. I'm going to have to figure that out and fix it ASAP. I will not lie on the ground, a broken rag doll.

Gritting my teeth, I raise my head a few scant inches to peer through the razor-edged drift blasting across the terrain as color leaches from Fae skin.

The immobilized Fae turn to alabaster ice then explode in silvery splinters, raining down on the courtyard, glittering like billions of tiny diamonds in the snow.

My lips curve.

An entire court, effortlessly destroyed. With a mere thought.

My thought.

I drop my head back to the snow and lie, shaking, waiting for my bones to return, eyes narrowed.

Is she watching me from her castle on high? Did she see what I just did? Does she understand that I am the queen and she is a thousand kinds of fool to think she can take *anything* from me, ever?

Above me, the leaden sky darkens and night obliterates day, as a deep, starless black claims the kingdom. High above, within that blackness, thunder rolls, and the temperature plummets painfully. I ice where I sprawl.

I didn't do that. The bitch princess did. How dare she? After what she witnessed? I shake myself and shatter the ice. Laughing softly, I vanquish her darkness and restore the day. It stutters a moment; I can feel her trying to seize control of it.

She fails. I laugh again. She may have dredged up a forgotten ward or two, but she's no match for me.

Barrons makes no move to help me up.

He's pissed.

He'll get over it.

Can you put the Seelie back together again? he says finally.

With immense effort, I roll my head to the side and gaze up at him with a gaze as sharp as knives and frozen as winter. *Why would I?*

———•◦•———

I droop on the lip of the toilet (which I haven't tried flushing yet because knowing my luck I'll get a water fountain) and drag a trembling hand across my mouth.

I feel as if I just vomited up every meal I ever ate in my life.

Not in quantity but quality. I've been puking for an hour. Far past dry heaves. Not even a thin drool of bile is left, yet my stomach retches and my body convulses.

Barrons is sitting with me on the floor in the bathroom at Barrons Books & Baubles, leaning back against the doorjamb, long legs stretched out, arms folded across his chest, eyes full black.

No whites. Not even a flicker of crimson. Full obsidian.

He's been watching me in silence since we sifted back to the bookstore. He hasn't said a word.

I know why.

He can't stand close to the kind of power I summoned without it affecting him, too.

That makes him a liability.

Wait—what?

I'm the liability.

I begin to weep.

My body feels sickened, poisoned, because I welcomed something that is anathema to me. I invited it. I allowed it to flow through me and became one with it.

This was very different than possession by the *Sinsar Dubh*. Then, there was a sentient, hungry blackness that plotted and planned, twisted and tempted, undermined and manipulated, seized control of me and forced me, until I finally figured out how to resist it.

But today was all me.

My choice.

My fury. My fear. My unchecked emotion.

I welcomed a power that was destructive. It held no kindness. Only cruelty. I sought vengeance in its basest form. I destroyed tens of thousands of beings. With a mere thought. That which earlier elated me now horrifies me.

I begin retching again and cry harder. I choke and snuffle, my throat burning, stomach on fire, heart a stone in my chest.

One would think, as much as my body has transformed into something very nearly Fae, altered by Cruce's elixir, I wouldn't suffer so, but I do.

"It's the human in you," Barrons says tightly. "Glad to see some small shred of it remains."

I meet his dark gaze.

He searches my eyes a moment then some nuance of his face softens, and his eyes lighten to midnight irises on silver. "Welcome back," he says flatly.

"You, too," I say quietly. "I'm sorry."

"Elaborate," he says in the same flat tone.

He's searching my eyes in a way I don't like and never want to see again. "I lost control of myself."

"How did it feel?"

I must be excruciatingly, ruthlessly honest to repair us. To repair me. "For a moment, it felt glorious."

He inclines his head. "Go on."

"The aftermath was cool, clear, and triumphant. I felt powerful as a god."

"Yet now you sit puking."

"I hate myself."

"Wasted emotion. Try again."

I search for the right words. The moment is precarious. "The price is my soul. I would lose it in time. The finest parts of me would exist no more." I'd be lost. I wouldn't even really remember who I'd once been.

"You don't keep puking. The more often you use that kind of power, the more palatable it becomes. It stops harming you, begins to feel good."

"Because monsters don't feel shame or grief or regret. And each time I use it, it turns me darker."

"Yes."

"How did *you* combat it?" I felt it rising up in him, answering my call. Yet coolly, remotely, he thrust it away. He could have joined me, adding fuel to my fire.

"You choose. Hero or villain."

"You told me you're not the hero."

"Not the villain either."

"What else is there?"

"A person that gets up every day and tries as hard as she can to live up to what she believes in. Aims for the stars. Misses sometimes. Tries again. Harder. With more commitment to protecting others and less selfishness."

"I have to put the Seelie back together again."

"Worry about yourself for the moment. It's not as if they're going anywhere." He pushes up from the floor and stands gazing down, searching my eyes as if he still isn't sure who I am.

I never want him to wonder who I am. He knows who I am. I

like him knowing who I am. I didn't just betray me, I betrayed us today.

He must see something of the real me in my eyes, because he extends a hand to help me up. "Ryodan and Christian are waiting at Chester's."

I wipe away tears. "I have to brush my teeth."

"You're the queen. You have only to think your mouth clean and it is."

"I have to brush my teeth," I repeat.

"Then we sift. Time is of the essence."

"It's only five minutes. Let's drive. Or better yet, walk."

"Those you love are in peril."

So am I, I don't say. *And my weakness put all of us in greater peril.*

I see the first flicker of warmth in his eyes, and I understand something then. At some point, if I continued using dark power and went fully dark—

I'd join you in hell. Black eyes flash crimson. *And I'd prefer not to. So, toe the motherfucking line, and don't make me cross it, Ms. Lane.*

Pain rips through me. He'd follow wherever I went rather than live without me. I understand that.

We're tethered. Bound beyond reason.

And because of that bond, we owe each other an enormous debt of care and kindness. Whatever one of us chooses becomes the other's reality.

The love I feel for him restores to my bones the grace of steel, to my spirit the resilience of hope.

It's the strength of love that holds darkness at bay. I wonder what Barrons once loved so greatly that he was able to claw his way back across that thin, dark line, long ago.

He smiles, but it doesn't reach his eyes. *We're not the same. It wasn't what you think.*

What then?

You'll figure it out. In time.

19

Frozen inside without your touch

IXCYTHE

Now she was truly princess of none.

The queen destroyed her entire court.

Ixcythe clutched the icy sill of the window, swaying, staring blindly down at the destruction of her subjects, and began to keen.

Behind her breast a mushroom cloud of fury and grief expanded, growing in size and intensity, and she knew, if she failed to somehow reverse or release the maelstrom within, she would shatter into thousands of jagged bits just like her court.

The queen had used the sacred True Magic against her own subjects; the species she'd been chosen, was *privileged* to lead. As Ixcythe watched in horror, torn chunks of Fae had rained down, many flung far beyond the courtyard walls. Some had been pulverized to dust where they stood, and, even now, their ashes were vanishing on a frigid breeze.

Then the queen and the beast left. Sifted out. Never looked back.

As if those bits weren't still alive.

Still sentient and suffering; shreds of their consciousness in each severed atom, eternally aware, in eternal agony.

Until, of course, the changes wrought by the Song would mercifully erase them from existence, destroying them forever, as if they'd not once been gods, as if they'd not once ruled the universe.

The blasphemy of it. Their own queen had exterminated them, turned them into creatures that would actually consider *death* a mercy. It was too much to bear.

Ixcythe keened harder but, silenced by her own spell, was incapable of making the slightest sound, denied even the release of wailing, and the mushroom cloud within bloomed with radioactive toxicity. She flung back her head, mouth stretched impossibly wide on a scream, stomach heaving. Hell was raging without being able to make a single sound.

It made her feel as if she didn't even exist.

It was bad enough that the Autumn, Summer, and Winter Courts had devolved into mindless savages, but at least, then, the three of them had been equal. None of them lesser, none of them prey.

But if Azar and Severina discovered Ixcythe no longer had a court, no army to raise, didn't have a single courtier she could punish, torture, or coerce into doing her bidding, that she was completely and utterly alone in her kingdom of ice—

They'll destroy me. It's a matter of time, she whispered, but no words came out, only puffs of frosted breath tinged with blood. She began to choke, gurgled and spat out a lethally edged shard of crimson ice, could feel more chunks of it backing up in her throat.

Emotion was deadly in her current state. She was so enraged, so betrayed—and by D'Anu, so very, very *afraid*—that, rather than transforming her environment with her pain, she was icing her own essence, doing to herself precisely what the queen had done to her courtiers.

In moments, she would freeze solid and explode if she didn't get herself under control. She was self-destructing. It was ludicrous that such a thing could even happen.

Humans! This was *their* fault. Over and again they'd manipulated, cheated, and abused the Fae.

Snarling, she cracked the rigid ice frosting her skin, whirled toward the only human present, and raised a hand to drive an ice pick through its brain.

Gritting her teeth, gnashing them with fury, she stopped herself at the last second, the weapon inches from its head.

She needed the human. Bloodied, broken, and poisoned, it was her only chance.

Retracting the ice pick took every ounce of self-control she possessed. She summoned it back slowly, inch by careful inch, rotating it as it came, turning it on herself, welcoming it into her flesh, using the pain of her body to distract from the pain in her breast.

After several long, shuddering moments, she realized the physical pain was, perversely, feeding the nuclear ice that threatened to detonate at her core.

For the first time in her existence, Ixcythe tried deliberately to summon warmth to her form. As her gift of an icy breeze had cooled Azar's rage and restored his reason in the Grove, she now needed a gift of heat to thaw her arctic storm. If she blew herself up, the many injustices to their kind would never be avenged. The queen would destroy them all, and in time the Fae would cease to exist, be forgotten, dwindle into myth that no one even believed.

Closing her eyes, she began to paint a picture in her mind of a day—still winter, but late and on the cusp of spring—a melting garden, as she strolled through it beneath a pale (the horridness of it) sun. She lavished the vision with detail, adding tiny white snow blossoms thrusting up from the melting drifts, birdsong in the distant forest, the wan rays from the faint blue orb heating her flesh—

She despised heat. She loathed the sun.

Ice was obdurate, proud, and beautiful. Ice held its shape, yielded nothing, like a great glacier, crept and crept and crept, until it swallowed everything in its path.

But the very thing that had saved her so long ago was destroying her now.

Over and again, she endeavored to create an image of warmth in her mind, and over and again, the ice she so revered rushed in, and the vision collapsed beneath the weight of her frozen heart.

She was incapable of being anything other than what she was.

Icy. Unyielding. Hard.

Abruptly, just when she thought all was lost, at the very moment the edges of her essence began popping with hairline cracks, ice rumbling with ominous thunder, she felt an unexpected tendril of heat brush her flesh. It was uncertain, gusting far too gently for her needs, but, as she forced herself to welcome it, the heat gained confidence, and a sultry breeze swirled around her essence, slipped beneath her skin, and penetrated to her core.

Shivering, she tossed back her head, eyes closed in bliss, welcoming it fully. Against all odds, she'd triumphed, managed to summon heat, and would live to war another day.

Let me in.

Ixcythe's eyes flew open, and she whirled, scanning the room.

Here, at the window.

Hand to her breast, she spun again. Azar was framed in the glass, suspended far above the ground.

I felt your grief and rage and came. And yes, Severina will try to destroy you. But you're wrong as well. I will not. The queen will do the same to my court that she's done to yours. We will stand together. You have the human. The queen will bring the Elixir in exchange.

Why would I trust you?

I just healed you. Thawed you with my heat.

No, you didn't. I did it myself.

Ix, you couldn't summon heat if your existence depended on it. As you just proved.

Never call me that.

But he was right and she knew it. It wasn't her. She was far too cold and had been for too long. She would have exploded if Azar hadn't sensed her pain and come. But why save her? It was the way of rulers, of all the Fae, to turn on those weaker and destroy them. She was indisputably weaker.

Princess of none.

For now, be consort of Autumn. I will leverage my court's power behind you. We'll take back the Elixir and restore both our kingdoms.

Ixcythe searched the banked embers of his gaze. *Why would you do that?*

Once, he said slowly, *we were lovers.*

She flinched. She recalled that time, had been astonished and horrified to discover it nestled within her memories. She also recalled the many times Severina had tortured her, when Ixcythe's power was diminished by the queen's punishment. *Memories, begone,* she wanted to scream.

She remembered, too, what happened at the end.

Ice was indomitable. Ice was peace.

Once, I meant the compliments I paid you. Once, Azar said heavily, *I loved you.*

Ixcythe jerked as his words knifed through her breast. She despised emotions and everything they did to her. They made her weak, vulnerable, foolish, and always ended in betrayal.

You remember. Say it, Ixcythe.

Never. She'd blow herself up before admitting that, once, she'd loved him, too.

Love was the greatest weakness of all.

I don't need you, she snarled.

You have no one, Ix.

I have the human. And if you try to take it or my castle, I'll destroy you. You've never been a match for me.

Azar sighed, gusting another warm breeze around her, one that lingered caressingly on her icy curves. *I'll be at the Grove when you come to your senses. We will summon the imposter queen together.*

He vanished.

20

Hail, Hail, the gang's all here

MAC

939 RÊVEMAL STREET.

The irony isn't lost on me. In French, *rêve* means "dream" and *mal* means "bad." How it must have amused Ryodan, eons ago, to set up base camp on a street called Nightmare. I wouldn't be surprised to learn he'd hoisted the original sign himself.

Ryodan did more than rebuild Chester's aboveground. The underneath was treated to a face-lift, as well. The entrance to the subterranean club no longer lies beneath two heavy trapdoors and down two awkward-to-navigate ladders. Now an elegant (albeit cobweb-dusted with more of those sticky webs that seem to be on everything lately) ivory staircase descends to a luxurious modern foyer, tastefully appointed with ivory and charcoal furnishings. A black marble floor, so highly polished it serves as an obsidian mirror, leads to black matte doors embellished with panels of wrought iron twisted into complex designs that open to reveal dozens of unique sub-clubs below.

The past washes over me in waves as I stand in the inner foyer and stare past the balustrade at surprisingly busy clubs (although it should no longer surprise me; the party not only continues rocking at Chester's through the worst of times but rocks even harder then). I remember when I first discovered the club, back when I was too naïve to understand the necessity of keeping your friends close, your enemies closer.

Over there, I chatted with the bartending Dreamy-Eyed Guy while the Fear Dorcha lurked menacingly on a stool next to me; there, down to the left, I stood behind a bar myself and mixed drinks during a time of crushing indecision; and there, high above, I shattered the glass floor of Ryodan's office, while under the control of the *Sinsar Dubh*.

Despite having some of the worst times of my life inside these walls, Chester's is part of me. My home has become an amalgamation of many places: Barrons Books & Baubles is my bedroom, Chester's is my living room, my parents' townhome in Dublin is my kitchen, a water tower that overlooks the city, with Dani at my side, is my favorite coffee shop. Arlington Abbey is my library. And somewhere, a few miles to the south of Nana O'Reilly's cottage by the sea, the grave of one of my ancestors, Patrona O'Connor, is my chapel. I'd like to light a candle there and say a prayer one day. Hopefully, by the time I do, I won't have betrayed my entire bloodline.

Barrons and I hurry through packed dance floors and bars, up the wide glass-and-chrome stairs that lead to Ryodan's office.

"You didn't sift?" Ryodan growls the moment the door hisses open. He's seated at his desk in the dimly lit office, a study in shadows. Lor stands behind him, arms folded. Christian is to his left, an enormous, dark, winged silhouette against the backlit glass wall. "You sifted to see your father, but now you fucking take your time. Dani is missing."

"So is my father," I growl back. "And they were both in your care, under *your* watch, with *your* wards for protection."

We stand glowering at each other a moment, then Ryodan smiles faintly. "Good to see you again, Mac."

I return the smile. "You, too." I incline my head at Lor, uncertain of my reception. The last time I saw him, I used the queen's power to manifest a machine gun and killed him.

"Mac."

"We good?"

He flashes me a grin that doesn't meet his eyes. "Got serious doubts about you. Babes never get enough of me."

"I mean after—"

"Yeah," he cuts me off tightly. "We're good."

The ghost of Jo stands between us. He gives me a long look and speaks inside my mind in the way the Nine have. *You didn't say you were sorry.*

And you didn't say you forgive me, I reply.

But he knows I am.

And I know he will.

To Christian, I say, "You're wearing prince again."

"Anger makes it more difficult to maintain my Highlander form. They took Dani. I may be stuck as prince for a while."

"It appears the Fae regained their memories." Barrons eschews niceties and gets straight to the point. "That's why they were able to sift past your wards," he says to Ryodan. "Powers that were forgotten long ago have been rediscovered. This isn't the playing field we've known for millennia. We've no idea what they're capable of."

Not entirely true, I think. One court isn't capable of anything any more. I saw to that.

Ryodan says, "Are you certain?"

"As certain as I can be without direct confirmation from a Fae."

Which, for Barrons, was 99.9 percent certain, and I agreed. It was the theory that best explained the anomalies we'd encountered.

"How much memory, how far back?"

Barrons replies grimly, "Quite possibly, all the way."

Christian unleashes a string of curses. I feel the same. We always had an advantage: Barrons and Ryodan could hold all the Fae at bay with their dark magic. Now we're sitting ducks, and the Seelie can find us anytime, anyplace they want.

"Why take Dani and Jack? What are they after?" Christian says.

"My mother, too," I add tightly.

"Your mother is fine," Ryodan says. "At least, last time I checked on her."

"What?" I say blankly.

"She wasn't abducted. She drove into one of those drifting pieces of Faery that are difficult to see."

"IFPs. Interdimensional Faery potholes," I murmur. While the Song of Making eradicated the black holes and healed the Earth, it didn't do anything about the places where Faery and the mortal realm crashed into each other on Halloween, creating distorted pockets of reality that are nearly impossible to spot. Once I figured out how to use the Song to sing the walls back up, and separate realms again, the IFPs would presumably disappear.

Lor says. "She got turned around and couldn't find her way out. Took her two days to get back."

"Two *days*?" I was aghast at the thought of my mother being lost alone in Faery for so long, but I also knew, depending on what fragment she'd gotten lost in, she was lucky she survived at all. There were fire cyclones, ice tornados, slices of underwater worlds. Relief floods me. Mom is okay—the Seelie don't have her. "I thought you'd tethered them all." The Nine had used their arts to bind the IFPs into permanent positions, and the *sidhe*-seers had passed out maps (I'd snagged one for each of my parents) letting people know where they were and how to avoid them.

"It was a drifter. We think the old gods are cutting them loose again. Doing something that makes them faster, trickier to dodge," Ryodan says.

"Why would they?" Christian says.

Ryodan shrugs. "Add to the chaos."

"Where is Mom now? *Here?*" My voice rises and my hands ball into fists. "Tell me she's not here. Clearly, you can't protect anyone here."

"Careful," Ryodan says softly. "I gave Christian the fight he wanted for those words. Happy to give you the same."

"You wanted it, too," Christian growls. "I merely accommodated."

"You won't touch a hair on her head," Barrons says just as softly.

"Rainey's not at Chester's," Ryodan tells me. "I don't know where she is at the moment and prefer to keep it that way. Fade, Kasteo, and Daku are guarding her. They won't leave her side. They won't rest. They won't eat. They'll keep her safe."

I blink. My mother is with three of the Nine. That's got to be as weird for her as her being stuck in an IFP.

"She's probably cooking for them, the lucky fucks," Lor grouses. "Woman makes hoecakes like no other."

"You can't possibly be talking about food at a time like this," I say.

Lor shrugs. "Man's gotta eat."

"I know what men like you eat, and it isn't hoecakes."

"Nobody's calling you on the carpet for your eating habits, honey. Get all of Jo outta your teeth?"

"Need I remind you of another time, another place, Bone-crusher?" Barrons murmurs with silken menace.

"Dani," Ryodan says flatly, "Is. Missing."

"So," I say just as flatly, "Is. My. Father. Can't Dani use your version of IYD? The spell will take you to wherever she is, even in Faery." It would, unfortunately, also put Barrons out of commission, as he's linked to that spell and would be drafted to the same location so he could kill Ryodan and get Dani out.

"She was taken nude from our bed. No sword, no cellphone. The tattoo vanishes when she shifts. I've stopped putting it on her."

Shit.

After a moment of silence, Christian says, "Your time in Faery was four days mortal-time. Notice anything strange when you walked into Chester's?"

"Yes. There's not a single Fae in here," I say. "Wait," I add, frowning. "We were only gone four days?" I glance at Barrons. "Shouldn't more time have passed, considering how long we were in Faery?" An afternoon once cost me a month.

Christian says, "I've been hearing rumors for the past few years that ever since you sang the Song of Making, the passage of time in Faery began to change, slowly at first, then escalating. It would seem the ancient melody deemed the temporal disparity between our realms, with no walls to divide them, a flaw and has been correcting it, bringing both realms into alignment."

Fascinating. And good. I wholeheartedly agreed with the Song's assessment.

"There's not a single Fae left in Dublin," Ryodan continues. "According to my sources, there's not a Fae left anywhere in the mortal realm, and that disturbs me. They live to prey on humans. Yet every bloody one of them is gone."

"Which can only mean one thing. They're preparing for war," Christian says.

I say, "The Winter Court was already at war. With itself." Quickly, I detail what Barrons and I discovered in the icy kingdom, omitting the action I took once Christian's missive arrived.

"One more reason you think they got their memories back," Ryodan says. "I'm inclined to agree."

"Let me make sure I got this straight," Lor says, grinning. "The Song restores their powers and memory and what do they do—go to war with each other over ancient feuds. Man, gotta love this shit."

"It's possible the princess was on the battlefield, unrecognizable," Barrons says.

I shake my head. "She turned day to night."

"That wasn't you?"

"No. She was in the castle. I could feel her. Somehow, she's not as afflicted as the rest of the Fae."

"Royalty are the oldest, with the longest memories, but they're also the strongest, more capable of controlling their lust for vengeance over ancient slights," Barrons says.

She'd better be able to control it, I think darkly. *If she hurts my family . . .*

"I'm royalty," Christian says. "And I'm not afflicted."

"You're young. You've never dumped memory," Barrons says.

"Besides, you're not Seelie. You're the last living Un," I say.

"I prefer to think of myself as a singularity, neither court," Christian says. "It's reasonable to conclude the same thing that's happening in the Winter kingdom is happening everywhere in Faery. They're all missing because they're too busy trying to kill each other." He laughs. "Lor's right. How bloody perfect is this? Christ, I'd've ordered an internal war up myself if I'd thought it was possible."

"It's not funny," I say. "You didn't see what they're doing to each other. It's horrific."

"If it keeps 'em the fuck outta our hair, honey, who gives a shit?" Lor says. "Besides, if it's true, that leaves you only a handful of royalty to bring to heel."

"Or push over the edge and get them to try to kill each other, too." Christian laughs again. "Mac, it's perfect. Problem solved. Let them keep fighting each other while you figure out how to use the Song and seal them away forever."

"Rabid and insane, just like the Unseelie?" I demand. "I'm trying *not* to repeat the mistakes that were made in the past."

"Are you saying you think the Unseelie shouldn't have been sealed away?" Christian says. "They killed *billions* of humans the night they broke free."

I sigh. "If they'd never been imprisoned to begin with, they might have had a chance. The odds were against them from the beginning. Mistakes were made from the moment the king created them."

"I can't believe you're defending the Unseelie," Christian says.

"Not defending. Just saying there is no black or white in this world. Everything, and each of us, is shades of gray. And you *are* Unseelie."

"Leavened by my humanity. Majorly, hugely leavened. Gray listing fiercely toward white."

"This isn't about the Unseelie." I try to steer the conversation back on track. "They're gone. It's about the Seelie—"

"Who turned on each other over ancient grudges. Fucking idiots. Let them war. Move on," Lor growls.

"I'm ready to discuss the terms of my freedom." Naked not-Mac manifests in the middle of the office, nude and beaming.

For a moment, none of us moves then, "What the fuck?" Lor explodes. "You got a doppelgänger, Mac."

"It's Fae," Ryodan growls. "Another bloody fucking Fae sifted past my bloody fucking wards. What the bloody fuck."

"Christian, get her out of here," I snap. "This isn't the time or place."

"I didn't bring her here." To the librarian, he says, "You choose *now* to appear? It's been days since you drifted into that bottle. I haven't heard a peep from you since."

"I was mulling my options."

"Well, go mull some more."

"I've quite finished."

"How did you even find me here?"

"I imprinted on you," naked not-Mac says. "I can find you anywhere."

"That's disturbing as hell," Christian growls.

"I'm ready to be free," she says brightly. "Let's discuss."

"Who the bloody hell is she, why does she look like Mac, and why the fuck is she naked?" Barrons says in a dangerously soft voice.

"She's the librarian of the Unseelie king's library," I tell him hastily. "I forgot to tell you about her." To Lor I say, "Stop staring at her like that. Christian, dress her. And tell her to keep her clothes on."

Abruptly, the librarian is clothed in a simple, short shift that's nearly translucent.

"I apologize," the librarian says. "It's difficult for me to get used to draping things about myself. I'll try to remember." Her face clouds, and she says fervently to Christian, "I *will* remember, from now on, I promise."

"You *will* return to your bottle," Christian growls.

The librarian blanches. "You said I could be free."

"You told her that?" I exclaim disbelievingly. "Are you crazy? I told you to cork her."

"It's complicated. She came to my bed, and, well . . . it's a long story."

"It's not that long," the librarian says with a roll of her eyes. "Certainly not what I expected. Lasted all of two minutes."

"You had a Mac-facsimile in your bed," Barrons says with silken menace. "You fucked her."

"No!" Christian roars. "As if I would," he adds defensively.

"You wanted to," the librarian says. "You only got funny about it because I look like her." She glances at me. "He was extremely hard." She glances past me at Barrons. "Oh, my goodness," she murmurs. "Aren't you quite the . . . whatever you are. Gracious."

"More than I wanted to know," I murmur. But I do know, I saw him that way once, myself, in the Unseelie king's stadium-size bed. I disregard her comment about Barrons and the way she's looking at him. It's justified.

"What the hell is going on here?" Lor says. "Why does it look like Mac?"

The librarian bristles. "I'm not an 'it.' I have a name. Lyryka. And I look like Mac because Death hates it when I look like the one called Dani." She gathers steam as she goes, growing even surlier. "And since Death is my new master, I have to obey him, because apparently I'm always going to have a master. I have no idea why I'm always going to be imprisoned, enslaved, and bullied when clearly no one else is, but there you have it, the sorry state of my existence."

"She looks like Dani sometimes," Ryodan repeats icily. "Naked. She was in your bed, too." He turns a gaze sharp as knives on Christian.

"No, she bloody well wasn't. And it's not my fault," Christian thunders. "I broke a bottle. Breakage of a bottle does not equate liability for leakage. I can't be expected to control the contents of every damned bottle in the world."

"Didn't you break the Crimson Hag's bottle, too? Bitch killed Barrons and Ryodan," Lor reminds.

"That was Dani," Christian says irritably, "and she didn't break it, she uncorked it."

"I had that one perfectly well labeled," the librarian says disbelievingly. "Why would you open it? What is *wrong* with you people? Can't you read?"

Christian bristles. "Dani opened it before I even saw it. Besides, who the hell puts the labels on the bottom? They belong on the side."

"They obscure my view on the side. Besides, you can't even remember which bottles you put your beer in," the librarian says irritably. "I thought Death was supposed to be brilliant. To what further indignities must I submit in order to remain free?"

Lor begins to laugh.

The librarian turns to study him a moment then says, "Death won't give me sex. Perhaps you will?"

Lor stops laughing instantly. "Been with one of you crazy Fae fucks. Ain't never gonna happen, babe."

The librarian sniffs and turns back to Christian.

I decide I must be losing my mind, because it actually offends me that Lor rejected the librarian. There's the whole lumping of all people into a rejected category because of a single unsavory experience that is completely unfair.

I drift inward, opening my senses, probing delicately at Lyryka. What is she? Where did she come from? Why is she currently reasonably sane, when the rest of the Fae aren't? "You've never drunk from the Cauldron, have you?"

She whirls on me. "Stop that!"

Interesting. She feels me poking about her edges, trying to ferret out her secrets. For all her externally imposed constraints, she's powerful. I wonder if she was bottled for that very reason.

I keep prodding lightly at her essence. Inexplicably, Cruce pops into my mind. Perhaps because I'm currently wishing he were alive so he could either take over the Fae or teach me the things I don't know.

Her eyes widen; she looks stunned and blurts, "You know my father?" Then she claps a hand over her mouth, looking astonished and horrified.

I narrow my eyes. "Cruce was your father?"

She's quiet a long moment, eyes narrowed, as if thinking furiously, expression morphing from fear to anger and back again. Finally she shakes her head vigorously, as if completing an argument with herself and says, "So he says."

"Says," Barrons says pointedly.

Present tense. Not past. "Did he—does he let you out?" I press.

She lapses into frowning silence again then says, "I'm forbidden to speak of him."

"You just did."

"You startled me and I blurted. An image formed in your mind while you were prodding at mine."

She gleaned an image from the High Queen's mind. Barrons cuts me a warning look. *Get your mental barriers up,* he growls silently. *Now.*

I fortify my mind against her. "When did you last see him?" I ask.

"It's forb—"

"Answer the queen's question and I won't put you back in the bottle," Christian cuts her off.

She's quiet, glancing at each of us, then counters warily, "For how long?"

"Each day you obey me, I'll grant you one more day," Christian says.

She stares into the distance a long moment before murmuring, "My father will do worse things to me than you, if I disobey him. If he learns that I told you he sired me . . ." She trails off, swallowing audibly. "You must never tell him."

I don't need Christian's lie-detecting skills to confirm she's afraid of Cruce, whether he's her father or not. I cut Christian a hard stare, and he interprets it correctly.

"I'll stand between you and Cruce if he tries to harm you."

The librarian's gaze flies back to him, eyes wide, and her face lights up like a small sun. "You would protect me? Not let him punish me?"

I give Christian another pointed look.

He sighs heavily and says, "To the best of my ability, yes—"

"Your ability is *everything*!" the librarian exclaims.

"—I will keep you safe and let no man—"

"Or woman or being of any kind," she clarifies hastily.

"—punish you. I won't allow anyone or thing to harm you. However, if you betray me or any of my friends, I'll harm you myself."

"That was a formal vow," the librarian says, looking awed. "Exchanged between royals."

Christian sighs again. "Aye, I ken it."

"That means you're my protector now. Bound to that oath."

His gusty sigh ruffles my hair, and he cuts me a glare. "Aye. I ken it, bloody hell."

Lyryka turns back to me and says in hushed tones as if she fears even speaking the words aloud, "I saw my father earlier today."

"Truth?" I ask Christian.

He nods.

To be absolutely certain we're on the same page, same paragraph, and same bloody word, I say, "You saw *Cruce* today. In the very much alive flesh."

Peevish again, which I'm beginning to think is Lyryka's natural state, she snaps, "Which word didn't you understand?"

"Spell it out for me," I command coolly.

Rolling her eyes, she says, "I saw Cruce today. In the very much alive flesh."

PART II

Rarely do we achieve the exquisite clarity of recognizing, with our intellect, a moment in time as pivotal; a moment upon which we can reflect, from a distant point in the future, and say: if not A, then not B.

Such as, if my car hadn't broken down that night, I would never have met my husband, subsequently our three children would not have been born. Or if I'd not failed the bar exam, I'd never have chased my dream of becoming a concert pianist. Or if I hadn't decided I couldn't possibly go to sleep without ice cream, as PMS as I was, and dashed out to the convenience store late at night, I wouldn't have gotten mugged and knifed and left with PTSD.

Those kinds of moments.

I think we feel them in our bones as they present themselves.

It might be a sudden chill at the nape of your neck, or an unexpected internal shift of pressure inside your skull, accompanied by a brief light-headedness; perhaps it's merely a puzzling sense of foreboding and dread.

I think so much more goes on in our subconscious than we know but, because we're driven by a desperate need to perceive life as manageable, rational, and within our control, we reject those inexplicable warnings that root our feet to the ground (for no reason our brain can discern—and doesn't the brain always win that argument) and make us deeply uneasy about whatever we're going to do next.

You must listen for those moments.

You must pay close attention.

If an elevator door slides open and you get a sudden, mystifying chill as you gaze in at a "perfectly normal" man, don't board. Don't let good manners subdue the atavistic wisdom of your beast. Walk away. Take the stairs. Surround yourself with other people as quickly as you can.

Run when your blood tells you to run.

FROM THE JOURNALS OF MACKAYLA LANE-O'CONNOR
HIGH QUEEN OF THE FAE

BLOODDREAM

───── • • • ─────

Time after time

I T'S THE FOG THAT gets me lost.

The fog in Dublin is unlike any I've ever encountered. It seems almost sentient, as if intentionally seeking out the darkest, most unnerving corners to infiltrate and obscure, and has a way of transforming even the most familiar landscape into something ominous and sinister.

Distracted by inner turmoil, one moment I think I'm headed straight for the Clarin House, plowing blindly down block after block, the next I'm in a dwindling crowd on a street in an unrecognizable part of town. Good grief, I've been in Dublin less than twenty-four hours, and already I'm lost.

Abruptly, I'm one of only three people on an unnaturally quiet, fog-obscured lane that affords only intermittent glimpses of my surroundings. Mist encases me, wisping in tendrils, gusting in thick banks, swirls about my ankles, and clings damply to my face.

I have no idea how far I've walked. By now, I might be miles from my lodgings.

Vowing to never go blasting blindly down unknown streets again, I make the quick decision to follow one of the other pedestrians; surely they'll lead me back to the Temple Bar District.

Buttoning my jacket against a light drizzle, I pick the nearer of the two, a fiftyish woman in a beige raincoat and a blue plaid scarf. I move in close, worried I'll lose her.

Two blocks later, she's clutching her purse to her side and darting nervous glances over her shoulder. It takes me a few minutes to figure out what she's frightened of: me.

Belatedly I recall what I read in my guidebook about crime in the inner city on my flight from Georgia to Dublin, two days ago. Innocent-looking youths of both genders are responsible for much of it.

I try to reassure her. "I'm lost," I call. "I'm trying to get back to my hotel. Please, can you help me?"

"Stop following me. Stay away," she cries, quickening her pace, coattails flapping.

"All right, I'm staying." I stop where I stand. The last thing I want to do is chase her off; the other pedestrian is gone, so I need her. The fog is growing denser and more menacing by the second, and I'm in an unknown country with no idea how to find my way back to the only place with which I'm familiar. "I'm sorry I scared you. Can you just point me toward the Temple Bar District? I'm looking for the Clarin House. Please, I'm an American tourist, I just arrived in Ireland yesterday, and I'm quite lost," I say, with growing desperation.

Without turning or slowing in the least, she flings an arm in a general leftward direction then disappears around the corner, leaving me alone in the fog.

I sigh. Left it is.

Taking stock of my surroundings as I go, I step up my pace a bit. I'm heading deeper into a dilapidated, industrial part of town. Storefronts with the occasional apartment above give way to run-down warehouses on both sides of the street with busted-out windows and sagging doors. The sidewalk whittles to a narrow catwalk and is increasingly trash-littered with every step.

I begin to feel strongly nauseated, I suppose from the stench of the sewers. There must be an old paper factory nearby; thick husks of porous yellowed parchment tumble and drift down the streets. Narrow, dingy alleyways are marked at entrances with peeling painted arrows, pointing to docks that look as if the last time they received a delivery was twenty years ago.

Here, a crumbling smokestack looms, vanishing into the fog. There, a car sits empty with the driver's door ajar. Outside the door is a pair of shoes and a pile of clothing, as if the driver got out, stripped, and just left it all right there to go for a walk through the neighborhood nude.

Creepy.

It's eerily quiet. The only sounds are the muted muffle of my footsteps and the *drip-drip* of gutters emptying into drainpipes. The farther I walk into the decaying neighborhood, the more I want to run, or at least give way to a jog, but I worry if there are unsavory denizens of the human sort in the area, the rapid pounding of my heels against pavement might draw attention.

I'm afraid this part of the city is so deserted because the businesses moved out when the gangs moved in. Who knows what lurks behind those broken windows? Who can say what crouches beyond that half-open door?

The next ten minutes are some of the most harrowing of my life.

I'm alone in a bad section of a foreign city with no idea whether I'm going the right way or headed for something worse.

Twice I think I hear something rustling about in an alley as I pass. Twice I swallow panic and refuse to run.

It's impossible not to think of Alina, of the similar location in which her body was found, a dirty dead-end alley, dotted with murky puddles and piles of trash. My sister died in a heap of refuse. Left alone like a heap of unwanted rubbish. I can't shake the feeling that something is very wrong here, and it's something far more wrong than mere abandonment and decay. This part of the city doesn't just feel empty. It feels forsaken. As if I should have passed a sign ten blocks ago that says "Abandon Hope, All Ye Who Enter Here."

I'm growing increasingly nauseated, and my skin is starting to crawl. I hurry down block after block, in as straight a general left-ward direction as the streets permit. Though it's only suppertime, rain and fog have turned day to dusk, and the few streetlamps that aren't broken begin to flicker and glow. Night is falling with alarm-ing swiftness. In moments, it will be as dark as pitch in the long, shadowy stretches between the weak and infrequent pools of light.

I begin to jog.

On the verge of hysteria at the thought of being lost in this awful part of the city at night, I nearly sob with relief when I spy a brightly lit building a few blocks ahead, blazing like an oasis of light.

I break into the run I was resisting.

As I approach, I see all the windows are intact, and the tall brick building is impeccable, sporting a costly first-floor façade of dark cherry and brass. Large pillars frame an alcoved entrance inset with a handsome cherry door flanked by stained-glass sidelights and crowned by a matching transom. The tall windows down the side are encased by matching columns of lesser size and covered with elaborate wrought-iron latticework. A late-model sedan is parked out front beside an expensive motorcycle.

Beyond it are storefronts with second-floor residences. There are people in the streets.

Perfectly normal-looking shoppers and diners and pub-goers.

Just like that, I'm in a decent part of the city again. Thank God, I think.

BARRONS BOOKS & BAUBLES proclaims the gaily-painted shingle that hangs perpendicular to the building, suspended over the side-walk by an elaborate brass pole bolted into the brick above the door. A sign in the old-fashioned, green-tinted windows announces OPEN. It couldn't look more like the perfect place to call a taxi if it sported a sign that said "Welcome Lost Tourists/Call Your Taxis Here."

A deep, velvety baritone floats from the night while I'm still about twenty yards from the sanctuary of the bookstore. "Mac-Kayla."

I skid to a halt, mystified. How could anyone in Dublin know my name? I've been in Ireland all of one day. The voice came from a shadowy alley to my left. A chill kisses my nape and my heart pounds and I suffer an intensely disconcerting déjà vu. Although I know I haven't—I've never even left the States—I feel I've been right here before, in this precise spot, at this precise moment, and something stupendously life-changing is about to happen. The moment reeks of *kairos*, a Greek word that means "the opportune moment, a pivotal time, the necessary instant"; a sliver of *chronos*, the Greek word for time, when great things might be accomplished.

Great good or great evil.

I stand, debating. Do I yield to curiosity, glance to my left, and investigate the mystery, or do I hurry toward the building that blazes bastion in the night and beckons me on a level I don't understand?

There's a ponderous, palpable weight hanging about my neck, as if this tiny, seemingly inconsequential moment, this decision and how I make it, could define and redefine the rest of my life.

It's possible the man standing in the shadows knew my sister, and that's how he knows my name—an irresistible temptation.

"Do you wish to know of Alina?" he says.

I gasp, and my heart begins to hammer. I turn to stare into the shadows but can make out only the vague silhouette of a tall man. Do I wish to know of Alina? I wish to know everything, and then I wish to kill her murderer with my bare hands! He destroyed my life, my parents' lives, my entire world when he took Alina from me!

A bell tinkles as the door of the bookstore opens, and my gaze flies back down the street.

A tall, dark, powerfully built man steps out. I go unnaturally still as if every cell in my body just devoted one hundred percent attention to him, sapping all my energy, leaving nothing left for essential bodily function.

The man to my left curses softly. "MacKayla, you must come with me now! Time is of the essence."

I can't move. My feet are glued to the sidewalk.

The other man stops on the sidewalk, bathed by the exterior lights of the bookstore. He's about thirty or so, six foot two or three, with dark hair and golden skin. His features are strong, chiseled. I can't pinpoint his nationality, perhaps Old World Mediterranean or Basque ancestry. He wears an elegant dark gray suit, a crisp white shirt, and a tie. He's not handsome. That's far too calm a word to ever describe him. He's carnal, he attracts, radiating strength, and self-possession. A man who knows exactly who he is, what he wants, and would swagger into Hell to get it, the kind who divides people into three camps: on his side, by his side, or in his way. And pity the fool that gets in his way. He's intensely magnetic. I'm both drawn and repelled.

He glances up, down, all around, as if sensing something, looking for something. I get the oddest feeling that he's . . . not quite human.

Abruptly his head whips my way, and he gazes into the shadows, directly at me, with eyes as black as midnight. For an instant, I think I see a flicker of crimson in them. But it was only a trick of rain and reflection.

Electricity crackles in the air between us.

"He's dangerous," the man in the shadows murmurs.

I remain frozen, pierced by the weight of the dark man's regard, an insect pinned to his paper. I can't look away. I can't move.

We stare at each other a long moment. Then he murmurs, barely audible, "You. You're here."

"What?" I whisper.

"Are you coming in?" He gestures to the door.

"How do you know me?" I manage.

"It's a long story."

To the shadows, I say very quietly, "And you—how do you know me?"

"It's a long story," the man in the shadows replies with a soft laugh.

I'm immobilized by indecision, by the weight of the moment.

"He owns the apartment your sister leased," says the voice from the shadows. "Beware, MacKayla. He's dangerous."

I turn toward him as he speaks. "Show yourself."

I shiver when the man steps forward into a pale pool of light. Tall, golden hair and skin, exotically beautiful, dressed in jeans, boots, and an ivory sweater, he's the epitome of civility, elegance, and courtly manners. "I am V'lane, MacKayla. I will help you with your quest, answer your many questions. But we must go, now, before he—he's coming! Choose, MacKayla. You must choose now!"

I glance back at the dark man, who's stalking toward me, shaking my head as if I might somehow shake a decision into it.

My heart is thundering, deafening in my ears.

Who are these men? How do they know me? What do they know about my sister?

How do I choose?

I don't know what to do.

As the man from the bookstore nears, I waffle in indecision. The dark man frightens me. The blond man seems somehow less . . . dangerous to me, both in body and soul. The dark man gave me little to go on, the blond offered information about my sister. The dark man rattles me in ways I don't understand. The blond man doesn't affect me on the same visceral level.

At another time, in another place, I would know that's because the dark man could lay siege to my heart.

I will never know such a time after this night.

"You must hurry, MacKayla," V'lane urges. "Come. I will tell you of Alina. I will teach you all I know. I will help you get revenge."

Somewhere in this city is the monster that brutally murdered my sister.

I want his head on a platter. I want him dead and six feet under. He will not be permitted to walk this world, take the life of another innocent, shatter another young woman's world.

Revenge. Yes. That's what I want.

I turn to V'lane.

"No," the dark man roars. "You can't trust him. He's dangerous!"

It's too late. I've made my decision.

When V'lane offers his hand, I take it, and, together, we vanish into the night.

21

Give him a pair of eyes with a "come-hither" gleam

MAC

- Mom is safe.
- Dad is missing.
- Dani is missing.
- Where is Shazam/Y'rill? Ryodan has no idea. Shaz was out hunting when Dani vanished. Is he missing as well? What kind of being is capable of capturing the last remaining Hel-Cat/Hunter? The thought is inconceivable. But with Dani missing, if Shaz wasn't taken, why hasn't he appeared?
- Cruce has a daughter, Lyryka, who was sealed in a bottle, according to Christian, nearly three quarters of a million years ago. Keeper of the Unseelie king's library. A wealth of information or a mess of myth with little basis in fact? Who is her mother? Why did he put her in a bottle?
- It appears the Seelie have regained their memories. Why didn't they just drink from the Cauldron again?
- For that matter, where *is* the Cauldron? It's mine. I should

know where the queen's things are. Must locate Cauldron, Stone, and miscellaneous OOPs.

- I blew up the Winter Court. I'm concerned the remains are still aware and in pain. Must address that but each time I go to Faery I lose too much time in the mortal realm. Put that on brief hold?
- I suspect Winter has Dad and Dani. But why? What does she want? Why hasn't she sent word to me, demanding ransom? If she gives them back unharmed, I'll re-create her court and negotiate a truce while we come to terms about my reign.
- Barrons is right, assumptions are dangerous. The ward I hit trying to sift to mom was not a ward at all but the impenetrable cosmic distortion of an IFP. They're impossible to sift into or out of. I gave up too easily on Winter's ward, because I didn't recognize it and thought it was what I'd hit earlier. Can I sift to Dad and Dani?

I stop writing and nibble the cap of my pen.

While Barrons and Ryodan are busy reinforcing the wards that protect Chester's, I'm sitting cross-legged on a plush charcoal sofa in a seating cozy located in an atrium of sorts (more of his new decor) on the same floor as Ryodan's office, trying to make sense of things by resorting to an old habit: writing down bulleted lists on a notepad I pilfered from Ryodan's office.

Last I saw Barrons, he was getting tattooed, which means he's going to employ dark arts to create a place for us to shelter. Despite the bookstore's relocation in the clouds, we are forced to admit it may no longer be effectively warded.

I'm surprised I made it this far without yet writing down the fact that disturbs me even more than Dad and Dani's disappearance, because I believe, if Winter is sane enough to have escaped her court's carnage, she's also sane enough not to harm them.

I turn the page to a fresh one, carefully inking the thought I've been putting off. It's a mindblower.

• Cruce is alive.

I was certain the Song of Making killed Cruce when I released it, along with the rest of the Unseelie. Aoibheal had been adamant the melody would destroy the entire Shadow Court. I stare at the words, trying to make myself believe anything other than the worst about this staggering fact.

It doesn't work.

We had a deal, which Cruce hungered to see through to completion with every ounce of avarice he possesses, and that's pretty much all the avarice in the world. Cruce *is* avarice. More than anything, he wants the True Magic of the Fae, hungers for the crown. He plotted, deceived, and manipulated for a small eternity to seize it, and nearly succeeded. As V'lane, he interred Aoibheal in a prison of ice, to finish her off, believing the True Magic would then choose him. He went ballistic when Aoibheal escaped her fate and bequeathed her legacy to me. He would only help me learn to use the queen's powers to save our world in exchange for a full transfer of the power and crown to him, once the Earth was safe.

I agreed.

Fifty-two pages of complicated legal jargon penned by my father and Ryodan detail that agreement. Signed in blood. Sealed by exchange of precious metals. The Compact is ironclad, and we are irrevocably bound by it.

Which means he has every right to walk in here this very moment, saunter to my couch (because apparently Fae aren't warded out anymore, which offends me as deeply as it incenses Barrons and Ryodan), and demand that I transfer my power to him immediately.

I can't welch. I discovered, while sequestered, that if royals negotiate a properly executed compact then try to renege when the other party demands their due, the reneging royal's power is suspended, allowing the compliant party to forcibly seize their pledged boon. Compacts are the only inviolate thing I've discovered about the Fae. All else is up for grabs to he or she with the most power.

If Cruce takes the True Magic from me now, my ability to search for Dad and Dani will dwindle to virtually nil, along with what leverage I possess to negotiate an exchange with Winter. I'll be unable to restore her court. I'll be powerless, with nothing to offer. Cruce will have all the power. I'll have to negotiate with him for help. Beseech his aid. How he'd love that!

How I'd hate that. I'd be in a subservient position, and Cruce would exploit it endlessly.

I wouldn't even be able to sift to Faery. I would no longer be able to sift at all! I'd have to rely on Christian or Inspector Jayne or even Cruce himself. And without the power of the queen, how well could I protect my two human-turned princes? This is a mess. Despite recently wishing he were alive, I'm furious that he is.

If he'd shown himself years ago, come to me shortly after the Song was sung and demanded his due, it would have felt up-front and trustable. We'd made a compact, fulfilled the terms, delivered payment.

But after hiding from us for all these years, never showing himself or coming for the power, if he were to saunter in now, I wouldn't trust a thing about it.

In exchange for the magic, he agreed to remove the Fae from our planet forever and never harm us. (I have no clue how he planned to get them off-world. Their power would be enormously diminished in the process.) I wonder if that's why he hasn't come—because if he never requests the transfer, he's not bound to his agreed-upon duties, and he's decided he'd rather have something else. It occurs to me that he, too, draws his power from the Earth. Did we actually spell out that he had to leave this planet, or did we use a vague word like "world"? If the Compact contains a single nebulous, twistable phrase, he'll work it into any shape that benefits him and only him.

I nibble my pen, musing.

Barrons said the Unseelie king's power is still undecided. Perhaps Cruce is waiting because he thinks the king's magic will choose him, and he'd rather have that than the queen's. But what would be the point? There is no Shadow Court. Cruce would be ruler of none. I don't see the Seelie embracing an Unseelie king any more enthusiastically than they've embraced me.

Any way I look at it, secreting himself away spells trouble for us all.

I force myself to write:

- If Cruce demands the True Magic from me, I have to relinquish it.

That hurt to write. Years ago when I'd agreed to the Compact, I couldn't have foreseen a time like this. I believed things would return to relative calm, even near normalcy eventually.

As if.

Besides, if I hadn't agreed to the Compact, our world would have been devoured by black holes, and I wouldn't even *be* here to bitch about things.

I stare at the page for a few seconds before forcing myself to bottom-line another truth, one that's disturbing me on a far deeper level than I'd anticipated.

- I'll be just-Mac again.

A woman with no queenly powers, only *sidhe*-seer gifts, the boon of rapid healing and extreme longevity.

Funny how, so often, we don't fully appreciate the things we have until we're about to lose them. I hadn't realized how much I enjoy having the perks, like sifting, that accompany the crown. I love the connection I feel to the planet. I was looking forward to learning more about what I could do with the True Magic. As much as I would prefer not to hold responsibility for the Fae, as fraught with challenges as my reign is, I like the benefits of the power Aoibheal bequeathed me. Besides, who's to say I won't succeed? Challenges motivate me, intrigue me, make me work harder. I might get the walls sung back up between realms, create a sort of governing party within the Seelie, then attend on infrequent occasions for dispute resolution and seasonal feasts. There's a part of me that hungers to succeed at this, to find the way forward for both species, no matter the difficulties.

A chill kisses my nape; the air behind the sofa crackles with a potent charge.

Then Barrons's hands are on my shoulders as he bends over the back of the couch, brushes his lips to my ear, and murmurs, "You will never be just-Mac. You don't need magic to be a queen. That power is in your heart. Never forget it."

"There you go, snooping in my notes again," I tease as I tip back my head with a faint smile. "I thought you were busy."

Eyes dark, face grim, he says, "I felt your distress."

Via the link of our brand. I frown. "Barrons, why hasn't Cruce shown himself? Why hide, why stay off-grid unless he's doing something he knows we'd try to stop? *What* is he doing? All he ever wanted was the True Magic. By all rights, it's *his* now. He could have taken it at any time."

"Perhaps his desires changed."

"But why conceal his existence?"

"Stop worrying. Sleep now. You need your strength. It will all become clear in time. Cruce will never harm you."

Because Barrons will never let him doesn't need to be said. Cruce raped me. Barrons wants him dead. He'll never let him touch a hair on my body, ever again.

Then he's gone, and I return my gaze to the page but realize, as the words begin to blur, that I'm far more exhausted than I realized.

Barrons is right, I need to get some rest while I have the chance. God knows what's coming next or when I might have another opportunity.

I toss my notepad and pen onto the coffee table, lean back on the sofa, prop my feet on the coffee table, and let my eyes drift closed for just a second.

I need to try to assail Winter's ward again, and I have far too many worries on my mind to ever fall—

I pass out before I finish the thought.

22

⸱ ● ⸱

I'm not no crocodile like the one in Dublin Zoo

DANI

I KNEW, AT A YOUNG age, exactly what LIFE was, which I always saw in capital letters, smelling of the rainbow-colored cotton candy Mom brought home, back when things were still good.

LIFE is the most amazing, thrilling, fantastical ride in the amusement park.

Albeit one with a guaranteed mortality rate.

You *will* crash and burn on this roller coaster. It's inevitable, and you don't get to know how or when. A slat might break, and the car derails when you're barely out of the gate. A storm might explode from a perfectly clear blue sky and wipe out everyone on your section of the track. Maybe you're born with a defective heart and know, from the age of eight, you're a walking time bomb. Or you're the last person alive in your car, riddled with pain and ready to see what comes next.

There are no certainties but one.

Death will come.

My philosophy has always been: feckin' A—all the more reason to ride the hell out of it! Milk life for all you can get. Howl with laughter, scream with fear. Get sloshed on every color of the rainbow.

My philosophy hasn't changed.

My mortality, however, has.

Thanks to one grumpy, emotional, needy Hel-Cat who is also an epic dragonlike Hunter that soars the deepest expanses of space and contains vast stores of wisdom and power inside her enormous body, this roller coaster ride will never end for me.

I'm a shapeshifter who will, one day, be fully immortal.

A shapeshifter who *still* can't shift, which offends every ounce of my abundant ego.

I never fail. That's practically my middle name: Dani Never-Fails O'Malley. I screw up, do things like unstopper flasks I shouldn't, but when I set my mind to something, I succeed.

It's inconceivable and irritatingly, infuriatingly—I can barely think the word—humbling.

I've been trying since day one but can't make the leap of converting my one hundred and forty pounds into the massive tonnage of a Hunter, or vice versa.

I get it on a hypothetical level; I've seen it done. I *know* it can happen. Y'rill has shown me over and over, tried endlessly to talk me through it, telling me to find my "breath of fire" and "heart of scales."

I still can't do it.

And I really, really, *really* want to shift right now.

In human form, which I currently am, I can still die. I have a lot to live for: Shaz-ma-taz, Ryodan, Mac and Barrons, immortality, space exploration, saving the world on a regular basis. The amount of time it takes to become fully immortal varies from Hunter to Hunter. And here's the real kicker: You don't even know you've passed that threshold and become unkillable in your original form until you almost die—but don't. I suspect I'm going to need to nearly die quite a few times to be convinced. One or two times might be a fluke, a near miss. Three or four or ten and I might start to believe it.

Everything comes with bloody uncertainties.

For the first time in my life, I want a rule book.

I, Dani O'Malley, would like a rule—the horror of it! I'd like to know a concrete rule such as: after two years, or five years, or a decade, I'll be fully immortal in both forms.

I frown. Maybe I wouldn't like to know that, because, then, I might be tempted to be careful with myself for that period of time, which would seriously dick with my head.

I sigh irritably. Life was a lot simpler when I had nothing to lose and nothing to live for but the sheer rush of living. Then I began loving people and caring about things, like whether I lived or died, and my essential principles started getting squished and contorted. I used to think adulthood sucks. I'm now convinced of it. I miss the days I swaggered around, little belly sticking out, full of myself and oblivious.

Yeah, well, not everything about those days. Mostly just my attitude.

It occurs to me I might be regressing, given my current situation, taking a broody page from one of Jericho Barrons's books.

But some things trigger me, hard. I'm a redhead. Easily triggered comes with the hair. We're fiery folk. Most of the time I file "easily triggered" under "perfectly normal, bodacious response to life." Not something like PTSD.

Still. There is one thing that can really get to me. Even after all these years.

With a groan, I lean back against the wall, gingerly stretching my legs. Everything hurts. I slammed into the perimeter so many times my body is one big bruise.

I'm alone. Naked. No sword. It's back in Chester's. That makes me feel way more naked than naked does. Depending on who's got me, naked can buy me a moment of brain-stutter in a male enemy. I'll take any advantage I can get.

Just like years ago, I'm all I've got.

One moment I was in bed with Ryodan, the next everything went black, then I woke up here. And it's still black. It was difficult at first to convince myself I'm awake because it's the kind of blackness that is blindness. There's not one speck of light, not even one speck of slightly-not-black. It's total ocular deprivation.

I must have been unconscious, but have no idea how I was put under or why, or who has me. Someone noodled me about. It offends me on a mitochondrial level, turns all my cells into bristling Tasmanian devils, bouncing from foot to foot, raging for a fight.

I have no bloody idea where I am.

But one fact is as solid as the unbendable, unbreakable, inescapable, very thick bars I kept smashing into.

Someone snatched me.

From *Ryodan*. From *inside* Chester's.

Noodled me about like I was a kid. Not a ferocious Hunter/superhero.

Metal bars surround me.

There are thick, impossible-to-dent-even-with-my-super-strength slabs at the bottom and top.

I don't need lights to know where I am.

I'm in a cage.

I knew the moment I came to. Live long enough behind bars and you become intimately acquainted with the tiniest nuances of imprisonment; the way the air movement stutters at evenly spaced intervals. It's a bare puff of a difference, but such things become your whole world when there's nothing else to feel.

But hunger.

Surely my captors will feed me.

There's going to be hell to pay when I get out of here. And I *will* get out of here.

I wonder—whoever's done this to me—do they know my past, or was their choice of incarceration merely a happy coincidence for them?

If it's a happy coincidence, I'll be more merciful.

When I kill them.

23

I was once like you are now

CRUCE

"MacKayla Lane knows you're alive," Masdann said as he sifted into Cruce's bedchamber.

Cruce turned from the fire that blazed in the hearth. "I've told you not to sift into my chambers. Unless I summon, use the door."

"I believed this news of critical import."

It was. Undesirable at that. He'd been staring into the flames, perfecting the details of his next moves, which, until this moment, had included how and when he was going to reveal himself to Mac, an act he'd been anticipating for a long time. "How is that possible?" Lyryka would never risk his wrath, not after what he threatened to do if she disobeyed him, not that he would. Prickly but sweet as an eternal child, she hungered to please him. He was her entire world. He'd made certain of that.

"I do not know."

"What makes you think she knows?"

"She was sitting on a sofa when I moved in behind her to see what she was writing."

"Sitting on a sofa, where?" Cruce demanded.

"At Chester's."

Cruce's eyes flashed. "You went to Chester's again without explicit orders from me to do so?"

"If you wish me to pass as him surely enough to convince even her, I must know her innermost thoughts."

"Have I failed to make myself clear? If I have not given you an order, you do not take action," Cruce snarled.

"Am I enslaved then," Masdann asked, but without the inflection of a question.

Cruce stared at him a long moment then slowly began to laugh. "Ah, Masdann, you surprise me."

"You question my loyalty, my liege."

"I question everyone's."

"That leaves you no one to trust, a perilous state of affairs."

"Trust is expectation that another will behave in keeping with prior actions. They rarely do. Do you feel enslaved?"

Masdann was quiet a moment, then said, "I exist only to serve your needs. Is that not enslavement? How is it different from the stories you've told me of the prior king?"

"It is only for a short time longer. Until we've accomplished our aims."

"Your aims."

"My aims that will establish *your* place in the world. Have patience, Masdann."

"'Patience' is another word for 'I'll tell you when.' Again, how is this different from the stories you've told me of the prior king who said 'only until my concubine is immortal and fully Fae'? How long did that take? Oh, wait, it never happened."

"Unlike me, the prior king wasn't seeking the Shadow Court's freedom. He wasn't fighting to raise you to the light. He sought a personal and selfish aim."

"Desire for a woman lay at the core of things, then as now."

"A small part of a larger plan."

"Your desire to possess her is lesser than your desire for our freedom?"

"You've never questioned me before. Has something changed?"

"I've seen what lies above and am intrigued and eager to live. You think motive defines results."

Cruce inhaled sharply. "You do not walk in my dreams!" It wasn't a question but a sudden suspicion. He'd thought those exact words recently. His prince could walk in dreams that shaped the dreamer's thoughts and actions. An excessively dangerous power if he chose to abuse it.

"Does the creator fear he's created something unmanageable?"

"Are you challenging me?"

"I'm saying the reason you oppress someone is irrelevant. They're still oppressed and hunger to be free. We've been waiting for years."

"You know nothing about years!" Cruce snarled. "Let me tell you what it's like to live for tens of thousands—no, *hundreds* of thousands—of years believing, pledging your loyalty, waiting, always waiting for that one day that never comes. What are three or four years to you? You know nothing of suffering!"

"Perhaps I know nothing of such lengthy periods of time, but I know you're becoming like him. The one you despise. I'm not permitted to do anything of my own accord. I exist only to fulfill your commands. If that is what my life is to be, tell me. Don't promise me freedom only to withhold it in the slightest ways. I serve you, always. But I have dreams of my own. As do my brethren."

A long silence spun out between them. Cruce studied Masdann's features, wondering if he'd inadvertently captured too much of the original's arrogance, independence, and determination. Was he, like the prototype, too wild to ever be tamed, too free to be broken? Arguing for his brethren's rights, just as he, Cruce, had done so long ago. Had he created his own rival?

There was truth in Masdann's words. The Shadow Court was newborn, and, until now, the lavish underground world he'd created for them had been enough. He'd not hobbled them with insatiable hunger. They were capable of deriving pleasure among their own kind. But eons ago, three or four years of imprisonment had seemed cruelly long to Cruce, too. Yet time had crawled so slowly by, dragging on and on, that he'd become inured to the passage of it. His faith in his king had faded. His rage had grown.

Was he doing the same to his own prince? "What freedom do you wish?" he said.

"The freedom of trust."

"Ah, only the greatest freedom of all," Cruce scoffed. "Ask for the world, why don't you?"

"You made me. You know me better than anyone. You fashioned me to want the world. That was what you intended, yet now you deny it. You created a hunger you forbid to be fed, gave me the power to navigate a realm where all is possible yet ask me to live in a realm where nothing is. Only what you choose to allow me. Befriend me or make me your enemy. Destroy me, if you must. I will live no other way than trusted and free. You want the woman. I will deliver her to you with her heart aflame with desire and love. But only if you trust me—the one who walks in the deepest, richest, most magical of realms—to learn her, know her, understand what she needs. You gave me great power. Let me use it."

"Did she think you were him?"

"Yes. And now we know for certain it's possible for me to move intimately close within their world, undetected."

"And if she mentions to Barrons that she saw him at a time he knows he wasn't there?"

"I may have given her a suggestion to forget the encounter while dreaming."

"Did you kiss her?"

"No. But I may. Can you abide?"

Cruce's eyes flashed with sudden thunder, and his wings rustled warning. "Only in the Dreaming. Never in real life. That is forbidden."

Masdann inclined his dark head, lips lifting faintly at one corner.

"Real life is, I suspect, but another dream, my liege, wherein emotional decisions are rarely any wiser than they are in the waking. Still, as you wish. Am I free to attend her as I deem necessary to secure your aims?"

Cruce weighed his options. His prince was right. He needed to either destroy him or set him free, and he couldn't bear the thought of destroying him. Before long, Masdann would be free anyway. They could reach that moment as allies. Or enemies. Once, Cruce had loved his king. And he'd begun to bristle at incessant promises of a future that never came to pass. Poisoned by the arrows of time and neglect, love became hate in time enough.

"You are free to attend her as you deem necessary to secure my aims. But once my goal is met, you will no longer reveal yourself to her. She will never lay eyes upon you again," he emphasized. Neither prototype nor copy; Cruce would see to that.

"As you wish." Masdann inclined his head and turned for the door.

—— • • ——

After Masdann left, Cruce stared, brooding, into the flames. MacKayla knew he was alive. He'd missed the opportunity for his great reveal. It mattered to him. He'd wanted to study her when she first laid eyes on him after so long, probe for hidden joy beneath her confusion. Had she grieved him? Had she told tales of the great Cruce, as he'd instructed, who'd been willing to sacrifice his own existence to save the world? No matter that he'd known the bracelet he demanded when they signed the Compact, coupled with a certain chamber in the Unseelie king's castle, would likely keep him alive.

He'd not been *certain.*

And therein lay worlds of sacrifice.

He'd always planned to one day create his own Shadow Court. He spent millennia refining what bits of essences he would employ, studying the king's notes, trials, and results, making his own notes on how to improve, securing the ingredients he required, purloining many without their owner's knowledge, secreting them away. The raw material from Barrons had been difficult to acquire as the bastard hungered to kill him, and could. Cruce had kept him at a giant's arm's length for a small eternity.

But that day in the rain, when Barrons discovered Cruce had fucked MacKayla, too, they'd ended up at each other's throats, and his small theft had gone unnoticed.

Masdann contained part of Jericho Barrons's very essence, the physical matter of which he was fashioned.

It was no wonder he was difficult to control.

It was on that day Cruce realized MacKayla had feelings for him. She'd never told Barrons they'd had sex. She'd concealed it, a hidden jewel in her memory, hers alone to revisit and relive. She'd wanted the other princes dead yet never tried to kill *him*. He would set her free from the male she'd imprinted upon merely because he'd found her first.

"Masdann," he murmured.

"My liege?" The prince appeared at his side.

"Did you read all that MacKayla had written?"

"Only a few sentences penned at the top of a new page."

"I want to know everything she wrote. Did you put her to sleep?"

"Of course. Our deepest fears and desires surface like submerged swans from the lake of midnight slumber to take flight in astonishing and revealing ways."

Cruce began to command him to read and report back, but chose to rephrase before he spoke. Masdann had reminded him that courtesies mattered among royalty for good reason. With beings as powerful as Fae, a light tread engendered priceless loyalty. It occurred to him that he was unable to recall the last time Masdann had called him anything other than "my liege." Once he'd called him king. "How would you feel about reading the entirety and reporting the contents to me?"

Masdann's smile lit his dark face, a fierce sun blazing on the coldest of winter days. "It would be my pleasure. My king."

———— • • • ————

Hours later, Cruce sprawled on the chesterfield sofa before the fire, where, one day, Mac would find her place beside him, in a place that would feel familiar to her, but afforded a far better view. His fireplace, rather than being inserted into a mere wall, was framed by the cosmos itself. The vastness of space yawned behind the flames, brilliant with glittering stars. Big minds liked big views. Ah, yes, she would feel at home here.

Lyryka had betrayed him. He had no doubt the simpleton had slipped. She possessed no guile, no ability to play games within games, a weakness he rued. As he'd feared, she was too naïve, too trusting to be used as a tool in the world beyond her flask, despite his clear instructions. He'd have been wiser to hone her into a sharper tool, indoctrinate her to suffering at a young age rather than cosseting her. Still, she'd done her best. It wasn't good enough. He'd hoped to be able to use her to learn the deepest secrets of the Keltar, keepers of the lore, and the Nine, who were capable of killing the Fae. He'd selected the two forms to which he'd restricted her to sow chaos. The enemy, befuddled by mysteries and inconsistencies, always proved more malleable. But from the moment of her birth, Lyryka had been a disappointment. He no longer had need of the library. Though he'd hoped she would prove of use in his current endeavors, she'd cheated him of a prized moment. Still, she'd done her best, and it would soon be time for him to keep the promise he'd made long ago.

Despite having lost the element of surprise, it was difficult for him to be upset by much of anything, because the rest of the news was so auspicious, the best for which he could have hoped.

The Seelies' memories had—as he'd suspected they might, hence his theft of the Cauldron of Forgetting—been restored. He'd removed the Cauldron of Forgetting some time ago, to prevent them from drinking again.

He knew what the restoration meant. But MacKayla didn't. She'd inherited the power of a queen who had never possessed the full history of the Fae, and there was much Cruce had not shared with her. MacKayla didn't know the Fae had once been wildly, disastrously emotional beings, far back, when they were mortal, before they'd drunk the Elixir of Life. Cruce knew Fae origins better than anyone, except for the king and Lyryka, given the work Lyryka had done for him over countless millennia, scouring the Unseelie king's library, distilling facts and reporting to him.

Emotion had returned as well.

Coupling that with their abduction of Jack Lane and Dani O'Malley assured him of one more delightful fact, for which he'd hoped but been unconvinced.

Mortality for the Light Court was not far behind—and they knew it.

Events had come to a head at one of several possible critical junctures he'd foreseen years ago, when MacKayla had sung the Song of Making. The queen and humans had been so certain the Light Court would escape unscathed, deemed perfect as they were.

Cruce had not been nearly as certain, and he'd postulated what the ancient melody might do to his "fairer" brethren.

It had done exactly what they deserved.

It was destroying them, too.

His original plan, based on a different conjunction of events—in which the Seelie remained immortal—was to rule with MacKayla, king to her queen.

But this delightful twist of fate—for which he'd hoped and planned but been uncertain might come to pass—changed everything. The Seelie would die out, there would soon be no Light Court, and no need for a queen.

In this conjunction of events, he would claim the True Magic and rule the only true court of the Fae with both the queen's and, soon, the king's power.

The Highlander pup would never inherit the reign. There were two ways he might kill the prince-who-should-never-have-been, and he was, as yet, uncertain which method he would employ.

Barrons would be out of the running once Masdann lured him into the Dreaming and stranded him for eternity in a padded room, leaving his body a useless, catatonic shell.

The old bastard would finally have to pass the dark crown to his legitimate heir, his finest prince, and only full-blooded Unseelie prince that remained: Cruce.

Before long, the Shadow Court would be the only Fae in existence, Cruce would be king, MacKayla would be his consort, and all would be right with the world.

24

I trip through your wires

KAT

DEEP IN THE UNDERNEATH at Arlington Abbey, four levels down, three of the abbey's governing body, the Shedon, gathered in a stone passageway, staring into a brilliantly lit chamber beyond.

"By the saints, that can't be what I think it is," Katarina McLaughlin exclaimed, horrified by the sight that loomed beyond the open doorway.

The pull of the chamber on the other side was nearly irresistible, even to Kat, who'd nearly perfected the art of resisting irresistible lures. Standing in the corridor, she felt she was being stretched thin, tugged and distorted, dragged inexorably forward whether she wanted to step through that doorway or not. Time ran differently beyond the narrow threshold at her feet, with a palpable temporal distortion rippling before their eyes.

"It fits the description we've read," Enyo Luna said.

"Who else knows it's here?" Kat demanded.

"Only Rhiannon, and she won't breathe a word of it," Colleen

MacKeltar said. "Not that she's able to at the moment. She's been in bed since yesterday. We had to carry her up to her room after she shattered the ward protecting the chamber. The undoing of it nearly shattered *her*."

Kat scrutinized the pair of *sidhe*-seers. These were two of her most levelheaded, focused members of the Shedon. And they were hiding something. "Where was Decla when it happened?"

Colleen and Enyo exchanged an uneasy look, then Enyo said, "Helping Duff at the catacombs."

"It was just the three of us," Colleen said.

Kat shook her head. She couldn't hold Enyo and Colleen responsible for Decla wandering off. She knew why Decla would prefer to work near the dead and also knew when the independent *sidhe*-seer got it in her head to strike off on her own, nothing and no one could stop her. *It's more peaceful*, Decla would say. *They didn't need me. Everything was fine.*

But it wasn't. The Shedon and their teams had an unbreakable rule: Never split up while exploring the Underneath. Stay together at all times. There were sound reasons for that rule.

There was a secretive, treacherous city beneath Arlington Abbey, riddled with corridors that narrowed to passages barely wide enough to accommodate a child turned sideways before exploding into streets as wide as ten-lane thoroughfares. It was packed with nooks and crannies, crypts and strange multistory abodes that hinted at long-dead, unusual denizens of inhuman ilk. It housed catacombs and caverns, opulent libraries and eclectic conservatories, chambers filled with thousands of impossible-to-open trunks, or gadgets stuck to a ceiling too high to reach without scaffolding, more chambers crammed with items they could neither identify nor assign any apparent purpose.

It was as if all of the universe's unwanted, dangerous, and obsolete things had been relegated to a cast-offs warehouse beneath their home. And from the looks of things, that warehouse had been accumulating cosmic detritus since the dawn of time.

Each new section to which they gained access offered only more doors, more challenges, mysteries, and dangers. Here were stairs that led to a blank wall. There were doors that opened on yawning abysses—or worse, appeared to have a floor, which was but a masquerade concealing a deadly abyss. In the past two and a half years, they'd lost seven women to one threat or another.

Until Kat, herself, nine months ago, had formed teams based on invasively deep empathic readings of their psyches, careful and thorough assessments of their gifts and curses, strengths and weaknesses.

Since that time, they'd not lost a single woman.

Yesterday, however, they might have lost one.

With a talent for neutralizing wards and spells, Rhiannon was delicate-boned, kind, and wide open, with no barriers protecting her mind and heart. She was obsessive, selfless, and constantly getting hurt, physically, emotionally, or both.

Decla was lean and strong, with a supernova-bright, diamond-hard mind, and a healthy sense of self-preservation honed from a young age. She had gotten her bachelor's from the School of Hard Knocks, had a master's in sight, and a PhD in death. Decla could see death shadowing another person, had, for quite a few years as a child, believed everyone saw it. Once she'd begun talking, she'd learned the hard way they didn't and, worse, didn't appreciate that she did.

She was ten when she discovered her gifts came with a seductive side. If she acted quickly enough, she could intercept and redirect death.

To someone else.

That was the price.

To save one person, she had to choose who would die instead and escort the shadowy companion only she could see to that person. Stand with it and ensure the act was completed. And death, when it came to the wrong person, was far more terrible than it would have been otherwise, as if death resented the redirection and lashed out with fury at the interference. Kat had no idea how many times Decla had redirected it by the time the twenty-seven-year-old had had the breakdown that sent her fleeing to their mother-house in Ireland in search of a teacher, forgiveness, and a way to learn to control and live with herself.

Decla and Rhiannon reinforced each other, were doubly strong together, chinking each other's weaknesses.

"Rhiannon spent five days working to break the ward on the door before she succeeded," Colleen said.

"How did she break it?"

Colleen and Enyo exchanged another guilty look, then Colleen said, "We weren't exactly standing right here in this exact spot when she neutralized it."

Kat sighed. "In which exact spot were you standing?"

"We were down there." Enyo pointed about twenty feet away, to a small metal door in the stone wall of the passage. "Inside, digitally scanning scrolls."

"You know better than to leave a *sidhe*-seer alone in the Under-neath."

"She'd been at it for five bloody days, Kat," Colleen groused. "You know how she gets. The more difficult a ward is to defeat, the more fixated Rhiannon becomes. She wouldn't give up. We kept begging her to walk away. Leave it, forget it. There are countless other things to discover down here. Our goal is to create a detailed map, not break into every single chamber, especially when half the ones we get into contain something we either don't understand or nearly kills us. We couldn't stay here with her every single minute watch-ing. We were nearby. We could hear her murmuring."

"We didn't think she had a chance of breaking it. She'd tried everything. Then we heard her scream," Enyo said. "She was uncon-scious when we found her."

"Why wasn't I told any of this until now?" Kat said.

"It happened yesterday while you were at Draoidheacht. You looked exhausted when you got back last night. We know how hard your days with Sean are. We took turns standing guard all night and brought you down the moment you came into the breakfast hall. Is it what we think it is?" Colleen said.

Kat stared through the doorway for a long moment then said, "The instant Rhiannon can function, bring her back down here to re-ward the door. Stronger than it was before. If she could break it, someone else might be able to, too. Until she secures it, I want both of you standing guard. Stay together at all times. That means—"

"I know, I know," Colleen said, groaning. "Buckets for toilets. Power bars and water bottles. No cellphones, no distractions."

Kat said, "Tell no one else it's here."

"It *is* what we think it is, then," Enyo pressed, dark eyes glittering with a bit more fascination than Kat would have liked. Enyo was the adventurous one. Born inside a tank in the middle of a war zone, she thrived in dangerous situations, sought them a bit too eagerly for her own good.

"I've never seen it myself, but Mac and Dani have and, from their descriptions, I would say yes." What other monumentally risky things were they responsible for safeguarding? What else had been dumped on their doorsteps? She was beginning to regret that they'd ever begun the mapping of the Underneath.

First, they'd discovered that the *Sinsar Dubh*, the ancient, sentient, evil book of dark magic created by the Unseelie king, had been housed beneath their floors for millennia, unknown to all but the inner circle of the Haven.

Then, a few years ago, they'd discovered the Light Court of the Fae had long ago entombed countless ancient earth gods in the Underneath, as well.

Adding insult to injury, one of those very gods, Balor, reinvigorated by the Song of Making, had the temerity to set up his war camp in the secretive and sprawling city beneath their home.

That was the catalyst that had propelled the Shedon, the governing body of the abbey, to begin aggressively exploring and cataloging what else had been hidden beneath their feet.

Now this. For heaven's sake, was each and every one of the most dangerous parts of the universe secreted away beneath their beds?

"It's a bit difficult to look away from," Colleen murmured.

"That's only a small part of the problem," Kat agreed. It did more than obsessively compel the eye, it seduced. It whispered in silken, urgent tones, *Oh, do come in. Stroll my lovely corridor, gaze upon yourself and all things possible, herein lie the doorways to your wildest dreams. Everything is here. Everything you ever wanted. Come in, come in!*

But it was corrupted. One's odds of finding nightmares down that eternal hallway were far higher than realizing one's dreams. Christian had gotten lost in there and would have died, if not for Mac. Dani had been cheated of five years of her life before finding her way home.

The chamber into which Rhiannon had finally managed to gain access opened onto an endless, dazzling expanse of gold.

Gleaming golden floors. Towering golden walls. No ceiling to be seen. The gilded walls shot up to a dizzying height, vanishing beyond the eye's ability to follow.

And on those glittering walls hung millions—no, billions—no, an *infinity* of mirrors of every shape and size.

Four levels beneath Arlington Abbey, Rhiannon had shattered the ward that kept this very dangerous and very-necessary-to-reclose door from opening onto the vast temptation and seduction of the Hall of All Days: the cosmic nexus the Unseelie king had constructed a million years ago as a sort of interplanetary/interdimensional travel agency for the Fae. Once, one had only to gaze into one of the mirrors, choose a destination, and step through.

But Cruce's curse had corrupted all the traveling Silvers, and now the destinations the mirrors reflected bore no relation to the reality one found on the other side. One might choose a tropical beach and end up on a fire world with no oxygen, only death by instant incineration. Some even claimed, from inside the Hall, one could travel forward or backward in time, if one knew how.

Staring at the infrequent piles of crumbling bones littering the Hall, Kat reminded herself of yet another danger the Hall held—if you stopped moving, failed to choose a mirror, the Hall lifted a memory from your mind and wove it into a reality around you. You could get lost in the illusion, never eating, never sleeping, until you died.

A gust of cold air abruptly blasted through the doorway, and they shivered.

"That happens sometimes," Enyo said, closing the door hastily. The moment it was shut, the chill lessened but it was still colder in the passageway than it should have been, and they could hear the sound of a distant wind moaning beyond the closed door. "Any idea what causes it?"

Kat said grimly, "Mac told me when someone or something enters the Hall of All Days from one of the mirrors, it kicks up a fair bit of a storm in the Hall."

"You mean things are entering our Underneath and walking around in there?" Colleen said. "Possibly headed our way?"

"Which is exactly why you're going to be standing guard with the door closed and securely barred until Rhiannon seals it again," Kat said. When Mac told her stories of the Hall, she'd admitted she'd wondered at its sheer size, wondered just what kind of being could reach the enormous mirrors high up on those towering walls.

Kat fervently hoped they never found out.

———— • • ————

"Mommy, I haven't seen the Spyrssidhe in *ever* so long," Rae said worriedly, as Kat helped her get changed into her pajamas for bed.

"You like the Spyrssidhe, don't you?" Kat smiled, as she slipped Rae's shirt off and smoothed her hair. Her smile faded abruptly as she spotted the marks marring her daughter's back. After an absence of more than three long, lovely, reassuring years, the spots on her daughter's shoulders had returned.

This time, they were different. Bigger. Angry, textured red welts.

Precisely where a pair of wings might grow.

"Are you itchy?" Kat asked softly.

"No."

"Your back doesn't itch?"

Nibbling her lower lip, Rae shook her head.

"What did you do today?"

"Played dolls with Anna at school. She likes to play Faerie queen. But her queen is mean and picks on everybody. I don't think that's how the queen really is."

"Did you go outside?" The only other time Rae had sported such spots, Kat told herself it was an unusual reaction to pollen; her daughter had sprawled in the grass, perhaps gotten bug bites.

"No. Teacher wouldn't let us. Too rainy."

"Then how do you know the Spyrssidhe aren't around?"

"They come to my window at night. But they haven't in so very long! I'm afraid something's wrong. I asked Bess today and she got her umber and went out and looked in their houses. They're empty. She said she was going to talk to you about it."

Kat hadn't seen the head of the abbey's daycare today. Ciara had collected Rae and brought her to their suite of rooms.

"I'll check on the Spyrssidhe tomorrow."

"Promise? You won't forget? I'm worried. I think something's wrong. I can feel . . ." Rae trailed off, nibbling her lower lip.

"What, honey?"

Rae shrugged and held up her arms for her pajama top. As Kat slipped it over her shoulders, she slid her palm over one of the spots. It was rough and leathery. And hot, very hot. "Your back's not bothering you at all?"

"No. It feels good. Like it's getting stronger. But I *am* growing up," Rae said proudly. "I'm almost *five!*"

"And we're going to have a big birthday party for you."

"And everyone at the abbey will come. Even the Spyrssidhe," she announced brightly. "Even Daddy."

Kat flinched. In nearly five years, Rae had never said anything about her father. She'd never asked why, though all her friends had mothers and fathers, she had only a mother. Kat hoped it was because she felt so loved that she wanted for nothing, missed nothing. "What do you mean, Rae?"

"He visits me in dreams," she said as she burrowed beneath the covers and pulled the blankets up to her chin. "He says we'll meet soon. I think he means my birthday. Oops! I wasn't supposed to tell you that. He wants it to be a surprise. Don't tell him I told you."

No, no, no. This was not happening. No one was visiting anyone in dreams. The only person (and she was using that term very loosely) she knew who could visit in people's dreams was dead, destroyed when the Song of Making was sung. With each passing year, Kat had grown more certain of it, relaxed a bit more.

"What—" Kat broke off, recalibrating her voice to a calmer tone and tried again, "What does your daddy look like in your dreams?"

"Not much like me at all," Rae said, and yawned. "But he says I'll look more like him when I get older. So, I guess, maybe when I'm five. I'm sleepy, Mommy. Forget I told you and act surprised, okay?"

25

— • • • —

All I have to do is dream

MAC

S PRAWLED ON A SOFA at Chester's, my dreams are strange and uncomfortable things.

It's no surprise that I dream of the last subject about which I wrote.

Cruce.

Barrons is there, watching everything, absorbing the tiniest details, as I relive my many encounters with the Unseelie prince called War.

The first time I met Cruce, he was masquerading as V'lane and trying to persuade me to help the Seelie queen (whom he'd already interred in a coffin of ice, in the Unseelie prison, to die, but I didn't know that then). A prince of the Dark Court stood before me that day, camouflaged by three of the king's amulets, lying through his teeth to me.

In the museum when Cruce used the *Sidhba-jai* on me, making me strip again and again.

The night he drove the Shades from Barrons Books & Baubles,

and saved me from the gruesome death-by-Shade Fiona had arranged for me.

In Faery, when he gifted me with an afternoon of playing volleyball with an illusion of my sister on powder sand. I'd lost a month of mortal time for that "gift."

The day he told me the history of the Unseelie king and his concubine, minus many critical details, such as his part in it.

The night he returned me to Ashford, Georgia, and I stood outside our house listening as my parents discussed the prophecy about me.

Our encounters go whirling by, faster and faster . . .

The many times he kissed me, embedding his true name in my tongue so I might summon him.

The day he lied, claiming he was with Aoibheal, protecting her while I was being raped by four Unseelie princes when, in truth, he was one of my rapists.

Beneath the abbey, the night he mocked the king for not figuring out Cruce stole his concubine, wiped her memory with a cup from the Cauldron, then hauled her off to Faery, a blank slate of a long-abused mortal woman, where they both lived concealed among the Light Court for hundreds of thousands of years, and the king went quietly mad, believing she'd killed herself to escape him.

The moment the king iced Cruce, imprisoning him beneath Arlington Abbey in the precise spot he once imprisoned the *Sinsar Dubh* so long ago. His two most dangerous creations, entombed in the same place, entrusted to the protection of *sidhe*-seers who twice failed to contain his disasters, but why would he expect them to succeed, when he himself hadn't?

The afternoon I kissed Cruce, convincing him, at another time, under different circumstances, I might have chosen him, and he might have changed for the better, in exchange for his half of the Song.

Barrons lingers long on that memory, eyes dark and intense, likely because of the guilt I feel about it. Of course, my subconscious would keep Barrons there, studying every damned nuance. I'd had to compartmentalize and box so many parts of myself that day that the woman who kissed Cruce hadn't been me at all. Merely the necessary version of me, who would save the world, no matter the cost.

I'd gotten the job done.

Then the Unseelie king is in my dreams, rising up enormous and dark, made of starry stuff, planets and nebulae rolling like tiny pearls in his gigantic wings, obliterating all else, sweeping away Barrons and Cruce, tiny dust motes caught on the straw broom of his gargantuan will. They leave unwilling but they leave.

Then it's just the king and me, and my dream is so bloody lucid, I'm once again standing on the first world, gazing up at the half-mad creator of so much beauty and ugliness, of truth and lie, of clarity and confusion, that I hear mighty Hunters gonging deep in their chests as they glide, wings barely flapping, past the moon, smell the lush perfume of the night-blooming jasmine, as I dwindle to minuscule inconsequentiality in the enormity of his presence.

Unlike other Fae, the king feels to me like a force of nature, sprung from the very fabric of the cosmos itself, as elemental and primitive and necessary as space between stars, the stars themselves, the thunder, the lightning, the sun, the passage of time.

I have no idea what he is, but he's not Fae.

I wake with a violent start that sends me sprawling from sofa to floor, cracking my head on the coffee table as I go down.

The residue of Barrons, Cruce, and the king clings darkly to me, thick and viscous, and I know the taste and feel of this dream, like my cold-place nightmare, will stalk me throughout the day.

The words the king spoke to me in that split second before awakening blaze supernova bright in my mind.

You seek a loophole. The rules governing Fae compacts pertain only to the original Light Court. Cruce is not.

I've long believed dreams are a subconscious method of collating the facts and events of our daily lives, where like is stored with like and conclusions are drawn that elude the cluttered miasma of our conscious brains.

On the heels of this powerful, revelatory dream, I know it's true.

Somewhere in the queen's files, I must have noticed something that made me suspect that which governed the Light Court was applicable only to the Light Court. Perhaps drawn from an amalgamation of many parts of many files, never fully spelled out, but implicitly understood.

As my dream king had pointed out, Cruce is not Light Court. Boo-yah. Got him.

Murmuring a silent thank-you to the cosmos for showing me what I needed to see, I push up, grab my notepad and pen, and dash off in search of Barrons.

———— • • ————

"I want to try sifting to Dad and Dani," I told him.

Barrons is sitting in Ryodan's office, shirt slung over a chair, while Ryodan tattoos his back with obsidian and crimson runes that will protect him against the high price due for dabbling in black arts.

"You realized it was the IFP you hit earlier, not a ward," Barrons says.

"Yes." Mental note to self, never try to sift into an IFP again. Barrons was right, the fractured state of the fragment of Fae reality had drained me, as if it was trying to seize my power to restore itself. "I may be able to get inside Winter's castle. I gave up too easily. Ward Chester's more securely or rescue Dad and Dani?" I present the options. I know what I consider top priority.

Barrons snorts. Ryodan tosses his knife on the desk, shoves aside the tray of ink, and says, "Fuck Chester's. I'm in."

"You should stay here," I say to Ryodan. "We'll lose time again, even though it's not as much as it used to be. What if Dani's not there? What if Shazam comes looking for you? What if something happens with Mom, or Cruce shows up?"

He regards me in silence, silvery eyes icy, bristling. I feel impatience and fury shivering beneath his skin, hunger for vengeance, hunger for battle. Someone took Dani, and he's seeing red.

But he's also seeing black and white and gray, because Ryodan always sees the big picture and will work his way past emotion to the coldly logical, most effective move at this moment. His man, the king, the ruler, the consummate chess player, is more dominant than the beast. Barrons's beast is more dominant than the man.

"Fuck," Ryodan says finally. Then, "Fuck," again as he slams his fist into the desk.

"Christian opened a portal, slid a message through, losing zero mortal-time doing it. If you need to contact us, use Christian. I'll send you a message the same way, and let you know when we find her." *If* we find her, but I didn't add that.

Ryodan nods, tightly. "Go. Before I change my fucking mind."

———— • ● • ————

I focus on my dad, constructing a rich memory. The first time he put me behind the wheel of a car to teach me how to drive. Mom almost had a conniption fit. She'd have made me wait until I was sixteen, but I'd been helping Dad detail his car for a couple of years, and he'd seen the hunger in my eyes. I was born loving muscle cars.

The 1970 Ford Mustang Boss 302, V-8, had a grabber orange exterior, black interior. Rear-wheel drive, perfect to play on snow-free southern roads. I adored every muscular inch of it. I can still feel Dad's hand on mine as he guides me through the gears and teaches me to feel the transmission hit the sweet spot. The interior of the car is filled with the smell of the peppermints he so loves, the light scent of his aftershave, the brimstone smell of exhaust. The sun dapples the windshield, the drugging scent of summer in the deep South blows in the open windows, ruffling my hair.

Winter's ward is a bitch. But not insurmountable. I *had* given up too easily. We go slamming into it hard enough that it knocks the breath out of me, but we don't bounce away, back to Chester's. Instinctively, I go limp, don't fight it. Instead, I embrace the power rippling around the castle, open myself to it, greet it as High Queen of the Fae, honoring its power, offering to blend and merge and leave it a bit richer for having passed through.

It's that easy, merely required an offering of my energy, no counter-ward, rune, or spell necessary. I'm beginning to suspect the reason the queen is the most powerful is she simply has the most generous connection to the earth-magic, and as the Fae hierarchy descends, each lesser Fae has a less potent connection. My rule is ascertained merely by the fact that I hold the ability to draw more power than any other Fae.

We manifest inside the North Tower. Winter stands with her back to us, facing the window, unaware of our invasion. She's a study of glittering ice, long, silvery hair crusted, dress dripping; the skin of her long, thin hands white, blue-veined, and frosty with long iced talons.

I drag my gaze away, scan the circular room, and spy my father, bound to a chair sculpted of ice, head lolling forward, skin bloodless and pale except for where it's crusted with frozen blood. He's badly injured. Dani is nowhere to be seen.

Daddy! I scream silently.

The enforced silence ratchets my fury to an unbearable pitch. I'm denied the simple release of screaming.

How did Winter suppress sound? There's a flatness to the air, a feeling of two-dimensionality, as if the spell she employed stripped out the very molecules that enable resonance.

Again, operating on instinct, since it worked with the ward, I take a similar approach, but instead of offering power to the spell itself, I offer a gift of my energy to the emptiness of the air, encouraging it to restore itself.

As I open myself, I realize the air is hungry. It *wants* substance back. It doesn't like being flat and two-dimensional.

Power rushes from my body into the circular tower, into the air beyond it, farther, into the too-silent kingdom and, abruptly, the sound of my scream is exploding from my lungs, echoing off the frozen walls.

Winter whirls from the window, snarling with rage.

I'm horrified to realize I just fucked up. Massively.

Offering power isn't without a price, especially not when you send it out to an entire kingdom of empty air.

I'm drained.

I'm not even certain I can muster the energy to sift us out of there. It's all I can do not to droop on myself and slump to the floor. I barely have the strength to stand.

Buck the fuck up, Ms. Lane, Barrons sends silently along our bond, *and perhaps next time, consider attacking the actual spell, not restoring Nature itself with your bounty, which is clearly not boundless.*

I'm still learning.

But his admonishment rams steel up my spine. I draw myself up straight, thrust back my shoulders, and return Winter's snarl.

Kindness and cruelty, Barrons reminds.

How long until my power returns?

No bloody clue. Although I suspect it would help if you planted your bare feet on soil. That's where your power comes from.

My cruelty would have been a direct attack on Winter herself.

My kindness, restoring her court.

Unfortunately, at the moment, staring into the eyes of my enemy, a woman who currently has far more power than I do and holds captive my father, who's clearly dying, I'm not capable of doing either of those things.

26

— • • • —

If I could through myself set your spirit free

KAT

___

THE LAST TIME I went to Draoidheacht to visit Sean I didn't
text Christian to ask him to sift me from the abbey to his
drafty castle. Rather, I made the journey from Ireland to Scotland
the long, hard way, ten hours of driving and two hours on a ferry.

I'd been craving time alone to think, and gotten it in spades.

This time, however, I've a more profound motivation for packing
Rae into the car and making the trip, which isn't without risk, given
old gods roaming the land and IFPs drifting about.

I don't want my daughter to see an Unseelie prince for the first
time until she sees Sean.

As we enter Christian's fifty-thousand-acre Highland estate,
crossing the ward makes me shiver, and Rae exclaims, "What was
that, Mommy? Are we there yet?"

If I never have to hear the words "are we there yet" again in my
life, I'll count myself a blessed woman. Still, buckled securely into
her safety seat, Rae has handled the long trip well, with a few brief
naps and her customary bright-eyed enthusiasm. She was riveted

by the scenery, the changing sky and land, the ferry ride, and bab-
bled happily most of the way, making up stories about everything
we passed.

I decided shortly after her birth that my daughter would not be
raised sheltered. I want her to see everything, taste and try everything, know she can be whatever she wants to be, and whatever she
chooses to be (so long as it's not evil) is perfectly perfect and all I
could want for her.

I will see my daughter happy. Loved. Fulfilled. Eyes wide open,
heart whole and strong.

The night she told me her daddy visited her in dreams, I let her
fall asleep without further questioning—not because I'm a good
mother and knew she needed rest more than I needed answers, but
because at that particular moment, I was a coward.

I didn't want to know if "daddy" had great black wings.

It had taken me a week to work my way around to being ready to
find that out. A week during which I'd not questioned her and she'd
not mentioned her father again. A week Rhiannon spent slowly
regaining the strength to get out of bed, during which we'd dispatched scouts, trying to locate a glimpse of a Spyrssidhe without
success. Rae was right. The diminutive, spritely garden Fae were
missing, their homes hastily abandoned.

"That, my love," I tell Rae, "was a ward. A powerful protection
spell that—"

"I know what wards are," she says and rolls her eyes. "The teach-
ers talk about all kinds of stuff at school. I just never felt one like
that before. The ones at the abbey are different."

I make a mental note to plan an impromptu visit to Rae's day
care in the near future to find out just what her little pitcher ears are
overhearing. She's a voracious sponge, soaking up everything, putting together facts in alarming and often insightful ways. "We're
nearly there."

"I love adventuring with you," she says, beaming. "Can we do this
all the time, Mommy?"

"Yes," I say, and it's a vow I will keep. I want to show my daughter the world. I want to watch her face light with joy as she discovers the many wonders.

"Why is all the grass burnt?" she asks a short time later, after we've parked and I'm helping her out of the car.

"There's a man here who has a power he's having a difficult time learning to control." I try to tell Rae the truth, as much as possible. I won't shield her. I won't grant her the grace of hiding, like I did this past week.

"But why does he burn the grass?"

"He has so much power that when he merely walks across the earth, it scorches, deep into the soil."

"But what about the worms? Do they die?"

"Yes, Rae, they do."

"I don't like that. He doesn't sound like a very nice man to me."

Oh, dear God, what was I doing bringing them together like this? Escorting Rae into a room with an Unseelie prince who couldn't control his power and—if Rae's dreams were true and Cruce was alive and he wasn't lying—a prince who wasn't even her father?

"He's the very best of men," I tell her quietly. "We grew up together. He protected me and watched out for me. But one day, he inherited a power he never wanted and has been having a hard time dealing with it."

"Do you love him?"

"Very much."

"Then I'll love him, too," Rae says matter-of-factly, tucking her hand into mine. "But he *must* stop killing the worms," she says earnestly. "All things like living. Even the things that frighten us."

My wise little daughter.

I delay, of course. I can't help myself. If we walk into Sean's tower room and she recognizes the dark, winged figure of an Unseelie prince—which she's never glimpsed before—I'll know Cruce is somehow still alive and is her father.

If she walks into that room and doesn't respond in a familiar way to Sean, I'll be able to breathe again properly for the first time in a very long and difficult week. I'll be able to tell myself she's been having mere dreams, not visitations.

It's not possible Sean has been visiting Rae in her dreams. Not only does he lack control of his power—assuming he possesses the ability to infiltrate the Dreaming—but he wouldn't bother to do so. Since our first meeting at Draoidheacht, he's not once asked to see her, never mentioned her again. We scrupulously avoid the topics of Cruce, Rae, paternity tests, anything but the weather, the castle, and the like.

We've not made love since we got back together, and I'm not even sure we are back together. I visit. He tolerates it. We fail to learn to control his power. Rinse and repeat. That's our life together. The man has walls around himself that are insurmountable, even for me. There've been times I've grown angry with him, although I conceal it, that he can't find it within himself to control his power but somehow found the power to wall out the greatest empath in Ireland.

I weary of loving so hard and being unmet. I weary of hoping, always hoping.

I stroll Rae through the castle at a leisurely pace, showing her the various weirdness and wonders as we take the long, dallying way to Sean's aerie in the sky. Rae's enchanted by the gloomy, strange castle, ducking inside hearths big enough to hold five tall men standing upright, dashing up and down stairs, growing impatient as I snatch back her hand time and again when she tries to touch one of the many inexplicable things in Christian's eclectic collection of artifacts.

But finally, holding hands, we ascend the dusty, circular stone stairs to the tower in the old, ruined part of the castle that Sean calls home.

"*Brrr!* It's chilly up here!" Rae exclaims.

I remove my scarf, wrap it around her neck, and button her little jacket. "The man you're going to meet is a bit different than most," I caution her. I've never permitted her to lay eyes upon Christian. I warned him off years ago. Today, for the first time, Rae will see an Unseelie prince.

And I will see her reaction.

And I'll know.

I inhale deeply, exhale slowly, and reach out a hand that trembles only slightly to open the tower door.

When we step inside the drafty, icy stone tower, Sean is nowhere to be seen. After a puzzled moment, I catch a flicker of motion beyond what rippled green glass remains, jagged and broken in the window frame, the flash of black feathers, a hint of dark skin, tattoos racing across the surface.

He's outside on the roof, perched on the gargoyle-adorned parapet, brooding down at the blackened estate below.

Sean rarely flies. Christian says learning to savor their wings and the gift of flight is a big step toward attaining peace with what they've become.

I wonder if Sean is flying more, if he's trying, or if he's as surly and defeated as ever.

"Sean, would you mind coming in?" I call through the shattered glass.

"I'm not in the mood for a visit today, Kat," he replies heavily.

He's never in the mood. "Please. I'd like to show you something."

Rae squeezes my hand and whispers, "He hurts, Mommy. I can feel it. "

My empathic daughter. "I know," I whisper back.

"I'll cheer him up," she says, dark eyes round and serious.

I hear a gusty sigh then another flicker of movement, then he's nearly to the door that opens onto the walk, and my heart is hammering like a drum, and he's moving into the opening.

"Mommy, you're squeezing my hand too hard!" Rae says.

I relax my grip then he's there, framed in the doorway, the sullen light glancing off his tall, dark Unseelie prince form.

Will he terrify her? Will he make her smile?

This is it.

The moment of truth.

Sean's gaze barely grazes me, but flies instantly to Rae with her black Irish, curly, dark hair and lovely gold skin that tans so easily, her dark eyes so much like his used to be. His alien, iridescent gaze clouds with rage and fear and something else I can't identify. He's muted himself, as he always does when I come, so my eyes don't bleed, shielding Rae as well.

For a moment, the three of us stand frozen, and I can't make myself glance down at my daughter.

When I finally manage it, my heart sinks heavy as a stone to the bottom of a terrifyingly dark loch of fear and revulsion and . . . och, so much love it doesn't matter whose she is!

Rae is mine and I love her more than life itself.

Her face is as radiant as a new dawn, her eyes shimmering with delight as she drops my hand and races across the tower toward him.

Sean stiffens. "Get her out of here," he cries hoarsely.

But it's too late.

Rae flings her arms around Sean's legs and hugs him, laughing.

Then she tips back her head and smiles adoringly up at him. "Daddy, you're *here!*"

27

Understand she's a force of nature

DANI

As I regain consciousness in slow degrees, enormously grumpy and discombobulated, I think that I really, *really* hate that there is someone or something in the universe that can knock me out without me even knowing it, until I wake up again. That's Supreme Bullshit with capital letters.

Grumpy and discombobulated is how I've greeted ninety-nine percent of the mornings of my life. I'm cranky, cross, and confused for at least five minutes after I open my eyes. Which is odd, given my eternal optimism that tomorrow will always be the best day of my life.

Mom used to say it's because I expend so much energy freeze-framing while I'm awake that it's impossible for me to ever get enough sleep. I think it's simpler than that. I just resent sleeping. It's time killed, countless aborted minutes strung into hours, during which you could be doing something bodacious and amazing. I wake up every single morning to the sobering and chafing aware-ness that I've wasted hours of time. Now that I'm nearly immortal,

I feel no different. Sleep is a massive pain in my ass, doubly so when I'm keelhauled without warning into the murky waters of slumber.

Sprawled on my back on a hard floor, I stretch, and my spirits are swiftly buoyed by the discovery that I'm no longer sore. They plummet again as I contemplate just how much enforced slumber that must have taken.

Who's captured me? Who even *could* capture someone like me who can hear people approaching half a mile away?

Does the Sweeper have me again? Did he learn from the last time he abducted me that he has to keep me unconscious or I'll escape? Still, how is he knocking me out? I have no memory of zombie-eating wraiths straitjacketing me.

Bloody hell! Is Mac here somewhere in a similar cage?

I never got comfortable with the Sweeper simply vanishing and never trying to fix us again. It felt as if we got off too easy. If I were a writer, I'd have made that demon bite my characters in the ass at least one more time, you know, like the dead serial killer who comes back from the puddle of blood on the floor the moment you believe he's out of the picture; my life consistently unfolds as bizarrely and traumatically as movies and books.

Arguably, though, Mac's and my problems were shortly thereafter rectified. Her inner *Sinsar Dubh* was defeated, unifying her brain, and Shazam and Ryodan unified my heart, merging Jada and Dani into a woman as fearless in love as life in general. We're no longer divided like we used to be, ergo, nothing to fix, not that there was in the first place, and now I'm even grumpier, thinking about how that awkwardly ambulating heap of junk actually dared think itself superior to me. My hands clench, and I growl softly, thinking when I get out of here I'm going to hunt down that clattering pile of rubbish and—

"Yi-yi?" comes a tremulous whisper from the darkness.

My heart thuds and stops beating and, only when I force myself to breathe slow and deep several times, does it resume.

One of my few consolations in this cage is that, at least, it's only me mired in this mystifying mess. I can handle being caged. I'll get out. I always do.

Goodbye consolation.

I whisper, "Shazzy-bear?"

He vaults through the darkness and lands on my stomach like a ton of bricks, and my bladder is full, as usual. With another groan, I wrap my arms around him, hugging him close while he nuzzles his face into my neck and begins to sprinkle me with copious amounts of tears.

I hate that he's here. I love him more than life. He—and Y'rill—is my best friend/playmate and the mother I never had.

He cries like me, dramatically and violently, with lots of snot, gulping, snuffling, and occasionally choking because he gets so worked up, despite me stroking his fur and murmuring reassurances.

As Y'rill, she's the one taking care of me; making sure I don't crash into a meteor as I push my flying skills to the limit, or go spinning off in a zero-gravity somersault straight into the incinerating atmosphere of a sun. As Shazam, I'm the one taking care of him; making sure he doesn't eat entire civilizations or abduct other species to mate with.

We're a match made among the stars. Literally.

"Nothing is going to harm you, Shaz-ma-taz. I promise. I've got you, I've got you," I tell him, over and over.

"Can't promise!"

"Just did."

"Can't keep. Bars on our cage. Both stuck now!" he wails.

"Good thing I'm a pro at getting out of cages. I'll get us out of this one, too."

"Not!" Shazam cries, anguished. "Nobody can get out of *this* cage! Too powerful!"

Frowning, I say, "Shazam, do you know something about this cage? Do you know where we are?"

He yowls so loudly and piteously that the hair at my nape stands up on end. I've heard Shazam make pretty much every sound possible for a morbidly morose Hel-Cat, yet never one quite so packed with fear and finality. He genuinely believes we have no chance at escape. Yes, he's pessimistic in his Hel-Cat form, yes, he's overblown and wildly emotional, but there's something . . . different this time. I feel it in my bones. And I don't like it one bit.

"Shazzy, where are we?" I demand.

He melts into a puddle of fatness and futility against me and whimpers incoherently.

"Shazam Mega-Hel-Cat O'Malley, you will answer me this minute!" I order sternly. "Who is holding us here?"

"Will not."

"Who?" I snarl.

He snuffles and burrows deeper into my arms. Finally he sniffs and hisses, "Hunters!"

Okay, that's not what I expected. "Why on earth would other Hunters put us in a cage?"

"Because there's a price!"

"For what?"

"Meddling," he says in a muffled voice, as he rubs his face against my skin, cleansing snot and tears from his fur.

"In what exactly?" What have we done this time?

"Helped you become."

"So?"

"Told you. Not allowed!"

I ponder that a moment, then say, "If they must, they can turn me back into a human. No foul, no penalty," I offer. I'll hate being just human again. And I'll have to find another way to become immortal. But I'll get used to it, and there will be no punishing or penalizing or even rebuking Shazam on my watch. He/she did what he/she did out of love. Motive matters.

"Not all they do." He collapses in great hiccupping sobs, tail frantically thumping the floor.

"Shazzy, it's going to be okay."

"Is not!" he cries.

"What else do they do?" I repeat patiently.

"I meddled with time when I threw your star," he mutters.

"We'll apologize and promise never to do it again," I say firmly.

He exhales a gusty sigh that ends in a whimper. "Not that easy, tiny red. There are rules."

The old me would have said, "Feck rules, they're made to be broken!" The mature me says instead, "Rules need to be tested and redefined as beings evolve."

"Not for Hunters. Rules are. Unbreakable. Irrefutable. There is always a price."

"Spell it out exactly, Shaz. What's the price?"

"A small one," he says weakly. "Because I am now a small thing, never to be Hunter again! I can no longer shift. They took it from me." He flings himself from my arms and sprawls on the floor next to me, belly up, covering his eyes with both paws, shaggy-furred body shaking with sobs. "Hug me! Hold me! I hurt everywhere!"

God, I love him. He says aloud the things I used to think but never vocalized. How many times I lay in my cage as a kid thinking: *Hug me, hold me, I hurt everywhere.* Mom. Please. Let me out. Until I learned to turn it off. Shazam can't turn it off. He is the way he is, needy and loving and fragile and strong and perfect in my eyes. I gather him into my arms, thinking, *I can deal with that.* Again, it's not my preference, but I love Shazzy in any shape or form and I'll be happy as long as I get to keep him with me, always. "Not a problem. We'll take care of each other. It'll be like old times. We'll be Dani and Shaz again. We had a great life. Remember? *Shaz the mighty fur-beast lived up in the . . .*" I begin to sing but trail off hastily because it's insult to injury at this point, since he won't be living up in the air anymore, and now I'm going to have to rewrite our Shaz-tastic theme song, which really pisses me off because it's catchy as hell. Why can't they just leave us alone?

"Won't," Shazam moans.

"Won't what?"

"Have a life."

"Why not?"

"They will return you to Earth when it's done."

My blood ices. "When *what's* done?" I ask, very quietly.

He's silent a long moment then says, "When I'm dead, tiny red. Price is my life, and you watch them kill me. Punish us both. I knew when I did it. Told them I'd do it again. I see you, Yi-yi. I don't want to die and never see you again. I can't bear it!"

I hug him close, snarling, sounding like a Hel-Cat myself. How dare the Hunters? Who are they to take a life just because a few rules were broken? Overreact much? Don't they know the meaning of the word "proportionate"; as in the punishment should fit the crime, not one iota more?

Killing someone for breaking rules that hurt *no one* is not proportionate. I might be able to get my head around them returning us to our original state; that feels more like an eye for an eye, but a whole *life* for an eye? Hunters are a highly evolved species, beholders of the universe's complex patterns, seers of how it all interconnects, weavers of the epic red threads that link together destinies.

Shazzy loves me. And if there's one thing I know about love, it's that it makes you break rules. And if there's one thing I know about rules, it's that they need to be revisited and questioned or they become rote, outdated mandates and laws that applied to a society that once existed, but exists no longer because it evolved.

Ergo rules must evolve, too. The universe, and everything in it, is in a constant state of flux. When's the last time anybody challenged the Hunters' rules?

Once, I stabbed Y'rill, and it immobilized her for a time. I'll stab them all if I have to in order to—

Bloody hell, I don't have my sword. Or clothes. Or food.

Ryodan will find us. He'll walk in with Mac and the Nine. We'll kick ass ten ways to Sunday, it'll be epic and badass, and we'll stalk out of here.

Unless we're, like, on a planet several galaxies and a gazillion light-years from the Earth, interred at the heart of a dark star, surrounded by countless black holes, guarded by an army of K'Vrucks, which is entirely possible given the nature of Hunters. That could present a smidgen of a problem.

No worries. I'll get us out of here.

My lips curve, but it's not the kind of smile a sane person would return.

It's the smile of a woman who survived a hellish childhood, was brainwashed by a monster of a headmistress, defied and irritated Ryodan for years and got away with it, was nearly frozen to death, defeated the Hoar Frost King, emerged stronger from five long years lost in the most dangerous of worlds within the nexus of the Silvers, killed two Unseelie princes, rescued Mac from all four of them, withstood the loss of Dancer, destroyed Balor, and became a mighty Hunter who sails the stars.

I am a bloody motherfucking force of Nature herself.

Allow the Hunters to kill Shazam?

Never. Going. To. Happen.

28

---・・・---

In da Gadda da vida

MAC

"RESTORE MY COURT, AND I will tell you how to save your father," Winter commands imperiously. "I've poisoned him. You must follow me if you want answers." When she sifts out, her venomous smile lingers after the rest of her body is gone, and mocking laughter echoes off the frosted walls.

"Can you follow her?" Barrons says grimly.

I can't take my eyes off my father. Both arms are hanging at unnatural angles, his skin crusted with bloody ice. All his fingers are twisted, some backward. The bitch broke his arms and crushed his hands. No doubt slowly and painfully. Rushing to his side, I drop to the floor and press my fingers to his wrist, which yields nothing, then his jugular. Five seconds tick by before I feel a heartbeat, seven more seconds until the next. His pulse is sluggish and weak but there. If she poisoned him—and I have no reason to think she'd lie—I don't dare lose her. If Winter is convinced I can follow wherever she sifted, I possess that power, and hopefully I have just enough mojo left to get me and Barrons there. Gently, I lift my father's head to see his face. He's been badly beaten with two black eyes and many lacerations. "I think so. Can you heal him, Barrons?"

"I can speed the repair of his broken bones." He presses his hands to the sides of my father's skull and begins to chant softly. When he finally stops, he says, "He will remain in a suspended state for a period of time. I have no idea how long the spell will last in Faery."

Tears roll down my cheeks, freeze into crystals, and tinkle to the snow-drifted floor. "What about the poison? Was she telling the truth?"

Barrons scrapes a few crystals of iced blood from my father's arm, where it's broken so badly I can barely stand to look at it. Bone is protruding from jagged, frosted flesh. He rolls the crystals across his tongue a moment before murmuring, "I don't recognize it. With memory restored, their knowledge predates mine."

"Can you neutralize it?"

"No."

"What is it doing to him?"

"The toxin is targeting a single organ, his heart."

That bitch! Jack Lane's heart is the finest thing about him, and he's made of only fine things. "What does that mean?"

"In time, it will harden and cease beating."

And my father will die. "How long does he have?"

"I am unable to gauge that."

I stare up at him, equal parts fury, grief, and entreaty blazing in my eyes.

"You don't want me to," he growls.

"Dageus looks fine to me," I say stiffly.

"And Chloe? Is she also fine? How will Dageus fare when Chloe dies?"

I flinch. If Barrons turns him into one of the Nine, my father would live forever. My mother would die. Alina and I never lacked for love, always felt treasured and cherished, but we also knew the love mom and dad felt for each other was soul mate love, eclipsing all else, and they wanted both of us to know that kind of love.

"Try exhausting preliminary options before flinging yourself onto a runaway train headed for the last resort, Ms. Lane."

"You don't think being what you are is terrible."

"Jack Lane would think so," Barrons says flatly. "Dageus has a darkness your father lacks. That darkness is necessary to live as we do. Do you have enough power to sift? Can you follow her?"

"I can't just leave—"

"She wants something from you. If Jack dies she won't get it. Use your head, Ms. Lane. Turn off your heart. No love, no rage. This is a game. You play to win. Jack would expect no less of you. Box that shit and sift us. Now!"

He's roaring at the last, and it does exactly what he thought it would, lights a fire inside me. I snatch his hand, close my eyes, focus on Winter, and we're—

Standing in a small, verdant glade in the middle of a towering, triple-canopied forest, with a humid, perfumed breeze ruffling the leaves high above us. I stagger and nearly go down. Barrons catches me, yanks me upright, and slips an arm tightly around my waist. Unfortunately, as I suspected, getting here took the last ounce of power in my possession. Wherever we are, we'll be staying awhile. Fortunately, I have my spear and a natural born Fae-killer at my side. I can stab from a prone, badly injured position. I've done it before.

Barrons moves behind me, his back to mine, lending me his spine for support, and we circle in defensive formation, searching the forest beyond the clearing.

Winter is nowhere to be seen, but she's here. I can feel the proximity of her rage, cruelty, and hunger for vengeance.

My dad is alone in Faery, tied to a chair of ice, suspended for now, but dying. I clutch the hilt of my spear tightly, as I flash back to the memory of saying goodbye to him earlier at Chester's, gripped by the foreboding they might be the last words I would ever say to him.

Is my queenly power of premonition so frighteningly subtle that

I might mistake a warning about our future for no more than my own imaginings and fears? If Winter kills him, will I be able to restrain myself from raining down destruction on all the Fae? Impossible to rule them if my father dies at her hands!

I frown. Winter is moving away from us, not toward. Why? Does she expect us to follow?

Remove your boots, Barrons orders, via our bond. *This world bristles electric with power.*

I will them away but nothing happens; I'm too drained. I have to bend and untie them, then sit on the ground to tug them off. The moment my bare feet touch the grass, I tuck my spear into my holster and sprawl on my back with gratitude and relief.

There's a motherlode of power at the core of the planet, dense and rich and beautiful.

Barrons gazes down at me, one brow arched, as if to say, you think to face your enemy, lying down?

I pat the ground next to me. "I can't feel her anymore other than in a general 'she exists and is the consummate bitch from hell who's soon to be returned there' kind of way. She aggressively moved away from us. I think she's looking for someone or thing. When she gets it, she'll return. That works for me." I'll drink my fill of power and be ready. He settles on the ground next to me, on high alert, scanning the terrain.

"I'll feel her when she approaches," I assure him. "Barrons, my father—"

"Is currently suspended and feels no pain," he cuts me off.

"But you said it won't last and the poison—"

"I'll tell you the moment I feel the spell shatter. Until then, worrying about his condition yields nothing. Cease doing it."

"Easier said than done," I grouse.

"Work harder at it then."

Unyielding, demanding man. But he's right. I know the importance of boxing things and shoring up reserves for the next thing. I've had to do it time and again. Problem is, boxing worry about my father makes me feel like a terrible daughter and lousy human being.

"Your feelings. Not reality. Were Jack here, he would advocate the same, commend you for being strong enough to cease thinking about him when you can do nothing to help him at the moment."

Right again. I let my eyes drift shut, playing tall, tender grass through my fingers, and focus on drawing power gently from the planet. I want to gulp it, greedily suck it down, but sense not only would that be wrong but met with strident rebuke from the planet itself. "Where are we?" I change the subject.

"I have no idea. It smells similar to Earth long ago. Unspoiled, pure. I doubt you'll find a sentient biped here. Nature at her finest. Nothing but beasts."

"Do you feel it, too? As if this place is one of a kind?"

He's quiet a moment then says, "If the human Garden of Eden exists, this is it."

Exactly. I can't put into words how being here makes me feel, but I guess, in a nutshell, I'd say totally free. No pain, no fear, no grief, no time. Only hope and love and the present moment. It's delicious. It's overwhelming. It's fortifying beyond belief. Especially after the endless, back-to-back battles I've been fighting.

"I have to send Ryodan a message. There was no sign of Dani at Winter's castle."

"Rebuild your energy reserves first."

God, I want to talk to Dani! Catch up, learn all about her new life. But in order to do that, we have to find her first. Oddly, I don't worry quite as much about Dani as I would if it were anyone else. She's as close to a superhero as it gets, doubly now with Hunter in her veins, and I can't imagine anyone or anything that could possibly kick her ass. She's been through the Hall of All Days, survived five deadly years Silverside as a teen. Resourceful, brilliant, superfast, and strong as ten men, she's been through more than anyone I know. If something harms her, my vengeance will know no bounds.

We sprawl for a time in silence, warmed by the sun, being replenished by the power of the pristine planet. It's so much lovelier and more tactile than any overblown Fae illusion of a paradise. It's as if I can feel the purity oozing from every ounce of nature surrounding me. Here, there is no war, hatred, envy, greed, or discrimination. No ugliness, no violence. Here, things simply are what they are in their natural state and delight in being as they are, unfettered and without fear of persecution.

Eventually I open my eyes and gaze up.

High above, birds and velvety-pelted creatures frolic in the multicolored limbs of trees that tower like vast, leafy skyscrapers against a brilliant blue sky. The rush of water tumbling over rocks in the distance is melodious, mesmerizing, and I imagine dozens of waterfalls tumbling hundreds of feet to sparkling lagoons below. Birdsong fills the air with lovely arias, their many and disparate melodies—not competing but blending into the theme and motif of a sumptuous orchestral feast.

I hunger to explore. I could live here one day. Run with my beast. When things finally get back to—

"There's no such thing as normal," Barrons says. "You keep thinking that. You suffer *hiraeth*."

"Here-eyeth?" I echo.

"A Welsh word that means unattainable longing for a place—or perhaps more accurately a state of being—that never existed. Nostalgia for something that never was. You experienced calm, happy security as a child and keep thinking when you fix just one more thing, you'll feel that way again. Good luck with that."

He's the pin in my balloon sometimes.

"Find a better balloon. One that's real. Life is messy, complicated, and difficult. Relish it as it is. Quit expecting it to change. You might find you feel, well, normal then," he mocks. "And realize life never was normal. You were just happy. Be it again. Your choice."

He drives me bugfuck sometimes.

Soft, dark laughter rolls. "In the best of ways."

I drowsily concede the point while also conceding that I feel like

I'm getting drunk off the planet. I'm more relaxed and peaceful than I've been in years. Everything is going to be all right. We're just one step away from—

I stiffen and explode up from the ground in a smooth, powerful surge. "She's coming, Barrons!" I exclaim. And she isn't alone.

———— • • •————

When Winter appears in the glade, I know it can only be the prince of Autumn accompanying her. His skin is chestnut, his waist-length hair rich mocha, his eyes flame, and his tall, muscular body radiates the heat of a fiery forge. He wears brown trousers low at his hips, soft suede boots, his upper body bare but for a torque of gold around his neck. I notice Winter positions herself some distance away. Glazed with ice, I imagine were she to stand too near, she might echo the cry of a fictional witch from the land of Oz.

They are each other's opposite, although, I suppose, not antithesis. That would be summer to winter, autumn to spring. Yet as they stand near each other, Winter, so icy and pale, Autumn so dusky and warm, it drives home to me how elemental the Fae are, the embodiment of the seasons themselves.

I wonder for the dozenth time if they weren't once vastly different than they are now. What creator would craft such elemental beings only to leave them sadistic and empty? What being would grant such a dispassionate and soulless species the priceless gift of the Song of Making? It doesn't compute.

"What have you done to my father?" I demand, as we face off at a distance, Barrons and I at the east end of the clearing, Winter and Autumn at the west.

"An ancient toxin," Winter says coldly. "The name doesn't signify. You possess no knowledge of it."

"Because your memories have been restored by the Song," I say. "And the queen's files don't go back that far."

If surprised by my insight, they conceal it, and, undeterred, Winter hisses, "There is no antidote."

"You said I could save him."

"You can."

"How, if there is no antidote?"

The prince steps forward. "I am Azar, prince of the Autumn Court. That is Ixcythe, princess of Winter. You may save him by passing the queen's power to Ix—"

"Never," I cut him off flatly.

"Then he dies," Azar says just as flatly.

"Then he dies," I agree coolly, although inside my heart is raging. Not only would I have no guarantee they would restore my father once I was no longer queen, but I would imperil the entire human race. It will slay me alive to enforce this decision, but I will, and my father would expect—no, *demand*—no less from me. Jack Lane would be ashamed of me if I did otherwise. Possibly even despise me.

Ixcythe's eyes narrow to icy slits. "You sentence your father to death. We won't stop with him. We will take more of those you love."

"Try," Barrons says softly. "You want endless war? Endless casualties? No, wait, it won't be endless. I'll take ten of your court for every one of hers you touch. The others of my kind will take ten each as well. And Mac, well," he breaks off with a snort, "she destroyed your entire court in an instant, with a mere thought. The Fae will be extinct in no time, the world ours."

Ixcythe turns to Azar and hisses, "I *told* you that was what she wanted!"

He slants her a fiery look. "You attack first and are surprised when she attacks back?"

"I didn't attack first!" Ixcythe snarls. "She destroyed my court!"

"After you took her father."

"She took the True Magic from us! And you agreed with my plan!"

"We were supposed to take the mother. You couldn't even get that right!" Azar snaps.

"We couldn't find her, and how would that have made any difference, you fucking moron?" she snaps back.

"Negotiate, Ixcythe," Azar growls. "She holds the queen's power. She's not going to give it to you. Get past your fucking jealousy for the first time in your frigid existence and put the fate of our—"

"Fuck you, Azar, you overblown bag of hot air!"

"Fuck you, Ixcythe!" Azar snarls. "You have no one. You are princess of None. You think you can stand against me? I'm all you have, so I suggest you pussy up and make me happy if you want to survive!"

"Pussy up? Did you just tell me to *pussy up*?" Ixcythe explodes, teeth bared, eyes glittering sharp as icy razors. "You were honored far in excess of your lowly station to even get remotely close to my glorified—"

"You were so stiff and cold it was like fucking a glacier. I don't know what I ever saw in you."

Ixcythe opens her mouth then closes it after a long moment. She curls her hands into fists and pierces the flesh of her palms with sharpened nails. Blood wells on pale skin, drips to the ground. Nostrils flaring, lips peeled back in a snarl, she hisses, "I apologize, Azar. Your autumn lands are—"

"Right. All that nonsense. Winter is lovely, too," Azar cuts her off tightly

They whirl as one to glare at me.

Shock and horror vie with the nearly uncontrollable urge to laugh. "Oh, God, I was right!" I exclaim, stunned. It was one thing to suspect it, entirely another to see full-blown evidence of it. "Memory isn't the only thing the Song of Making restored. It's given you back emotions!" And it's my worst nightmare come true. A race of grudge-holding, wildly volatile, immortal savages.

"Oh, *fuck* you, bitch!" Ixcythe snaps and vanishes.

I struggle to wrap my brain around the horrifying development, flashing back to the scene in Winter's courtyard. I'd told myself the depth of brutality was merely the marriage of ancient grievances to immense power. But there'd been a personal savagery to their attacks that had nagged at me and, now, made perfect sense. They'd remembered their grievances, with the full capacity to *feel* them.

Azar sighs heavily. "Ixcythe can be a handful."

"You think?" Sarcasm drips from my voice. "What about you? Why have you remained?"

"I petition the right to speak on Ixcythe's behalf. On behalf of all Fae."

"Where is the other mortal you took?" I demand. "Her name is Dani."

"We took only one. We have no other humans."

"I don't believe you. Dani vanished from Chester's before my father did."

"I can only assure you that Ix and I did not take her. As you saw in Winter, our courts are beyond rational action. That leaves only Severina, the princess of Summer, who might have abducted your mortal, and although Sev's beauty is blinding, her warmth staggering, her physical attributes far exceed her mental endowments. *Vastly* exceed."

"You don't think she's powerful enough."

"She's powerful enough. Intelligent enough. Not motivated enough. Severina is unfocused, easily distracted by a ray of sunshine, the promise of pleasure, and more often than not, she lazes about in a summer-intoxicated stupor. Little penetrates."

Sounded like the perfect version of summer to me: sunshine, pleasure, intoxication. Or at least, to the Mac I once was. Although I lack Christian's lie-detecting abilities, I sense no lie in Azar's words.

"What about the other princes and princesses?" I press.

Sorrow flashes across his dark, regal features. "They are dead." He's silent a moment then says, "I rue their loss. Emotions are not easily borne, when presented with such a vast store of memories. Our ability to feel faded slowly over a long period of time, along with our ability to sire offspring. When you lose something in minuscule degrees, you scarce notice. Until it's gone. Then you no longer even understand what you lost."

I feel the truth of his words in my bones and incline my head. "You may speak."

"I do not believe the Fae can accept a human queen after discovering we were long deceived by both a human queen and an Unseelie masquerading as one of our Seelie princes. Compound that betrayal with the return of emotion and memory, and you have a species tested to its limits. You saw what was happening at the Winter Court. We seek a boon. My queen," he drops to his knees and fists his arms across his chest in a gesture of fealty, "we *need* a boon if we are to have any hope of avoiding a war that will only result, as your guard astutely observed, in our extinction. Unless Ixcythe speaks the truth, and our extinction is what you desire."

In all the time Barrons and I wasted at the Fae court, I was never once alone with a Fae, one-on-one. They'd besieged us en masse, distracting us with chaos and spectacle, neatly avoiding any and all talk, while they studied us and plotted to destroy us. This was my first opportunity at meaningful dialogue with a royal. "I do not desire your extinction. I desire a peaceful solution that affords a life worth living for human and Fae alike."

"And how do you envision such a thing coming to pass?"

"Ideally, I would sing the wall back up between realms. You would have your share of the Earth, the mortals would have theirs."

"A return to the old ways, which the majority of our kind found repugnant. Few would entertain it. Those that did would be outcast."

"The new way, in which you preyed upon mortals, was equally repugnant to a majority of mortals, and none would entertain it. Neither species can prey upon the other. That is nonnegotiable."

"What is negotiable?"

"My lack of interference once the realms are separate. I would leave you to govern yourselves." Gratefully. Sealed safely behind walls. If only I can figure out how to sing those walls back up.

"In order to attempt such a negotiation, we require a boon."

"What do you seek?"

A scrap of parchment materializes in the air before me and flutters to the ground. I don't stoop to collect it but read it where I stand. The Light Court wants me to return a number of items and agree to multiple concessions. Not *one* boon but many.

The items are: the four Light Hallows: cauldron, stone, spear, and sword. All Seelie objects of power currently in museums or private collections. All elixirs and potions held by the queen.

In addition, I must agree that I will never don the formal crown of the High Queen of the Fae, nor carry the scepter nor wear the ermine cloak. All jewels in the queen's bower will be gifted to Ixcythe. The stable of unnatural beasts that carry the Wild Hunt will be bequeathed to Azar. The kingdom belonging to the High Queen will be razed, and a quarter of it apportioned to each of the courts. I will reveal the secret location of the Queen's Aerie and relinquish it to Ixcythe. All other items in my possession belonging to the Fae that are unnamed, or unknown, will also be returned. And when the time comes for me to pass, I will return the True Magic to a full-blooded Fae princess.

I frown, studying it. I know they don't expect me to meet all of their demands. They've frosted the cake with countless planned sacrifices.

What do they *really* want?

I mentally cross off the things they know I'll never give them, any more than I would be willing to pass Ixcythe the True Magic.

None of the hallows.

I don't dare cede the queenly accoutrements of my station. The crown, scepter, and cloak might hold power I require at some point in the future.

The stables I'll yield. The Wild Hunt will never be run again. Not on my watch.

The jewels mean nothing to me unless they confer necessary power. I'll carefully examine each before deciding.

The elixirs and potions don't matter. I have no intention of using—

Clarity slams into my brain with the devastating impact and ratcheting pain of a thunderbolt striking my skull. A mushroom cloud blossoms in my heart, threatening immediate detonation.

Ixcythe said she would tell me how to save my father from the poison she used.

She also said there is no antidote.

I know what she wants.

What she *needs*.

If the Song of Making restored memory and emotion—why would it stop there?

I see no reason it would. Apparently, it deemed the Seelie imperfect and began fixing them, slowly but ineluctably, undoing everything about them, taking the ancient Tuatha De Danann all the way back to what they once were before they stole a potion from another race.

The Fae are becoming mortal.

Oh, not yet, as evidenced by Winter's Court but—for beings accustomed to immortality—much too soon.

Of all the things on this list, there's only one thing Ixcythe truly wants. I have no doubt, were she to secure it, she'd instantly go to war with me for all the other items, too.

The only reason Azar is attempting a discussion with me, the only reason he's willing to kneel before me in subjugation, is because the Fae are *dying*.

And in order to force me to bring them what they need, they created a situation where someone I love is doing the same.

I no longer need Ixcythe to tell me how to save Jack Lane.

He'd have to drink the Elixir of Life. The very drink that turned the Fae into the immortal monsters they are. The drink they now desperately need in order to assure their return to that state.

The drink Dancer refused even though he knew he was dying, for good reason.

Because it will eventually destroy my father's immortal soul and eradicate all emotion, making him no different from the savages I'm expected to rule.

I narrow my eyes, fury raging in my veins.

Then a new thought occurs to me. I smile faintly.

I can simply let them die.

And technically, I won't have killed them.

They'll wipe one another out, scour the world of their stain, as they continue to devolve.

No harm, no foul. I remain a powerful queen. The Earth and humans are safe. Cruce is still a problem, but I'll figure that out.

I lift my gaze from the parchment and look at Azar.

The moment our gazes lock, he surges up to his feet, abandoning his gesture of subservience.

Must be the hellfire in my eyes coupled with the mirth shaping my lips.

"You said you didn't desire our extinction!" he hisses.

"That was before I realized you sentenced my father to choose between a terrible death and a vile existence."

"Ixcythe spoke the truth—how repulsive you find us! Your father would become like us, and you consider that lofty elevation a vile existence," he says bitterly. "I demand you return our power and leave us in peace!"

"You would never leave *us* in peace. I'm all that stands between our species, and I will never relinquish the True Magic. I am your queen. Get. Used. To. It," I grit. "For whatever *very* short period of time remains to you."

I take Barrons's hand and sift us out of there before I do something I'll regret.

Or worse, don't regret at all.

29

I will follow

KAT

I STAND AT THE TOWER window, gazing out, hand pressed to my lips, watching Sean and Rae as they talk outside on the parapet.

She's persuaded him to take her for a flight. It wasn't difficult. That child has but to tip back her head and smile, and people melt. She has such a sunny disposition, is so good and loving, it's hard to believe she's from the Dark Court.

But she is.

My mind is reeling.

This day has bestowed upon me both an enormous gift and an enormous curse.

My Sean has returned. The ice around his heart thawed when Rae threw her tiny arms around his legs. His eerie Unseelie prince eyes widened, flew to mine, and I watched the icy shards within them heat and pool into a liquid silver then abruptly, they were warm, rich brown again.

I gazed into my beloved soulmate's eyes for the first time in years.

Then those lovely dark Irish eyes were wet with the sheen of tears as he stared disbelievingly down at the child he believes to be his daughter.

"I don't frighten you, lass?" he'd asked Rae.

"Oh, Daddy, you're silly! You're beautiful! You have *wings*! And all those pretty colors under your skin!"

Then he was kneeling beside her, and she was staring at him with fascination and love, touching his face and petting his wings, brushing her hands over the kaleidoscopic tattoos at his wrist, and he was regarding her with such astonishment and love, I felt my heart might burst from happiness.

Then Sean was locking gazes with me, saying silently within my skull, *Thank you for telling her I'm her da. I'll be her da, Kat, and I'll be a grand one.* He pauses a moment before adding, with tones of shame and regret, *I've wasted time. I blocked her from my mind, couldn't bear to think of her, and she's so big already! I missed so much. You were right. Cruce is dead, and it doesn't matter who her father is. I'm honored to fill the role. I'm sorry I was such an ass. I never stopped loving you, Kat. It's what kept me holding on.*

Sean adores children. We once dreamed of having half a dozen.

But the curse . . . if there'd been any doubt in my mind at all, it vanished when Sean said he'd blocked Rae from his mind.

It wasn't Sean visiting her in dreams, making plans to meet.

Another prince did. Apparently, Sean looks enough like Cruce that Rae believes *he's* her father. Perhaps Cruce visited in heavily shadowed dreams. She only glimpsed wings, a tall, dark man with kaleidoscopic tattoos and wintry eyes. The Unseelie princes look alike, especially to a child dazzled by the exoticness of wings.

Rae's father is Cruce. He's still alive, and for some reason, he's been biding his time without revealing himself, which terrifies me. The deceitful prince of War is the consummate divider, the ultimate manipulator. He does nothing without purpose.

If he said he would see Rae soon, he will.

Which leaves me in an impossible bind. If I tell Sean that Cruce is alive and is her father, I'll lose him to the ice and darkness again. I couldn't reach him. Rae did. Losing her will send him right back down into the depths of despair.

Cruce *will* come for Rae. Of that I have no doubt.

I must tell Sean. I can't protect her by myself. I need both human–turned–Unseelie princes, Sean and Christian, to help me, to have any hope of guarding my daughter against the ancient, powerful prince.

A flutter of motion on the parapet draws my attention back to the day beyond. Sean is cradling Rae carefully in his arms; they're perched on the edge of the wall, his enormous black wings opening, preparing for flight.

He glances back at me, smile flashing bright in his dark face, and raises his brows in question.

I nod. *It's okay, go,* and he blows me a kiss and turns away.

It frightens me that she's in his arms, about to be airborne. But I want her to soar in every way possible, fear nothing.

When they lift off, I hurry out onto the walkway and stand, clutching the stone sill, watching them. Sean knows me well and, rather than flapping high into the sky on their first airborne adventure, he glides in a smooth, wide, circular sweep to the lawn below. Rae laughs with delight as they soar gently down. He deposits her on her feet, takes her hand, and they begin to walk the blackened earth, a giant, dark, winged and tattooed man with a tiny, beaming, curly-haired child at his side.

How I've dreamed of seeing them together like this. Her hand is swallowed by his, her eyes sparkling, cheeks rosy with excitement.

Rae chatters earnestly up at Sean, nonstop, and I laugh softly. She can talk. And talk and talk. After a few minutes, he looks startled, then thoughtful. He stops walking and squats on the scorched earth, facing her as she presses whatever case she's making, his wings arched up high, trailing across the ground.

He's beautiful. His wings suit him when his eyes are warm brown. Dear God, I do not want to lose him again! I want to make love with him, plan for our future, stroll the coastline and fields of flowers holding hands, have all those long conversations about anything and everything, like we used to have so long ago. I want my best friend back.

After a moment, Rae takes his other hand and they close their eyes.

I catch my breath, wishing desperately I'd been able to hear what she's been saying. I know my daughter. She's driven by a need to heal any unhappiness she senses. There are days at the abbey when she wanders the halls, randomly touching people, and I've noticed their smiles linger for hours after she's gone. Bess told me since Rae began coming to day care, fights among the children reduced to almost nothing, and on the rare occasions one does occur, it resolves swiftly.

She has spots on her back where wings will one day be. She is the daughter of the most powerful Unseelie prince in existence.

She's going to be an amazing woman.

I narrow my eyes. They're motionless, holding hands. What does she have Sean doing?

A faint glow of light begins to emanate from Rae's skin. Her head falls back, lovely curls (that drive me mad trying to untangle after a wash) tumbling down her back, and she's smiling, and I watch as the light passes from her tiny hands into Sean's. It seeps slowly up his arms, into his shoulders, across his chest, filling and filling him until even his dusky wings shimmer with light. I've never seen her do anything like this before. How did she know how to do it?

I gasp.

Abruptly, the blackened estate is but a memory. The lawn stretches green and lush as far as the eye can see. In the blink of an eye, the destruction of the soil was undone. Does my little Rae have so much power? Is it their power joined that accomplished the miracle?

Overhead, the dark thunderclouds that have squatted heavily

and sourly above this castle the entire time I've been coming, part and go wheeling off to the far corners of the horizon, leaving a vast expanse of blue and the first sunshine this land has seen in years.

The moment the warmth of the sunlight touches their skin, both open their eyes, and Sean looks around, stunned. A smile explodes on his face, and he sweeps Rae into his arms, surges up from the ground and begins spinning them both about.

"You *did* it, Daddy!" she exclaims. "I *knew* you could!"

"You did it, Rae. You freed me," he replies, eyes sparkling. "I'd not have known what was wrong with me, if not for you."

Will he revert to what he was? Will the ground blacken again and the storm return the moment he knows the truth?

I make a swift decision.

I want a day.

A single happy day with the family I might have had. One that will have to keep me warm for the rest of my life. One I will replay over and over when I'm old and weary. And likely countless times before those final years arrive.

I slant my face up to the sun, smiling, determined to savor what joy there is in this moment.

Now nothing hurts. Now Sean is the man I once knew. Now they think we're a family, and they're happy.

I am, too.

I will milk this day for all it's worth.

A flicker of motion draws my gaze back to the lawn.

I glance down, thinking Sean must have expanded his wings, preparing to take Rae on another flight.

But that's not the case. Sean and Rae have their backs to the source of motion, don't even know it's there.

I try to scream, to warn them, but my lungs have collapsed and refuse to expand, though my mouth stretches wide. I struggle to inhale with all my might but can't.

Not fair! Too soon! I shriek silently. I just wanted *one* day—was that so much to ask? One. Bloody. Day.

But it's not to be. Cruce must have sensed their reunion, or perhaps he's been spying on us all along. Minutes. We got mere minutes of happiness as the family I so desperately want to be.

When a third Unseelie prince sifts in to join Cruce on the lawn, I'm still unable to make any sound, and I wonder frantically why Christian's perimeter alarm isn't going off. We need him here— right now! How can there be *three* princes?

Does this mean *all* the Unseelie are alive? Did the Song not kill them? Did they just go into hiding?

My fear takes a darker turn.

I can't feel this new prince with my *sidhe*-seer senses.

If I weren't looking straight at him, I'd have no idea he was there. If he were glamoured, I wouldn't even know he was Unseelie. How is this possible? Who *is* the third prince? His head is canted down and I can't see his face. I need to see it, commit it to memory, describe him for the other *sidhe*-seers.

It seems I've been frozen, unable to breathe, for hours, but mere seconds have passed, and Sean and Rae still have no idea two princes stand behind them.

Cruce looks up at me then.

A chill shivers through my soul.

His dark gaze is triumphant, and I realize he'd planned this all along.

He let me raise her until he deemed her either old enough or interesting enough to be useful.

Cruce with a crying baby? Never.

Cruce with a powerful new tool to exploit? Of course.

That's what Rae is to him, all she will ever be. I despise him. I want him dead. Mac needs to kill him.

Inclining his head, he flashes me a dark, mocking smile.

The four of them vanish.

My lungs are no longer compressed.

I scream and scream.

30

I'm not America's Sweetheart

MAC

I SIFT US BACK TO Chester's, in a battered and violent mood.

Ixcythe wasn't there when I detoured to her castle.

My father was gone, too, leaving no trace of him but blood on snow. And we still have no bloody idea where Dani is.

Overriding Barrons's objections, I had what I thought was a brilliant idea and tried to sift to my father, figuring if Ixcythe wanted to play hide-and-seek, as juiced as I was from the last world, she'd wear out long before I did.

Unfortunately, the princess of Winter is well acquainted with a fact I discovered a short time ago.

One can't sift into an IFP.

The bitch.

Once again, I got knocked flat on my ass and lay, paralyzed with pain, shivering on the floor of Winter's castle until I was strong enough to sift us out of there.

I also learned it's impossible to pinpoint the location of a random IFP containing my father with any queenly power I possess.

Those unprecedented fragments of Faery didn't exist until our realms collided on Halloween.

Winter has the upper hand.

For now.

Somewhere, in a fractured fragment of Faery, my father is dying. If she continues to torture him, I'll eat her alive like Jo, only with full cognizance as Mac, not in the blind grip of the evil Book. I have no doubt she'll soon send word, telling me where to bring the Elixir of Life in exchange for him. He'd better be in exactly the same condition or better.

I have serious doubts about being able to convince my father to drink the Elixir. Jack Lane take a potion that will ultimately destroy his ability to feel love for his wife and daughter, plus any chance at an afterlife?

Not seeing that. He's a man of strong faith, and family is everything to him. I'm not even sure I'd try to convince him. It's possible I'd try to talk him out of it, sobbing my heart out the entire time. Without emotion or soul, he'd no longer be my father, or Rainey Lane's husband.

It's all my fault.

And, somehow, I have to tell my mother.

——— • • • ———

A short time later, we're sitting in a conference room on one of the deepest levels of Chester's. Ever the businessman, Ryodan has meeting rooms in his lair that marry the same sleek blend of muscle to elegance as the rest of Chester's. Appointed with modern charcoal and black furniture, and a long oval zebra-ebony table at which we're seated, it's impeccable and tasteful, although it could use a maid service to dust away more of those sticky cobwebs that are everywhere lately.

After learning there was no trace of Dani at Ixcythe's castle and the Seelie claim they didn't take her, Ryodan informed us we were only gone a day, and Barrons and I conclude the rumors Christian has been hearing about the Song resolving time disparities between realms are correct.

While we were gone, Ryodan re-warded all of Chester's in case the Fae somehow shattered his underlying spells, then focused his efforts on adding wards to a single room in the club he believes is impenetrable.

Barrons, Ryodan, and I are sitting in that room now. Lor and those of the Nine not guarding my mother are out searching for Dani and Shazam.

The urbane owner of Chester's leans back in his chair, arms behind his head, muscles bunching beneath his crisp shirt. His silver eyes are flinty, cold. When I met with Kat at Draoidheacht, she gave me only a brief sketch of what happened with Dani while I was away, but I know Dani and Ryodan consummated a long overdue, volatile yet pretty much perfect relationship, against enormous odds, after thinking they might never get to be together. I know, too, they've snatched only brief times as humans since. Now Dani's gone, stolen from his bed, and he will raze everything in his path until he gets her back. We all will. Dani is family. "The Seelie are becoming mortal again," he murmurs. "Do we have any idea how long until they are?"

I slice my head to the left, fisting and unfisting my hands convulsively.

His eyes narrow. "Do you know where the Elixir of Life is, Mac?"

I slice my head again. "No. I need to search my files. I don't contain the queen's memories. I hold endless notes in an endless filing system that's impossible to navigate." The last time I queried my inner store of knowledge about the tonic that made the Seelie immortal, I'd gotten tens of thousands of files, all tabulated under the name of whatever Fae signified most largely in that file. Big help there. The queen is a walking repository for . . . well, in my opinion, a flood of complete detritus, as if part of her duty as their leader was to carry the entire history of the Fae within her. Every last damned detail. If life ever gets back to normal, I'll implement a new filing system and dump the obsolete.

There's no way to query: *Where* did the queen keep the Elixir of Life? I can only query the potion itself then begin sorting through each bloody file, hoping I get lucky.

Ryodan says, "We'll find Dani and your father and let the Seelie fucks die. No way we're making them immortal again."

Amen to that. "Cruce is still alive. I want him dead, too." All Fae must die. Queen's edict.

"You *knew* Cruce was alive?" Kat exclaims behind me. "How long have you known? Why didn't you tell me? I might have been able to protect Rae!"

I whirl in the direction of her voice. Christian, Kat, and the librarian just sifted in and are standing near the door.

Ryodan surges to his feet, snarling. "Did you have *any* difficulty at all sifting in?"

Christian shrugs. "I didn't feel a thing. I figured you'd taken your wards down for some reason."

Crimson flames leap in Ryodan's gaze. "That was some of my finest work. The wards on this room should have slammed you back to Draoidheacht and left you unconscious. It took more blood than I care to waste."

"Get her out of here," I say to Christian, jerking my head at my doppelgänger. "Are you crazy? That's Cruce's daughter." How dare he bring Lyryka into Chester's again?

"I'm aware of that," Christian says coolly. "He abducted Rae and Sean from my lawn at Draoidheacht. Apparently my wards don't work either. Nor does my perimeter alarm. Bastard has a way of bypassing or neutralizing everything."

I close my eyes. It just keeps getting worse.

"It gets worse, Mac," Kat voices my thought.

"Christ, *seriously*?" My eyes pop open.

"There was a prince with Cruce that I've never seen before, and I couldn't sense him with my *sidhe*-seer senses. If he'd been glamoured, I wouldn't have known he was Fae. Mac," she continues urgently, "there's an Unseelie out there *sidhe*-seers have no way of detecting. Do you know how much damage even one Unseelie prince like that could do to us?"

Yes. If he was intelligent and determined, he could wipe out our entire order of *sidhe*-seers in time. My world is crumbling around my ears.

Seelie have become emotional, mortal, and regained knowledge of wards and powers we don't possess.

New Unseelie have appeared that we can't sense or keep out.

More of my people have been taken, and we don't know where *any* of them are.

Scowling, I pinch the bridge of my nose, thinking. How is it possible that there's an Unseelie that's undetectable by *sidhe*-seers? The Unseelie king created us specifically for that purpose: to be able to sense *all* Fae, Light and Shadow Court.

I close my eyes again, heart sinking.

There's only one explanation.

The aberration wasn't made by the Unseelie king.

It was made by someone else, a new type of Unseelie we were never calibrated to sense.

There's only one being in existence with both the talent and ambition to create a new type of Unseelie: the prince called War who stood and watched while the first Unseelie Court was made, took notes and secreted away ingredients and ultimately betrayed his king by stealing his woman and trying, eventually, to steal the Seelie throne.

"Mac, quit icing my bloody club," Ryodan growls.

"*Brrr!* Turn the temperature back up," Kat complains.

I open my eyes to find my fury has crusted the conference room, and everyone in it, with a thin layer of ice. Frosty stalactites are sprouting from the ceiling. Even the cobwebs in the corners glitter with frost. Absently, I will it all away and warm the room. "I know where the prince came from and why Cruce let us think he was dead. He cloistered himself in a chamber like mine where he used the king's recipes to build a new court." The moment I say the words aloud, I know it's true. It's too logical not to be. It's why he never came to claim the True Magic. He didn't want it. He was busy building a new Shadow Court, to seduce the Unseelie king's power into choosing him.

The king's power is far greater than the Seelie queen's, but it wasn't until after I sang the Song, shortly before I sequestered, that it was up for grabs. Once the Unseelie king abdicated power and stepped down, he didn't choose a successor. Five years later, the king still hasn't decided. Which shouldn't surprise me, because time means nothing to the ancient, half-mad entity.

Now I'm furious with the Unseelie king, as well, for leaving us in this predicament, for letting his power continue to surf about, not choosing.

"What in the world is *that*?" Kat exclaims, staring up.

I tilt back my head and see a dense black fog seeping into the room from above ornate crown moldings. It slithers in through cracks, paper-thin, and assembles itself into a sooty cloud, roughly five feet tall and fifteen feet wide. I probe gently at it with both my *sidhe*-seer senses and the queen's. Pulsing with gargantuan power, it holds a sentience that unnerves me. Vast, dispassionate. *Familiar.* I've rolled in that great being's wings too many times not to recognize the essence of it and, as he's so fond of saying, *can't eviscerate essential self.* Or conceal it.

The kingly power just drifted in, and hangs above our heads. Did my mere thoughts summon it? Can I talk to it? Curse and rail at it? Reason with it?

"It must have followed me here," Christian growls, staring up at the ceiling. "Sorry, Ryodan. I have no bloody idea where it came from. But I believed it trapped."

Ryodan's eyes narrow to slits. "Followed *you*. Trapped where?"

"It's been hanging around Draoidheacht. I've seen it three times now. I suspect it escaped from one of the Unseelie king's artifacts. But I thought it was bound to the castle, to that artifact from which it escaped."

Ryodan laughs softly. "You don't know what it is."

"I'll sort it out, and find a way to ward it within my keep."

"Good luck with that," Barrons says dryly. "It's the Unseelie king's power. It's been spending time at the bookstore, as well."

"*That's* the king's power?" Christian blinks up at it then looks back at Barrons. "I can understand it hanging around you, but why the bloody hell would it watch me?"

"Apparently, it thinks more highly of you than you do," Ryodan says, amused.

"I barely know how to use my power. I just learned to control it."

I say, "Good. Cruce has competition. The king hasn't chosen yet, and he's considering two other contenders, Barrons and you, Christian." Personally, I don't see anyone but Barrons getting it. Assuming he wants it. The mural on the ceiling of the bookstore was painted long ago showing me as the Fae queen and Barrons as the Unseelie king. I'd give my eyeteeth to know who painted it and why.

Kat says, "Perhaps it's undecided because Cruce only managed to create a single—"

"No," I cut her off. "I know him. If he has a prince, he's got an entire Shadow Court. He'd never create royalty first. He'd build from the bottom, perfecting, just like the king before him." And he'd make sure it was bigger, better, and more badass.

"Then you sing the Song and destroy them again," Kat says firmly. "I get my daughter and Sean back. Christian or Barrons gets the Unseelie king's power. End of problems."

"I may never figure out how to use the Song, and who's to say Cruce didn't perfect his court this time? Perhaps the Song wouldn't destroy them." To Barrons, I say, "Am I right in thinking there are more chambers like the one I sequestered in?"

Lyryka clears her throat. "There are seven chambers beyond time.

The king created multiple rooms for his concubine, each better than the last until, finally, he constructed the White Mansion, where she could live forever, without aging."

"You do know she'll be reporting everything she heard to Cruce if she gets the chance," I say to Christian. "She must not have that chance. Bottle her. Now."

"It's equally possible I won't tell him a thing," Lyryka says tightly.

"I won't let her out of my sight. If I'm otherwise occupied, I'll cork her flask. Satisfied?"

Far from it, but the look in Christian's eyes tells me I'm in for a fight if I push, and I don't want to fight with my friends. "Where are these chambers?" I ask Lyryka.

"Five are in the Unseelie prison, three of those five are inside the king's castle. The other two are in the White Mansion."

"The ones in the king's castle would be perfect for Cruce's needs," I muse. "The king's laboratory is beneath it."

"I stacked Silvers long ago to the one you sequestered in, which was in the White Mansion," Barrons says. "You spliced it off and moved it to the bookstore. It's no longer inside the prison."

Lyryka says testily, "I was unaware one of them had been moved. I need to notate the correct tome. Precisely which one did you move, and precisely where did you put it?"

Nobody answers her.

"Would Cruce have been safe from the Song of Making if he was in one of those chambers?" I ask Barrons.

"Assuming the Song destroyed all Unseelie, and assuming I am Unseelie since I'm Cruce's daughter, it's logical to conclude being sealed away, even in a spelled bottle, prevents death by Song," Lyryka says. "You can ignore me if you wish, or you could make use of me. I have an enormous amount of information at my disposal."

"So do I," I mutter. And that's part of the problem. Internal in-undation of minutiae.

"Those are the odds I would have played," Barrons says. "He also demanded the bracelet from you when you formalized the Compact. Perhaps the two, together, afforded protection."

I conclude grimly, "That's where Cruce is. In the prison, with his new court." I glance at Lyryka, wondering if she'll confirm.

She throws her hands in the air and snaps, "How would I know? I've never been out of the Library and, until recently, I wasn't even sure I believed there *was* anything in existence besides the Library. My father tells me nothing, unless he's giving me an order."

I don't need her confirmation. I know him. It's just like when he pretended to be a Seelie for hundreds of thousands of years, hiding in plain sight. Patience is his middle name. Manipulative, devious fuck is his first. "Whatever he's up to, he's going to take action soon or he wouldn't have let Kat know he was still alive." I narrow my eyes at Lyryka. "*Or*, his daughter told him she'd slipped and told us, so he knew his time was up. *Or*, he had her supposedly 'slip.'"

Lyryka protests, "I didn't tell him, nor did I—"

"Oh, give it up, we don't believe you." To Barrons, I say, "We can access the prison through the White Mansion."

"Unacceptable," Barrons says flatly. "You're the only one who can pass through the king's mirror in the boudoir, and we don't know if you'd survive it now, without the *Sinsar Dubh* inside you. The Silver may no longer recognize you as containing essence of king. And you're not going alone anywhere, Ms. Lane. Not in your current frame of mind."

"Get a fucking grip on your priorities, Mac," Ryodan growls. "You can't postpone finding Dani just to march off to the Unseelie prison and kill Cruce because you're angry."

"It wouldn't be just because she was angry," Kat says sharply. "Cruce took Rae and Sean! Who are you to decide in what order we recover the people we love?"

Ryodan's eyes glitter with crimson ice. "The one who loves Dani, and she's goddamn first."

"My father is," I correct.

"*Then* who?" Kat demands. "Dani then Rae then Sean? Mac, she's a *child*."

I ignore them and demand of Barrons, "How did you gain access to the prison?" I don't know how to find Dani or the Elixir at the moment, which means I can't find my dad, but I *do* know where Cruce is. My options are to go sit somewhere in a corner and search my files or go kick Unseelie ass, and at the moment kicking Unseelie ass, or any offensive ass, is highly appealing.

"One of the Silvers tucked into the wall behind the bookstore leads there." He adds pointedly, "Only if I employ a specific spell on the surface. Otherwise it leads elsewhere."

Clever, clever man. He plans for everything. As I should have. And he just made it clear I can't dash off to confront Cruce by myself because I need him to employ the necessary spell to grant me access. I glance back at Lyryka. Or rather, at myself. I can't bear the sight of a Fae and certainly not one that looks like me. "Bottle her," I order again. "I'm ordering you as queen to keep her sealed away."

"I believe she can help us, Mac," Christian tries again. "She's intimately acquainted with every book and artifact in the Unseelie king's library."

"I gave you an order." He could say I'm not his queen. That technically that he's Unseelie. But after holding my gaze a long moment, he chooses not to go down that path.

"I *want* to help," Lyryka says with desperation in her voice. "Please don't lock me away again. Please give me a chance."

My laughter is brittle and sharp as knives. "I'm sure you want to help. So you can steer us in the wrong direction while your father implements his plans to take over our world with his new court." To Christian, I say, "Pull your head out. She's Cruce's spy. His weapon. Carefully shaped and calibrated by him to do his bidding. Nothing more. Her worth to him lies only in how he can use her. No one is important to Cruce but himself."

Lyryka flinches and says bitterly, "Perhaps after a small eternity, I've begun to figure that out myself."

"Stop looking like me!" I snarl at her. "Change your glamour to look like someone else!"

She stares at me a long moment then says quietly, "The only other person I can look like is your friend, Dani. I understand she's missing, and I'm not certain that would be more comfortable for you."

Right, she's using quiet and reasonable tones, and I sound like a hot mess. I *feel* like a hot mess, and my head's going to explode if I don't get some breathing room without so many people and problems in it. "Oh, for fuck's sake, she won't even show us her true form because her allegiance is to Cruce, and you want to let her *help* us? You're all batshit crazy!" I surge to my feet, whirl, and stalk out the door, slamming it behind me.

—— • • ——

"I took Rae to see Sean for the first time today."

I flinch. I don't want company, so I say nothing. Keeping my back to Kat, I continue staring over the balustrade, at the many sub-clubs of Chester's, seeing nothing but my mother's face superimposed on a dance floor as I tell her Jack Lane is dying.

"In retrospect, I realize how foolish that was of me. I think it was bringing them together that made Cruce come."

Still, I say nothing. If she thinks her mistake of taking Rae to Sean is as terrible as what I've done, she's mistaken. The world is in chaos, four of the people we love are missing, and I've killed my father.

"I knew all along Rae might be Cruce's child. It didn't matter. I love her more than life. She's my daughter, regardless of who her father is." She pauses a minute then says, "I imagine there's another mother somewhere that might say the same about Lyryka."

"You did *not* come here to argue for the librarian." If Christian doesn't bottle her, she's going to taste the cold iron of my spear.

"Merely to point out that while you may be losing the father you've had the privilege of loving for decades, I just lost the daughter I had only five years with. You can choose to wallow in self-loathing, or you can recognize that there are many who suffer. There's a whole world out there, and they've incurred horrifying losses since the walls came down. Many lost their entire families. If everyone who ever had something awful or painful happen to them turned ugly, and possessed the kind of power you do—which I feel stirring in you like a dark cyclone capable of mass destruction—how long do you think our world would survive?"

"Oh, God, please just stop talking, Kat."

"With immense power comes immense responsibility."

"You think I don't know that?"

"You're the Fae queen."

"Painfully aware of it."

"But you're more than that, Mac. Though you wear no crown and hold no formal title, you're our leader. We look to you for guidance. We have faith in you. You've seen us through seemingly impossible situations and, whether you know it or not, we follow you. You always find a way when it seems there's none to be found."

I have a sudden lump in my throat. I didn't know she felt that way about me. Most of the time I feel like I just bumble about and get lucky with the help of my amazing friends. The truth is, nothing I've ever done would have succeeded if I'd been alone. "It takes all of us, Kat. Not just me."

"My daughter was stolen by Cruce. He took Sean, and I strongly doubt he means to let him live. Your father is dying. Dani is missing, and we have no idea where she is. Get back in that conference room. Open your mind to the possibility of Lyryka helping us. Christian says she's passed every lie-detection test he's given her. I, too, probed her with my gift of empathy. Her feelings for Cruce are a mixture of fear and growing anger amid the lingering confusion of one with Stockholm syndrome. He was her entire world for her entire life. Now she knows there's another world, where everyone is free, and she's gotten the chance to see it. How do you think she feels about Cruce now? Imagine Dani being in a cage for hundreds of thousands of years with nothing but the telly to watch, finally escaping. Would you put her back in?"

I wince. "I can't deal with the librarian right now."

"But you will."

I sigh. "Yes, Kat, I will."

Kat switches gears with, "Ryodan's right. We need to prioritize and implement swift, decisive plans. Be the woman we know you are, the one your father raised you to be."

"Ouch."

"If the shoe fits."

I sigh again, heavily, drop my face into my hands and rub my eyes. I know I'm behaving abominably. But of all the things that have happened to me, this one is deeply, horridly personal.

He's my father. My *daddy*. My champion, my hero.

Was his fate locked in the moment Aoibheal passed her power to me? Barrons, Ryodan, and Cruce all see so far ahead, anticipating countless moves on the chessboard. What's wrong with me that I can't?

"How old are you, Mac?" Kat queries softly.

Odd question with an odd answer. I have no idea anymore. "Twenty-four or twenty-five, I think." Today, I feel a hundred.

"Cruce is nearly a million years old. How old are the Nine?"

"Are you a mind reader now, too?" I mutter darkly.

"You and Dani have responsibility dysmorphia. When you compare yourself to others and deem yourself inadequate, you sabotage the very strengths and talents you need to succeed. Barrons is coming," Kat says. "I told him I wanted a moment with you first. The two of you are the strongest women I know. Compartmentalize your emotions, or figure out how to release them. If you don't, they will destroy you. With the amount of anger I feel churning in you, you might destroy a fair portion of our world, as well. We'll get through this, Mac. And, whatever the future brings, we'll be there with our arms around each other, wiping away each other's tears, celebrating our triumphs, always forging on. Together. We need you."

I say nothing for a long moment. By the time I turn to say quietly, *Thank you, Kat,* she's gone.

———— • • ————

I don't return to the conference room.

Not yet.

Kat is right. I'm mortified by the mess I am. I'm out of control and about to do something stupid if I don't center myself. I need to either compartmentalize my emotions or vent them. This hit too close to home. My friends have been threatened many times but this is the first time since Alina's death that I've had to face that I might lose another member of my small family. I keep praying Dani is off somewhere, perfectly fine, not involved in any of this. I have no idea how to go about trying to track her. Is it possible Cruce took her, too?

As I'm racking my brains for a way to center myself, it occurs to me that, after spending so much time drifting in inner thought, void of all sensation, it's simultaneously wonderful and terribly painful to be in the physical world, jarring on levels I didn't expect. I've felt no emotion for suspended centuries, and now I'm being flayed alive by them.

I returned to Dublin from absolute quiet, long peace, and solitude to chaos and heartbreak. First I learned my mother was missing. Then I learned she wasn't, but my father was. Then I learned Dani was gone, too (and we still have no idea where she is!). Then I destroyed the entire Winter Court, discovered my father brutalized and dying, learned the Seelie are going to die unless I save them, learned Cruce is still alive, that he's created a new court we can't sense, that Rae and Sean have been taken, and, apparently, my life is back to the normalcy of "new day, different, vastly intensified battlefield."

I need a moment to remind myself of the good parts of being in the physical world, so I can gather the strength to address the difficult ones. I remember the many difficult things I've faced in the past, and how spending time at the bookstore always seemed to recharge me.

After firing off a quick text to Barrons, asking him to meet me back at Barrons Books & Baubles, followed by another to Ryodan, asking him to reconvene our meeting in four hours—at which time I will be one hundred percent the woman I need to be—I sift into the calming interior of Barrons Books & Baubles.

I've done most of my best thinking here, curled on a chesterfield before a fire, sipping hot cocoa.

I stand a long moment, eyes closed, inhaling the scent of the many things I love.

The gleaming hardwood floors that always exude a hint of lemon polish, the outdoorsy, horsey smell of aged leather, the peaches-and-cream aroma of Alina's candles that I scattered throughout the store, the spice of Barrons that lingers in the air, the intoxicating scent of books and glossy, new magazines and pencils and Post-its and notepads; all the tactile pleasures of an old-fashioned, Old World bookstore.

Barrons Books & Baubles is home.

Opening my eyes, I move to the front door, open and shut it, smiling as the bell tinkles. I hurry to the cash register, remembering my many days standing behind it, ringing up sales on the antiquated device. Absently, I dust cobwebs from it, pop the drawer open and closed, enjoying the sound, further grounding myself. With each physical aspect of the store I focus on, I feel a bit more solid, more capable of addressing the many problems on my plate.

Turning, I invite the gas fire to flicker on then cross the room and drop down on the chesterfield. As an afterthought, since I've decided immersion in the physical things I love about this world might help me get my shit together, and my proverbial shit is feeling sadly all over the place, I manifest a cup of rich, dark hot chocolate in my hand.

I miss being a sales clerk at a bookstore. It was so much—
SIFT ME IN!

Explodes inside my head at such horrific volume, I drop my cup to clutch my head against a sudden, blinding migraine, and dump steaming hot cocoa all over my jeans.

"Ow!" I yelp, burned and pissed. It was Barrons, via our bond. He needs to work on his volume.

I push up, hurry to the window, and peer out. Far below our invisible floating home, Barrons stands, looking up. *Now, Ms. Lane, before passersby begin to wonder why I'm standing here.*

I've never tried to sift someone to me before and don't know if I can. Rather than waste time trying, I sift down, snatch his hand, and return us to the bookstore.

"Why didn't you take the Silver?" I ask, as I change from my still steaming chocolate-drenched jeans into fresh ones with a mere thought (gotta love some of those queenly powers).

Eyes narrowed with fury, he growls, "Because every single one in the White Room—including the bloody Silver that was our only bloody fucking way into the Unseelie prison—has been shattered."

31

---•◦•---

Take your protein pills and put your helmet on

DANI

WHEN I WAKE THIS time, I'm alone in the cage.
Shazam is gone.

I crawl around every inch of darkness, feeling for him, calling his name, wiping angrily at my eyes with a fist.

I hate everything about this.

Perhaps the darkness most of all. At least in my cage as a child, there was some degree of light, if only the wan glow of late-night telly gone off air.

I'm beginning to realize it isn't just ocular deprivation but full sensory deprivation.

I'm starving, thirsty, and have nothing left in me to pee out on the floor in a corner of the cage.

I could be anywhere for all I know. Or nowhere. Tucked away in a Hunter-bubble beyond time, like Mac in her chamber. Holy hell, I wish she were here. There's so much I want to tell her, show her. I've been missing her for years. I want my family back together again.

Before I fell asleep, of my own volition this time, with Shazam curled in my arms, like the countless times offworld I hugged him close as we drifted off with no idea what dangers the morrow might hold, he told me the Hunters would soon convene a trial, and they adhere to the strictest letter of the law.

They would present their case.

Shazam would get a chance to present his.

The decision would be made.

But, he'd told me tearfully, the decision was already made. The laws were simple, precise, and always enforced.

If a Hunter interferes, in any way, with the birth of a child, that child is returned to their natural state. All memory of everything pertaining to being Hunter is stripped away, including all memory of the birth mother in any form.

If a Hunter abuses their ability to manipulate time for personal gain, they are destroyed.

Period, the end, exclamation mark! he'd told me around great, gulping sobs.

There has never been an exception made or a more lenient sentence given.

Stretching, pressing a hand against my achingly empty belly, I envision a huge marshmallow filling the hollow cavity, soaking up the acidic juices, dampening the discomfort of starvation. Been here, done this.

Then I compartmentalize my brain, partitioning it into units, disposing of the ones that serve no purpose. Not the other, not Jada, but Dani grown. Those parts that long to weep or rage with my usual abundance of emotion are pointless and will accomplish nothing, ergo boxed.

Clinically detached, I ponder the two applicable laws.

The one about interfering with the birth of a child is easily argued. I can think of seven different ways to highlight flaws in that, especially in light of some of the information Y'rill shared with me.

The one pertaining to the manipulation of time for personal gain is trickier. I'd like to know the exact wording of that law.

I concur that any being with the power to alter time can do irreparable damage to the universe and concede laws governing the use of it are necessary.

However—and howevers have always been one of my strengths—human law makes allowances for motive and extenuating circumstances, matching degrees of criminality with degrees of punishment.

I will argue to lessen the charge, thereby diminishing the punishment Shazam receives for his crime, which is, in a nutshell, loving me more than he loves life itself. Terrible crime, there, eh?

As if that kind of love isn't a miracle. The finest of a mother's love, a best friend's love, unconditional and pure.

I jerk and nearly freeze-frame out of my skin.

My environment changed!

Light just exploded into my cage, blinding at first, on the heels of prolonged darkness. I blink repeatedly, squinting, waiting for my eyes to adjust.

I realize, in slow degrees, the light isn't blinding at all but sparkling and faint. My eyes couldn't handle the faintest of glows after such intense absence of light.

"Holy shitballs," I curse with a scowl.

One question answered.

I know where I am.

It's the fourth worst possible option of the two hundred and forty-three I'd considered.

I'm in a cage that is suspended in the vast infinity of space. Tiny, so tiny.

Below me looms a brilliant gold-and-lavender planet.

Above me, a field of stars.

To my left, the kaleidoscopic stain of a brilliant, three-columned nebula.

To my right, a few miles away—or perhaps a few hundred miles;

impossible to gauge distance in space—another cage is suspended in the vacuum of the cosmos.

Inside that cage, Shazam stands, looking small and achingly alone, clutching the bars, staring across the miles of blackness at me, violet eyes enormous with fear, weeping.

I call to him, but he can't hear me.

I mouth with exaggerated expression: *I see you, Yi-yi.*

He weeps harder, doubling over, banging his head against the bars.

They may have turned the lights on for us, but we can't talk to each other. Our cages are cocooned by faintly shimmering force fields, providing the oxygen we breathe.

Until they've finished with us.

They might simply eject us into space in our natural forms, ensuring a swift and complete death for the last remaining Hel-Cat in existence and one soon-to-be-forgotten superhero.

As I stare across the darkness at my beloved Shaz, fear fists around my heart.

Me, the Mega. Afraid. Funny how love does that to you, makes you greedy for all the time in the world. Makes you care whether you live or die. Makes you hunger with all your being for just one more hour, one more day, one more bloody lifetime, because not even eternity will be enough time to love like I do.

The Hunters have imprisoned us in a place where it's virtually guaranteed none of my friends will find us, drifting in the vast expanse of space.

For all I know, they've removed us from time as well.

We're needles in an infinite, cosmic haystack.

Assuming they let me live, not only do they plan to take Shazam from me, they intend to steal all my precious memories of our life together.

I would no longer even recall that Shazam ever existed. All our splendid adventures Silverside, the years of healing love, just gone.

While, on one hand, that would spare me the endless pain of

knowing how much I'd lost, on the other hand, they are *my* emotions, it's *my* love, and it's *my* goddamn pain.

No one's taking it from me. I've earned every wound, every cut, every scar. Each time I've bled has made me the woman I am.

Epic and unbeatable. Not to be cowed.

I. Never. Give. Up.

They turned the lights up.

That means the trial is about to begin.

It ends one way: Shazam and I will leave here alive.

32

---

*Speed increasing, all control is in the hands
of those who know*

MAC

WHEN WE SIFT INTO the conference room, I'm relieved to find Lyryka gone.

I glance at Christian. "Bottled and corked?"

He nods but doesn't look happy about it, and I realize the librarian got under his skin, and it's more than the mere fact that he made a vow to protect her. He was standing up for her before he took the oath. Interesting. At some point in the future, I'll address the cruel terms of her confinement, but at the moment I have too many other problems on my plate.

"I've not yet been contacted by Ixcythe, and I can't do anything to recover my father until she sends word," I say as I spin a chair backward near the conference table, settle into it with my legs around it, arms folded across the slatted back. Except search my files for the location of the Elixir, which I plan to do in any downtime I have.

Barrons's dark eyes gleam, which gratifies, but I don't need him to concur. I know I made the right decision, the only decision I could make, given who I am and how much these people mean to me.

"It's impossible for me to decide who to go after first, Sean and Rae or Dani, because choice implies priority of life and would be a messy decision any way I made it. So," I reach in my pocket and pull out two small squares of paper, folded, and offer them to Kat and Ryodan, "each of you choose a piece of paper from my hand, but don't open it yet."

Ryodan inclines his head at Kat, gesturing for her to go first. He takes the piece that remains.

I extract a quarter from my pocket next. "You both hold a piece of paper that says either 'heads' or 'tails.' Whichever way this quarter comes up, whoever is holding that piece of paper, that's who we go after first. This is as impartial as I can make it. You have even odds." I flip the quarter high in the air, catch it when it comes down, and slap it onto the table. "Heads. Open your papers."

They do.

Kat inhales sharply and Ryodan says, "I'm sorry, Kat. We'll go after Sean and Rae the moment we have Dani."

"It was fair," Kat says, gray eyes disappointed. "We had an equal chance. It was a good way to do it, Mac."

"What now?" Ryodan demands.

"I focus on Dani and try to sift to her."

"I'm coming with you," Barrons says flatly.

"Alone. I'll dip in and come straight back, hopefully with Dani. But I'm not taking anyone with me on the first attempt. If I hit something like the IFP—"

"I can withstand it," Barrons growls while Ryodan snarls, "It's my choice."

"No, it's not," I reply. "I'm not endangering anyone else until I get the lay of the land. We can't afford for either of you to be out of commission. Once I ascertain it's safe, if I need help, we'll go back as a team. I won't fully appear. I'll remain misty and unseen. Reconnaissance only."

"I don't like this," Barrons growls.

"I hear you. Sometimes I don't like your decisions."

We glare at each other, but I see the instant he accepts what I made peace with some time ago: we must allow each other the freedom to implement actions without compromise at times to preserve the independence that makes us strong as a team.

With a faint smile, I close my eyes and summon a memory of Dani. It's hard to choose as there are so many vivid ones. I select a memory that holds both pleasure and pain because it captures her joy and one of the many unbearable brutalities to which she was subjected in her youth.

We're sprawled on the chesterfield at Barrons Books & Baubles. I'm painting her stubby fingernails black. There's chocolate icing on her face from the birthday cake I baked for her, and she's surrounded by a pile of presents I shoplifted from abandoned stores with no one left alive to run. She's wearing a bracelet given to her by Dancer, and her cheeks are flushed with happiness, her eyes sparkling, and that gamine grin has been dancing on her face for hours.

My lovely, strong, wounded, irrepressible Dani who shines so damned bright. I love her like a sister.

Later that night comes the brutality: I learn she was used as a weapon to kill my sister.

I move from that memory to one of us sitting on top of a water tower. She's Jada, cool and remote, refusing to let me in. I give her a cup of coffee that's too hot, and there's that porcupine scowl I sometimes purposely provoke because she has the most bodacious reactions, and sometimes it's the only emotion she lets me see. We argue.

But she *stays* to argue.

And I know our love is strong, worth fighting for to both of us, and one day we'll share it again.

The abbey, the night I see her looking so frighteningly pale and defenseless, heartbreakingly young, unconscious and sooty in Ryodan's arms after she nearly burned herself alive to rescue a stuffed animal.

Later, when we're both strapped to a table, about to be operated on by the Sweeper.

Realizing I would give my life for her. Do anything, incur any price to keep her alive and buy her time to chase her dreams. To love and be loved, as she always deserved.

This time, sifting feels different.

I die then I'm there and alive but in a sort of in-between place.

Neither at point of origin nor destination.

I feel myself being stretched long and impossibly thin, going, going, farther and farther.

Where the hell is she?

Where the hell am I?

I slam up against a barrier that's impenetrable yet oddly resilient.

There's no way past it, nor, however, does it harm me or slam me violently back.

Hastily, I recalibrate from trying to sift "to Dani" to merely "near Dani."

Abruptly, I'm *there*, and I'm concealing myself but I can't breathe, and it's so bloody damned cold I feel myself instinctively trying to snap back to the conference room, but I fight to stay because I need some way—any way—of identifying this place that is the *last* place we would ever have looked for her, and I don't dare manifest.

And all I can think is how incredibly grateful I am that I refused to allow anyone to accompany me. It can often be a week or more before Barrons returns after dying.

I glance left and right, up and down, swiftly committing it to memory, then abruptly—

Shit! Everything is *pain*! Crushing, pressing down on every cell in my body, colder than I knew cold could be!

I can't breathe, I can't breathe!

I recoil violently, trying to retreat, but I'm so crushed by pain. I'm not sure which way is backward or forward and I screw up, manifest fully, and go somersaulting out of control.

Then some invisible thing slaps me and knocks me backward at the speed of light and I see stars rushing past as I rocket into what can only be a wormhole and I *still* can't breathe and—

My world goes black.

PART III

Every action generates a reaction.

There is no action we can take that doesn't impact the world around us.

Bottom-lining it: there are consequences.

I used to drop in at the local bookstore back home in Ashford, Georgia, every Friday after school and, with the sun slanting in mullioned windows across old pine board floors, spend hours searching for a new book to read.

The store had a poster hanging on the wall that drove me nuts. I'd look at it and think scornfully, "Are we mice or men?"

It was a poster of a black door liberally sprinkled with stars. On that door was a gold knocker, inviting you to rap firmly against the edge of the universe.

The words on the poster were from "The Love Song of J. Alfred Prufrock" by T. S. Eliot.

Do I dare
Disturb the Universe?
In a minute there is time
For decisions and revisions which a minute will reverse.

I hated it because it reeked to me of indecision and nervousness. I was a woman who would tackle the world boldly, plunge right in.

I get it now. I, too, study that knocker and think hard before I reach, and that doesn't make me a mouse. It makes me a woman tempered by time and loss, who's grown into her wisdom.

There are consequences.

And consequences have a perniciously persistent way of always coming back to bite us in the ass.

FROM THE JOURNALS OF MACKAYLA LANE-O'CONNOR
HIGH QUEEN OF THE FAE

FAEDREAM

* • *

Dream a little dream of me

I'M A CREATURE OF darkness.

Like my lover I have great black wings. We fly the night skies together, marveling down at our world.

Once, we were golden and bright, the pair of us. His, an illusion, mine a skin in which I was never truly comfortable.

He found me in the alley that day, moments before I might have hurried, unaware of the vast dangers awaiting me, into the shop of our enemy.

He taught me to see the Fae. Taught me to defeat them. When we discovered the *Sinsar Dubh* inside me, together, we employed spells to control it. It was never the dark sentience of the king within, or MacKayla Lane, but a deft blend of the two.

I spent the first twenty-two years of my life infatuated by summer and sunshine, white beaches, rainbows, and sunlight glittering like diamonds on aquamarine waves.

Only to discover I worshipped the light with such fierce devotion because I always sensed what I really was and feared that woman. She was strong, powerful, relentless, and passionate.

Dark.

When he came, darkness fell with the sacred, silken hush of

raven wings closing around me, silencing the divided chaos in my head, muting the garish colors, and in darkness, I find only beauty.

Stars against a midnight sky. A full moon on blue velvet. Once, I wore pink and yellow, but white, black, and cobalt are my favored colors now.

His colors.

Cruce set me free. Taking a page from my sister's journal, he calls me his Queen of the Night.

Drawing my ermine cloak more snugly around me, I stroll the streets of our midnight kingdom, face tipped back, reveling in the moon's gentle, luminous glow.

I pass the many creatures of the Shadow Court, and their beauty and elegance never cease to amaze me, creations sprung from the brilliant mind of my lover. Our streets throng with revelers, some gathered in groups, others slipping off to mate. Our court can sire children. One day, Cruce tells me, we will have children of our own.

"MacKayla." Cruce's melodious voice sends shivers up my spine. An inexhaustible lover, he focuses on me as obsessively as he focuses on all else. Our hours together, when he's not busy with court or his creations, are intense, passionate, blissful, exhausting.

I glance down the street and watch as he approaches, noticing the admiring glances of the females as he passes, the envious ones of the males, yet none dare challenge him and none ever will. Cruce is not a man to be crossed.

A young king, new to his power, he's not vast and strange as the ancient being we stripped of rule and banished to die on a harsh and forbidding world. Cruce tells me he needn't ever become so vast and surreal. The first king's original form was not Fae, and it was only through greed and carelessness he achieved gargantuan proportions. Although my lover is ambitious, he's no fool. He knows when enough is enough, and we have all for which we could ever hunger, right here and now. With each other.

Darroc is with him, and later I'll meet my sister to moonbathe by the pool and talk. My only regret is that my parents didn't live to see us together again. But they are impossible to bring back, thanks to our enemy's Machiavellian spells.

Still, it was consolation that, with the *Sinsar Dubh*, we were able to restore both Darroc and Alina, and the four of us govern this vibrant, thrilling kingdom that never stops growing, expanding, more stunning and magical with each passing day. I never get enough of it.

Here is everything you could ever dream, all that you might dare, in part due to—

I slant my gaze away.

"Why is *he* here?" I demand of my king.

"We've been refining my plans for new additions to our world. His power grows, he hones his craft as a sculptor."

"I don't like him. I don't understand why you made him."

"Don't gaze upon him, then. I relish being reminded of the one that lost you. The one that never deserved you and betrayed you in every possible way."

I don't. It reminds me of my naïveté, of the losses we suffered at his hands. *He* is the reason we can't restore my parents, so Cruce says.

"We bested him in the end," Cruce reminds me with a dark smile. "Recall, he and the others suffer in eternal limbo, neither living nor dying, but there, eternally aware that they are nothing."

Because we destroyed the Earth and the Seelie and, armed with the king's power, we made our own home, far across the galaxies.

Sometimes, I dream he's still out there.

Jericho Barrons.

He's roaring at me that Cruce set me up, that the Earth has not been destroyed, that my lover manipulated the press, slanted the facts, snared me in a web of lies, and Barrons never betrayed me. Would never betray me. Did not kill my parents. Did not nearly kill me. Still exists. Still waits.

And in those dreams, Barrons tells me he can bring me back to the world if only I'll pull my head out of my ass and realize this eternal night of peace and seduction is but a dream of someone else's weaving, and I'm not really happy but trapped in a hell where I'm Cruce's amusement, nothing more.

Barrons whispers to me of love that knows no bounds, exceeds all, is etched into his very genes, the stuff of which he's made, and to trust him, no matter how improbable events seem, or how different he might appear, and he waits for me still.

But I am lost, he explains. Cruce has trapped me in a controlled midnight slumber and, like Lyryka in a bottle, visits only when he's bored; and he gets bored with everything because nothing will ever be enough for the prince who eternally hungered to be king.

And the world is passing me by.

And those I love will die.

And if I don't choose to awaken, if I don't fight with all my might, with all my fury, and all my love, if I don't somehow force my eyes to open and break the spell I'm under, I will spend eternity in a hell that masquerades as a heaven, in which I pass ninety-nine percent of my life slumbering in a blank oblivion and only the tiniest slice of it dreaming.

When Cruce wills it.

And Cruce, Barrons tells me, will tire of this charade one day, and I will never dream again, but drift, as blank and lost as Cruce pretends Barrons does.

Then, *shhh!* he whispers and presses a finger to my lips before he departs. *Remember this until we meet again.*

I know Barrons lies. I refuse to believe him. I refuse to gaze upon the face of his doppelgänger Cruce made for his own amusement when we meet.

Still . . .

I remain hushed with the imprint of Barrons's fingertips upon my lips; when Cruce and I are together again I say nothing of what he's told me.

And there are nights, after Cruce leaves and I lie in our bed alone, that, for some reason, I don't instantly fall asleep as I usually do.

On such nights, I hear a hushed and distant chanting, as if some-one is casting a spell, working feverishly to append a concealed space of time onto the end of a dream, to buy me time to think.

And in that stolen space of time I wonder . . .

Am I alive, queen of a midnight kingdom?

Or am I asleep, dying slowly in a dream?

33

24601

LYRYKA

I SPRAWL ON THE FLOOR of my new bottle that sports the label MACALLAN RARE CASK. Considerably larger and more accommodating than my last, it holds several inches of pungent liquid at the bottom. The only thing I don't like about it (besides that I'm in it at all!) is Death's infernal labeling technique. He desperately needs guidance; he's plastered a huge label on both front and back, obscuring my entire view of the world beyond. Were I to scrunch down, I might peer beneath it, or perhaps I could peek from the neck of the flask.

Irritated, I prop my feet against the glass, wriggling my toes against the side, fold my arms behind my head, and scowl up at the offensive cork.

I've been stuffed into yet another container, corked and shelved. Queen's orders. On a low shelf, no less, as if Death doesn't yet realize I'm always top shelf, regardless of the bottle that houses me.

Increasing my irritation, I find the scent of Macallan, whatever that is, overpowering and . . . yet . . . somehow intriguing, so I tip my head sideways and take a greedy slurp.

I bolt upright instantly, choking and pounding my chest with a fist. When I can finally breathe again, I'm astounded that I don't exhale the sparks of red-hot embers, like a fiery dragon.

By the Goddess, that scorched!

I inhale slowly and carefully, wheezing, chest on fire, wondering if I just drank poison. While I wait for the burning sensation to subside, I resume fuming.

Life in all its grandness is happening out there beyond the glass.

And the wonder of it—Death took a formal oath to protect me! That means he has to, whether he wants to or not!

I, Lyryka, have a protector.

Inconceivable and thrilling.

My debut landed me smack in the middle of epic events, surrounded by heroic characters of all sorts and, just as the plot is beginning to thicken with major snarls that require all hands on deck to employ the deftest of finessing, what do they do?

Shelve me.

I'm an avid reader. I understand plots and know how to finesse them. They *need* me.

Who am I kidding? I need *them*. I require more information, answers to countless questions.

My head is spinning, in part from the fumes, but in larger part because of the things I learned in their company, as I was battered by one astounding and disturbing revelation after the next.

The original Unseelie Court was destroyed, yet I knew nothing about it!

I believed the Unseelie still existed. According to my father, they were hunting him, which was why we had to remain hidden.

But the Unseelie are no more.

They've been gone for some time.

No one hunts my father. I assume no one hunts me either, now.

Why, then, am I still not free?

My father created a new Shadow Court.

I can scarcely wrap my mind around the fact. It makes me sick in the pit of my stomach. He has a court, with real, live courtiers, and a kingdom where he lives, interacting with others, having a life.

I imagine he takes lovers, eats and drinks and converses and touches.

I've never been touched. (Death rejecting my bid for sex doesn't count.) I ache to be touched. My father never did. During the eons of my incarceration, there were no hugs or pats of affection such as those I read about in books.

My father is actively seeking the king's power. Yet that power has not chosen him, and is considering two other beings. I find that illuminating and disturbing. Were my father the wonderful, powerful Unseelie he claims to be, surely the king's power would have chosen him by now.

After all, he's the only pure-blooded Shadow Court prince of the three.

He abducted two of my new acquaintances' friends.

One of them is his *daughter*.

By a human.

A *half-blood*.

This fact makes my stomach hot and sick, too.

I suspect he took this new daughter of his off to live at his new Shadow Court, permitting her freedom, alongside his courtiers, no doubt eating and drinking and touching, and one day, she, too, will take lovers.

At a court I didn't even know existed.

In a kingdom I've never seen.

My new acquaintances don't trust him and want him dead.

I don't trust him either.

There isn't a single book in the Library about an Unseelie prince named Cruce. I've searched high and low for stories about my father. The few times I inquired about their absence (and was always treated to a look of scathing rebuke!) he claimed his grand exploits remained unrecorded because he's been forced to hide, that we have long shared a separate yet similar cruel isolation.

Lie upon lie.

In Fae and mortal realms alike, he who controls the press controls the world. I believe he took all the books that captured him in verse and volume to be certain I would never discover who and what he really is.

A tyrannical, selfish bastard who orders me to do this or that, find this or that, *don't* do this or that, and never, *ever* show your true form, not even to him, who has no intention of releasing me.

In addition to containing no volumes about my father, the Library has not received any new editions in quite some time. I had no idea Aoibheal was gone and had passed her power to a mortal queen, no idea there were hybrid princes and the like. He kept me from knowing what was going on in the world. I wonder if he banned all the messengers that deliver new tomes. Perhaps he killed them. I wonder if books and artifacts have been piling up outside the door of the corporeal Library for a long time. I would never know.

How did the Fae queen put it?

Her worth to him lies only in how he can use her. No one is important to Cruce but himself.

Seething, I push up from the floor, summon a mirror, and hang it on the inside of the bottle.

I drop glamour and revert to my true form and, as I settle into it, I sigh with pleasure.

Smiling, I turn this way and that.

Then I stand still, locking gazes with my reflection, facing truths irrefutable and long overdue.

34

Cannibal class, killing the son

CRUCE

"COME, CHILD," CRUCE SAID to Rae, patting the sofa beside him.

"Where did you put my daddy?" the tiny girl demanded. With a wary expression, she remained where she was, arms crossed, jaw jutted, staring defiantly up at him, dark eyes snapping.

Cruce said, "He's not your father. It was I who came to you in dreams. Sean isn't even full Fae."

"Neither am I," the child said matter-of-factly.

Cruce smiled. "Though your wings have not yet come in, you know what you are."

"The Spyrssidhe told me. I smell good to them."

"Did you tell your mother?"

Rae shook her head. "No. She worries a lot. I thought I'd wait till I was older."

"She needn't worry anymore. You'll live with me."

"Why?"

"You need someone to teach you about being Fae. She can't do that."

"Why? She knows a lot about the Fae. That's what the whole abbey is for."

"She can't teach you the things I can, show you the wonders I will show you. Would you like to see our kingdom?"

"This isn't my kingdom. I live up there." Rae pointed at the ceiling. "With my mommy and daddy."

Cruce growled, "I'm your father, and I'll—"

The child puffed out her lower lip, eyes darkening with anger. "No! I want my daddy back, and you are *not*. And if you hurt my daddy, I'll hurt *you*."

Cruce was silent a moment, staring down at the truculent beast, wondering if all children were such grand pains in the ass, as the old king had said on more than one occasion. Was it possible, he wondered, that this child truly was Sean's and not his?

But he sensed his own essence within her, the same as Lyryka. He was certain she was his. And, unlike Lyryka, Rae would one day look as magnificent as any Unseelie royalty. She might be a half-blood, but she pulsed with the power of a pure Fae, as potent as any in his court. He was avid to learn what new talents she possessed.

Perhaps, he mused, the blending of Fae with *sidhe*-seer—who'd been tinkered with by the king himself, and had precious drops of his blood coursing through their veins—yielded as pure an Unseelie as a coupling among their own kind.

If so, there was an entire abbey to be plundered and a new Shadow Court to plunder it, thereby adding *sidhe*-seers gifts and knowledge to their arsenal. "Why do you think Sean is your father, not me?"

"Because he loves me," Rae said simply. "You don't love anyone but yourself."

Cruce threw his head back and laughed. "Ah, child, you and I will have such grand times." Then he murmured, "Masdann."

The prince appeared.

"Put the little princess to sleep and keep her there until I'm ready to speak with her again."

"No!" Rae cried. "I don't want to sleep! I want to go home! I want my mommy and daddy!"

"As you wish, my king," Masdann replied.

After the child was subdued and lay slumbering upon the sofa in an enchanted dream, which Masdann would deftly shape, altering her beliefs about her origins, Cruce stared down at her, musing, for the large part quite pleased.

"How long will it take to reprogram the child?"

"You seek to alter powerful underlying beliefs. That requires repeated, traumatic sojourns in the Dreaming."

She was as lovely as any Unseelie, and Cruce imagined MacKayla would enjoy having her. If mating with a *sidhe*-seer created such offspring, mating with the soon-to-be ex-queen would create an entire stable of noble, blooded allies.

"Convince the child MacKayla is her mother, and I her father."

Perched on the sofa beside Rae, Masdann inclined his head. "Would you care to join us in the Dreaming?"

Cruce shook his head. He had another daughter to attend. A more difficult one.

Lyryka.

Many eons ago, when Cruce was a young prince and the king was otherwise occupied, before the Seelie queen knew the Unseelie existed, Cruce attempted to birth his own court within hers.

He'd theorized that, unlike the Seelie, the Unseelie might sire children, since their immortality sprang from different sources. The Unseelie had never drunk the Elixir of Life. Why wouldn't they be able to sire bairns? A handful of the Seelie were still fertile, though fewer children were born with each passing century.

To test his theory and further his aim of infiltrating the Light Court, using spells and artifacts unearthed from the king's library, Cruce abducted a Seelie prince, donned his glamour, and seduced the verdant princess of Summer.

V'lane was not the first Light Court prince he impersonated, nor would he be the last.

When the princess discovered she was carrying a child, she was eager to gain audience with the queen to share the thrilling news. After millennia of barrenness, a royal bairn was to be born!

But Cruce persuaded the princess to conceal her pregnancy, urging that others at court might, out of jealousy and spite, attempt to harm their unborn child. He proposed they slip away, birth it in private, then present it at court, to everyone's envy and dismay.

He'd taken the princess to a faraway isle and remained at her side until their daughter arrived.

The day of Lyryka's birth was not one of his finest.

He'd imagined their child might be dark-skinned—which was why he'd chosen the tawny princess of Summer, not pale Winter— perhaps have unusual eyes, possess abilities not seen before among the Seelie, but all the differences would be explained away by the Fae's continuing evolution, their powers diversifying, increasing, their forms adapting to new and greater magic.

The Seelie had no reason to think any other type of Fae existed but them. They wouldn't discover the Shadow Court for another forty-two thousand years.

Because the child would be unmistakably Fae, the queen would be delighted to have a new prince or princess and embrace whatever variations with which their offspring came. Cruce had come to understand the Light Court well in the time he'd spent there. Their minds were as void of imagination as their bodies of passion. When they encountered something they couldn't explain, they readily accepted the first lie that reinforced their version of reality in which they reigned supreme in all ways.

Translated: The Seelie believed they were too superior to be deceived. Exploiting that egotistical weakness, he'd fed them lie after lie, cementing a foundation for future lies.

He'd toyed with the idea of impregnating many Seelie females, to increase variations, ensuring even the most questionable of his offspring would be accepted, and one day the Light Court would be so diluted with his seed, he would rule it through all four royal houses.

But his union with a Light Court Fae proved a bitter disappointment.

As if the universe itself reviled their union, it marked the child in a manner that ensured he would never attempt it again, one that betrayed his and his court's existence.

That very day, Cruce tested another of his theories. If a Seelie was entombed in the ice of the Unseelie prison, he suspected that Seelie would eventually die, their essence leached away by the antithetical nature of the Shadow Kingdom.

It wasn't as if he could let the princess live after what she'd seen.

That test, at least, proved successful, and, in a world where Fae could be killed by only one of three weapons (no one knew about the third but he and the king), Cruce was pleased to discover a fourth weapon of which not even the king was aware. Over time, he'd used that weapon on his enemies again and again, most recently interring the ex Queen Aoibheal/Zara.

The princess was still shrieking with horror at the sight of their babe, raging at Cruce's betrayal, demanding answers, threatening to go to the queen, when he sealed her in a coffin, warded it shut, and buried her deep beneath the ice. She'd survived mere months; she had ceased fighting at the end.

After entombing the mother, Cruce sat back and pondered the troublesome babe for a time before gouging a chasm deep in the ice in which to toss it.

It was a kindness to kill it.

Yet, as he continued to study it, aware of his own essence within it, he decided perhaps the experiment wasn't a complete waste, and the child could be of use. He had need of a dedicated ally to work toward his goals.

He would be her world. She would love and obey him. He was, after all, her father. The only being she would ever know. And, one day, far in the future, he would do her another kindness. When it was time. There were few kindnesses a child such as this could expect in her life.

Although immortal, he had infinite plans for his future, and he loathed wasting any part of the present. He'd been spending long hours in the king's library, searching obscure scrolls, absorbing their ancient history, tracking down spells, determined to match the king in knowledge and power.

Before long, the child would be old enough to catalog the jumbled collection, absorb and distill information, regurgitate it swiftly, sparing him the drudgery, freeing him to turn his attention elsewhere. She would uncover artifacts of importance in the vast, shambolic library where things were piled haphazardly; nothing was where one thought it should be, and many things weren't even *what* one thought they should be.

She could organize the place. She would have eternity to do it, and nothing else to occupy her time.

He would afford her a life, such as it was, and she would be grateful for it. And one day, far in the future, he would release her from her bottle for the last time. That day had come.

It was time to bring Lyryka home.

35

Is she not right? Is she insane?

IXCYTHE

I XCYTHE MANIFESTED IN THE too-bright castle of the Summer kingdom, wincing, narrowing her eyes against cruel, razor-sharp rays of sunlight.

How she despised this place.

It was sweltering, the sun a violence to her eyes. Her gown began to drip the moment she sifted in, further incensing her.

She'd materialized in Summer's ballroom, which was draped with garish swaths of colored silks that spilled from ornate columns and framed no less than seven large, brilliantly sparkling, three-tiered fountains, adding yet more light and humidity to the already overpowering, steaming clime.

Her nostrils flaring with repugnance, she adjusted her core temperature, stabilizing her gown. A ballroom for holding dances and feasts and other manner of revelry. The absurdity of it. It was no wonder Summer had long failed to secure a seat on the High Council. No wonder her court was weak and simple. She was as much a wastrel as that human god of the Bacchae, Dionysus!

She was pleased, however, to hear the unmistakable sounds of battle beyond the castle walls. Though Severina had barred her keep against her court, she'd not mastered the complex art of vanquishing sound.

Leaning forward at the waist, hands behind her, summoning icy daggers behind her back, Ixcythe hissed, "How dare you summon me?"

Severina regarded her impassively from the other end of the long ballroom. "Azar told me you betrayed emotion to the queen. The human imposter now knows we are becoming mortal."

"She would have figured it out anyway," Ixcythe snarled. "It was but a matter of time."

Severina surprised her by allowing, "I agree. And we have more pressing problems to address."

Ixcythe stiffened, sensing Azar's arrival a moment before he appeared. She felt as if all her nerve endings were exposed, hypersensitive to every facet of her existence. Life, with emotion, with memory, staring into a future that promised death was a constant barrage of fiery blades to the coolness of her skin.

While holding the poisoned human in the fragment of Faery, into which no one could sift, she'd discovered the beast that consorted with the imposter queen had tampered with it, suspending it, preventing it from moving even one breath closer to death. Clever, useful beast. She could smell him on the human.

He'd used magic with which she was unfamiliar, and she'd wasted hours trying to undo his spell, to no avail, all the while her desire to possess the canny beast growing. Whatever magic he'd used upon the human prevented her from even touching him. It was as if he'd erected an invisible rubbery barrier around his entire body, several inches above his skin. The poison wasn't affecting him, and she could do no damage to him. She was encountering resistance and failure at every turn.

"You summoned?" Azar demanded, looking at Ixcythe.

"*I* did," Severina corrected sharply. "Winter is not the only one with information to offer and plans to refine."

Azar's gaze swiveled to the Summer princess. "Why have you brought us here?"

Her mouth curved in a triumphant smile. "Because *I* succeeded where you failed. I have found the Elixir of Life."

Ixcythe's eyes narrowed and she straightened, retracting the daggers of ice back into her hands. "How dare you drink it first?" she hissed. Did the simple princess of Summer think she could withhold it from them? Dare she provoke two royals to attack her at once?

"I didn't!" Severina denied heatedly. "I summoned the two of you the instant I returned here with it."

"Where did you find it?" Azar demanded skeptically.

"At the queen's castle, beneath a floorboard in her boudoir."

"I ripped out the entire floor of that castle," Ixcythe thundered. "There was no flask hidden in it."

"It would appear, in your frenzy of emotion and carelessness, you missed it," Severina snarled. "It was buried beneath a mound of rubble."

Azar studied her, embers of disbelief in his gaze. "Why didn't you drink it?"

"Where is it?" Ixcythe demanded icily.

Severina withdrew a flask from the folds of her gown. "Our first queen could not have imagined a time such as this might come to pass when all the Tuatha De Danann would require it again." Her sunny eyes darkened with the fury of storms as she held the flask aloft for them to see. "There is a single drop left. Enough for only one of us."

Ixcythe went motionless.

Across the ballroom, Azar, too, went unnaturally still.

Ixcythe knew why. Both were contemplating attacking Severina, seizing the flask and gulping down that last precious drop, unwilling to betray their intent by the slightest motion.

The moment was perilous.

Both, too, she knew, were reconsidering it for the same reason Severina hesitated to take it.

It would be one thing if Ixcythe might drink it and live forever, ruling an immortal court.

But *all* the Fae would die over the next few centuries.

Leaving her no court to rule.

No mirror, no reflection of her existence.

Leaving her utterly and completely alone. As surely alone as if trapped within the dark heart of a mountain.

Severina inclined her head, golden gaze dripping mockery. "Precisely why I didn't take it, Ixcythe. We do not fare well, alone, do we?"

An understatement at best. Prolonged solitude was a death sentence for a Fae. Unseen by others of their kind, they would fade, grow transparent and insubstantial and, with each passing eon, slip deeper into madness, until they collapsed into dust and vanished on the wind. Humans once penned a tale in which a Fae required clapping and belief to survive. It wasn't far from the truth. Such solitary confinement had been meted out as punishment from time to time.

It took a Fae a small eternity to die alone, the largest portion of it spent stark, raving mad.

Ixcythe shuddered, remembering. Each time the queen had enforced that punishment, it served to remind her couriers they were immortal by her sufferance. They could be disposed of, slowly and horrifically, if they crossed her. Or even just tortured for a few centuries. If commanded to choose between fates, Ixcythe, indeed, all Fae, would choose death by spear or sword over the terrible, lingering demise.

"Perhaps," Azar growled, "we can study and re-create it."

Ixcythe laughed, brittle and bright. "Have you forgotten who we are? We forswore studies an eternity ago."

"We abduct humans, force them to study and re-create it," Severina offered eagerly.

Ixcythe shook her head, rejecting the idiotic idea. "We would all be dead long before their technology reached levels sufficient to create such a potion. Humans are still in the dark ages, compared to the species that created the Elixir. It was the result of tens of thousands of years of scientific achievement, by a highly evolved society that then eschewed the rewards of the very science they'd prized."

"It is said," Severina pressed, "the species from whom we stole it still lives on that world. We visit them again. Seize many flasks this time. Of the three of us, one is stronger. More determined to succeed. Ruthless. A natural born leader."

Ixcythe raised a brow and mocked scornfully, "You think so highly of yourself?"

Severina replied, "Whether I care for you or not, Ixcythe—and we both know I don't—I think that highly of *you*. If one of us is to drink the potion then make the taxing journey to that world to collect more of the Elixir, it is you who must do it, Ixcythe."

Flattery. There was a game here, of that Ixcythe was certain. The princess of Summer preyed upon Winter Fae every time they drank from the Cauldron and erased memory, during those perilous early years they floundered, unable to distinguish friend from foe.

"I know my strengths and weaknesses," Severina pressed. "I lack your determination and focus. Azar is powerful, but you are, by far, the most cunning among us. If anyone can restore immortality and save our species, it's you, Ixcythe."

"You trust that I would bother myself to elevate the rest of you once I was immortal?"

"None of us wish to spend eternity alone," Severina reminded. "I seek immortality for all the Fae. I believe you do, too. You are our best chance to succeed, and I'll do everything in my power to help you. Including relinquishing to you the last precious drop of the Elixir."

Ixcythe gathered her gown in both hands and strode across the ballroom. By the time she'd reached Severina, Azar was there as well.

He met her gaze, eyes narrowed. *Be wary, Ix,* he said silently within her mind. *Sev is not your friend.*

Inclining her head, Ixcythe plucked the flask from Severina's hand. She turned it this way and that, studying it.

They'd all seen the bejeweled flask that contained the Elixir on those rare occasions the queen (particularly Aoibheal, who'd had an unnatural fondness for humans, which had recently become all too clear) had dispensed it to one mortal or another.

This was, indeed, that flask.

Or a very clever replica.

Cleverness wasn't one of Severina's strong suits.

At the bottom of the flask, a thin bead of liquid rolled. Severina was right. There was only enough left for one of them.

"You'll do it?" Severina pressed. "You'll drink it and find us more? You'll save our species from extinction?"

Ixcythe slipped the flask into her gown. "You were right about me, Severina," she said.

Severina nodded, eyes alight with hope. "I knew I was. Drink it now. Let us all share in the glory of your restored immortality!"

"I *am* more cunning."

"You are," Severina agreed. "Vastly more cunning than I. Drink it now so we can all savor watching you regain what we all will have soon."

"And I have a vastly more clever idea of what to do with the last remaining drop of the Elixir of Life," Ixcythe purred with a cruel smile.

Azar's autumn eyes gleamed as he intuited her thoughts. "Of course you do, Ix. I concur."

Ixcythe favored him with a smile. Once, the pair of them had been more than lovers. They'd finished each other's sentences, completed each other's thoughts. "The queen possesses far more power than I. She has the ability to sift worlds. Once, she even possessed the ability to sift time. She can obtain a new flask of Elixir more quickly and certainly than I."

"Yet she lacks the proper motivation," Azar murmured.

Ixcythe nodded. "She is mortal, with human emotion, driven by passion to protect the wrong species. She doesn't understand us. Can't fathom why we wish to be the way we are."

Azar laughed softly. "We give *her* the last drop, scorching away emotion, destroying her soul."

"Make her like us. *We* become her people. Those she will fight to save."

"This is a terrible idea," Severina hissed. "You can do it *now*, Ixcythe. Drink and be restored! Save us!"

"You have great faith in me. I, too, know my strengths and weaknesses. I may not succeed. But a queen will."

Severina argued, "But if we use it on the queen, it will take too long for her emotion—"

"Not so long," Azar cut her off. "We'll survive longer. Within a few decades, she'll barely be human, and find the thought of living forever without company as unpalatable as we. Once we're immortal again, we find a way to depose her and seize the rule."

"This is a dreadful idea," Severina cried. "One of the stupidest I've ever heard. There are too many variables. Countless things could go awry. *I* should be the one to say what to do with it. *I'm* the one that found the potion."

Ixcythe cast her a withering glare. "I'm the one that *has* the potion." She challenged with icy menace, "Or are you fool enough to try to take it from me?"

Azar shifted position, moving to stand before Ixcythe, honoring her with his stance, crossing his arms, legs splayed wide, in the protective position of a royal guard. "Make that fool enough to try to take it from us both, Severina," he growled.

"You're making a mistake. I warn you, it will turn out disastrously and only call down more suffering upon us. I will play no part in this foolish fiasco."

Eyes flashing with anger, Severina vanished.

Smiling, Azar took Ixcythe's hand. "We don't need her. We never needed anyone else, Ix. The two of us will secure the future of the Fae then . . ." He trailed off, raking her with an appreciative, frankly carnal look.

She snatched her hand away. "Don't touch me again without my permission, and clear your mind of such unsavory frivolity. We have a far more difficult seduction to plan."

36

Déjà vu, I've just been in this time before

MAC

"WHERE THE HELL IS Dani?" Ryodan snarls the moment I open my eyes. He towers over me, hands fisted, glowering down, silver eyes narrowed and cold. "Why didn't you bring her back with you? Is she hurt? Is she in danger? Answer me! Where the bloody fuck *is* she?"

Barrons is on the floor beside me. "Give her a fucking minute," he growls.

Ryodan cuts him a savage look. "She *had* a minute. She's been out for five. Her eyes are open, she can bloody well talk."

I stare up at Ryodan, marveling because I've never heard him ask so many questions in, like, *ever*, nor have I seen such unguarded emotion. His hands are fisted, three muscles jump in his jaw. I realize Dani has been gone for *weeks* and he has no idea why or where she is. There's been no enemy to attack, no castle walls to storm. It must be eating him alive just as it would Barrons. I missed so many significant events while I was gone.

Dani's relationship with this aloof, brilliant man was consummated without my being the tiniest part of it. I've not heard a single detail from her, and I want a *lot* of them. I feel as if my daughter ran off and got married while away at college, leaving me shut out and trying desperately to reinsert myself into the picture.

Ryodan loves Dani with the same unwavering commitment and ferocious loyalty that Barrons loves me. Good. Because I have no idea how to rescue her, and I hope to hell the man who eternally has a deck of aces up his sleeve holds a few killer cards to play now.

Groaning, I shove myself to a sitting position but don't try to get up yet. I'm shaky and weak. "How long was I out?" I ask as I reach up to feel my face. When I'd gotten slammed into the wormhole it felt like my brain sloshed brutally against the confines of my skull. I'd been certain bones were broken, but my face seems okay. Unfortunately my stomach isn't faring as well, prolonged somersaulting turned it into a vat of aggrieved acid, and I can't recall the last time I ate. I've been rushing from one crisis to the next since the moment I left the chamber. I don't even know how many days I've been awake, or whether to count Fae-time or mortal. Or even how much sleep I need. Will I simply topple over and pass out at some point? I'm starved, exhausted, and bitchy-hangry.

I feel like crying. It's too much: the savage, emotional, dying Fae; our only way into the Unseelie prison shattered; the impossible choices I'm being forced to make; Cruce ruling a new Shadow Court that *sidhe*-seers can't detect; my father dying in a place I can't access; my mother unaware Dad is doomed and I'm the reason; Sean and Rae in the underworld with the villain, and now, oh, God—Dani!

What I saw when I sifted to that deadly place demolished my heart.

I wish she'd seen me, but she'd had her back to me the entire, all too brief time. Not that I was exactly visible (although a Hunter obviously had no problem detecting and whacking me back to Chester's, I'm pretty sure, with its enormous tail), but we're talking about Dani's super senses and, perhaps, if she'd been looking, she'd have glimpsed my faint outline and known we'd located her and would get there, one way or another.

As I'd battled to remain suspended in that suffocating place between places, one foot poking through the door into an environment in which no human, or even Fae, could survive, horror and fury had crashed over me in towering waves.

I glance back at Barrons. *Do you die in the vacuum of space?*

Dark eyes grim, he inclines his head. *I once took a cursed Silver that dumped me in the midst of an asteroid field. I swelled to twice my size and froze to death.*

I close my eyes. I want to scream my fury to the heavens, demand whatever mad gods arrange events to correct them right now because this is the biggest load of crap ever.

Dani is in a *cage*.

Locked away behind bars. *Again.*

Alone.

There were two cages floating in space, miles apart.

In the one nearest me, Dani stood tall, defiant, naked, back to me, weaponless, hands fisting with fury, staring across the vast starry blackness at the other cage where Shazam clung to the bars, shuddering, his great violet eyes gushing faucets of tears.

I didn't need empathic skills to feel their pain.

I can never forget Dani nearly burning herself alive trying to save a stuffed substitution of Shazam. None of us will ever forget it. Their reunion was one of the happiest days of her life. Her delicate features had glowed with joy, supernova bright.

Dani and Shazam love with the pure, unconditional love of mother and child.

I know Dani. She'll give her life to save Shazam.

Which means we have to figure out a way to save them both, *fast*.

"If Mac doesn't start talking, I'm going to rip her bloody fucking head off," Ryodan says, very softly.

A thick, animalistic rattle, atavistic and chilling, rumbles in Barrons's chest.

"Figuratively," Ryodan adds tightly. "Not literally."

"Wise man." Barrons's voice comes out hoarse and unnatural, as if around teeth too large for his mouth.

"By the saints, you're one of the beasts that fought beside us at the abbey!" Kat breathes, stunned, staring behind me at Barrons, and I don't need to turn to know that his eyes are glittering bloodred, fangs are protruding, his face is darkening, and he's sprouting the stumps of horns, betraying his beast. His half brother spoke words that threatened my life, though we both know Ryodan would never harm me. Deep in the belly of this club, Barrons, Christian, Ryodan, and I once swore a blood oath to be eternal allies, protect one another, unite to battle common foes, never turn against one another, and guard one another's secrets as our own.

Ryodan cuts Kat a lethal look. "Forget you said that. Or that you saw what you *think* you saw. Which you clearly didn't see. Because if you did, I'd have to kill you."

"Right," Kat says instantly, averting her gaze from Barrons. "Absolutely. Didn't see a thing."

"The Hunters have Dani," I tell them. "She and Shazam are caged, separately, a few miles apart."

"Where?" Ryodan demands. "On what world?"

I shake my head. "Not on a world. They're suspended, floating in space."

"Bloody fucking hell, who comes up with this shit?" Christian curses.

"Alive, though," Ryodan roars, as if daring me to deny it.

"Alive," I say hastily. "Sorry, I should have said that first."

"Unharmed," he insists with irrefutable certainty.

"Not so much as a scratch on either of them," I assure him.

He plunges both hands into his short, dark hair, eyes narrowed, lips drawn back, baring his teeth, looking nearly as animalistic as Barrons on a seriously bad day, and begins to prowl the conference room. "Then, why didn't you sift into her cage and bring her back? Why is she not here?"

"There was a force field of some kind around both cages," I tell him wearily. "Keeping me out and likely keeping in the oxygen they're breathing. I couldn't penetrate it. I tried to sift to her, but it was impossible, so I had to recalibrate to sift near her. Then I had to kind of . . . hang between here and there because I couldn't breathe, and if I'd stayed any longer, it would have killed me. I'm not sure I wasn't dying when the Hunter swatted me out of there. I'd lost control of keeping one foot in both places. I stumbled. I didn't see a Hunter, but I caught a whiff of brimstone and the cold increased dramatically when something enormous knocked me into a wormhole of sorts. I woke up here."

"But why would the Hunters cage Shazam and Dani?" Kat exclaims. "It doesn't make sense."

Ryodan clips tightly, "Shazam broke the rules for Dani. I wondered if there'd be hell to pay. Looks like there is."

"How are we going to get them back?" Kat asks, her eyes glistening with the sheen of barely repressed tears.

I realize she's exhausted, too. Her daughter and soul mate were abducted by Cruce, and Kat loves Dani as deeply as I do. On top of that, she feels everyone else's worry and pain, despite her stoic nature and immense mental barriers.

I sense the disturbance of space and time at the same instant Christian stiffens and whirls toward it.

A slot opens in the air, a piece of parchment flutters to the floor.

I don't even see Barrons move toward it. He's simply there, holding it, scans it, and looks at me. "You need to eat. You need rest."

"Read it to me," I growl. I felt the icy draft of air that chased the missive through. I know Ixcythe was on the delivering end, and apparently she'd been spying on me when Christian used the technique to communicate with us in Faery.

"You haven't stopped since you left the chamber," Barrons growls back. "Your body was shaking even while you were unconscious. You're weak."

"I. Am. Never. Weak. Read it," I repeat grimly, pushing to my feet, concealing the wobble in my legs rather superbly, if I must say so myself.

A muscle works in his jaw, then he shoves the piece of paper at me.

We will return your father to you.
Meet us in the grove where we met before.
Come alone.
Don't keep us waiting.
We won't.

I glance at Ryodan, feeling as if I'm being ripped in two.

"Describe everything you saw. I need landmarks."

The information is why I fought to remain. I describe the precise colors and shape of the triple-columned nebula, down to the last detail of it, the gold-and-lavender planet, the layout of the stars.

"Go," he says then, flatly. "I've got this. I'll work on getting Dani back. You contend with your father."

"Bring her home, Ryodan." My words contain the urgent fervency of a prayer.

His smile is cold and dangerous, and I realize if anyone can figure out a way to take on the Hunters and win, it's this man.

"Bet your fucking life on it, Mac."

———— • • ————

"You do know you're not going alone," Barrons says as we close the door behind us and begin walking down the hall.

I glance up at him. "I had no intention of it. Ixcythe doesn't make the rules."

"You're eating before we go."

I summon a power bar from the stash I keep at the bookstore in case Dani drops by, rip it open, shove it in my mouth, and chew once before swallowing. It takes less energy to summon something that already exists than creating it from scratch.

"And now you're eating like Dani," he says dryly.

"But I'm eating."

"You need to sleep."

"Not happening, Barrons. What do you think her game is?"

"Finish that bar, eat a second one, drink some water, and we'll find out."

I roll my eyes but follow his advice then also dash into a bathroom to pee and splash some water on my face. I stare at myself in the mirror a moment and snort. I may be part Fae and hard to kill, but I still have smudges of exhaustion beneath my eyes. That's bullshit.

Since I've been to the grove before and know the layout, I sift us into protective cover at the edge of the forest, the better to scope out the enemy. I expect to find either an army of Fae waiting for us, or no one to be seen.

I'm wrong on both counts.

Ixcythe and Azar are seated in the middle of the glade, the epitome of relaxed elegance, at a long table decked with linens, crystal, and china, covered with a mouthwatering spread of food, appetizers, lusciously ripe fruits, desserts, and a ruby red bottle of wine.

God, I'm hungry. The power bars didn't make a dent, and sifting takes energy.

I glance at Barrons.

Eat nothing. Trust nothing.

Agreed, I reply.

"Come. Join us," Azar calls. "We feel when you sift in."

As we leave the cover of the forest and approach the table in the clearing, I demand, "Where is my father?"

"You know where he is," Ixcythe says, popping a frosted grape in her mouth, wintry gaze raking me from head to toe with blatant contempt. "You can't sift to him. That tells you all you need to know. Well, not all, but it does tell you I'm holding him in one of the fragments Darroc caused when he brought down the walls between our realms and our worlds crashed together." Her gaze moves to Barrons and heats up instantly. She regards him with frank lust while murmuring to me, "I told you to come alone."

"And knew I wouldn't."

"You always bring the beast. I would, as well. He's quite fascinating. I would like to have him for myself."

Barrons says softly, "Get to the bloody point. What do you want in exchange for Jack?"

Ixcythe narrows her eyes. "Manners matter. Sit. Join us. We wish to discuss our future."

Barrons smiles faintly. "We've already established your future is mortal. And very short."

She shrugs. "If you consider five hundred years short. The Song hasn't undone our immortality yet. It might be another century before it reaches that point. That's six long centuries the woman you serve might pass peacefully. Or spend it incessantly looking over her shoulder, while you try to protect everyone she loves."

I say, "He doesn't serve me."

"Of course he does. Why else would he remain at your side?" she counters.

"Difficult for your kind to comprehend that there's more to life than rulers and serfs, predators and prey," I say. "You want to believe he serves me because a servant's loyalty can be bought or swayed, and that might give you a chance at him."

Barrons gives her a smile that's all teeth and savagery. "Not in any reality, princess."

"Now you merely intrigue me more," Ixcythe purrs.

"Get to the point," I echo Barrons's command.

"I agree," Azar snaps. "Get to the fucking point, Ix."

Winter's gaze moves, with obvious reluctance, from Barrons to me, her eyes narrowing and cooling markedly. "We're willing to accept you as queen."

"Convenient," I scoff. "Since I already am. Whether you accept it or not."

"What Ixcythe means to say," Azar says, cutting her a pointed and furious glance, "is that we hope you are willing to guide and care for our species. You now know that memory and emotion have been restored and that, in five to six centuries, our species will go extinct. Will you see to us until then?"

"See to you how? Have you given up your quest for the Elixir?"

"No. And we won't," Ixcythe says. "We hope, in time, you'll change your mind. And, in time, we will learn to live together, and humans will no longer fear us. We also acknowledge that the Unseelie"—she emphasizes *Un* heavily—"destroyed a significant number of humans. That number was in the billions, I believe. While the Seelie have infrequently preyed upon humans, we are responsible for a fraction of a percentage of lives lost. A mere few thousand lives can be placed at our feet, over our eons of inhabiting this planet. *Billions* attributed to the Shadow Court. Quite a difference, wouldn't you agree? We are not monsters. You look at the pair of us and see the deaths of billions of mortals. Yet it was not the Light Court that caused those deaths. The amorphous ones, the tusked, slithering, crawling, and lumbering ones—" She breaks off, shuddering. "It was the ugly and vile Fae that slayed so many of your kind."

"We were deceived, my queen," Azar insists. "Cruce posed as one of the Seelie for hundreds of thousands of years. An *Unseelie* infiltrated our court. He was the one that urged us to become savages, who spoke fervently in the support of Aoibheal while campaigning privately to perpetrate new, increasingly aggressive attacks on humans, as the Unseelie are wont to do in far greater excess than the Seelie. It was he who reinstituted the Wild Hunt. He placed a token on the throne, ruled us through it."

Right, blame everything on the person you believe is dead, I think acerbically but remain silent, letting them talk, screening for subtext.

"We were misled and manipulated," Ixcythe asserts with imperious ire. "Is it any wonder we are angry? Any wonder, after Cruce and Aoibheal, we distrust all humans and would prefer to govern ourselves? How would you feel if one of the Light Court Fae was in charge of your species, responsible for making all the decisions that govern you? A Fae that knew little to nothing of humans? Would there not be resistance? Would you not, when your way of life was threatened—the *only* way of life you'd known and enjoyed— seek leverage to restore to your people the rights and privileges they once had?"

Well. She had a point there. Perhaps even two.

"Adding insult to injury," Azar presses her point, "we've lived for hundreds of thousands of years, yet we're to be governed by a being that has lived what? Scant *decades*."

Another fair point, I concede, a fair concern. "I see your points of view. And, as I stated earlier—and also the first time I came to court and was met with nothing but deceit and hostility—I seek a way for our species to coexist peacefully." I pause to lend emphasis to my next words. "I'm also open to one day returning the queen's power to the Fae."

Azar's eyes widen then swiftly narrow, and he studies me intently through half-closed lids, similar to the fashion in which Cruce often regarded me. "Why would you do that?"

"Do you really think I want to govern you? Aoibheal thrust her power into me in order to neutralize the *Sinsar Dubh*. That was virtually her entire reason for doing it, plus a significant amount of spitefulness. Cruce was there when she did it, demanding she pass the power to him. You think you're angry that you were misled? Aoibheal, whose real name is Zara, by the way, was once human and loved her mortal life and family. She loved her world, and she loved the Unseelie king. She was stolen from that king by Cruce, who raped her, wiped her memory, lied and told her she was Fae then thrust her into the rule of a species that not only wasn't hers but had savaged her repeatedly. She was a bit pissed off, too."

"The significant lesson there is that mortal and Fae don't mix," Ixcythe says sharply.

"Agreed," I reply just as sharply. "And precisely why the walls that once stood between realms served a purpose. But if you wish me to concede that you've been misled and misguided, you must concede there are legitimate grievances on both sides, and both parties have reason to be angry and defensive. From that position, we may find our way to an arrangement where we all prosper."

"There's truth in your words. Sit." Azar waves a hand at the chairs. "This is the discussion we need to have."

I glance at Barrons, who nods, then pull out a chair and drop into it. He remains standing, slightly behind me and to the left, regarding the Fae with a narrowed, intent gaze. "Did you know," I say, "in order to gain the other half of the Song, in order to sing it and heal the planet to which you are tethered, I had to agree to pass the queen's power to Cruce?"

Ixcythe's hands fist, her eyes narrow with fury, and she hisses, "You said you would return it to us one day!"

"I have no intention of passing it to him. There's a loophole in our Compact."

Azar shrugs indolently. "He's dead anyway. The Song killed all the Unseelie."

"Cruce is not only *not* dead, we recently learned he created a new Shadow Court." My doubts about whether they knew he was alive are instantly erased. Both gape, mouths ajar for several moments, then they explode from their chairs and begin roaring, at each other, at me, accusing me of helping the Shadow Court, accusing each other of knowing and working in collusion with Cruce, accusing me of failing to protect the Seelie. I'm surprised they don't fall on each other in their fury. They genuinely don't have the faintest idea how to handle emotion. They lived without it far too long. This species that was once cool and composed and scarcely telegraphed a mere hint of motive now has motive written all over their faces.

I lean back in my chair, folding my arms, waiting until they run out of steam, eying the spread of delicious-looking roasted meats, olives stuffed with garlic and cheeses, an array of seasoned vegetables and crusty breads, three types of delicately sauced fish, the plumpest, ripest fruits I've ever laid eyes on, but most of all—an impossibly tempting cake that has my name written all over it and beckons as insidiously as an Alice in Wonderland potion, flashing the words: EAT ME.

I sigh, mouth watering.

It's seven layers of deep, rich chocolate cake, garnished between each layer with a raspberry compote, and topped with an inch of frothy pink frosting, embellished with delicate curls of dark chocolate and lightly dusted with cacao. I mentally scoop it onto a plate and begin to devour it, bite by decadent chocolate bite, tuning them out.

When finally they lapse into silence, I drag my thoughts from the confection and say, "The Shadow Court is our shared enemy, as you yourself said, responsible for billions of human deaths. And although Cruce's court has not yet attacked, with him as their ruler, I'm certain it won't be long before he attempts to assert dominion over our world." It's what he's always been after. Ultimate rule.

They search my eyes, gauging my sincerity.

"She means it, Ix," Azar says finally.

Ixcythe sighs and slumps heavily into her chair, drops her face into her hands, rubs her eyes in such an uncannily human gesture that I, once again, wonder if human and Fae began existence more alike than not. Finally she lifts her head, wintry eyes glittering with icy crystals of rage and fear. "They will destroy us once we're mortal! You *must* give us the Elixir again. My queen, you can't leave us powerless against them. Is that what you wish? The Shadow Court to endure and prosper while the Light Court goes extinct? Would you choose them over us? If you return our immortality, we will go to war against them. *With* you."

I glance at Barrons, who growls silently, *If you so much as touch that bloody cake, I'll smash this one, too. You will not eat in Faery.*

I nearly snort with laughter, remembering the fiasco of a night when I'd tried to give him a pink-frosted chocolate birthday cake. *I have no intention of eating it. I was just looking at it. Take a seat, Bar-*

rons. They're finally open to discussion. I glance longingly at the cake before sifting it to the far end of the glade. Out of sight, out of mind.

We're going to be here awhile.

———— • • ————

Hours later, the four of us have hammered out an agreement. It's far from complete. We still have significant issues to resolve.

But we've agreed upon enough that I have hope we will eventually find a way to share the Earth for the next five to six hundred years. Talking with them made me realize my surest bet is to figure out how to sing the ancient Song and rebuild the walls between our realms. Then I could seal both Light and Shadow Courts away (and I'd probably have to give the Seelie the Elixir again, because I'm not willing to let Cruce kill them all), and they could deal with each other. I now have a deeper understanding of why the first queen imprisoned the Unseelie. They were rabid, dangerous. I can only hope Cruce created a more rational, less savage court.

Ixcythe and Azar made a number of valid points. So did I. Though, in repayment for what they've done to my father, I'd like to let them die out, I'm not willing to let the Shadow Court be the only one that survives. I have no idea, quite honestly, what I'm willing to do to prevent that. I need downtime to think things through.

"An exchange of tokens is necessary to finalize terms," Azar says.

"What token do you offer?" I say coolly.

Ixcythe says, "I will return your father. You may take him back to the mortal realm. The spell the beast placed upon him holds. He has not worsened."

"He's still dying, though."

"The Elixir will prevent that."

"It's not an option for my father," I say flatly.

Ixcythe is silent a moment then says, "There may be an antidote. I need time to search."

"What do you seek in exchange?"

"Restore my court. They suffer, in fragments, drifting across my kingdom, aware and in agony, as they will continue to suffer until the day their immortality is undone. *Centuries* of suffering."

Inwardly I wince, though I betray nothing. "What about the statues in your labyrinth, Ixcythe? Don't they suffer eternally, too?"

She begins to snarl, catches herself, and says, "The statues are none of your concern. They deserve to be where they are for one transgression or another."

"You mean one mere slight or insult against you or another. I agree to restore *all* the inhabitants of the Winter Kingdom. That is nonnegotiable. Only if you bring my father here right now so I may take him home with me."

"Restore my court first."

"No."

Without another word, Ixcythe vanishes. When she's back, she has my father with her and dumps him roughly to the ground. Again, I refuse to betray emotion, merely scan him to make sure she hasn't injured him in a new way then glance at Barrons, who inclines his head infinitesimally. *He is as well as he last was. My spell still holds.*

Ixcythe pours four glasses of wine and slides two across the table to us. "We are not yet done. We must formally consummate our truce. Otherwise it can be reneged upon."

"How do we formally consummate it?"

She smiles faintly, with a ravenous look at Barrons. "In the old days, we required a public mating to seal it. I'm willing to accept that."

I roll my eyes. "I'm sure you are."

"You do know I could kill you. You would let me so near?" Barrons says, eyes glittering with bloodred sparks, looking ravenous himself but not in a sexual way.

Ixcythe tosses her head, gaze icy and smug. "Not on this world.

Within the Sacred Grove of Creation, no living being can be killed." She glares at me pointedly. "Not even with your spear. It is why we chose to meet here."

I say, "The Sacred Grove of Creation? Elaborate."

"It was once the home of She Who Sang the Song. The one who entrusted the ancient melody to our first queen. We lived here with the Goddess, long ago. The Spyrssidhe were conceived in this grove," Azar replies.

A fascinating piece of Fae history I didn't know, and it goes a long way toward explaining the lovely Spyrssidhe.

"This planet is protected. Nothing can be killed here," Azar continues.

"Then the Light Court could live here and never die," I point out.

"Nothing can be *killed*," Ixcythe repeats scornfully. "You're as bad as Severina. Dying of natural causes does not constitute being killed. We would die here as quickly as on Earth. Come, we must seal our fragile truce."

I arch a brow. "No one is mating with anyone, and I think you know that."

"A toast is an acceptable alternative," Ixcythe proposes and raises her glass. "Provided our oath is formally spoken. We must all repeat the same vow before we drink. It needn't be elaborate or specific, merely something like: to new beginnings; together we will find a way to share the Earth and prosper."

I raise my glass, swirling the ruby liquid in the cut crystal, studying it. Abruptly, a dream of sorts, or more of a waking nightmare that I had while sequestered in the chamber beyond time, crashes into me with the suddenness and savagery of a tidal wave, smothering me in terrifying detail.

I'd met with the enemy, accepted a glass of tainted wine, believing peace possible.

They'd poisoned me with a drop of the Elixir of Life. I'd become as cold and dispassionate as the Fae. I destroyed humanity and trapped all of the Nine but Barrons in a hellish limbo because Barrons somehow ended up as the Unseelie king and had stood facing me, immense sadness in his ancient gaze.

Mac, you've forgotten everything, he said in my nightmare. *Let me take you back.*

But I hadn't forgotten everything, and I'd hated that I'd ever even been born, all too aware that soon I would no longer even hate it. I'd be fully Fae and lost.

Forever.

I wonder now if that "nightmare"—I'd actually had several of them while confined—is more evidence of the queen's much too subtle gift of premonition.

If so, and I'm going to escape this one, it implies—if my fear of my father's impending demise was also a premonition—that his fate, too, can be avoided.

It also implies that Azar and Ixcythe have been lying through their teeth to me the entire time we negotiated.

Perhaps nothing can be killed here. But I could certainly be slipped a drop of the Elixir of Life. That wasn't killing me. That was rendering me immortal.

But, assuming they'd actually found it before I did, why would they try to make me fully immortal? What would it gain them? It didn't make any sense.

Locking gazes with Ixcythe, I tip my goblet sharply to the side and pour the contents to the ground.

She explodes to her feet, screaming, "Stop! Don't waste it! I'll drink it, by D'Anu, just give it to me! Give it to *me!*"

The moment the liquid hits the ground, the grass blackens, thick, noxious smoke rises, and Barrons and I leap from our chairs a split second before the grass bursts into crimson flames.

Ixcythe stares at the ground for a long, frozen moment, then her gaze whips to Azar, her eyes narrowing with fury, face tightening to inhuman proportions, skin on jagged, sharp bones. "Severina tried to *poison* me! If I'd drunk it while we were still at her castle—*I will flay that bitch alive!*" she snarls with incandescent rage.

Barrons manages to collect my father's body before I even notice he's moved.

I grab his hand and we sift out.

37

- • -

I get knocked down

MAC

WE PUT MY FATHER in the same room at Chester's where he and my mom once stayed, during that dangerous chapter of my life in which the corporeal *Sinsar Dubh* stalked me, trying to mow down those I loved.

Now the Fae are doing it again. The onslaught is personal and never ending.

On the second floor of Chester's, down a honeycomb of glass-and-chrome corridors that sport reflective surfaces and create a carnival hall-of-mirrors effect, in a suite of rooms with transparent walls set to opaque, we tuck my father gently into bed. I can't smooth his hair. I can't touch him at all. He looks like he did back in Winter, bloodless, pale, and cold. The spell Barrons wove around him creates an unseen barrier between my hand and his body that hovers several inches above his skin. The only difference is the bone in his arm no longer protrudes through skin. Whatever Barrons did is slowly healing his physical injuries.

I'm grateful for the protection. I hate it.

We stopped, first, before returning to Chester's, amid heated arguing, at the Winter kingdom. *Kindness and cruelty,* I'd argued. *This is my kindness,* I'd told Barrons. *Besides, I can't let them suffer. It's not who I am.*

I nearly drained myself restoring Ixcythe's court, leaving enough power to get us safely back to Chester's but little more. I suspended her subjects, unharmed, frozen in battle. I altered each being in the labyrinth, freed them from whatever hellish torment Ixcythe had frozen them in the midst of, then suspended them before they could finish thanking me and realize I wasn't exactly setting them free. Yet.

I would, one day, return and retrieve the many humans, then release the many prisoners from her frozen river, as well.

Now I slump wearily into a chair next to my father's bed and stare up at Barrons.

"What was the point of trying to give me a drop of the Elixir?"

"Ah, you figured that out. With Fae, it's games within games. Severina must have convinced Ixcythe and Azar that she'd found it, and there was a single drop left, thinking perhaps they'd war with each other for it. Rather than take it themselves, leaving one of them to live longer yet eventually die insane and alone, they unwittingly foiled her plan and chose to slip it to you in hopes of scorching your soul and emotion, turning you into the queen they want you to be so you would somehow procure them a full flask of the Elixir and restore them all."

I murmur, "It might have worked. Had it been the true Elixir."

"You had no intention of drinking it. I could see that."

"I had a . . . premonition . . . while sequestered. It was as if I saw that precise sequence of events unfolding and the horrific future that followed."

"What future did you see?" he asks quietly.

"I destroyed humanity and trapped the Nine in a hellish limbo. Except you. You were the Unseelie king. You despised me yet offered to take me back somehow. You wanted to give me a reset."

He's silent a moment then says, "You didn't drink. And it wasn't the Elixir. Which means it's still out there somewhere."

"Still not an option for my father." I turn my gaze back to Jack Lane, musing that I really need to tidy his room. Dad's accustomed to the meticulous tidiness of my mother, who cleans and dusts and sweeps whenever she's feeling emotional, which is pretty much all the time. There are cobwebs even on the posters of his bed. When I wipe absently at one of them, it greedily attaches to my fingers and clings, sticky and distastefully moist. I scrub it from my skin on the side of the upholstered armchair and say, "When I find it, I'll offer it to him. But I know him, Barrons. He won't take it. And if he considers it, I'll talk him out of it." I lapse into silence then say bitterly, "So, Ixcythe was lying about everything. Even her claim that there might be an antidote to the poison she gave him?"

"Most likely," Barrons concurs grimly. "They'd have spun any lie to get you to drink the glass of wine. I was more concerned they might insist you eat that infernal pink cake they'd sliced."

I glance at him, lips twitching despite the currently miserable state of my existence.

Then he's tugging me up from my chair, slanting his mouth hard, hot, and hungry over mine. I melt into the strength of his body, meeting his hunger with ravenous, desperate need. I have no idea how long we kiss. I gratefully succumb to the heat and lust of the moment. When, at last, we part, I feel restored enough to face what I know I must.

"Have Fade and Kasteo bring my mother to Chester's. Ryodan needs to figure out how to ward this room securely. If he needs more blood, he can have mine. If nothing else, I'll slap crimson runes all over the place."

"They might work. Fae harbor intense revulsion for them, and they did succeed in confining Cruce and Christian."

"It's possible," I concede. "I suspect I'd have to cover the entire room and doubt I could summon that many at the moment. I'm also not certain what havoc they might wreak on the club." There was a door and threshold I'd once sealed with those same runes, when I'd stayed at Darroc's penthouse, determined to get the *Sinsar Dubh* and use it to achieve my own vengeance. I'd passed that building since. It had morphed into a terrifying ramshackle hulk of cavernous, shadowy rooms with pulsing red walls; a true haunted house if ever I'd seen one. "If Ryodan can't secure the room, we may have to try it." I glance back at my father and murmur, "When you release the spell, how quickly will he die?"

"I have no way of knowing. His heart had just begun to stiffen when I placed it."

"Speculate," I say woodenly.

"We have no idea how rapidly the poison progresses. But, applying logic, if such a thing can be applied to these Fae: Ixcythe knew you'd need time to find the Elixir. The question is how much time was she willing to allow you. She'd have to hedge her bets. She wouldn't want him to die before you found it; you'd no longer be motivated. I have no doubt they searched all of Faery for it, but were unable to locate it, which means she knows that either you have it and will require time to be persuaded—and what better persuasion than watching your father slowly and painfully die—or you need time to search more thoroughly than they did. If I were Ixcythe, I'd allow you at least a week or two mortal time, possibly as long as a month. But, Mac, that's assuming she's rational. I'm not convinced she or Azar are."

Valid points, and exactly what I'd concluded. Still, I'd been hoping I missed something or he had one of those brilliant, miraculous answers of his to offer. "Mom's going to insist you remove the spell so she can talk to him. Can you suspend him again after?"

"I can."

I turn away and head for the door. We have a great deal to do before my mother gets here and my world devolves into the waking nightmare of me telling her Dad is dying, and it's because of me.

———— • ◦ • ————

"We need Lyryka," I tell Christian when he sifts into Chester's in response to my text.

Barrons and I are ensconced in a plush seating cozy in the re-decorated version of the Sinatra Club, which is now the Jimmy Durante Club and affords the only subdued atmosphere in the sordid, fascinating place, as well as the best platter of Guinness-battered fish-and-chips I've tasted since I've been in Dublin.

In the far corner, a chanteuse croons that she'll be seeing us in all the old, familiar places, while at the bar, half a dozen humans sit, tossing back shots, staring fixedly at us. They nearly topple from their stools with excitement when Christian sifts in.

They'd been loudly expressing their displeasure at the closing of the Fae nightclub, Elyreum, when Barrons and I arrived.

Now four men and two women stare hungrily, gazes moving from me to Christian to Barrons and back again, and I know it's only a matter of time before they work up the nerve to approach.

"It never changes, does it?" I murmur. "They know the Fae prey on humans; still, they flock like sheep to the slaughter."

"They think they're in love with death. They like to stand next to it, flirt with it," Christian says in a low voice. "Then they realize they're actually facing it, and suddenly Death is the frightening entity it's been all along. But, until that moment, they feel more alive than they ever have. It isn't death that attracts them, it's the rush of cheating it. Problem is, once you gain Death's attention, he rarely looks away. Until he gets what he came for."

I glance at him. His words were delivered without an ounce of bitterness, and with a tinge of regret. He says levelly, "I am what I am, Mac. I've made peace with what I've done. I control it now. I won't kill again unless there's a necessity, meaning an obvious enemy for whom there's no other acceptable fate." He jerks his head toward the bar. "And I will never entertain the attention of such fools."

I realize, a bit miffed, that as queen, I don't have nearly the effect on the patrons at the bar that Christian does. They're far more enamored of his towering darkness and inky wings than my wingless, ethereal Fae countenance. Why didn't I get wings? They're also, I realize, far more enamored with Barrons. What is it with humans and tall, dark, dominant men?

I arch a brow with a wry smile. I can answer that. I'm drawn to them, too. Once, long ago, I found Christian to-die-for attractive. Barrons *is* to die for.

"Where do you want me to bring Lyryka? Surely not here. Those idiots are about to head over to us at any moment."

"Ryodan's out," Barrons says. "Mac's going to finish eating. We'll meet you in his office."

The humans on the stools have finally fortified their nerve after not nearly enough intelligent discussion and too many shots. Puffed up with alcohol-induced courage, they slide from their stools and begin sauntering toward us.

Rolling my eyes, dipping into my greatly diminished reserves of energy, I sift Barrons, myself, plus my platter of fish-and-chips to Ryodan's office.

———— • • ————

"What can you tell me about poisons?" I ask without preamble when Christian sifts in with Lyryka.

Her brows climb her forehead. "Is there someone you wish to poison?"

"The Seelie poisoned my father. I seek an antidote. Do you have any other form you can wear besides mine or Dani's? It's disconcerting to look at myself while talking to you."

She frowns. "I'm trying not to draw my father's attention at the moment. Adopting a different form might. Do you know the name of the poison?"

"Ixcythe wouldn't tell me."

"Oh, *Ixcythe*," Lyryka exclaims, visibly distressed. "She's an unsavory sort, featured in many Light Court tales. A bitter and cruel woman, she's been trying to wrest control of the kingdom of Winter for eons."

"She has it now."

"That's dreadful! She hates humans and most all Fae, too. She was once the lover of Azar, from the Autumn Court. He chose advancement over her, consorting with one of the Summer Court Fae . . . what was her name . . ." She trails off, frowning, "Seraphina?"

"Severina," I correct grimly.

"That's it! The two of them set Ixcythe up, let her take the fall with the queen for their treachery, although I have no idea what they did. She was sentenced to five hundred years, sealed inside a mountain. Not long enough to kill her, but more than enough to make her stark raving mad. When the queen finally released her, Ixcythe spent another hundred years or so, addled, easy prey for any sadistic Fae at court. Eventually, she regained her sanity but was permanently damaged. She never forgave any of them. They say she has a list of enemies and has been sealing them, one by one, into monstrous frozen sculptures in a labyrinth as she grows in power. It was all-out war between the three of them until finally the queen wearied of it and forced them to drink from the Cauldron so she might have some peace."

Good grief, no wonder there was such animosity between them. Ancient love, ancient feuds, all recalled at once. "How do you know this? I heard the Fae aren't big on writing things down."

"The queens always have multiple scribes, some human, some Fae. They keep detailed records of events, perhaps in case a traitor manages to force a cup from the Cauldron on them." She wrinkles her nose. "Which is silly because once they forget, they'll forget they ever made such records. I vastly prefer the human accounts, but if you want the closest to the truth of things, you have to take the stories with a grain of salt, as both sides embellish liberally, offering skewed perspectives."

"Okay, let's get back to Ixcythe and the poison."

"She will never tell you what it is," Lyryka says. "Eternal grudges and permanent punishments are Ixcythe's theme and motif in virtually every story penned about her."

I change the subject. "Hunters. What can you tell me about them?"

"What do you wish to know? And can I just say, I'm *so* grateful you've decided to let me help you," she adds brightly. "I think you'll find me quite an asset, and I'm positively thrilled to be part of the team. I was deeply concerned you wouldn't release me again. Cruce may be my father, but . . ." She trails off and looks away. After a moment, she goes on, "You were right. He has no love for me. He locked me away from the world, and used me while he went on living. He built himself a new court. He made himself a new daughter." Her features harden. "A wiser man would never have released me and allowed me to discover the true nature of reality."

I was just convincingly lied to by two of the Fae and have a difficult time believing Lyryka is any different. I glance at Christian.

"Truth." He looks at Lyryka. "How do you feel about your father?"

Her hands ball into fists. "I despise him."

"Truth. What would you like to see happen to him?"

"I'd like to put *him* in a bottle for a million years," she says in a low voice. "But I wouldn't because I know how awful it is. So, I guess I want to see him in a position where he can never harm anyone again." She's silent a moment then says, "I'm afraid that's only possible if he's dead."

"Truth," Christian says vehemently.

"Hunters," I steer Lyryka back to the topic. "Two of my people are being held in cages in the vacuum of space by Hunters. Hunters can survive in space. Humans and Fae can't. How do we get to them?"

Lyryka's eyes get a far-away, glazed look for several moments. "I can't simply spout everything in the Library, nor do I know if the things I read are true or somewhat embellished. Authors frequently lie to lend their story a more appealing and dramatic flair and, oh, narrators, don't get me started on them! Such *sneaky* bastards. Not even the king himself can hold all the information in the Library, which is why he created it. Often, when my father asked me to find something, it took weeks of searching. I had the place organized to make my quests as expeditious as possible but," she cuts Christian a scathing look, "Death completely disheveled my filing system! Now part of the Library is in Scotland while part is still, I assume, within the White Mansion."

"We have no way of getting to the White Mansion at the moment," I tell her. "Cruce shattered the Silvers."

Lyryka continues, "The king used to ride the most powerful and ancient of Hunters. One known as K'Vruck, whose fiery breath is said to deliver death unto all beings. He's the end of all things, the Omega. Whatever the king is, he can survive in space. The environment doesn't affect him. But he liked to take his consort into the heavens so he could show off his creations. They say K'Vruck had some way of keeping her alive, so she didn't suffocate, freeze, and balloon as humans do."

To Barrons, I say, "We need to find K'Vruck. He could protect both Dani and Shazam in their original forms." His phone was in his hand, and he was already texting Ryodan.

I frown, eying the librarian. There's a thing that's been nagging at me for a while. Not as pressing as other matters, but I sure would like to know. "When the king abdicates power and chooses a successor, does that successor become like the king?"

"I'm not sure what you're asking."

"Will his successor become enormous and . . . weird and . . . half-mad . . . and well, you know, like large enough that existence is surreal in his presence and planets roll around in his wings and he's so huge he has to split himself into many humans in order to communicate with us?"

Lyryka laughs and claps her hands delightedly. "Oh, my, you've met the Unseelie king! Good gracious, that must have been a thrill!"

Hardly how I'd describe it, but I nod gamely because I desperately want to hear her answer.

"It's said the king became the creature he did through neglect, carelessness, and greed. He chose to keep expanding and changing, always hungering for more until he grew beyond manageable proportion. Legend holds he was once vastly different. Not Fae, not mortal, something else entirely. Whoever inherits his power will grow into whatever he or she is as their essential self. Moderation begets stasis for the most part. Greed begets change and excess."

"So if the person who becomes king is not greedy . . ."

"It's plausible they would remain relatively unchanged. In time, they, too, would grow wings but," she glances at Christian, "I suspect, more like Death's."

"Does the queen of the Seelie have wings?"

Her laughter tinkles silvery. "The queen has anything she wants to have. You are in control of your appearance. Summon wings."

"Can I get rid of mine?" Christian asks curiously.

"Oh, good gracious, why would you want to? I quite like them. They're lovely." To me, she says, "All royalty has wings. Even Seelie."

"I've never seen a single winged Seelie prince or princess," I disagree.

"They conceal them."

"Why?"

"They can be cut off," Lyryka says grimly. "In the past, such was done to depose the ruler of a royal house. The royals learned to displace them. Never use them. They don't really need them for anything. They can sift. Removal of their wings vastly lessens their powers."

I snort. No wonder Cruce was so adamant I restore his wings. "Is there a way to summon a Hunter? Specifically, K'Vruck?"

"I don't know. I'd need to search."

"Do you know anything about Hunter law?"

"I believe there's a book somewhere that mentions it, though not in any great detail. The king was the primary narrator where Hunters are concerned, and good gracious, what a jumble of stream of consciousness those volumes are! One moment you're reading a tense, descriptive action scene, the next he's segued into some complex philosophical monologue that, while not quite what I was anticipating would follow, I end up pondering days later. He wasn't interested in laws and such. His motifs, even by his own accounts, were benign neglect and amused nonchalance."

To Christian, I say, "Take her back to your castle and begin searching for a way to locate and summon K'Vruck. That's how we get Dani back."

Lyryka says irritably, "Perhaps you might *ask* me to help you as opposed to telling a man to order me about? I'm standing right here in front of you, after all, and I've been answering your questions fully and truthfully to the best of my ability. I'm being pleasant and helpful, eager to be of use. You might try returning it in kind. It's the whole vinegar and honey thing you mortals wax on about. I'm not averse to being thought of as a fly."

"Lyryka, would you mind searching your books for the information I requested?" I say dryly.

Her smile is radiant. "I'd be *delighted* to provide assistance! Thank you *so* much for asking!"

— • • • —

Hours later, I'm sprawled on the sofa where, previously, I snatched the only forty minutes of sleep I've had, and dreamed of Cruce, Barrons, and the king. I blink and rub my eyes, acknowledging that I'm beyond exhausted. Mom is supposed to be here in a few hours, and this is not how I want to greet her. I want to be rested and fortified or I'm going to burst into tears the moment she walks in.

I haven't had a decent night's sleep in two centuries and an unknown number of days, and I swear those two centuries of not sleeping are catching up with me. I'm not going to be able to keep functioning if I don't curl up somewhere quiet and dark for at least six hours, soon.

After warding my father's room to the full extent of his ability in a tight time frame, Barrons headed out to help Ryodan secure a Hunter, but our skies have been empty of the great beasts for some time now. According to word in the club, the last of the icy black dragons soaring above Dublin vanished roughly six months ago, about the same time Seelie began pulling out of our realm.

I guess we got boring then, what with no planet-threatening wars, evil books, sadistic wanna-be vampires, sociopaths, Lord Masters, and Cruces lurking around.

I frown, thinking, well then, the Hunters should be headed back soon, because every manner of villain is exploding from the woodwork.

Abruptly, my skin sizzles with a faint electrical charge, my pulse quickens, my blood heats, and I know Barrons is standing behind me. Then his hands are on my shoulders, and he says, "You need to sleep."

"I need to stay awake so I can talk to mom when she gets here."

"Which won't be for hours."

"I can't sleep. My mind won't shut up."

"Work on that. I have to go back out. I only returned for tattooing implements to place binding spells on the Hunter's hide."

"You found one!" That's a relief.

"If you won't sleep, at least get some fresh air. Take a walk, stroll the city," he says softly. "Reconnect to the world you love, to Dublin. It fortifies you."

Then he's gone and I'm alone, and suddenly I can't bear being inside Chester's one minute more.

38

I've got you under my skin

CHRISTIAN

OCH, CHRIST, LYRYKA IS bubbling, eyes sparkling as she bustles about the chapel at Draoidheacht, sorting through stacks of books, peeking beneath faded tapestries, peering behind mirrors, rummaging about in chests, murmuring things like "Oh, no, not *you*, silly," and *"There* you are, my dear old friend," and "They asked for *my* help and, by the Goddess, I'm not about to let them down."

As I sprawl atop a haphazard stack of enormous, ancient, cobweb-dusted tomes, chin on a fist, watching her, I realize, much to my consternation, the woman bloody well charms me.

I frown, thinking I'm glad she looks like Mac, because it keeps me from letting her close and serves as a constant reminder that I have no idea what Lyryka really is or what she looks like and, as mercenary as Cruce is, he'd have fucked the Crimson Hag if he thought she might provide him with a useful tool as a result.

I scowl, realizing there are legends about the Hag trying to do just that—create offspring with Unseelie princes, and legends frequently hold a sizable element of truth. Is that why Lyryka doesn't want to show me her true form? Because she's a darker version of the hideous, vicious creature that staked me to the side of a cliff and gutted me over and over, knitting my entrails into the hem of her gown?

Gripped by suspicion, I roar across the length of the chapel. "Are you familiar with the Crimson Hag, the one Dani inadvertently released?"

Bent over, head poked in a steamer trunk that's as wide as a baby grand and half as tall, Lyryka replies absently, "You needn't shout at me, and I'm sorry, but your questions simply must wait until I've procured answers for the queen. Her needs take priority over your curiosities." Then she bolts upright and turns to stare inquisitively at me. "Unless . . . is the Crimson Hag another of the cornucopia of villains by which your small confederacy is currently threatened?" She looks intrigued and enormously invigorated by the thought. "Goodness, *that* would be a fascinating and unexpected plot twist!"

"The Crimson Hag is dead."

"Well, there's a cheery bit of news!" Lyryka exclaims and turns back to the trunk.

"Answer my question."

"What was your question?" she mutters into the trunk.

"Are you familiar with the Crimson Hag?"

She snorts. "Who isn't? She's quite notorious."

That wasn't an answer. Figures. She's hiding something. I snarl, "Was the Crimson Hag your mother?"

Lyryka freezes, bent over, then drops a stack of books she's holding with a thunderous thud, snaps upright and whirls to face me, fists at her hips, eyes flashing fire. "Of *all* the creatures that might be my mother, what on *earth* would possess you to select that monstrous madwoman as a likely candidate? Do I bear some familial resemblance to her in either persona or temperament? Do I strike you as mentally unhinged? Sadistic and revolting? Is my taste in fashion so appalling you believe I secretly pine for a gown of clinging, wet, glistening guts? Do I *look* like the knitting type? I mean, really, *what* is your *problem?*" she snarls right back at me in a heated rush of words.

I open my mouth then shut it again. Then I say tightly, "Nothing. I merely wondered."

She hisses, "Well, try wondering something *nice* about me, not something mean!" and turns back to the trunk. "Like maybe," she mutters into the chest, "how beautiful I might be. Or perhaps how unique and what a lovely person I am on the inside, because I can tell you, aside from being permanently irritated because I'm permanently underestimated and ordered about by those who aren't any smarter than me—and frankly many of whom, and yes, in this specific instance I mean *you*, O Great and Idiotic Death, don't seem to be even remotely *as* smart—that I'm quite the loveliest, kindest person I've ever met."

"You're not a person. And you've only met a handful of people, so it's not as if you have many points of comparison," I counter irritably.

"I haven't met *any* people," she explodes with such vehemence that dust rises in a small cloud from the trunk in which she's conversing. "Strictly speaking. Not even that *sidhe*-seer, Kat, who gave my father his new daughter is entirely human, and as a footnote, append this asterisk to all our future conversations: I was employing the word 'people' in the broadest conceptual sense. Agreed-upon definition of terms is critical for successful communication. And you knew exactly what I meant, you frustrating, pigheaded oaf!" She plucks a book from the trunk and straightens, rapidly fanning the pages. "The Crimson Hag," she growls. "Seriously!" She stops rifling the book and sniffs with dismay. "Oh, no, who dog-eared you, my lovely? You haven't been read in centuries. How did I miss this?" She places the book with great care on a nearby table, murmuring gently, "I've no time for you now, but I promise I'll fix you later."

It occurs to me as I watch her conversing with a book, these tomes, these trunks, these artifacts are her family, her friends, her entire world. Of course she talks to them. They're all she had to talk to. And, I've no doubt, the characters within those books also became like family, friends, her world.

Bloody hell, the woman has gotten under my skin.

She whirls, a delighted expression lighting her face. "You *like* me!"

I surge to my feet, glowering. "It's not polite to go poking about in other's thoughts!"

"Oh, *you* can cry truth or lie on everyone around you, but I'm not allowed to put two and two together in logical fashion? You were worried the Crimson Hag is my mother because you're sitting over there wondering what I really look like, and the only reason you would be wondering that is if you find me intriguing enough that you're becoming curious about my true form. Which tells me you're thinking about giving me sex but not while I look like the queen, and that leads you to wondering if I possess a form you would enjoy giving sex to and, I assure you, you most *definitely* would. I'm magnificent. And all of that," she stabs a finger at me for emphasis, "I determined through the process of simple deduction, concluding you like me. *Goodness*, what a day this is turning out to be. I'm making friends and being found interesting."

Then she thrusts her head right back in the trunk again and begins murmuring to the bloody books, as if I've been dismissed.

I growl, "You skimmed Mac's thoughts and lifted the image of Cruce from her mind."

"That was different," she tells the trunk. "She broadcasts. You don't. You're a closed book, intensely private. The queen is open, like me. Perhaps females are different. I require more experience to refine that thought. Oh," she exclaims, straightening again, cutting me a look of excitement, "this one just might have some of what we're—" She blanches and gasps. Her eyes go vacant, and she stands so completely motionless, it's as if the very life was abruptly sucked out of her.

I devour the space between us in three half-flying strides and grasp her by the shoulders. "Lyryka," I say urgently. "What's wrong?"

There's no response. I shake her gently. Her eyes are eerie, opaque green, turned inward, with no signs of life. "Lyryka." I repeat her name over and over, then begin rubbing my hands briskly up and down her arms as if to restore circulation and thereby life, and reclaim her from wherever she's gone.

Then she's back and staring up at me with a panicked expression. "My father is here. In my bottle. Summoning me."

"Good, I'll shatter that fucking bottle and—"

She shakes her head violently. "No. You mustn't. It will only make things worse and won't harm him. I must go." She gives me an anguished look. "Please tell the queen I'm sorry. I didn't *choose* to abandon her in her hour of need! This is dreadful, she's going to think me unreliable and unhelpful."

"What happens if you refuse his summons?" I demand.

She pales even more. "He's shown me what he will do to me if I disobey him. There's an abyss in some horrid place that has only three colors, black, white, and blue. It's cold and dark and there are monsters in it."

"He will *never* put you there. I'm your protector, remember?"

"You're touching me," Lyryka breathes wonderingly, staring down at my hands on the bare skin of her arms. "It feels *wonderful*."

"You've never been touched?"

She shakes her head, seeming dazed by our contact. "I always wondered how it would feel. It's even more delicious than I imagined." Her eyes widen in alarm. "I have to go! Now. Or he'll come out, and I don't want him to see you. Not yet," she says urgently. "You don't even know what you are, and it's not fair. He never played fair. He lied and concealed and used. I *hate* him." She grabs my head with both hands, pulls it down, presses her lips to my ear, and delivers a frantic rush of words.

Then she's gone.

I stand, stunned and disbelieving for a moment too long.

That's what I am? Holy fucking hell! No wonder Cruce wants me dead! No wonder he wouldn't teach me anything!

By the time I whirl on the bottle to demand the bastard release Lyryka to my care and never dare come near her again or I'll kill him and now we both know I *can*, the bottle is gone.

As is Lyryka.

39

And I'm gone, I'm gone

MAC

I WISH I COULD SAY exactly how long ago I first set foot on the Emerald Isle but, between time lost in Faery, months spent Priya, yet more of it careening illogically by in the White Mansion then sequestered for a few centuries, I have no idea how long ago I arrived.

Whenever it was—that night I checked into the Clarin House, exhausted, starved, and every bit as determined as I was terrified—and pulled aside the worn orange-and-pink curtain and stared out at the luminous, rain-slicked streets, I was prepared to despise the country that had stolen my sister's life.

Instead, I fell in love with it.

My love for the country of my birth has only grown, making me ferociously protective of her.

She will be defended against all marauding forces: black holes and Hoar Frost Kings, psychotic-Unseelie-king-offal and Crimson Hags, Gray Men and Women, Fae and old earth Gods. This land is sacred to me, as are its people.

Barrons was right. I needed to get out, boots on the ground, smell the salt-kissed breeze blowing in off the ocean, hear the lovely, lilting voices of street musicians, watch normal, everyday people, admire the neon-stained, crisp reflections of quaint buildings with brightly painted façades in still, reflective puddles on streets made of cobbled stones. As usual, there's been a recent rain, and dusk is near; the sky an ombre swath of black fading to cobalt then, nearest the horizon, orchid with deep violet undertones, the Fae-kissed light drenching rain-misted windows with a shimmering mauve. It's breathtaking and magical.

Thrusting my hands deep into the pockets of my jacket, I stroll, drinking it in.

At least for ten minutes or so, I do, as the day continues to darken.

That's all the longer I manage to hold my worries at bay, before thoughts of mom and dad ambush me again and, abruptly, I'm walking blind, lost in a bleak inner landscape, picturing my mother's face when I tell her daddy's been poisoned by the Seelie, and I have no antidote.

The tears I've been refusing fill my eyes, and I stumble through the lovely, violet gloaming, head down, unseeing, ducking and swerving to avoid passersby until, abruptly, I find myself alone on a quiet, cobbled lane.

I glance around, absorbing the peace, determined to internalize it and carry it back to Chester's with me.

Townhomes of Gregorian architecture, with gaily painted doors beneath half-moon windows, façades adorned with wrought-iron faux balconies, line both sides of the quaint lane. The moon has risen, full, round, and brilliant, rimmed with amethyst, refracting off wet streets, brightening the night.

Like my parents' house, these townhomes are meticulous but for . . . I narrow my eyes; good grief, there are cobwebs all over the façades.

What is the deal with so many cobwebs lately? One might expect to see hordes of spiders rushing to and fro, given the sheer number of webs on everything.

And that one! Holy hell, that can't be a spiderweb, I think, stunned as I hurry down the street.

It's enormous! From the roof, it drapes in a silken fall nearly to the ground and vanishes around the side of the house.

As I hurry around the corner, I skid to an abrupt halt, a chill kissing my spine.

Stretching from one house on the east side of the street all the way over to another house on the west side of the street, a glistening, silvery spiderweb, bedecked with fat pearls of rain, spans the roadway, some sixty feet in diameter.

I know spiderwebs. I found them fascinating as they sparkled in the early morning sun, shimmering on the exterior of the windows of our sunroom in Ashford, garnished with pearls of dew. This one is an elaborate, standard orb web fashioned of wheel-shaped, concentric outlines with spokes extending from the center and, at the very core of it, unusual geometric designs. It's so enormous it completely blocks passage down the street, unless one is willing to push through the billowy, ropy web, and the mere thought causes an atavistic shudder to ripple across my skin.

I may love spiderwebs, but I'm not fond of their denizens. My brain gets that wolf spiders eat cockroaches, but that doesn't stop my gut from responding with primitive terror when I find one nested in the bed linens in the closet. And don't get me started on the abundance of brown recluses and black widows in the Deep South!

Spiderwebs means *spiders*, and a web of this size means I'm looking for a spider that couldn't possibly have originated on Earth, and I wonder—did Cruce create a caste of spider-Fae?

I nearly smack myself in the forehead as a lightbulb goes off in my head.

Papa Roach was Ryodan's brilliant technique of eavesdropping, infiltrating hard-to-reach places, using creatures that survive masterfully in the smallest of crevices and are capable of swiftly scurrying back through the tiniest of cracks, bearing a full report of all that the nearly indestructible cockroaches saw and heard.

I know Cruce. He's the ultimate plagiarist, copying what others do if it proves successful and putting his own spin on it, which really pisses me off, because it's far more difficult to come up with the original idea than steal someone else's and spruce it up a bit.

But I'd stake my life that, taking a page from Ryodan's book, Cruce created a caste of Fae spiders, and *that's* why the sticky concoctions are everywhere. And those arachnid bastards have been lurking in our corners and cracks, spying on everything we do. That's how Cruce has always managed to stay ten steps ahead of us. The logic of my theory is inescapable. We never had a cobweb problem before. He creates new Unseelie and suddenly we do.

They're even in my bookstore, on the mirror, the cash register, in the elevator. More, in the conference room at Chester's, even in my father's bedroom, on the posters of his bed. I both admire and despise Cruce's cleverness.

I yank out my phone and fire off a furious text to Barrons, detailing what I've discovered along with a photo of the web, urging him to crush every spider he sees and destroy their silken traps.

Then I shove my phone back in my pocket, realizing, miserably, the only way to get rid of them is to roam Dublin tracking down spiders and stabbing them with my spear.

How will I ever get anything done if I have to hunt Unseelie spiders? How many of them did Cruce make? Are they recent arrivals? Are they preying on humans or is that yet to come?

I frown. Will my spear even kill them?

The devious prince of War created *new* Unseelie that *sidhe*-seers can't even detect. Who's to say the Hallows work on them?

Tamping down escalating panic and frustration, wondering how my world got so freaking out of control, I inch cautiously nearer, keeping a sharp eye out for the spider. I have to find the oversize

Fae-arachnid and kill it. Quickly. I can't leave a huge, undoubtedly lethal, venomous spider wandering our streets. From the enormity of the web, it's got to be the size of a small car.

When I'm ten feet away from it, a sudden breeze gusts a delicious scent into my face, and I marvel (and get seriously pissed, because kids are going to *flock* to these bloody things) that Cruce managed to drench the web of his new eavesdropping caste of Unseelie with the precise intoxicating aroma of crispy funnel cakes from the state fair, piping hot off the griddle, and smothered in confectioner's sugar.

Scent is memory, and attending the Georgia State Fair with mom and dad when Alina and I were kids, holding hands, wandering through the carnival-like atmosphere, holds countless comforting we're-a-family-and-deeply-loved memories. The aroma of the delicious confection is an invitation to lean in and inhale deeply.

Which I do.

After all, there's no spider to be seen, and I'm doing reconnaissance, and I'm about to tear down the web anyway. Force the spider to start all over again whenever it comes back, if only to make it waste time building a new web.

I never learn.

Assuming makes an ass out of me.

But some things are so deeply ingrained that we reflexively rely upon them without even realizing we're doing it, because what we're thinking is normal, logical, and true. It's the way the world works.

In the human realm.

Spiderwebs mean your enemy is a spider, right?

Not when you're dealing with the Fae.

The giant web drops with the suddenness of a thunderbolt from the sky and wraps around me with lightning-fast reflexes, cocooning me completely in its steely, inescapable embrace before I even realize what's happening.

No silken ropes here, they sear painfully where they touch my skin and bind as tightly as 550-pound braided fishing line. The web enfolds me, tighter and tighter, trapping my arms at my sides, preventing me from reaching for my spear, which I'm not even entirely certain can kill it.

I sift instantly to Chester's.

Or try.

Some element of Cruce's new creation is neutralizing even that power, keeping me from sifting and, as it continues to constrict, compressing my ribs, it forces the breath to explode from my lungs in a great *whoosh* of air.

Tighter, tighter, crushing me.

Horrified comprehension dawns, in that last instant before I pass out from lack of oxygen, that Cruce didn't create a new caste of Unseelie spiders to spy on us.

Playing on our all-too-human assumptions, baiting his trap with a well-beloved human scent, that wily fuck created a new caste of spider*webs*.

40

·•·

No exit

IXCYTHE

Ixcythe stepped back, regarding her work with satisfaction.

Here, too, in the kingdom of Summer, she'd muted sound, but only beyond the castle walls. The din of battle was getting on her last nerve, reminding her of the savaged, broken Winter Court she'd failed, but more important, it was competing with her ability to thoroughly savor the intoxicating sounds of Severina's blood-curdling screams.

Once, the dim-witted, treacherous princess of Summer had been more powerful than she, but that began to change when the Song was sung, restoring Ixcythe's more ancient magic, undoing the damage done during five hundred hellish years of torture, alone in a cold, dark mountain. Torture she hadn't deserved, as Severina and Azar well knew.

The day the queen finally released her, Ixcythe no longer possessed awareness such a day might come, and she'd stumbled, confused, blinded by the onslaught of long-denied light, back to court, gibbering mad, drooling, less than half corporeal, her magic drained beyond repair. She'd clawed at the insides of a mountain for too long, seeking escape with every ounce of power she possessed, gouging deep, useless chasms in millions of tons of solid rock, even causing minor earthquakes at first.

But not for long. Her power was eroded by isolation as swiftly as morning dew evaporating beneath a desert sun.

She'd never regained it. Full recovery from such a punishment could not be achieved. That was why the queen did it. To weaken those who stood against her, yet keep them present in Faery as eternal reminders to others at court.

But once the ancient melody began restoring them, undoing changes all the way back to the beginning, it had also undone the loss of power she'd suffered and, since she was one hundred seventy-three thousand years older than Severina, her magic was now stronger, a fact she'd been concealing, even from Azar. Who, unfortunately, was older than both she and Severina, which made it a very good thing he wasn't around.

Once, he'd chosen Severina over her, and she would never forgive either of them. Immortal, or condemned to die in five or six centuries, she would spend the rest of whatever time was left to her refining Severina's constant torment, tweaking it to ever-increasing heights of pain.

"But not me?" Azar says quietly behind her.

Ixcythe whirls. "Begone, you fool! This has nothing to do with you. You saw what she tried to do to me. If I'd taken her alleged 'Elixir of Life,' it would have burned me alive on the inside, *forever*. Incessant, inescapable agony. There is no antidote. It cannot be undone. That patch of grass in the Grove will blaze for all eternity, even in her hallowed realm."

She turns back to Severina with a cruel smile. "I'm merely returning the favor, doing to her what she tried to do to me." The Summer princess was bolted to the wall of her own garishly bright ballroom by lances of razor-sharp ice, through her feet, her hands, her gut, her head. Her once-lovely face was an eruption of ragged flesh and bone around a five-inch diameter icy spear. Ixcythe had been careful to drive it through the top of her head only, so her mouth might continue to scream and scream.

Then she'd begun to ice her, bit by bit, every inch of her stripped bare, bleeding flesh, with the cruelest, deepest, most burning ice she was capable of summoning. Working it up her thighs, driving ice-picks deep into her womb, the cheating bitch who seduced Azar! She could listen to the music of Severina's screams forever. Hum along with the divine melody. Add inventive leitmotifs of whimpers and begging to the guttural, flesh-rending cries. Back off a bit, make Severina think the pain might end.

Never.

Slam it back into her again in entirely new ways.

"Once, you painted the world in very different hues," Azar says quietly. "Do you remember what they called you in the Winter kingdom, before I betrayed you, when we were young?"

How could she forget? That was part of the problem, too. Memories. Wed to emotion. Irreparably bound to mortality. She knew who she'd once been, before they'd savaged her, the two she'd loved most. Azar, her lover, and Summer, her dearest friend. She and the golden princess had been fascinated by each other's differences, drawn to their opposite.

Gh'luk-sya drea. Tiny snow blossom, winter's beloved flower.

They'd called her that because she walked the kingdom, painting it beautiful with her growing power, carpeting it with delicate blossoms, tweaking the sky from cool slate to brilliant blue with sun refracting off dazzling drifts of snow. She'd wandered the forests, singing to herself, frosting limbs with delicate, lacy ice, enameling heavy pine boughs with diamond-faceted crystals.

"You killed the snow blossom, Azar. You and Severina did that *together*," she says bitterly.

"I know," he says sadly. "And there is neither excuse nor forgiveness. But, Ix, have you considered what our future might hold?"

"Every possible incarnation of it. And in them all I will torture this bitch forever."

"The queen will never give us the Elixir. She has no intention of using it for her father. She will allow him to die before permitting him to become like us." He's silent a moment then says, "I can't say that I blame her. As time passed, my passion for you dimmed. Power was the only thing that made me feel anymore. I'd tasted everything. I could no longer feel anything but the most violent of sensation. All that was left were games. We became driven by a nagging, unquenchable hunger for something, *anything*. But now, I remember how we once used to be, how I felt about you, us."

When he lapses into another long silence, she wants to clap her hands to her ears, scream at him to stop talking. She doesn't want to hear another word.

Yet she also feels as if she's been waiting to hear words such as these for half an eternity.

He says, "I don't want to lose it again."

She turns on him, disbelieving and horrified. "You would *willingly* remain as we are?"

"No. If possible, I would be immortal again. But not empty as we were. I never loved her, Ix. I wasn't capable of it by then. She was nothing more than a stone on a path I wish I'd never trod. And now, would never tread again."

"Are you asking me to *forgive* you?" she says incredulously.

"I'm merely saying that if the queen doesn't give us the Elixir, and she won't, there are only three of us left. You, me, and Severina. All our subjects are mad. We have no one but each other for the next five to six centuries. Is this how you wish to spend the remainder of your time?"

Her eyes narrow, and she gouges sharpened nails through palms, inhaling sharply. By D'Anu—he's right! What cruel fate would leave her alone at the end with those she despises most?

But yes, yes, and a thousand times yes, spending it like this, torturing Severina until the end, will be her masterwork.

Azar says, "It's rather like that piece penned by a mortal playwright, what was his name?"

"I have no idea," Ix growls. "You always enjoyed the mortal dramas more than I." She preferred the Fae ones, the tragedies in which she dealt out revenge after revenge.

"Jean-Paul Sartre. *Huis Clos.* Three humans trapped in a room forever providing more than enough torment to serve as their eternal damnation. Hell is other people. That's us, Ix. That's all we have now. The three of us. But it could be different."

"Not so long as that bitch lives and breathes!" She jerks her gaze back to Severina.

"Let me spend the next five hundred years making up for those you lost in the mountain."

"You are weak and pathetic, and I despise you!"

Suddenly, he's behind her, closing his hands tightly around her waist. Then, they're elsewhere.

He's sifted her to the Winter Kingdom.

"Get your hands *off* me!" She whirls on him, roaring, with such fury, thunder explodes in the sky, booming and rattling, bones on chains, and a thick, frosty snow begins to fall.

Azar brushes his hand against her hair. "I once told you the snow was a veil of diamonds made by Nature to adorn you, because nothing fashioned by Fae or man could ever hope to compete with the beauty of your hair."

"I said, don't touch me!"

He doesn't listen, merely slips his hands back to her waist and spins her in the opposite direction, facing the courtyard beyond the open gates.

She gasps. Her court has been restored. Each subject is again whole and unharmed, suspended in battle.

They're no longer suffering. Merely frozen in the moment before striking or being struck, no longer in pain.

And, if Azar is right, they will all die precisely the way they are, five or six hundred years from now.

"Did *you* do this?" she breathes. Is he so powerful now? Surely not!

"The queen did."

She opens her mouth, closes it, then finally demands incredulously, "But why would she do such a thing? It makes no sense! What is her game? Explain this to me!" The torment of her court, the lovely wintry subjects within her care, had been eating at her. She'd warred for eons uncounted to gain the right to wear the Winter Crown, provide for and protect her subjects.

And she'd failed them.

"I don't understand," she protests. "I didn't honor our bargain. I gave her nothing. I sought to destroy her soul. I sentenced her father to a slow and hellish death."

Azar replies, "She wasn't willing to allow your subjects to suffer for your actions. A wise decision. Emotion, Ix. The thing we gave up. It's necessary."

"Never. I will find a way to undo what has been done, and restore us all to what we once were. Even if I must do it alone."

"Count me out, then. I won't drink again, even if you find it."

Stunned, Ixcythe turns and stares up at him, searching his gaze, trying to decide if he could possibly be telling the truth, or if this is but another cruel ploy in yet another endless Fae game. The kind she would play forever, if left to her own devices.

"I rage at the loss of my immortality," he tells her. "But I now know the price I paid to gain it. We lost emotion in such slow degrees that we scarcely felt what we were losing. Bit by bit, we numbed, grew more hollow, incapable of being filled. I want two things of life, however much of that remains to me. To feel all emotions again, not merely the shallow impressions we manage to achieve thorough increasingly convoluted machinations. Genuine emotion, no matter how torturous or seemingly unbearable."

"And the second thing you want?" She has no idea why she asked. She hates him and always will.

He brushes a strand of hair from her face, and says softly, "To one day watch the *Gh'luk-sya drea* carpet her kingdom with flowers and etch young limbs with crystalline ice again, singing softly, as she passes beneath their boughs. Then I'll know, Ixcythe, that although you will never forgive me, the damage I did to the snow blossom has been undone."

41

***

There's nothing in the world that feels like coming home

LYRYKA

UPON A HIGH HILL that reminds me of the Hill of Tara, which I've seen in countless books, my father and I stand, staring out over a vast midnight kingdom that sprawls across hill and vale, as far as my eyes can see.

Houses rise and buildings soar, leaping from low rooftop to towering spire, alabaster against a black velvet sky that dazzles with an infinity of stars.

"What do you think of my Shadow Kingdom, Lyryka?" my father asks, smiling at me.

He's been smiling at me ever since I returned to the bottle, answering his implacable summons, leaving Death standing in the chapel, looking properly stupefied by what he just learned. What the prince of Death before him never knew, was never told. Once he checks in the tome to which I directed him, where I secreted away the last bit of information he needs, he'll come into his full powers.

Then we'll see which of the possible contenders the Unseelie king's power decides to choose.

Cruce, who I've been certain is the villain of this piece, is being *nice* to me.

Lavishing me with affection, hooking his arm through mine, even, on occasion, taking my hand. Plying me with food and drink, regaling me with stories and anecdotes that showcase the overbearing certainty of his superior wit and strength. Ebullient and charming, he's shown me wonder after wonder, telling me it's long past time he brought me "home."

Home.

I try to process the word.

Decide if I even want to be here.

Or whether home for me has already been found, in a different sort of place, with different people, in the broadest conceptual sense of the word.

Once Cruce discovers what I've done, what I've told Christian, he won't smile at me anymore.

Will he ban me from his realm?

Will he clash in war with Death?

At least now, it will be a matched battle, two princes at the full heights of their power.

Either way, my father will never forgive me. And, despite the beauty of his kingdom, despite it being a place where, once, I'd have hungered to dwell with such intriguing and fabulous companions as his new Unseelie, I'm not the woman I used to be. My acquaintances will never be welcomed here.

I stand with one foot in two very different worlds.

For hours, or who knows—perhaps we've been here for days, I've seen so many marvelous things I've quite lost track of time—Cruce has whisked me through dazzling streets and lanes of a midnight kingdom he constructed in the caverns beneath the Unseelie king's castle. Yet there's no sense of being underground here. The city is so vast, the ceilings vaulted so far beyond my ability to see, that the faraway sky, hung with planets, three lovely moons, and millions of stars seems as real as any that might grace an actual planet.

"Long ago, I watched the king insert a pocket of reality within a realm. I tunneled down, beneath the old king's castle, and did so here, seeding it, allowing it to grow," he tells me. "Humans and Seelie believed me dead and I kept it that way, buying time to build my court as the kingdom they deserve."

He'd sequestered, he told me, for centuries in the king's laboratory, fashioning hundreds of thousands of dark Fae, countless castes, each more lovely, powerful, and imaginative than the last. He'd left me alone so long because he needed to establish sufficient numbers to serve as an army to protect their world, to war against both Seelie and Man, if necessary, as well as give them time to acclimate to their new life.

"But I could have helped you," I protest. "Why didn't you bring me here long ago?"

He favors me with an affectionate glance that startles and, despite my reservations, which are many, thrills me. I've never been on the receiving end of such looks from him before. "You're always so sweet and willing to help. You *did* help, Lyryka. It was your research into the king's endless collection of chaotic notes and books that provided much of the knowledge I needed, your time searching, your answers that allowed me to perfect my kingdom, and the Unseelie that inhabit my city."

There it is again: *my*. On occasion, he says "our," but most often he uses the singular possessive pronoun.

If his words are true, then this is my kingdom, too. It was my groundwork that built the foundations.

"Where are we to live? Do we have a house?"

He laughs, richly amused. "A mere house for a king? No, Lyryka, I built a castle. Come, I'll show you." He takes my hand.

— • • • —

Hours later, after a sumptuous feast with my father during which I'd stoically refrained from inquiring about my half sister, unwilling to let him know I knew, I sprawl across the bed in the chamber to which he escorted me (and I believe, locked me in; I haven't checked yet but heard a suspicious click, as if he's forgotten I can sift now that I'm free of that infernal bottle) with the curtains billowing in a crisp yet temperate breeze that's the precise degree of perfect.

I place my book aside—one I found tucked on a high shelf in this chamber, filled with grand exploits by the Seelie prince known as V'lane—and stare out the open French doors at the sparkling lights of the city, wondering who is this being that told me I'm free, after an eternity of captivity, yet still forbids me to show my true form and who, despite sharing with me the many wonders of his kingdom, kept *me* unseen, both of us hidden beyond the vision of the many Unseelie we passed?

I'm their king, he told me when pressed, *and if they see me they'll present matters of business, disputes and the like. I want this time to be yours and mine, alone.*

I wanted to argue, protest: but I've been alone for *so* bloody long and I've had to hide who I am for the entirety of it, and it's time for me to be truly, *fully* free!

But, wisely, I held my tongue. Because, despite his seeming warmth, and sharing his splendid world with me, I can't shake the feeling that something's wrong with this abrupt plot-detour into happiness.

Stories don't unfold in such pleasant fashion. The long-suffering heroine, imprisoned by her father, isn't suddenly released to live happily ever after, at his side.

Irritated by my current circumstances, which were once all I might have asked of life—to be in my father's house, sprawled on a bed fit for a princess in a castle fit for a king—I push up, and hurry across the room to check the door.

As I suspected, it's locked.

Snorting, I whirl and hurry through the French doors, onto the balcony, considering reverting to my true form and, with my unique, lovely wings, soaring out over the city beyond.

As if I've tripped some hidden threshold alarm, my father appears beside me on the balcony, smiling down at me, and I have no idea why, but the look in his eyes doesn't match the curve of his lips, and it chills my blood.

"Come. There's one other place I want to show you."

I try to thrust my hands in the pockets of my gown, but he's swift and sure and catches one of mine in his; then we're—

—standing together, on a ledge, thousands of feet up, perched on the side of a great cliff, a bitter wind whipping my hair into a tangle.

It takes me a moment to get my bearings. "Is this where you once lived?" I exclaim, staring everywhere at once, with shock and disbelief. I recognize it from pictures in my books and descriptions. All Unseelie were once confined here.

Again, I'm seeing something I've only read about in books and, although I've quite the imagination, no written words could ever capture the palpable misery, horror, and despair of this place.

"A hellish half-life as it was. I want you to understand me, comprehend why I've done the things I've done. Why I worked so hard to create a superior court, a superior kingdom. I succeeded, did I not, Lyryka?" He startles me by asking, as if he cares what I, or anyone, think. "Did I not?" he repeats vehemently, and I realize it's not that he cares but that, by the Goddess, he wants applause. He wants praise, and I'm being cued to give it.

That was the true purpose of the tour of his kingdom. I was being prodded to gush and exclaim over his many achievements, gaze worshipfully up at him, as he paraded me past creations undertaken to demonstrate his superiority to the king; a test I'm quite certain I failed.

"How long did you live here?" When I shiver, he puts his arm around me, providing warmth with the heat of his wing. In the ancient, brutally cold Unseelie prison, there are cliffs upon cliffs of chilling, killing black ice, jutting up at nauseatingly wrong angles, divided by deep, narrow chasms and ravines. The entrances of thousands of dwellings are chiseled into the cold, unyielding ice and a sickly blue glow emanates from the seemingly bottomless ravine below us, as it belches a sulfuric blue-black fog. An arctic wind sluices down from high above us, biting deep to my core.

I tip back my head. No moon will ever rise here. No stars will ever be glimpsed. No light will ever grace this barren, desolate place. This was the first queen's ultimate cruelty. She created a monstrosity when she might have created any number of wonders, or even taken the time to pass the melody of the ancient Song of Making to a successor.

I'm staggered she created such a horror. The air itself hangs heavy and bitterly cold, saturated with the residue of pain, hunger, and bottomless need of those who once dwelled within their icy abodes, with undercurrents of the crushing truth that there is no satisfaction to be found, ever, in this place.

Futility is the oxygen here. There is nothing else in the air, if even air exists.

And I realize the Unseelie prison, despite my half-Unseelie side, is my antithesis. It's anti-life for one like me. I can feel it preying on the energy of the Light Court deep inside me, licking with rapacious tongue at my flesh and bones, trying to devour me, and I know, instinctively, I wouldn't survive long here. Shivering, I wonder why he really brought me to this place. Am I to gasp with horror, commiserate, and laud him for the many grand things he's achieved? Is more applause being cued?

Frowning, I wonder why, on a gut level, the prison seems somehow familiar, beyond what I read in books. As if I once tasted this despair and it seared itself into my memory, driving me to embrace the light side of myself with abandon.

Although half Unseelie, I'm light and bright and, despite my innate irritability, happy to be alive and experience yet another day, read one more book, dream one more dream, perhaps even—as of late—make one more new acquaintance. I've been especially happy, working with the small confederacy that requested my aid and who will never simply *take* everything from me, giving nothing in return before locking me away again.

Death is my protector.

The queen herself is light and bright and strong and has spoken of freeing me.

"Three quarters of a million years," Cruce murmurs. "That's how long I suffered this hell. But come. I have more to show you."

I could feel sorry for him. He wants me to. But I don't. Because what he just admitted to me was that, although all the other Unseelie were trapped here, he could leave. He has always been able to leave and live a life even when no one else could. I know he left. I know how old I am. He went to Seelie and seduced someone there while all other Unseelie were trapped in this hell.

And I was born. My mother was someone from the Light Court.

"The princess of Summer," he murmurs then.

I look at him sharply. Can he read my thoughts?

"You think them absurdly loud, Lyryka. You always have. You bear everything on your face. Every emotion, even the truth of your heritage."

I'm the daughter of Summer and War. No wonder I'm a disgruntled, perky sunbeam. I wonder, why did he *really* bring me here?

"I brought you here because I want you to understand how much I overcame. Given whence I sprang, I might have become a monster, like him."

Oh, father, I think, but hastily plunge this thought deep into a trunk, *how can you be so deluded?*

"But I'm not a monster. I created a court of beautiful things. Only a beautiful being can do such a thing. I will see my children raised to the light, walking openly in the world. I will see the Seelie bow to them, genuflect, and beg for their lives. And I will watch the

Light Court *die*, one by one until the only court that remains in this world is the only one of worth. And we will take all of Faery, my children and I."

"Does that include me?"

He favors me with another of those odd, remote smiles. "Ah, Lyryka, you will always be part of me and my plans."

That was an uncomfortable and not at all reassuring reply. How? Does he intend to extract my teeth, perhaps wear them on a string about his neck after he's disposed of me in some horrid fashion?

I shiver. I need to get out of here. Perhaps I'm being melodramatic—these icy, dark cliffs persistently and urgently invite one to plunge down any number of slippery slopes of paranoia—but I feel as if some terrible plan of my father's is about to come to fruition.

I do a foolish thing then. I try to sift back to the world of my friends.

It's beyond foolish, springing purely from instinct, not thought at all, for I know well the rules of this place. Only two of whom I'm aware are capable of sifting in, but no one can sift out of the Unseelie prison. Were it possible, all of the higher castes would have left. I have no idea how my father was able to escape on those occasions he did, but I know it wasn't sifting. Perhaps a Silver secreted away somewhere only he knew?

Then he's laughing and shaking his head at me as if I'm such a fool, and he grabs me and swings me up in his arms, and something bites into my hip with the sting of a bee, and his wings are opening, powerfully beating air, and abruptly we're flying, soaring over ridge and ravine; for miles and miles he flaps his great wings, carrying me in his arms.

Then we burst through a sort of façade of a scene, and he settles us on a ridge adorned with hundreds of square, raised platforms of blue-black ice that jut above the ground, and the vision makes me think, with a convulsive shudder, of the sight of a human graveyard, although there are no markers adorning the cairns.

In all the books in the Library, I've never once stumbled across mention of such a place within the prison.

"I keep it concealed. It *is* a graveyard. Of Fae," he says. "My enemies." He shrugs. "A few friends that got in my way. You may resume your true form now, Lyryka." He settles me on my feet.

I'm free to change at last, to be what I really am, and I'm horrified to discover, standing precisely as he deposited me without moving so much as an inch, it's too late.

I can't move. At all.

What has he done to me? *How* has he done it?

The sting at my hip—did my father poison me?

He sighs. "I forgot too much of that potion has an immobilizing effect. I may have overdone it, but it was to help you sleep, make this less disturbing for you. I can't ensure that you will slumber until the end because it would require additional doses and, as you can see—or rather can't see, because you can't turn your head now—you'll be beyond my reach, and I won't be returning. This is goodbye, my dear. The bright side is, as only half of you is Light Court, you should last only half as long as your mother. Perhaps a month, mortal time. It won't be long, Lyryka. Blink of an eye to ones such as we." He scoops me up, a mute, wooden doll, and carries me to one of the platforms. He places my stiff body on the slab of ice and begins to murmur the words of a spell.

I feel my body begin to change, my glamour dropping away, as he strips Mac's face and body from mine, to reveal my true form.

He stares down at me when it's done, and I see all too plainly what he thinks when he looks at me. Disappointment and contempt glitter in his starry eyes.

Because of what I look like. And only that.

I weep, but no tears fall. Not because of what he thinks of me, but because I'm denied the simple pleasure of flexing my magnificent wings one last time. Or even feeling them at all.

I'm in a waking stasis for now and, according to him, will soon sleep.

After that, if I understand him correctly, I will die. Awake, at the end.

Why? I think as loudly as possible.

"You're a half-blood," he says. "This is not what I wanted. You were to be the first of my secret army hidden with the Light Court but, from the day you were born, you were a walking, incessantly needy, crying, hungry liability. Your mother lies in the coffin to your left. I brought you with us the day I buried her, long ago. I nearly interred you the same day but relented. *I* granted you a life, Lyryka. *I* fathered you. *I* permitted you to live. When you think of me, remember that. I might have drowned you at birth, an unwanted mongrel. When the princess saw what she'd been carrying inside her, ah, my ugly, unwanted Lyryka, she screamed and screamed, denouncing you, threatening to expose me. I'd glamoured myself as her consort, you see. She believed I was Seelie. She had no idea Unseelie existed. I thought you would merely be a darker version of Light Court Fae, but you came out so utterly wrong, you betrayed the existence of our court. At the very moment of your birth, you betrayed *me*."

But they're long dead now. Yet you never released me. Why?

"Half-blood," he says with a shrug, eyes narrowing with distaste "The universe marked you a monstrosity. It knew, too, that you should never have been born. You will never be accepted. There is no place for you. No Fae could look at you without seeing their enemy court. You don't belong anywhere. I protected you from their scorn and savagery. I promised myself the day I buried your mother that I would grant you two kindnesses. I would give you a life, and a fine one, such as it was with your books. Then I would bring you home when it was time. It's time. You don't fit in this new world of mine. This is where you belong, beside your mother. You can rest at last."

But I haven't lived *yet!* I scream.

He doesn't care. He's done with me now, he's had his say, and he has a life to get back to, a new daughter who's pretty and looks like him, and a new court, and new plans, and I'm sinking into the ice as he presses me down and down, and I can neither fight nor scream nor rage nor kill him as I so deeply hunger to do.

Who is *he* to decide I don't fit or belong? Who is he to tell me no one will ever accept me? Who is he to label me wrong based solely on my *appearance*, of all things, as if that's what matters?

Who is he to decide whether I live or die?

All beings that live, no matter their form, have the right to live well and free.

I feel the ice closing around me and I can't breathe (although technically I don't need to), and it feels like suffocating anyway, just like drowning in Guinness—oh, by the Goddess, what I wouldn't *give* to be back drowning in Guinness inside a smelly bottle, about to seek Death's bed again!—feels like drowning, then Cruce's face is far away, beyond the smothering blue-black ice, and he's placing wards atop my tomb, and walking the circumference of my sepulchre, chanting and placing more wards.

And he's killing me, I know, because, already, I feel a hungry darkness lapping at my essence, draining my light and energy, and all I can think is, but he's wrong.

He's so very, very wrong.

I'm not ugly.

I'm not monstrous.

I'm good and kind, I'm passionate about creating, never destroying, I take excellent care of books, I don't dog-ear pages, I like to help others achieve their goals and attain success, and I love. And oh, how *delightfully* well I might have loved Death! (While also teaching him to label things properly.)

In sum, I am magnificent.

I think no more then, for despite my frantic attempts at resistance, sleep weights my lids closed with heavy coins of slumber for what may well be the last time.

42

Good morning, Worm, your honor

DANI

TELEPATHY IS HOW THE brilliant, space-faring beings known as the Hunters communicate and how they intend to conduct our trial.

I stare beyond the bars of my cage, at an even dozen of the icy black dragons, remembering the first time I saw one sailing, leathery wings flapping, churning ice, high above the streets of Dublin.

It feels like so long ago; I was so bloody young. On fire with life, irritated by everyone and at everything for not being as vibrantly alive and rambunctious as me, as I tried on one personality after the next, deciding who I wanted to be.

Those were some of the *best* days. I love the kid I was. Especially now that I have a clearer perspective on how I might have turned out. I kept alive what mattered most in me, didn't let the erosions turn into landslides.

The Hunters, with their massive satyr-like heads, long, curved horns, cloven hooves, and forked tongues, with their great inky black hides and wings and long, scaled tails, look Satanic, although they churn ice in their wake, not flames of hellfire. Regardless, I find them beautiful and don't want to stop being one. Nor do I want Shazam to never again get to be the entity known as Y'rill. I want a reduced sentence so we can remain the dual creatures we are. They could "clip our wings," so to speak, for a few decades, limit our powers. I'd agree to that.

Our jury of a dozen hang in space, effortlessly floating, without moving so much as a wingtip (bugger, I need to figure out how to do that—jealousy is me) arranged at even intervals beyond our cages.

These are the creatures that tend the great threads of the cosmos, traveling through space and time, occasionally tying together lives and events, watching epic events unfold. Being curious adventurers, whenever they feel the ripples of significant events converging in a single spot in some remote corner of the universe, they journey to the planet suffering birth pangs to watch the changes unfold. Just as they were once drawn to Earth, not long ago, when the walls between Fae and Man began to come down.

There are different castes of Hunters, Y'rill told me. At the bottom of their hierarchy is the caste the Unseelie king created in his laboratory: the V'Kan, who became bounty hunters of *sidhe*-seers. Because the Hunters were having difficulty birthing children, they allowed the king to use their essence in his quest to create life, hoping, in such fashion, they would birth more young.

According to Y'rill, the Hunters were offended by what the king produced, and the V'Kan are outcastes. If foolish enough to join their brethren in the skies, they are instantly sifted elsewhere (and never anyplace pleasant). For repeat offenses, they are destroyed. The true Hunters want nothing to do with the mercenary caste spawned by the king.

Still, they like the king. Y'rill says, a long time ago, he did them an enormous favor, incurring the debt of a boon, which he's never collected. I find that thought deeply concerning. Hunters can manipulate time, and I only hope the king doesn't one day decide he wants a complete reset. Mac says she owes him a boon, too. Again, concerning.

The Hunters want more children. But the strictness and illogic of their rules, coupled with the complexity of the birthing process, guarantees a disappointing outcome.

Back when I began turning black and could suddenly fling deadly lightning bolts with my hands, I had no idea what was happening to me, and I'm a woman accustomed to strangeness. I can't imagine how the average human might deal with the disturbing transition.

I could have rejected the changes at any time. Y'rill told me if I'd not been fully committed to embracing the transformation, if deep down I'd not *hungered* for it, it would have swiftly reversed, leaving me no explanation for those days parts of me blackened and I temporarily possessed a new superpower. I would never have known a great Hunter had chosen me to be her child. I would never have become the space-exploring dragon I am.

You will speak only when spoken to, explodes in my head, and I clap my hands to my ears, snarling, "Volume!" Bloody hell, they're louder than Christian in a pissy mood. We're not off to a good start. Already I'm bristling. Speak when I'm spoken to, my ass. "I'd like to see the letter of the law," I demand.

What part of "speak only when spoken to" did you fail to understand?

"Every bloody syllable," I reply flatly. "You've been torturing us, caged us, *starved* us, left us in the darkness, accused of crimes you've not even bothered to address, and you're supposed to be so bloody highly evolved that one has every reason to expect—"

Silence!

"—at least something to eat in their cage, even if it's only a thin gruel of virtually inedible protein-based food. And I can't hear Shazam. I have a right to hear what he says. Let me hear him."

SILENCE!

My ears ring, and I'm suddenly nauseated. "I'll keep my mouth shut if you let me hear Shazam when he speaks." I'm desperate to be able to talk to him, console him. Being trapped in a cage, watching as he weeps, is killing me. I hunger to comfort him, reassure him.

Fiery snorts echo inside my head. Many thoughts broadcast at once: *She's a difficult one. Why would Y'rill choose* her? *Perhaps it's not Y'rill's fault but the fault of that unmanageable one. Y'rill was a rule-follower until* she *came along.* Finished by the stern admonishment: *Y'rill will be held accountable for her actions. They were hers alone. Hunters are not influenced by others.*

"Bull-crikey. Everyone is influenced by others, if they love them," I growl. "The only thing Y'rill is guilty of is loving me. That's the only reason she did any of the things she did. Speaking of, where are your laws? I demand the opportunity to study and prepare our defense."

Suddenly there's sound as if they've connected our cages to a vast intercom system, and Shazam is sobbing violently. "Yi-yi, my Yi-yi, can you ever forgive me?"

"There's nothing to forgive, Shazam. I wouldn't undo a moment of our time together," I say fervently. "I see you, Yi-yi."

You will not address each other, only the court. If you violate that rule again, we will not permit you to hear what Y'rill says.

"But that's just the problem," I pounce instantly. I was ready for this, had my argument prepared. "You accuse Y'rill yet put Shazam on trial. Shazam didn't make the choices you intend to punish. Y'rill did. Therefore Y'rill should be the one speaking."

Silence for a suspended moment, then a burst of thoughts I can't make out followed by deafening silence as they terminate telepathic communication with me.

Bouncing from foot to furious foot, ignoring the borderline migraine I've got from starvation, excruciatingly aware I have precious little energy to spare, I snarl, "You can't just shut me out. Trials don't work that way. I have the right to be privy to the detailed thinking behind your decisions. Even humans allow that, and you're supposedly vastly superior. Heavy emphasis on the 'supposedly.'"

Twelve pair of fiery eyes swivel my way.

Shazam is no longer permitted to be Hunter.

"I know that's what you've decided. I'm saying it's wrong. Shazam is not a Hunter. He's a small being that doesn't possess the wisdom and intelligence of Y'rill. He can't express himself as clearly as she. It wasn't Shazam that committed the crimes of which he's accused. It was Y'rill. You're trying the wrong person. Y'rill must have the opportunity to speak on her own behalf."

One by one, the Hunters vanish, I suppose to reconvene elsewhere and discuss the objection I raised. I take their adjournment as a hopeful sign. And I hope also, when they return, they'll bring me the letter of their law and allow me time to pore over it.

"Shazam?" I say just as hopefully. There's no reply. They've disconnected us from each other again.

Sighing, I turn to gaze across space at him, and my heart sinks. Furry paws tipped with black talons wrap tightly around the bars against which he's slumped, sobbing.

I can't help but see myself, when I was young, in my own cage. How many nights I felt the same, small and alone, aching for comfort. I understand his pain, loneliness, and fears. Shaz and me, we're perfect together. I'm not losing him.

Abruptly, my cage goes dark, and I can no longer see beyond it.

Sighing, I slump to the floor, hear a clatter, and grope about frantically in the darkness, trying to find whatever I jostled.

I discover it, by plunging a hand into something cold and wet. "Oh, bloody hell, it's about time," I mutter. I don't even care what's in the metal bowl they deposited in my cage when they turned out the lights. It's a grain of some kind, swimming in a thin liquid. Holy Not-a-Happy Meal, Batman, I think irritably, if I'd known they were taking orders, I would have suggested a burger and fries.

I eat greedily, using my fingers to shove the messy stuff into my mouth, pausing to slurp sips between gulps, hoping they fed Shazam, too.

If not, that cruelty will also be addressed when they return.

43

Behold, I have become Death

CHRISTIAN

YOU ARE THE END of all Fae, Lyryka whispered urgently in my ear before vanishing, *the Unseelie king's version of the Seelie queen's* Far Dorocha, *driver of her Death Coach. You can kill them. Death was created as the king's private weapon. Only the king and Cruce knew what the prince was, and they never told him, never gave him the spell to attain his full power. Check the Boora Boora books. You'll find what you need there.*

I sit before a pile of those very books, which I've not yet opened because the moment I do, words and sentences will commence a determined, hostile march from between the pages. For whatever reason, the sentences in the Boora Boora books don't like being confined to the page; perhaps they think their story sucks and seek the opportunity to write their own, a new one in which events are more momentous and interesting. I've read a few books in my time that certainly could have used a bit of help, a few of which needed to be rewritten entirely.

Dani cracked these books open, long ago, in the king's True Library, the day she released the Crimson Hag. I'd been hovering near the high shelves, drawn for some unfathomable reason to peruse those tomes, listening as she snickered below. Her snickers turned to curses as she tried frantically to stuff sentences back into the books, and they stung her with the viciousness of fire ants, incensed at being mangled and manhandled.

The Boora Boora books come from a world that bears the same name, where nothing is what it seems. Rather like Earth, lately, and I wonder if, in time, the Song of Making might not awaken our stories, bringing all the characters that have ever been written to life. Bloody hell, I hope not. We've already got enough freakish characters on the prowl.

I take a deep breath and reach for the first volume, bracing myself, cursing Lyryka's sense of humor. No doubt she tucked the information I needed between these pages to mess with me. I smile faintly. She knew all along what I was. And it didn't diminish one defiant, perky, irritable ounce of her personality.

Assuming the spell works, I'll soon be as lethal as Mac's spear, as deadly as Dani's sword.

And, if it works, Lyryka will have given us a third weapon to use against the Fae, against her own father, which speaks volumes to me.

I eye the pile of books—seven in all—with irritation, fair certain, should I commence my search at the top of the pile, what I seek will invariably be at the bottom of the stack, and vice versa, so I remove the top three books, place them aside, and open the fourth.

I slam it closed violently, but not fast enough. A tangle of trapped sentences dangles from between the covers, twisting, turning, straining, and hissing at me.

Christ, they're fast and furious little fucks.

I glare at the closed book with the explosion of bristling sentences and shrug. I've got a shattered mirror somewhere in my keep, from which I've no doubt something dreadful has escaped, and I'll probably break another bottle soon. My castle is already a shambolic affair. How much more harm can seven books of marauding sentences do to my life, scurrying about my floors?

I should know better than to think questions like that, inviting the universe to answer. It's always listening, snickering behind a cosmic hand.

Resolved, I open the fourth book again, but this time I swiftly turn it upside down and shake the book vigorously, dumping the story onto the floor. Words spill in a snarl of sentences that writhe on the flagstones but quickly manage to extricate themselves from one another and dash off, speedy as snakes, for the far corners of my chapel, where they vanish into cracks in the stone.

And there, on the floor, where, seconds ago, a complete story was jumbled about, lies a folded piece of parchment with my name on it.

I snort, amused.

And, och, bloody hell, charmed.

I may be violently horny and frustrated as a celibate priest. Still, I'm charmed.

Christ, I wish I knew what she looked like.

Lyryka drew a tiny heart to dot the "i" in my name.

I unfold the parchment, expecting to discover the written words of a spell, but that's not what happens, and I understand, belatedly, why the spell was in the Boora Boora books.

The moment I open the parchment, words fly from the page.

Literally. *Fly*.

One moment the sentences are there on the paper, the next they're wrapping around my throat, nipping with sharp, pointy letters, puncturing holes in my skin, and burrowing into my flesh.

I surge to my feet, swatting at the damned sentences, but it's too late, they're inside me, and my mind whirls frantically, as I hope to hell my lie-detecting abilities are worth their salt and Lyryka isn't some kind of—

Ow!

While swatting at my neck, I just conked myself in the head with something, and I'm stunned to realize I'm holding an object that wasn't in my hand before.

It appeared out of nowhere, manifesting in my grip.

A sense of wholeness settles over me, as if something was missing, as if I knew all along my transformation to prince was incomplete, but had no idea what I lacked.

What I now hold in my hand was precisely what I lacked.

I imagine the original prince of Death spent his entire existence feeling, in similar fashion, vaguely unfinished, diminished. I wonder if that's why I had such difficulty learning to control my power.

My hand is fisted around the shaft of a reaper's scythe fashioned of antiqued, blackened silver, sporting a long, wickedly curved obsidian blade. It's as tall as I am, with eight lethal spikes around the hilt, at the point of ascension, where the shaft curves into blade. The shaft itself is the perfect thickness to grasp with my hand, its surface embedded with glowing, icy blue-black runes. It feels *good* in my hand. It feels alive, as much a living part of me as my wings.

I turn to glance in the mirror that leans against the wall and, as I do, I sense the ancient, sentient power of the Unseelie king.

Behind me, it nearly drapes my shoulders in a great, inky cloak, and I go motionless, as if I might somehow become invisible to it.

It oozes over my skin, smoky and dark. I hold my breath as it pokes and prods at me, as if taking my measure, and I will silently, *No, no, no, not me. I don't want you. I'm a Highlander, a Keltar druid and the prince of Death, and that's quite enough for me so please just go away and pick someone else.* Anyone *else. Except Cruce,* I append hastily and vehemently. *Please. Just not me.*

Abruptly, the king's power vanishes.

"Oh, bloody hell, thank you," I explode, punching the air with a fist.

I get to live another day just as I am and, if I have my way, I will *never* become the Unseelie king.

Spreading my wings, I raise the scythe at my reflection in a sort of dark toast to the future and smile.

Being the end of all Fae, specifically Cruce, is quite enough for me.

44

• • •

It's three o'clock in the morning
Baby I just can't treat you right

MAC
___

I STAND ON A BALCONY, beyond a pair of glass French doors, staring out at the dark city beyond, holding a book crammed with the exploits of the Seelie prince V'lane, just a little light reading for a narcissistic Unseelie prince. He's probably stocked his entire castle with volumes attesting to the numerous feats and greatness of his alter ego.

I lost consciousness when his web closed around me and woke to find myself in a bedchamber, in a castle high on a hill, that looks down over a city of night. My door is locked and, although there's no longer a hint of cobweb on my skin, I still can't sift. I can't do anything, not even manifest a crimson rune. I don't know how he's done it, but Cruce has stolen my powers.

I searched every inch of the bedchamber, looking for my cellphone or spear, anything that I could use as a weapon, while keeping an eye out for wards or runes that I might try to break.

Not only did I find no hint of weapon or ward, I'm unable to summon a single object. My queenly powers appear to have been stripped away. According to the king, that's not possible, but while I was unconscious, it seems Cruce found a way to do it.

God knows if there's a loophole, he finds and exploits it.

Further adding to my concerns, inside the cover of the leather volume I'm holding, Lyryka penned a note.

I think my father plans to kill me by interring me in the Unseelie prison. I have the worst feeling of déjà vu.

Sighing heavily, I try not to admire the view beyond the balcony, but it's difficult because Cruce replicated Dublin in his midnight kingdom, wherever we are. I know we're underground. I hate being underground and can feel tons of earth pressing down on me.

Though this is a city of night, the streets glow with the soft amber of gas streetlamps, identical to those in Dublin above. The windows of the houses and pubs are brightly lit, music spills from open doors, and the colors of the neon signs reflecting in puddles are the most beautiful, ethereal Fae hues I've ever seen.

It's a Dublin evening on steroids, lovelier than what lies above. From my high vantage, I can see Trinity College and the Guinness Storehouse, the Gate Theatre, the sprawl of the Temple Bar District, Dublin Castle, and Kilmainham Gaol, Ha'penny Bridge, and St. Stephen's Green.

Above, stars glitter like diamonds cast on a cloak of black velvet, and the sky is hung with the fiery lanterns of planets, three moons, and kissed with the kaleidoscopic stain of distant nebulae.

I can't fault his artistry.

Cruce likes beautiful things.

Mentally, I tally my problems: my father is dying and my mother is undoubtedly at Chester's by now; Dani is being held prisoner in a cage in space with Shazam; the Seelie court is raging out of control, I have no idea where the Elixir of Life is, or any of my other (ex?) queenly possessions; Rae and Sean are being held somewhere by the same monster currently holding me; Lyryka may, at this very moment, be dying in the Unseelie prison (entombed because I don't believe Cruce can use the spear, given it's a Seelie hallow and he's not king yet—I hope—and only the queen and kings can touch all the hallows) and I'm staring out at an entire kingdom of new Unseelie that *sidhe*-seers can't sense.

And I seem to have lost my powers.

And there are Unseelie spiderwebs all over our world.

The past few days were a blur of frantic discoveries, each more daunting than the last. Cruce, and the Seelie, pummeled me with one attack after the next the instant I left my chamber.

Cruce excels at sowing chaos, to gaslight and confuse. I now suspect he released Lyryka primarily to distract us. I wonder if he somehow sowed discord at the Seelie courts, inducing their battles. I wouldn't put it past him. With his spiderwebs, he always knew what we were doing. I wonder if he steered my mother into an IFP. I wonder, too, if he pilfered the queen's possessions, stole the Elixir so the Seelie couldn't drink again, perhaps tinkered with the Cauldron to keep them incapacitated by memories. I put nothing past him.

I sink inward, trying to access power, any power.

I'm relieved to find the great golden vault of the True Magic still stands within me. Unfortunately, I can't access it. He couldn't take it, but he managed to neutralize it somehow, seal it tightly away from me.

We were right. He cloistered himself in a chamber beyond time, where he spent centuries building his court and kingdom, putting his plans into motion.

And I realize Cruce knew, when he made me kiss him and convince him I might have loved him in another time and place, that giving me his half of the Song would cost him nothing, because he knew there were chambers beyond time in which he would be safe.

He always planned to give me his half of the Song. He just wanted to make me stroke his ego and work for it.

But why am I here? Does he plan to kill me, too?

The moment I think it, I know he doesn't.

He's fixated on me in the same way the king fixated on the concubine, except the king genuinely loved his concubine. Cruce is incapable of loving.

Still, therein lies power.

He thinks he loves me.

In this chamber void of useful objects, his delusion is my only weapon.

"MacKayla." Cruce is behind me then. Power rolls off him in dark, coursing waves, and I almost gasp but stifle it, abruptly certain the king's power is going to choose him. How could it not? I feel the stuff of which he's made, and it's staggering. Old court Unseelie, he can still be detected by my *sidhe*-seer power and, oh, God, how his magic has grown.

I half expect to turn and find the mad king regarding me, but when I spin, tipping my head back to meet his gaze, he's not yet the king.

Still, his eyes are starry and strange, and he seems vast and mysterious and oh, so damned strong.

If he gets the king's power, we're doomed.

"Cruce," I reply.

"What do you think of my kingdom?"

I turn to stare back out over the city. "It's breathtaking," I admit. "The Unseelie I've seen in the streets are beyond compare. You didn't create a single thing that isn't lovely. What powers did you give them?"

He laughs, pleased with my reply, and the interest I'm taking in his new court, and thereby him. "I bequeathed my children elemental powers similar to the Light Court, connected not to the Seasons, but facets of Nature in all her grandeur. You recently met my *Damhan-allaidh*. Clever and stunning, are they not? You should see how they move. Like silken ghosts in the night, they weave the most marvelous designs where they choose to dwell. Unlike the last Shadow Court, my children are not destroyers, but creators."

"I'd like to meet each of your splendid castes." And I would. Because when I get out of here alive, and Cruce is dead, these Fae, too, will be mine as queen to rule.

"In time. Everything for you, in time, MacKayla."

I turn again, meeting his gaze levelly. I am immune to *Sidhba-jai;* still, Cruce's sexuality is blatant, carnal, and electrifying. Not Jericho Barrons quality, yet immense and impossible not to feel. He's a prince at the full height of his power. How am I to kill him? My fingers itch for my spear. Old court, he would die were I able to stab him, regardless of the drastic increase in his strength and power. Should he become king, however, I'm not so sure it would work. I don't believe the king can be killed by anything. Long ago, Cruce glamoured my spear to keep me from knowing I had it. If that's what he's doing to me now, his glamour is beyond my ability to penetrate. I think of Barrons, a walking Fae-killer. He's the weapon I need.

"You will forget him," Cruce says with such unequivocal certainty that I shiver. Abruptly, I recall another of those waking nightmares I had while confined in my chamber. I think I suppressed it because it was so hellishly wrong.

I was trapped in a dream I believed was reality, and in that dream, I loved Cruce, was his willing consort and co-ruler but no longer the queen. We'd destroyed the Earth, imprisoning the Nine in limbo forever, where they were continually reborn only to die in the instant of rebirth, eternally aware of that single moment of life to death and back again.

We exterminated the Light Court, long before they would have died out, with inventive cruelty, as he'd meted out yet more vengeance for his countless eternal grudges.

We'd rebirthed my sister and her lover, Darroc. The four of us ruled the midnight kingdom.

But Barrons still existed somewhere far away, and was roaring at me, trying to wake me from my nightmare. Insisting none of it was true.

I narrow my eyes, wondering: Am I awake?

Or still cocooned in a silken web, deeply unconscious, dreaming Cruce's meticulously guided dream?

45

I'm on the hunt,

I'm after you

CHRISTIAN

WHEN I SIFT INTO Ryodan's office, brandishing my death scythe, Barrons and Ryodan surge to their feet, staring at me.

"What?" I growl irritably. "I don't look *that* different. I mean, my eyes may be a bit, well . . . wintry again but—"

"It's not what you look like," Barrons growls back, nostrils flaring as if he's sniffing me like the beast he is. "It's what we feel. What happened?"

I tell them what Lyryka told me, about the spell and what it did, what my scythe is capable of doing.

Then, as the great dark cloud of the Unseelie king's power begins to seep into Ryodan's glass castle in the sky of the nightclub, we all stare up at it, and Ryodan laughs.

"It almost chose you, didn't it?" he says. "What stopped it?"

I scowl. "I made it clear I have no fucking desire to be king. Ever. Apparently that matters. I'm wondering if the key to being chosen doesn't lie in wanting it more ferociously than the other contenders."

Barrons cuts a hard look at Ryodan. They begin some convoluted nonverbal communication that I ignore completely because I have more pressing matters on my mind. "How the bloody hell do I get into the Unseelie prison, with the Silvers behind your bookstore broken?"

"Why do you want to get into the Unseelie prison?" Barrons demands.

"I think Cruce has taken Lyryka there." I tell them what she told me about the punishment with which he threatened her, that the place he imprisoned her possessed only three colors (with which I'm all too familiar, having spent a small eternity there), and that the instant I came into my full power, Cruce felt it. Sean must have, too. It's as if we're linked to each other somehow.

"Mac's missing," Barrons says. "She vanished a few hours ago. I can no longer feel her in the mortal realm. She wouldn't have returned to Faery, not with her father dying and her mother coming in. That means Cruce took her."

"And we've yet to find a bloody Hunter anywhere in this city," Ryodan says.

"So?" I demand of Barrons, because that fuck's backup plans have backup plans to an exponential degree. "How do I get into the prison?"

"If you ever try to return where I'm going to take you now—"

"Try. Just try," I snarl.

The corner of Barrons's mouth twitches as if he's trying not to laugh, and it offends.

"Seriously? You're going to laugh at me? I'm Death. I can kill the Fae. I'm as lethal a weapon as the spear and sword. I think I'm pretty damned impressive for a Highlander from Inverness." I bristle with indignation. These two bristly beasts don't have so much on me anymore.

Now Ryodan looks like he's about to burst out laughing. Furious, I snap, "What the bloody hell is so funny?"

Barrons reaches out and pinches something from my shoulder

and holds it up. It's a hostile sentence, badly bent and hissing, reaching desperately for me.

"The Boora Boora books," Barrons murmurs. "Have you any idea what those sentences do when released?"

I shake my head. "I thought I brushed them all off me."

He snorts. "How many did you release?"

I shrug. "A bookful."

There goes the corner of his mouth again as he says, "Well. Good luck with that then."

"What do they do?"

"You'll find out."

I say irritably, "I was in a hurry."

"Clearly," Ryodan says dryly, as he, too, reaches out, and plucks something from my left wing. I'm beginning to feel as if I'm decorated with castle lint. I sifted from Draoidheacht to Chester's in such a hurry that I kicked up a small storm on my way out. Ryodan regards what he retrieved and cuts a look of dark amusement at Barrons. "Isn't that cute," he mocks. "Lyryka's got a crush on Death. For fuck's sake, she drew a little heart above the 'i' in his name."

Now both sides of Barrons's mouth are twitching.

"Give me that!" I snatch the note from his hand and slip it carefully into the pocket of my jeans. "It's not funny. It's bloody well sweet. I'll ask you one more time—"

"Come." Barrons turns for the door. "We all want something from Cruce. We're all going to the prison."

I glance at Ryodan. "What about Dani?"

Silver eyes glittering with crimson sparks, all trace of mirth gone, he says coldly, "New plan."

46

— • • —

I'm gonna walk before they make me run

DANI

I T OCCURS TO ME, as I sprawl in the darkness of my cage that, although the Hunters reverted Shazam to his original Hel-Cat form, since I've never been able to shift into that enormous, leathery skin, and Shazam said the Hunters *plan* to return me to my original state, that means they haven't done so yet.

They don't consider me a risk. They think I can't shift.

Underestimate me, I think with a smile, that'll be fun.

Running from something isn't always a cowardly thing to do. Not when it buys you time to figure out how to defeat what's threatening you. Sometimes, running is just plain smart. A mad dash to safety is a critical part of my plan, my reason for prodding them to revert Shazam to Y'rill.

But I have a bad feeling the Hunters aren't going to agree with my logic, although it's inescapable and airtight. They're going to force a lonely, emotional, needy Hel-Cat to try to justify the actions of a Hunter. Which is impossible. The two beings don't think the same.

Since Plan A is unlikely to work, it's time to get busy with Plan B.

If they refuse to allow Shazam to shift, my only other option is to shift myself.

If I can transform, my increased size will blow the cage to smithereens, freeing me. Then I grab Shazam's cage with my talons and make a mad dash for the border.

Who knows—perhaps I can add my gift of freeze-framing to the gift of Hunter wings. I've never tried. I'm still a small Hunter, which I suspect makes me more agile, and we spent months perfecting my flying skills. I may not be able to effortlessly hover yet, but I'm a pro at dangerous, tight maneuvers, zooming so snugly around sudden obstacles that I nearly give Y'rill a heart attack. Expeditious velocity is my drug of choice and my OODA loop—Observe/Orient/Decide/Act processor—is even faster as a Hunter than it was as a human.

I have no doubt I can give those ancient Hunters a run for their money. I bet they never even practice flying technique anymore. I bet they live in their stuffy old heads, complacent and as rigidly settled in their ways as they are their laws. Which is one more reason they need to bring in the fresh blood of youth. Without maximizing the gifts of one's fiery, fearless generation, a society stagnates.

By crikey, after countless failures, I will not fail this time.

Stretching out on my back, I fold my arms behind my head, close my eyes, and go inward with a cocky, *Hello, brain. Let's get inventive, try out some new stuff. I got big ideas this time.*

I greet each section of my brain, lobe by lobe. I've always been able to feel my brain inside my head and picture it in vivid detail. I don't understand folks who can't.

I can drift from region to region of it, choose to lightly skim the ridges and valleys of my cerebellum—which sizzles with constant lightning—or sink deep within, targeting any lobe: frontal, parietal, occipital, or temporal.

I can settle deeper still, into my ventricles, thalamus, hypothalamus, hippocampus, pons, medulla, and, finally, the most intriguing part of all—my amygdala.

When I was a kid, I used to concentrate on centering my heartbeat in the various parts of my brain as a sort of meditation, figuring why not feed it more blood and see if it grows? It's not as if I had much else to do. Whenever I stumbled on what seemed to be a light switch of any kind, I flipped it on, repercussions be damned. My brain was all I had to play with, and there was an undiscovered country in there.

I sink deep into my limbic region. It's quiet here, rich, dark, and fertile. I peel away the uncus and behold my amygdala, the many visceral inputs feeding it.

Fascinating.

This is where I always sensed the most significant anomaly in my genetic makeup. Something about my limbic region, specifically my amygdala, is different than most humans. I suppose thanks to Rowena's tampering plus the blood of the Unseelie king in my veins. I don't know precisely how my amygdala varies, I know only it does.

It's the most vibrantly alive part of me and, for a while, after I escaped my cage, I studied the human brain voraciously, poring over medical journals and scouring the Internet. I even broke into a morgue and stole a cadaver, did a bit of hands-on inspection, trying to decide why I wasn't like others. Unfortunately, I can't visually inspect my own brain without killing myself, so I'm still wondering. What I feel with my mind when I sink inward is probably very different than what it actually looks like. I seriously doubt I have lightning visibly crackling on the surface of my brain.

Then again, maybe I do.

It pisses me off that, when I eventually die, *if* I eventually die, I won't get to autopsy myself. How bloody fascinating that would be.

Here, deep in the center of my amygdala, I feel a different sort of heartbeat, as if it holds its own darkly beautiful circulatory system that pumps stardust through its veins, bequeathing upon that tiny section of gray matter abilities that defy explanation.

When I first began playing with my amygdala, it was a small, almond shaped thing. It grew and expanded over time, plumping to the size of a walnut in its shell. It throbs, fearlessly, with passion, power, and eternal optimism that anything at all is possible, if you want it badly enough.

I sink deeper, letting go of everything in the world, experiencing myself void of thought, existing only as a soul, whatever that is, and, as I continue to sink to the crux of my existence, I know for a certainty, I just *know* that I'm going to shift this time.

It's all about the stardust of which each and every one of us is made. We hold limitless possibility for creation, evolution. Everything is inside us, and if we bring forth the best of what is within us, it will save us. And if we don't, it will destroy us.

I have no more thoughts then.

I drift.

I am.

Not human. Not Hunter.

Not corporeal at all.

I've become the most powerful stuff in the universe: love and hope wed to focused will.

47

Sweet dreams are made of these
Who am I to disagree

MAC

I NO LONGER WONDER IF I'm dreaming.

I know I'm not.

I'm being talked to death.

If this were a dream, and Cruce could truly control me, we'd be in his bed and I'd be blankly, brightly exclaiming about his sensational attributes and prowess, not standing glumly at the balcony with a careful smile pasted on my lips and an appreciative sparkle in my eye, as he trots forth countless grand achievements in an unending parade meant to dazzle me.

I'm hungry. I need to pee. He's still talking. I hate him.

He darts with disconcerting swiftness from one subject to the next, each topic showcasing his accomplishments or espousing his many grievances.

He's changed. Become more arrogant. Increased power has intensified his innate tyranny.

Having torn a page from Lyryka's book, resolved to be honey, not vinegar, I feign attentiveness, I applaud, and the show goes on.

"Did you never wonder why," Cruce is saying, "of all the Unseelie created, only the princes and princesses were beautiful and not driven by insane, bottomless hunger?"

Despite my resolve to be honey, I can't help but retort dryly, "Apparently I missed something. Driven by insane, bottomless hunger is precisely how I'd describe you."

"Ah, there's a bit of your lovely fire." He laughs. "Good to see it again. I'd begun to fear the *Damhan-allaidh* had damaged you. I assure you, princess—"

"Queen," I challenge. I still possess the True Magic even if I can't use it, and he doesn't.

He arches a brow and continues, "—my bottomless hunger is quite sane."

A pithy retort is on the tip of my tongue, but I refrain, considering his words. He's right. The lesser castes: the Shades, the Rhino Boys, the Gray Woman/Man, the Many-Mouthed Thing, the Crimson Hag, the Hoar Frost King were all rabidly determined to feed in whatever manner they did without restraint or thought to consequence. Yet, Rath and Kiall, the other two Unseelie princes— once they'd escaped the prison—had achieved a degree of self-control and discipline. "Why are Unseelie royalty different?"

"The king didn't give any of the lesser castes what he gave us. Have you also never wondered *how* the Unseelie are immortal when we've never drunk the Elixir of Life?"

I stare at him, stunned. No. I didn't. It never once occurred to me, yet now that he has brought it up, I can't believe I didn't wonder. The Light Court drank the Elixir to achieve immortality, destroying emotion and soul in the process, but whatever the Shadow Court took had no such effect. Was there a *second* Elixir of Life—in addition to the imperfect one Cruce gave me—that didn't eviscerate essential self? And if so, might I give it to my father? "Go on," I encourage.

"Originally, when he began creating the castes, the king cobbled together a recipe using the blood of an immortal creature so hideous and vile he kept it sealed in a pit beneath his kingdom. That creature also bestowed upon the king's lesser castes a rabid, gluttonous appetite and ugliness. Over time, the king wearied of monsters and searched for something less debilitating to use. When he found it, he substituted that ingredient for us, bestowing immortality without detraction of any kind. It's the same ingredient I used to birth all my children, ergo their capacity for beauty, passion, and logic."

"And what ingredient is that?"

"Ah, my cunning MacKayla," he purrs with a dark smile, "I'll not allow you to make the Seelie immortal again."

Which means whatever it is, it's still around here somewhere. "Is it the same elixir you gave me?"

"No. I made that one, not the king. You're merely difficult to kill, not impossible. Perhaps, in time, I'll gift you the king's elixir as well. We'll see."

Aha, so there *is* a king's elixir. "Why didn't he use it for the concubine?"

"Immortality wasn't the only thing he sought for Zara, and the White Mansion kept her ageless. He wanted her to be fully Fae."

"Then why are Christian, Sean, and Jayne immortal? They haven't had the elixir or whatever the king used to make you."

"I've not yet deciphered that puzzle. It's possible the old bastard interfered. You never know what the wily prick's been up to."

Besides still not choosing to pass his power to you? I wisely refrain from provoking. "You mean shared some of the king's Elixir of Life with them? Why would he do that?"

"His motives eternally defy me. Perhaps it amused him to have mortals become immortal Fae replacements. Perhaps he knew I'd kill them if they weren't. Perhaps he decided we might benefit from diversity. Perhaps it was a passing, pointless whim. Perhaps he thought it would piss me off, and that was amusing enough for him."

"But they'd know if the king tinkered—"

"No more than you did. If the king felt like making humans immortal, he could spike something they ate without them ever knowing. Regardless, we, the Unseelie, *are* immortal." His smile is all teeth and smug satisfaction as he adds, "And now the Seelie. Are. *Not*. And the universe is as it should be. But enough talk for now. Come, let me show you more of my world."

———— • • ————

I'm exhausted when Cruce finally returns me to my chamber, where I toss myself on the bed and peer from between the curtains of my four-poster, past the drapes and out the now-closed French doors.

Dublin of Eternal Night, as I call it, is truly beautiful. I met caste after caste, and, in spite of myself, grew increasingly impressed with Cruce's creations. He created a court equal to their fair brethren that live together in families, as emotional, bonded couples with children, nurturing goals and dreams. Were a creator judged by his creations, Cruce would take grand prize.

But the Cruce that began birthing this court is not the being that now exists.

He changed along the way.

He's become nearly identical to the king, and I find it difficult to understand why the king's power still hasn't chosen him. If being as much like the original king as possible is the criteria, Cruce nailed it.

Arrogant, obsessed with his own agenda, self-aggrandizing, he's sacrificed the finest parts of himself to gluttony for ever-increasing power. He sees the beauty of his children only as a reflection of himself. And, before long, they will suffer diminishing freedoms, incur escalating punishments as they do what children do—evolve, hungering to find their own way in the world. He won't be able to permit that. His reflection must remain unchanging.

And the Shadow Court will be right back where it began so long ago: imprisoned, controlled, subjected to the whims of an increasingly absent, obsessed, half-mad king.

Lyryka was right. It's the nature of our essential selves that shapes the power we hold.

As we walked the misting streets of the city, passing the brilliant red exterior of the Temple Bar Pub, Cruce demanded I yield to him the True Magic. I asked why he even wanted it, given how powerful he already is. He replied all power was good, and it is rightfully his because he suffered at the Light Court for so long, and I agreed to do it, and he upheld his end of the bargain; therefore it was time for me to honor mine.

When I pointed out that the Compact was invalid because those laws apply only to Compacts struck between Light Court royalty and he was not, his gaze had darkened to full black, his skin had deepened to ebony, and I'd thought, for a moment, he might do me harm.

But he'd swiftly regained control of himself, laughing softly with icy eyes that didn't match his smile at all.

Then, abruptly, he terminated our tour, escorted me back to my chamber, and locked me in, even warding the doors to the balcony. He told me the True Magic was neutralized and I would never again be able to use it so long as I lived and, in time, I would certainly pass it to him. Then he told me he would give me three nights' sleep to come to my senses and yield both the True Magic and myself to him willingly.

Or what? I asked.

One way or another, he replied, with a tight, cold smile.

Then he vanished.

And I wonder, as I stretch on the bed, yawning, loathing the thought of sleeping in his midnight kingdom but so very, very tired, is this where things might go dangerously awry?

My waking nightmare/premonition weighs heavily on my mind.

If I refuse to yield to Cruce in real life, does he truly have the power to submerge me in the confused, enforced submission of an eternal midnight dream?

I battle sleep with everything I've got.

I don't win.

PART IV

When I was young, Dad used to read a lot, and occasionally he'd read a passage aloud that meant a great deal to him. One of his favorites (which I swear he read to me a hundred times) was from *The Collected Works of Kahlil Gibran*.

> *Your children are not your children,*
> *They are the sons and daughters of Life's longing for itself.*
> *They come through you but not from you,*
> *And though they are with you yet they belong not to you.*
> *You may give them your love but not your thoughts.*
> *You may house their bodies but not their souls,*
> *For their souls dwell in the house of tomorrow,*
> *Which you cannot visit, not even in your dreams.*

It always struck me as terribly sad, and I'd hasten to assure him, *But, Daddy, Alina and I* did *come from you* (this was before I discovered, biologically, we hadn't), *and we'll be yours forever, and there's no other place we'd rather be, and you're in every one of our tomorrows.*

Like so many other careful seeds he planted, I get it now. Alina and I, the new Unseelie Court, the Hunter's offspring, they dwell in the house of tomorrow, and any parent, any ruler, must understand his or her position is a shepherd of transition, no more, no less, as the student becomes the master.

One must know when to step up, and when to step down.

From the Journals of MacKayla Lane-O'Connor
High Queen of the Fae

SHADOWDREAM

— • • —

You held it all but you were careless to let it fall

I STAND AT MY FATHER'S grave, beneath a gray sky and a lightly misting rain, great black wings trailing the ground.

Wet, those great feathery appendages smell of silk, fine leather, and peaches-and-cream candles, which I find inexpressibly odd.

I buried Jack Lane in the cemetery at the abbey, with a vacant plot beside him for Mom. I'd say, hopefully, "one day far in the future," but for Mom's sake, I don't know if that's the best call. Dad's death sent her back into the same black depression she suffered when Alina died, and she can't even look at me. She didn't come to the service. Mom refused to leave the townhouse she shared with Dad. She told me she already said her goodbyes, but I know the truth. She can't bear to look at me.

If Daddy were here, he'd tell me something like, *Your mother loves you with all her heart, Mac, and she knows my death wasn't your fault, and one day, you'll be close again; give her time. It heals all wounds, baby.*

To which I'd say, *No, it doesn't. At best, time is the great leveler, sweeping us all into coffins, except for me, not me, never me. There will be no plot in this graveyard bearing my name, because I can't die. But everyone I love will, and the best for which we can hope is to find ways* to distract ourselves from the pain. *Time is neither scalpel nor bandage. Scar tissue is merely the wound's other face.*

To which he'd say, *Mac, the walls would have come down anyway, whether or not you and your sister went to Ireland. All of this would have happened, with or without you. Who's to say, had you and your sister not gone to Dublin, the four of us wouldn't have died at the Shade's hands, years ago? Been four of the billions of humans that were lost? You can't second-guess every action. You can only greet each day with a loving, true heart—and, baby, you do that.*

Funny, how clearly I can still hear his voice.

To which I would reply, bitterly, *No, I don't. My heart got dark at a critical moment. That's how I ended up here.*

And he would say something, anything that would make my grief bearable, like, *But if given one more second, the dark moment would have passed. It was a clusterfuck, baby. We all have dark moments. We get through them.* And he would remind me that getting to love, at all, even for the briefest of hours, is life's greatest gift, and hindsight is 20/20 (but not that dreadful human year many of us lived through). He would tell me that Barrons and the Nine know this, and I need to remember it, too. Take a page from their books. Learn to live with grief.

And I would have, in time.

I didn't get that time.

And Daddy's not here. That's the problem.

It's also the blessing. I don't want him to see me now.

I have no doubt Jack Lane is in heaven. But I don't want him looking down. I don't want him to see what I've done. Who I've become.

His slow, agonizing death destroyed me, too, but I don't get depressed when I lose people that I love with all my heart.

I get angry.

Furious.

Vengeful.

It happened when Alina died, it happened when I believed Barrons was dead, and it happened again when my father finally, with dignity and grace, requested the dual mercy of Ativan and morphine as he lay, feet blue and fingers dusky, struggling to breathe with a heart no longer capable of providing sufficient oxygen to his lungs.

In my defense, I tried. He's been dead only three days. I was struggling to convince myself that his death was not my fault and, even if it was, there was nothing to be gained by going postal on the world, but grief does funny things to your brain. Like, it turns it off, leaving you one big, stupid bruise of red-hot pain and confusion, unable to make the slightest decision.

You wander in a gray fog from day to day, and, on those exceptional days you actually manage to take a shower and feed yourself before going straight back to bed, you consider the day a major triumph.

I destroyed the Seelie.

All of them, even the Spyrssidhe.

I didn't mean to. I wasn't even in Faery when it happened. I was at the bookstore, curled in my bed, a mushroom cloud of pain and rage expanding far too large for my body to contain.

As I raged and wept, the great, dark stain of the Unseelie king's power drifted into my room, hovering above my bed, studying me.

I rolled over on my back, face wet with tears, teeth bared and snarled: I *want* your power, I want all your power, every bit of it, because I don't want a single Fae to have one ounce of it, and Cruce is still out there, dicking with our lives, planning some other dreadful disruption that will kill someone else I love, and, by God, he is *not* getting your power, and if I have it, I can destroy him for good, destroy *all* Fae, and our world will be the way it should be—only human life on this planet. I'll kill the old gods, too. This is *our* world. Give me your power!

In that kernel of time and pain that encapsulated all my deepest flaws—a moment that would have *passed* in time, you must remember, such moments pass—I crossed the line into "Oops, shit, it's too late."

One instant. That's what condemned me. An instant of craving power with all my heart coupled with a moment of hungering to crush my enemies.

I'm not perfect. None of us are. Like I said, mercifully, we aren't all powerful and those moments pass. That's what you have to hold on to.

But my life works a bit differently.

You must be careful with each and every one of your wishes, with where and how you direct your will. I hold great power; therefore my responsibility is greater, too.

My wish, all my wishes, were granted in that single second.

The king's darkness rushed into me and, as it crammed my tiny being with more than I could hold, the power exploded right back out and, because the thoughts were in my brain and the desires in my heart, I destroyed the Unseelie and the old gods.

I scoured the planet of all but human life. Made the world safe from the Fae.

I remember the look on Barrons's face when I stumbled, horrified, down the stairs, great black wings trailing the risers, and he must have felt what happened, because he was rushing up the stairs to find me.

We met at the landing.

I sifted out instantly, leaving him roaring at empty space, and came here, to the graveyard, where I don't dare remain long, because he'll find me. He'll go to all the places he knows I'll go. He'll stalk me incessantly until he finds me. He'll try to "talk me down." But there is no coming down, or back, from this. I will never forgive myself for the things I've done, and, when you can't forgive yourself, you can neither love nor be loved. You keep making the same mistakes, over and over. Like the king.

"Goodbye, Daddy," I whisper, wiping tears from my cheeks. "I love you. To the moon and back."

Then I tip my head and stare up at the sky, eying my new home.

Out there, among the stars. Avoiding the hell out of Dani because I can't face her either.

I wonder if this was why the king did it: created, constantly created. An act of atonement, not just for his concubine but for his very existence.

Because once—just like me—he destroyed the precious things entrusted to his care.

48

⸰ ● ⸰

And she ran to him and they started to fly

CHRISTIAN

WE SPLIT UP AT the Unseelie prison, Barrons, Ryodan, and I.

I recall the blood oath we swore beneath Chester's, when they revealed to me what they are, and what they'd done to my uncle Dageus. I now carry one more secret to guard.

Deep beneath the garage behind Barrons's Books & Baubles, Barrons has a powerfully warded room of Silvers that contains more than a hundred mirrors of all shapes, colors, and sizes, and one of them took us straight to the Unseelie prison. I couldn't discern where most of the others went; he rushed me past them at slightly less than the speed of light. But I saw one that featured continuously changing scenes, a few of which I recognized from history books.

He'd shoved me into a mirror, and we made our exit from within a towering wall of blue-black ice.

I know this place. I despise this place. How dare Cruce bring Lyryka here? The prison is her antithesis.

But I know he did. Cruce never makes idle threats. Threats from him are something he's already decided, and he's merely biding his time for the right moment, which usually means whichever moment causes the greatest harm to others while amusing him the most.

She was frightened of him, I could tell. I also know, if he brought her here, it's because he's done with her. What kind of monster could keep Lyryka in a bottle for three quarters of a million years? And if he hadn't been completely done with her before she told me I was Death and turned me into a weapon capable of killing him, he certainly is now.

Long ago, I would have iced the moment we arrived in the Unseelie hell, but I don't, and although Barrons and Ryodan do, they shake it off, cracking the ice by jogging in place.

Motion is key to surviving in the worst of Fae realms: keep moving, always moving. And if you think the next place might be better, think again. Hall of All Days, case in point.

Then Barrons and Ryodan incline their heads, turn, and take off, racing away, side by side.

"Hey, wait," I shout after them.

"What?" Barrons turns, growling, still jogging in place.

"Aren't we sticking together?"

"We have different goals, which must be accomplished in different places. Time is of the essence, Highlander," Ryodan grits over his shoulder.

I blink. They just explained something to me instead of stalking off wearing identical scowls. I know what that means.

Barrons cuts me a dry look. "It means we believe you can take care of yourself."

"No, it doesn't," I say with a faint smile, taking a page from Lyryka's book. "That wasn't an expression of faith, it was bloody well an explanation, and that fucking means you like me." Boo-yah. The Nine are my tribe now. And I'm keeping them.

With an amused laugh, I turn and strike off for the ridge where once before, what feels like another lifetime ago, Cruce buried the Seelie queen.

———— • • • ————

Lyryka isn't there.

I squat by the ex-queen's sepulchre, glowering, trying to decide how the hell I'm supposed to find Lyryka in the vastness of the Unseelie prison that stretches impossibly wide and long and once housed a million Unseelie or more. She never had a problem finding me. She said she imprinted on me in some fashion.

I rock back on my heels, knowing it's impossible to sift in this place, so it's not as if I can take a page from Mac's book and sift directly to a person—which I've never managed without a token— och, wait!

I reach into the pocket of my jeans and extract Lyryka's note, where she scripted my name, with great care, adding her charming heart over the "i."

Closing my eyes, I focus on the myriad aspects of Lyryka. Infuriating, funny, eclectic as hell, horny as hell (thank you very much— I wonder for the thousandth time what she looks like), a walking repository for countless Fae secrets, brilliant and widely read but innocent and trusting and seemingly so young, despite her advanced age.

I snort with laughter. Irritable. So bloody testy, but all it does is get my blood pumping hot and stalky. I adore when her nose crinkles and I know she's about to snap at me. No filter. What she thinks explodes out, both from her mouth and emblazoned on—

Got her.

I open my eyes. I'll be damned. I think she's calling for me. Drowsy and fighting sleep, but she keeps slipping back into it.

Direction doesn't compute here. No north, south, east, or west. I know only she's "that way" as I turn toward her.

I know also that I'll find her atop a high ridge, some hundred miles from where I stand, in a graveyard, concealed behind illusion.

Shoving her note back in my pocket, scythe tucked close to my side, spreading my wings, I explode into flight.

⸺ · ⸺

It takes what feels like an hour to figure out which part of the landscape is Cruce's illusion. I hack into icy cliff after cliff with my scythe before finding the sweet spot and, when I do, the runes on my scythe spit a shower of sparks, causing me to study it thoughtfully, suspecting the weapon might do more than merely kill the Fae.

Time drags because I feel her slipping away, over and again. Not dying, not even close, her light is too strong to be dimmed so quickly, even in this place, but Cruce must have drugged her, because she keeps getting faint, then I'll feel a violent struggle, before she gets faint again.

Then I'm through his illusion and I gape, stunned and furious, thinking, *How the fuck many Fae has Cruce killed?* I thought he'd attempted the murders only of Aoibheal and now Lyryka, but apparently he succeeded at murder, hundreds of times.

I soar over the graveyard, dialing into Lyryka's essence, and abruptly, her sepulchre is below me, and I'm landing lightly atop the raised platform of ice, scrubbing away snow to peer through the blue-black frozen lid of her coffin.

She's slumbering deeply now and—holy hell.

She no longer looks like Mac or Dani.

This, ah, yes, *this* is Lyryka. But of course it would be.

Christ, she's beautiful.

But duality always has been my poison.

It takes the blood of Death to break Cruce's wards and, the moment I do, they explode into the air and vanish, and I know instinctively they shot straight to Cruce, to alert him his wards were broken.

I smile, cold as Death.

Because. I. Am.

Let Cruce come.

Bloody hell, let the bastard come!

I scoop Lyryka from the ice, cradling her gently in my arms, and lift off again, heading back to the Silver to return her to the world in which she belongs.

Our world.

49

Copycat trying to cop my manner
Watch your back when you can't watch mine

MAC

I WAKE FROM A DRUGGED sleep, surfacing slowly, miserably, from a dark, bottomless loch of nightmares.

In each of them, I was Cruce's consort. In each of them, I hated who I was. I'd raged silently inside, seething with denial and fury, while my mouth shaped words I would never think, never say to him. Not in a million years.

It felt as if someone was controlling my dreams, trying to subtly reprogram me, convince me that I'd never loved Barrons, that it had always been Cruce and only Cruce for me.

I wrestle a tangle of quilt from my head that I somehow managed to nearly tie around my skull, I suppose while thrashing violently against the appalling events happening in my dreams.

"Ah, there you are," Cruce purrs. "I'd begun to think I might have to join you in that mound, help you extricate yourself." His eyes narrow, fixed on my face, then drop lower, darkening and narrowing with lust.

I know how I wake up. My mouth gets swollen when I sleep.

Mom always called it the "collagen kiss of youth." My hair is tangled and sticking up, but men seem to like bedhead and—oh, bloody hell, *that's* what he's staring at.

I get hot when I sleep and strip without waking. My boobs are on full display.

I instantly summon the glamour of clothing.

It doesn't work.

Of course it doesn't.

Cruce has neutralized my powers.

Yanking the quilt up over my breasts with a snarl, I pat frantically around beneath the covers for my shirt.

Cruce holds it up, smiling, but it doesn't reach his eyes. Then he tosses it over his shoulder to the floor. His gaze is hard, lust-filled, and hungry, and I wonder if his smile ever reached his eyes. Was he always glamouring them? Or did they change slowly during the centuries he spent cloistered here, working to expand his kingdom and power?

"Yield, MacKayla. You can't win. Not against me. I had you beneath me once, and you experienced nothing but pleasure. How were your dreams last night? You'll be getting a repeat tonight. And every night. Until you comply. Masdann tells me it's traumatic to the dreamer, reprogramming their reality. I may join him tonight in your dreams. Watch you struggle. Inevitably, you'll fall. He's reprogrammed others before. Give in, MacKayla. Accept defeat and make the best of things. Don't be plebeian. It's beneath you. Beneath creatures like us."

I stare at him, horrified, blanket clutched to my chest. "You created a prince that can walk in the Dreaming, didn't you? He's been messing with my dreams!"

What a fearsome power to hold! Was Cruce so great a fool? Like the king before him who fashioned amulets capable of weaving illusions even he couldn't penetrate, had Cruce created a weapon that might one day be his downfall? Did they never learn? How easily such a prince might slip into Cruce's dreams, convince him over time, he—the prince of Dream—was king, not Cruce at all. What a danger such a prince would be! Talk about holding a tiger by the tail.

Oblivious to his own idiocy, Cruce inclines his head, starry eyes glittering. "Yes. And he is mine to command. Masdann," he murmurs.

The next events are so bizarre and unexpected they seem to unfold in slow motion.

The door to the chamber opens.

Jericho Barrons walks in.

Cruce turns to smile at him.

I blink. Cruce *smiles* at Barrons. As if he's happy to see him. He doesn't instantly sift to establish safe distance between them. He merely smiles, sitting at ease, no more than ten feet away.

"You summoned, my liege," Barrons murmurs.

"I did, Masdann."

My eyes widen further, and my heart sinks like a stone, and I growl, "You. Did. Not. Make a prince of dreams that looks exactly like Jericho Barrons." And dresses like him, wearing an elegant Italian suit, crisp white shirt, and a crimson tie.

Cruce smiles. "Ah, but my lovely MacKayla, I did. And one day you will gaze upon his face and believe him your greatest enemy. And when such a day comes, you will never see him again. Masdann has been walking in your world, masquerading as Barrons. He fooled even Ryodan. He fooled even *you*. Twice on the sofa at Chester's, he visited you. *Twice*, he touched you, conversed with you. And You. Never. Knew."

If my eyes go any wider they'll surely pop from my skull. "That was Masdann? *He's* the one that told me to go for a walk and I ended up in your web?" I exclaim, stupefied. I refuse to believe it. I can't. That was Barrons. I know Barrons. No one could imitate Jericho Barrons well enough to fool me.

Cruce inclines his head. "Also Masdann who read your notes while you slumbered and reported the contents back to me. Masdann who guided your dreams that day, helping you recall each time we were together, encouraging you to warm to me."

I remember those dreams. I thought Barrons was watching me in them. But it was the prince that looked like Barrons who'd made me revisit my encounters with Cruce. It was Masdann, not Barrons, who'd lingered long on the kiss we'd shared to seal the Compact.

It was Masdann who'd touched my shoulders, reminded me that my heart was my greatest power. And it was Masdann, the second time he'd come to my sofa yesterday, telling me he'd returned only to get tattoo implements to bind the Hunter they'd found, and I should get outside, go for a walk.

I'm so horrified I can't speak.

Cruce created an Unseelie prince that looks exactly like Barrons, that possesses the ability to make me dream anything he wants, with the goal of reprogramming everything that I believe is true about myself and my world. And it might work.

"Even if it takes a hundred years," Cruce says softly, eyes glittering with triumph. "But I warn you, don't take too long. I grow impatient to have you willingly at my side."

Shuddering, I look from the prince that wears Barrons's face and body so convincingly well, to Cruce and back again. I might have had sex with Masdann and never known. He's a flawless copy.

"The *Damhan-allaidh* were of considerable assistance," Cruce tells me.

Here it comes, more bragging about how clever he is, but I'm more than willing to listen because my future is bleak; I'll gamely indulge him as long as he wants to talk. It's more time wasted that he's not messing with my head, literally, in dreams.

"They're ward-breakers, but you never figured that out."

So that's why every damned Fae in the book could sift into Chester's and Christian's castle.

"The moment Barrons, Ryodan, or Christian placed a new ward, the *Damhan-allaidh* neutralized it. Most were simple to break.

Wards are easily shattered when one possesses a powerful enough ingredient, which I used as the foundation of their caste."

"Are they sentient? Or are they like the Shades?" I ask, desperate both to keep him talking and to learn all I can about the castes I will one day escape. My gaze drifts to Barrons again and again. I can't help it. He's Jericho, but not. He's a complete stranger. He returns it impassively, saying nothing, a manservant, awaiting Cruce's next command, whatever it may be.

This is the being that's going to erase the love of my life from my mind and heart. Turning Barrons's face into that of my enemy. I'm powerless, naked, and have no cellphone. I'm trapped in a chamber with Cruce and an Unseelie prince from which there appears to be no escape.

"Highly sentient and quite lovely, don't you think? You should see the forms they can adopt. They're exquisite, inventive designers."

"If I cooperate, will you save my father?" It's the only thing I can think of to say at the moment. The appearance of the Barrons-prince, the fact that he fooled even me has totally fucked with my head. I actually talked with Masdann and thought the prince was Barrons. He *touched* me, and I didn't know it was an imposter. The complexity and cleverness of Cruce's plans are stupefying.

He clucks reprovingly. "Forget about such things as your old family. You have a new one, and soon the earth won't exist anymore, MacKayla. I have no use for it. I no longer need the power at the core. I have other sources and other plans. I've come to despise this world. It's time for it to end. Let it go. It doesn't matter."

My face must betray my abhorrence, because he adds, with a sigh, "If it makes you happy, I will grant Jack Lane a swifter, less painful death." To Masdann, he says, "Where is Barrons now?"

"Securing a Hunter. He and Ryodan intend to use it to search for Dani."

"I didn't think the Hunters were still around," Cruce says.

"Recently returned, drawn by momentous events unfolding. They cooperate with Barrons without even the force of binding spells," Masdann replies, cutting a look my way. "They seem to like him."

Wait, what? A tangle of thoughts explodes in my mind all at once.

Slowly, I tease them apart and line them up in order: Cruce said Masdann was the one who most recently visited me on my couch at Chester's, the one who sent me out into the streets, ultimately, to Cruce's web. That means Masdann was also the one who said he needed tattoo implements to bind the Hunter. But now Masdann is saying those very implements aren't necessary, and he knows it. And, if I hadn't been so worried about Dad, sitting on the couch when he'd said it, I'd have realized that myself, because Barrons and I discovered together the tattoos never did anything more than annoy the great dragonlike beasts. Trinkets, they called them. So why is Masdann *now* saying they're not necessary?

"There's no accounting for taste," Cruce says dryly. "The Hunters will leave again soon enough." He dismisses them from his mind and turns back to me. "I weary of waiting. I'm going to fuck you, MacKayla, while Masdann watches. And you *will* permit it, and you *will* respond favorably, because if you don't, I *will* dispatch my prince that is impossible to tell apart from the original Barrons to the world above where he *will* kill your father and your mother and everyone you love. Do you understand?"

I stare at him. It would work. My family and friends trust Barrons. They would let him close. And, given that Masdann can fool even me, and moves just like Barrons, he could mow down everyone I love, in no time at all.

"A nod to convey agreement would be sufficient, MacKayla," Cruce cues me coolly.

Swallowing bile, hands clenching fistfuls of blanket so tightly I'm surprised my fingers don't snap, I tell myself, in my best John Wayne voice, *Buck up, little buckaroo, and live to fight another day. He raped me once before. I'll survive. I'll fight in other ways, when he's not looking. I'll figure out what he's done to my powers and find a way to kill him. I have a fierce, brave heart, a titanium will, and I. Will. Never. Give. Up. Until I've won.*

That's my mantra, the words I will repeat over and over while he touches me, while I disconnect from my body and retreat into my mind, and I will withstand whatever he does to me, and play any role I must in order to permanently eradicate Cruce from our world and save it.

He plans to destroy the Earth. I will never let that happen. One way or another. Price be damned.

I jerk my head in a tight nod.

Cruce smiles. "I knew you'd come around. You're a survivor, like me. It's one of many reasons we're going to be perfect together. Masdann." He pats the bed beside him. "Come. Join us."

"I'd be delighted, my liege," Masdann purrs, moving across the room with the same sleek, prowling grace as Barrons.

I think woodenly, no wonder he fooled me. He's a flawless copy, down to the smallest of details.

Then Masdann is settling on the bed beside us, to watch while Cruce rapes me—watch me suffering the revolting horror with *Barrons's* eyes staring out of *Barrons's* face—and, as he settles near, he looks directly at me, and I nearly gasp but swallow it hastily, because crimson sparks just glittered in Masdann's gaze and, coupled with his Hunter comment, a suspicion explodes in my mind that's too divine to be true, but if it is, I dare not telegraph it.

When Cruce reaches for me, tugging the blanket from my fists, Masdann strikes, with Barrons-esque swiftness.

And I think—that's why Cruce would never let him near. He knew how fast Barrons could move. He risked it only once. The day they ended up at each other's throats in the rain, and I'd been the one to call Barrons off. Cruce had counted on that; he'd known I wouldn't let Barrons kill him because I still needed his half of the Song.

Clever, clever bastard—he was planning this even then.

Then Masdann is holding Cruce by fistfuls of his wings and he's—oh, God, is *that* how the Nine kill the Fae?

Barrons never let me see, always blurred himself beyond my vision whenever he killed one of them. Sure, I had my ideas, but that's different than seeing with your own eyes.

Masdann crushes his mouth to Cruce's, fusing their lips together. Cruce struggles violently against him, pummeling with fists, as Masdann inhales deeply, chest inflating to an impossible girth. I saw something similar, the day I released the Song of Making, when the *Sinsar Dubh* rode the Unseelie princess's body into battle against us, escaping our trap in the White Mansion and, to buy me time, Barrons sucked the *Sinsar Dubh* from her body, by locking mouths with her in a savage kiss. Masdann is killing Cruce the same way, draining the life like a psychic vampire. And for some reason, he's doing it more slowly than usual, allowing me to see.

Abruptly, the bedroom door opens again, and my gaze flies to the entrance.

Barrons just walked in.

I gape.

Or did Masdann?

I narrow my eyes. What the fuck is going on here?

Cruce bucks wildly in Masdann's grip, locked in the deep kiss that's stealing his life. His arms and legs flail wildly, his body jerks in an immense surge of resistance.

Then he's still.

When Masdann shoves him roughly away, wiping his mouth with the back of his hand, grimacing with distaste, Cruce collapses to the floor, pale, eyes wide and leached of color. He's deflated to half his weight, withered, a crumbling husk of a Fae, his skin wrinkling before my eyes, rapidly aging.

Dying.

I realize then, Barrons/Masdann/whoever-the-hell-he-is can control the way he kills to precise degrees. In the past, whenever

Barrons killed Fae, although he never let me see the act, I saw the bodies afterward. They were unharmed, exactly as they'd looked alive, merely dead. Normally, Barrons kills swiftly, mercifully, without inflicting damage.

This time, he damaged.

Forgetting my nudity, forgetting everything but this moment, I clamber from the blankets to the edge of the bed, peering over, not about to be denied the satisfaction of watching Cruce die.

"I took your life slowly, timing your death, Cruce," Masdann says coldly. "So you may witness one final thing." Barrons-on-the-bed glances at Barrons-at-the-door, and they share a smile.

Then Barrons-at-the-door moves to stand near Barrons-on-the-bed and gazes down at Cruce, who stares with shock and disbelief from one to the other. "My prince," he whispers. "How could you?"

"Never your prince. Free. The moment you created me, I was no longer yours. You bloody fool, you used part of Jericho Barrons's essence to make me. What did you expect?"

To which Barrons-on-the-bed adds coolly—and now I know he's the *real* Barrons, and has been all along—"Did you really think there was any version of me you could create, in any reality, in any universe that would not—first, foremost, and forever—be loyal to MacKayla Lane?"

50

Lost boys and golden girls

CHRISTIAN

LYRYKA TALKS IN HER sleep.

I sit beside her on the bed, staring down, unable to take my eyes off her.

She's magnificent.

Unmistakably the daughter of a Shadow Court prince and a Light Court princess and, if I don't miss my guess, I'd say Summer.

The daughter of War and Summer is divided vertically down the middle by a clean, straight line. And, given her age, she was born at a time when the Light Court had yet to discover the Shadow Court existed, thereby betraying Cruce's nature and existence by mere dint of her appearance. Solely because of her looks, the bastard sealed her away to use her, where she would never be glimpsed by anyone, and never betray him. And when he'd finished using her and built his new world, he'd buried her alive to die.

Half her face and body are Seelie, the other half of her face and body are Unseelie.

She sports the grace and quick-witted fun of Summer in wide-set eyes, the upward tilt of her nose, the quirky mouth that I can't wait to see smile, yet the resolute strength of soldiers of war marches across her high forehead and shapes her wide, strong jaw.

The left side of Lyryka is golden skinned and warm with an elegant, alabaster wing that shimmers in the low light of my bedroom. The right side of her is as dusky and ebon as I am, shoulder graced with a black velvet wing that smolders with cerulean fire. The hair on the left side of her face is blond, the hair on her right side is raven silk.

She takes my breath away.

Half and half, there's no way anyone could ever look at her and not know she's both Light and Shadow Court. A singularity, she's spectacular, and I'm avid to know what color her eyes are.

Abruptly, they're open, and she's staring up at me.

Her left is tiger-gold like mine, with copper flecks and a hint of mossy green; her right eye is such a deep, rich cobalt, it's nearly black.

"Hi," she whispers.

"Hi," I whisper stupidly back.

She searches my gaze a moment. "Oh, no," she moans, forlorn.

"You're safe," I assure her. "You're at Draoidheacht, and Cruce will never get anywhere near you again. I promise." I don't say, *because he's going to be dead*. She's recently traumatized, on top of hundreds of thousands of years of trauma, and I'm not about to add an ounce of emotional baggage. Cruce is her father, and our feelings about parents are complicated, even when they behave monstrously.

"That's not it," Lyryka says, blinking slowly, looking heavy-lidded and utterly fuckable, but mostly as if she's having a hard time keeping her eyes open.

"Rest. We have all the time in the world, Lyryka."

Her eyes drift closed and she murmurs, sadly, "Yes, but you want to give me sex right now. I can tell. And I can't stay—"

I laugh softly. She's out again. "Awake," I finish for her. And she's right. I very much want to give her sex. And hopefully when she wakes again, she'll let me. I have years of raging lust stockpiled. Still, I'm not ferociously horny like I was when I first realized I could have sex again. I'm on fire with desire, hungering to make Lyryka's first time everything she's ever dreamed. After slow, tender lovemaking we'll get down to hot and dirty fucking as I work devotedly to bring to life every fantasy she's ever had.

Bloody hell, she fascinates me. I look forward to getting to know her, to watching her live freely in our world, loved, accepted, and treated with the kindness and respect that has always been her due.

As I tuck the blankets snug about her, I brush a hand lightly over each wing. Her white wing is warm, soft, and deliciously silky. Her black one is cool, strong, the feathers a bit sharp and edgy. She's a walking dichotomy.

Och, I'm falling. Hard.

But right now, there's a bastard of a prince out there long overdue to come face-to-face with his baby brother. Death.

As I rise and turn for the door, a text swooshes in on my cell, and I tug it from my jeans.

Cruce is dead.

Well, fuck. I deflate. I have a serious hard-on for killing the prick. The text is from Barrons. *Bring him back,* I text back swiftly, *so I can kill him again.*

Tempting. Not. Heading back to Chester's with Mac.

Dani?

Ryodan went after her.

How?

You'll see. And I'm not your fucking tribe, Highlander.

Are, too.

Not.

Laughing, I pocket my phone. I turn and glance back at Lyryka, who's once again murmuring softly in her sleep. I regret that I wasn't the one to kill Cruce, but no matter. She's safe now.

I'm her sworn protector.

She has my life, my hot-blooded Highlander heart, and the icy finality of my scythe to stand as shield between her and all harm, at all times.

Lyryka will never be mistreated again.

Not on my watch. And my watch is eternal as is my oath.

"Dream well, lass," I murmur as I head for the door.

51

———— • • • ————

I might not be a savior and I'll never be a king

DANI

SHAZAM IS DEFENDING Y'RILL, and it's going as terribly as I suspected it would.

When the Hunters returned from their tête-à-tête, they'd not budged an inch from their initial position. Shazam would speak for Y'rill, the saffron-eyed Hunter Z'kor informed us, then they would remove the force field from his cage, subjecting my brave, weeping, loving Hel-Cat to the killing cruelty of space.

I know what happens to an unprotected human in space and, given Shazam's biology, I suspect he would die pretty much the same way, though it might take longer.

The gas in your lungs and digestive tract rapidly expands, inducing swelling. If, like an idiot, you instinctively hold your breath, the loss of external pressure will cause the gas in that breath to rupture your lungs. If you're smart, you exhale the moment you enter unprotected space.

The temperature is a brisk -454.8 degrees, but you don't freeze to death because your body heat doesn't evaporate quickly enough to kill you before something else does.

In roughly ten seconds, you lose vision. At about the same time your skin and tissue swell, as the water in your body vaporizes due to the absence of atmospheric pressure. You won't explode—movies embellish for dramatic optics—you'll stop at roughly twice your size. Skin is pretty elastic. If you're lucky and retrieved in time, the swelling will go down. You don't stay a balloon-human.

The moisture on your tongue may begin to boil. You might get a sunburn from cosmic radiation and suffer decompression sickness. A few seconds later, mercifully, you lose consciousness due to oxygen being dumped from your blood. You turn blue, circulation stops, and in another minute, you're dead by asphyxiation.

Your body doesn't decompose in space once the oxygen is gone, and conceivably your corpse might drift for a few million years.

Hel-Cats are an incredibly long-lived species. It could take Shazam longer than the average ninety to one hundred twenty seconds to die.

And these Hunters, our judge and jury, believe forcing me to watch him endure such a horrific death is an acceptable thing to do. I despise them. They're wrong, so wrong.

"I thought you were supposed to be so highly evolved," I break in bitterly. It's not as if I'm interrupting much. My beloved Hel-Cat is crying too hard to present any sort of case, and I know it's not because he's worried about dying as much as he's worried about me.

We'd die for each other. We share that kind of love. If not for Ryodan, I would willingly go with him. Take a chance on the possibility that Shazam, Dancer, and I would get reunited in the Slipstream, that mysterious, fluid place we go when we die.

But Ryodan. I'm torn in half. I love them both.

On the surface of my brain, I'm aware of everything, but deep in the core of my amygdala, part of me remains in the meditative state I achieved while awaiting the Hunters' return.

We are *highly evolved,* Z'kor says.

"Yet you would kill one of your own because she broke a few rules, out of love?"

Motive is irrelevant.

"Bullshit!" I exclaim. "Motive is critically relevant. Intention matters. Regardless of how hard we try, we all screw up every now and then, and I guar-damn-tee you that long before any of you became Hunters, you screwed up, too. You just don't remember that far back. Intention is the true, underlying desire that infuses our actions, and when we muck things up, if our intention is good, we learn from our mistake, refine our actions, and do better the next time. If the intention is bad, nothing is learned and the bad person remains bad. Y'rill's intention was *not* bad. It was pure. She protected me and did the things she did for no other reason than unconditional love. Something you great, cold bastards obviously have no concept of." I pause a moment, then my mouth says without conscious thought, without any intelligent control at all: "Fine. If Shazam dies, I die, too. If you are a species that would kill a being like Shazam/Y'rill for doing what he/she did, I want no part of being anything like you. If you remove the force field from his cage, you better fucking remove mine, too, because I won't live without him."

By the time I'm done, I'm shaking with emotion. I don't want to leave Ryodan, but this is pure bullshit. And if they kill us—

Holy hell, I gasp, astonished, it's happening.

I can feel it.

I'm shifting.

There's a great, fiery breath building inside me, and now I finally understand what Y'rill meant when she was always saying I had to find my "breath of fire" and "heart of scales." I could never wrap my brain around it.

I get it now.

The breath of fire is a new part of me I couldn't access, because I kept looking for it in my brain, and that great, logical mass kept insisting what I was trying to do was impossible. But the fire-breath doesn't reside in my brain, it's in my gut and it's expanding, spreading, rushing into my blood, heating it to scorching while leathery scales form around my heart as if to protect my circulatory system from exploding as the heat spreads to my brain, my organs, and beyond, transforming bones and muscle and skin.

Holy hell, my spine is changing and a tail is forming. It's the best feeling in the world, as if the cosmos is rushing into me, and now I understand why Hunters insist the mother never help the child shift.

It never felt like this when Y'rill changed me. In fact, I barely felt anything at all. I was Dani one minute, then Dani inside a Hunter body the next.

But this time, my brain is kicking up a few notches, and I'm watching countless dark grids I never managed to wake flare with light as new connections are made. It's exhilarating, dazzling, and humbling, and such a freaking rush.

I'm getting more brainpower. I'm also getting more . . . wow. I drift for a few moments, realizing I see things differently. I'm a bit less bristling with life and hunger for action, and more compassionate, a bit more . . . ew! Humble? Ick. I'm not sure I like this. It's as if my consciousness elevated and the quotidian concerns of life melted away, granting me a bird's-eye view of the world, whereas Dani is all about the details.

This is why Y'rill is so different from Shazam. She found her way through her transition. But I never experienced it. When Y'rill shifted forms for me, I remained exactly the same Dani inside, only my skins changed.

I'm growing and expanding and my cage is too small and it explodes and I explode from it. Roaring fire, I go rocketing into space and dive straight for Shazam's cage, on the verge of trying out freeze-frame in midair, and I'm just about to close my talons on the bars when—

Abruptly, I'm frozen in place, frozen in my skin, unable to move at all from the neck down, just like the time V'lane iced Rowena's body but left her head free so she could talk.

I turn my head to glare daggers of fire at the bloody interfering Hunters, but they're staring past me, all twelve of them, and the look on their faces makes me turn, too.

K'vruck.

The most ancient of Hunters hovers a few miles away, his great leathery sails churning dark ice. On his back, he carries the enormous, dark, noncorporeal cloud of the Unseelie king. Actually, he's not completely noncorporeal. Although the king is smudgy and indistinct, his wings are clearly visible.

The king and K'Vruck are so gargantuan, they seem a small, dark moon in the sky.

I've come to collect my boon, the Unseelie king says.

The Hunters say nothing for a time then Z'kor replies, *Are you certain this is the boon you would claim? There are many others, much larger, you might ask of us, which we would grant.*

It wasn't a large thing I did for you.

It was, Z'kor disagrees. *No being can decide for another what weight a matter carries.*

This is a large thing to me. You will free them, permitting both to retain their dual forms. You will strip them of the ability to manipulate time. They will be outcast for two centuries, denied the comforts of companionship with other Hunters. In two hundred years, they will be welcomed back into your fold. You will not interfere in their lives, in any way, during those two centuries, and, when they do return, all is forgiven.

Z'kor says, *You need not redeem your boon. We planned to release them anyway.*

Wait, what? They did? *But* why? I try to blurt the words, but my mouth is no longer capable of forming them, so I send telepathically, *I don't understand! I mean, don't get me wrong, I'm super bloody grateful. But why?*

Z'kor turns its head to me and says, *The transgression which con-*

cerned us was not Y'rill's. You have earned your new name. Welcome to our clan, Y'taine. Today, you are born. The moment you are able to control shifting yourself from your original form to Hunter is the true rite of passage. You felt what it did inside you. That is being Hunter.

Frowning, I say, *Are you telling me you would have killed Shazam/ Y'rill if I failed to shift? That's what this was all about? You caged us to force me to shift?*

Not why we caged you. Still, had you not shifted, we would have permitted you to believe we destroyed Shazam/Y'rill, then returned you to Earth, never to see each other again.

You were never planning to kill Y'rill? Despite my larger view of matters, I'm having a hard time processing this abrupt shift in perception: Y'rill was never on trial.

I was.

It was your punishment, Z'kor says, *and yours alone. You exploited Y'rill's love for you to achieve selfish ends. Y'rill was never the one on trial here. Intentions do matter. Yours were not pure.*

I'm abashed and deeply ashamed. I get what they're saying, and they're right.

However, it was love for another that drove you to demand Y'rill continuously shift you. We believe you will learn from today. You have now shifted of your own power and tasted what we are. We believe you worthy of being Hunter.

I'm so sorry, I say, and I mean it. I did exploit Y'rill's love for me, pushing her to break more and more rules, without thinking beyond my own hunger to have it all, be human with Ryodan. She kept telling me the Hunters would call due a price. I didn't listen. As long as I could talk her into it, I kept pressing with that devil-may-care attitude that despises any and all rules. And because Y'rill kept willingly shifting me, I never tasted the depths of a true transformation. Over time, I would have stopped trying so hard to attain it, perhaps never evolved. I was cheating, plain and simple. *I was wrong. I see that now.*

Do better.

I will, I vow intensely.

Dani Mega O'Malley, Z'kor says gravely, *we see you. We are aware of the trials you endured, and the triumphs you've achieved. Like Y'rill, we have tasted both your suffering and the enormity of your potential. You are an exceptional being. From time to time, we will make exceptions. But do not test our patience. A wise Hunter would wait a long time before doing so again.*

I nod just as gravely. *Can Shazam be Y'rill again?*

Already am, tiny red. I'm proud of you, my young Y'taine.

My heart glows supernova bright, and I whip my head around to see Y'rill hovering effortlessly behind me, violet lightning and love crackling in her eyes.

Come, the Unseelie king intones. *I will return you to Earth.*

We can fly ourselves, I tell him, realizing I can move again. I vibrate in place then bristle excitedly into formation beside Y'rill.

Work on her hover, Y'rill, Z'kor chides. *She's dreadful at it.* To me, Z'kor says, *Not from here, you can't. The arena where we gather is beyond your ability to reach and will be for quite some time. K'Vruck and the king will return you to Earth.*

Thank you, I tell Z'kor, and all the Hunters.

They bow their great dark heads, then they're gone.

I thump Y'rill with my tail, grinning from ear to ear. *You ready, Shaz-ma-taz?* I'm so happy, I burst into song: *Shaz the mighty furbeast lived up in the air, watching all of Olean, grouchy as a bear, Dani the Mega O'Malley loved that rascal Shaz—*

You said you would die with me, Y'rill rebukes. *Never say that again. I would see you live, always live.*

I see you, Y'rill, and I'm so, so sorry.

Let's go home, tiny red.

K'Vruck and the Unseelie king do something then that my brain can't process. Their wings expand and expand; then Y'rill and I are wrapped in them, rolling around, spiraling through time and space. From between feathers and leathery scales, I watch planets and stars go shooting by. We rush, faster and faster, then abruptly, we're not moving at all, but floating, rocking as I imagine it must feel like rocking in a womb, then we're spiraling off again then—

We're on top of Chester's. Back home in Dublin.

K'Vruck is gone.

The Unseelie king diminishes to roughly human size, though he remains indistinct but for the clarity of his wings.

Y'rill and I shift to our original forms simultaneously, and I beam at Shazam. "My shifting was effortless," I exclaim. "I can't wait to do it again." I drop to my knees, open my arms wide, and Shazam rushes into them, hugging me, sobbing with joy. I bury my face in his fur a long moment, drying the last of tears I didn't know were on my cheeks. I thought I was going to lose him. Then I thought we both might die. But he's in my arms, and I will never jeopardize his precious life again, in any form.

I tip my head back and gaze up at the king, who's still standing there watching us, and say, "Thank you for bringing us home."

He laughs, and his wings begin to shimmer with cobalt fire as he becomes corporeal before my eyes.

I've half a mind to clap a hand up to block my view, concerned it might not be safe to gaze directly upon whatever the Unseelie king truly is without going mad or blind.

But I don't, because he's corporeal now, and my mouth is hanging open.

And I'm staggered.

Stupefied.

Stymied.

Stunned.

Speechless, even.

I'm all the "s" words, I suppose.

The Unseelie king tosses one more my way. "Always. Stardust," Ryodan says with a smile.

52

My love, my life

MAC

I SIT IN A CHAIR beside Dad's bed, holding his hand, watching his chest laboriously rise and fall as he wheezes.

He keeps drifting in and out of sleep.

I no longer have any doubt the Song of Making reset time, aligning the flow of it to coincide in all realms. My day and a half at Cruce's castle cost me only an identical amount of time in Dublin.

My brain is simultaneously whirling and numb.

The moment we left Cruce's underground kingdom, I took one last look at Barrons standing next to Masdann then fled for my father's chamber.

Barrons understood. I can't process anything else. I'm all the emotions; exhausted and overwhelmed, angry and relieved, filled with gratefulness, riddled with grief.

I have a million questions, but they have to wait.

Barrons removed the spell suspending my father shortly after we returned. Mom is sitting on the opposite side of the bed, holding Dad's other hand.

Barrons said he believes my father has two weeks, at most.

Inwardly, I'm sobbing, but I refuse to let the tears fall. I won't add one more ounce of sorrow to the room.

Mom told me all the things Dad said, in one of the awful waking nightmares I had. "Honey, the walls would have come down anyway whether or not you went to Ireland. This would have happened, with or without you, just in some other iteration. It's not your fault. Who's to say we wouldn't have died years ago? Don't you dare blame yourself! Your daddy and I knew the risks. You and I will get through this. It won't be easy, it's going to gut both of us, but we'll hold on to each other as we grieve and find our way through, together. I love you, Mac."

To which Daddy added, with labored breath, "Baby, I had a good run. That's what you want to be able to say, whether death comes at twenty-eight or at fifty-eight. If you blame yourself for this, I'll haunt you, petunia. You're my beautiful, perfect little girl."

He's sleeping now. Their forgiveness and understanding slay me. I love them both so much.

"Why are there two Barrons?" Rainey Lane says.

I look at her. There are two Barrons. Oh, God. And I can't tell them apart. That disturbs me on levels too profound to face. I say, "It's a long story, and I need more answers before I tell it." I've been thinking, while sitting there, about how to cheat death, and I don't know where it is yet, but by God, I *will* find it. I say in a low, urgent voice, "Mom, there's an Unseelie elixir—"

"Your father won't take it."

"But it doesn't take your soul and emotion," I press heatedly. "It only—"

"Would make him immortal."

"Yes," I say flatly. "You could take it, too!"

Rainey meets my gaze, her eyes glistening with unshed tears. Like me, she refuses to add them to the sorrow of our vigil.

We're alike, she and I. We'll both smile right up to the end. We'll assure Jack Lane we will be just fine. Because that's who Mom is now, and I'm fiercely proud of her. She's tempered, composed, graceful. And that's how they raised me. Lanes are soldiers, we march into battle and live as others fall, but we don't allow ourselves to get lost in grief because, if you live a long life, death will come, grief will rain down over and again, and the only way to survive it and remain an alive, passionate being is to pay the price of pain every time. It's always going to hurt. But as long as you're still capable of suffering, you're still capable of joy.

"We have no desire to live forever, honey. We have strong faith. He won't risk losing Heaven, and neither will I."

I leap restlessly to my feet and scan the room, looking for I don't know what—a hard-core tranquilizer? Someone cleaned the cobwebs from the room. Thank heavens.

"Will you be giving the Unseelie elixir to the Seelie?" my father says then, and I whirl, scowling.

I fist my hands. "They did this to you!"

"My question stands," Dad, ever the barrister, says with a tired smile.

I stare at him in mutinous silence. If I say no, he'll berate me, and I don't want him wasting his precious breath. If I say yes, I'll hate me. If I say no, I'll probably hate me, too. The weight of the waking nightmares I had, where I pretty much K'Vrucked the world in every scenario, the only variation in the details, is a suffocating albatross around my neck. I know what I don't dare do. I also know what I'll hate doing.

"I want to hear it, baby. You know what's right."

Clenching my jaw, I grit, "I'm not doing anything to them. I'm just leaving them alone."

"Wrong answer."

"They did this to you. I'm not killing them. I'm merely letting Nature take her course."

"Wrong answer again. Tell me what your heart knows."

I rub my eyes and sigh. "That I can't judge and convict an entire species based upon the actions of two."

"Go on."

I feel like I'm on trial, before my father. We both are. Because he's judging himself as a parent by the decisions I now make.

"If I can find a way to help them that offers them the possibility for a good life—"

"—an immortal one like they had," he interrupts.

"—I will do all in my power to help them achieve it," I say woodenly, and I know it's true. It's the right thing to do. The problem is the Cauldron doesn't work, and I can't just give the Seelie the Unseelie Elixir, assuming I can find it. All the Seelie, with the three exceptions, those three hateful ones who did this to my father, are stark raving mad, overwhelmed by the weight of too many memories. It would be no kindness to make them immortal as they currently are.

"That's all I ask, baby. I know you'll make me proud."

He's asleep again, and tears are about to begin gushing from my eyes. To Mom, I mutter, "I have to pee," and race from the room.

I manage to close the door behind before bursting into tears.

To my consternation, Barrons is standing there, either about to come in or waiting for me to come out. Hastily scrubbing my tears away and turning them back off, I sidle away, pressing against the door. Is he Barrons? Or am I being fooled again?

"Which is precisely why I'm here," he says grimly, not missing my reluctance to get close to him. "We're addressing this. Now."

"I need to sleep." I'm not ready for this. I can't face anything else.

His midnight gaze glistens crimson. "I listened to Cruce saying he was going to fuck you while his prince watched."

I inhale sharply, realizing we were both deeply traumatized by events. He stood impassively by while Cruce told me the horrid things he was going to do to me, awaiting the perfect moment to strike. While Cruce spoke of his plans to erase Barrons from my mind and heart, rape me, erase *me*. And he's right, I don't trust myself to know which of them is him, and I must. "Fine. What now?"

"We go talk to Masdann. And put your fears to rest."

"Then we put yours to rest, too," I say quietly. I know what Barrons needs. And I know, even as bone deep exhausted as I am, what I need, too. I need to stretch out next to him, skin to skin. Hold him close and have him hold me, know he's my Barrons. And if I can remain awake long enough, make love slow, hot, and desperately tender, with the last vestiges of my energy until I pass out in his arms.

Knowing it's him. Not an Unseelie prince.

"I fear nothing," he growls, offended. Then his mouth twists in a wry smile and he adds, "Except that you might fear me. That I can't bear. Come."

———— • • ————

Masdann is waiting in Ryodan's office. As the door whisks open and I glance in, I'm once again stunned by how identical they are. Barrons is standing next to me, yet Barrons is also standing near Ryodan's desk, staring down at the club below. Both powerful, darkly beautiful, wearing the same face and form.

When he turns, I wince.

Their faces are i-fucking-dentical. How will I ever know for a certainty if it's Barrons at my side, in our bed, not Masdann?

"Greetings, my queen," Masdann says with a courtly bow. "I apologize for the deception, but Barrons and I deemed it necessary to protect you."

"How many of my dreams did you mess with?"

"Two."

"Which two?" I demand.

"The afternoon you slumbered on the sofa, when I guided you to show me your encounters with Cruce was the first time. The second was last night as you slumbered in Cruce's chamber. Though he did not enter the Dreaming with me, he sat in the chamber watching, and to preserve our charade I had to comply with his wishes. What I saw the first time solidified my resolve. You never loved Cruce.

You loathed kissing him. You compartmentalized yourself to do so."

"When did you and Barrons team up? How did Barrons even find out about you?"

Barrons says, "He appeared at Chester's before you left the chamber beyond time."

Masdann says, "I told Cruce that Barrons had already departed. Cruce wanted me to test whether I could fool Ryodan. I didn't want to fool Ryodan. I wanted his hackles up."

"He succeeded," Barrons says. "Ryodan knew it wasn't me. But only because he knew I'd not yet left the chamber, that I would never leave, until you had."

Masdann says, "Later, the afternoon I watched your dreams of Cruce is the day I revealed myself to Barrons."

Barrons says, "You were so worried about your father, I didn't want to bring up that Cruce was still alive, and there was no way to tell you about Masdann without doing so. Then Lyryka revealed his existence, but from that moment on—"

I say wearily, "We were so busy chasing one problem after the next, there was never a good time."

Barrons's gaze is dark and filled with shadows, and I see now how deeply worried he's been about me. "You were exhausted and grieving your father, and I didn't want to add to it. Masdann didn't believe Cruce would take you for some time. We hoped to eliminate him before he did. But between the Light Court's incessant machinations, Dani missing, your father missing, Sean and Rae being taken—"

"—we were too busy trying to put out whatever fire was directly in front of us," I finish bitterly. Both the Light and Shadow Courts had kept us hopping, distracted by one crisis after the next, starting the moment I left the chamber.

He inclines his head in agreement.

Masdann says, "I didn't drive you into the web. Had I known

Cruce was planning to take you, I would not have encouraged you to leave Chester's. I believed you would benefit from walking the streets of the city you love."

"The chamber Cruce held you in mutes power," Barrons says. "I couldn't communicate with you via our bond. Masdann told me what he said to you about getting tattoo implements for the Hunters, which was based on old information. Cruce didn't know we'd discovered such marks were unnecessary. I said what I did when I entered the chamber, hoping to tip you off that it was me."

It had worked, sort of. Then he'd flashed crimson fire in his dark gaze, and I'd been afraid to hope. Yet I had hoped, in spite of myself, what I was thinking was true.

"Look deeply at me, my queen," Masdann says. "I'm an Unseelie prince. There are significant differences between Barrons and me."

"*Sidhe*-seers can't penetrate the glamour of the new Unseelie Cruce created," I tell him.

Masdann says, "While Cruce did make us undetectable to your Order, you hold a deeper, much more powerful magic. Look with your queen's eyes, using the True Magic."

"Cruce neutralized my True Magic somehow," I tell him.

Masdann says, "The chamber did that to you, and only while you were within it."

More cleverness on Cruce's part. He'd counted on me trying to access my magic in the bedroom, wagering I'd not try again while touring his kingdom.

"Do as Masdann says," Barrons says. "If at any time you'd tried to penetrate Masdann's glamour, it would have worked. But you believed he was me, so you had no reason to try."

If it's true that the queen can see through the new Shadow Court's glamour, thank God. I gaze at Masdann, drifting inward, seeking the softly burning power of the True Magic, pleased to find it accessible again. *Show me what is true*, I command.

I smile faintly.

So that's what Masdann looks like.

The prince of dreams is identical to Barrons, with the same darkly chiseled face, height, and powerful musculature, midnight eyes and smoldering carnality. But great, black wings adorn Masdann's shoulders, sweeping down at his sides, and tattoos rush like brilliant clouds beneath his skin. He's darker than Barrons with an ebony torque around his neck. He's clearly Fae. Clearly an Unseelie prince.

Masdann says, "You can always tell us apart; you can discern the true forms of all the Shadow Court Fae. I've no doubt you'll be scrutinizing Barrons with the queen's power every time you see him for quite some time, and for that, I apologize. I will not impersonate him again. And in time, yet more differences will appear between us. At this moment, Jericho Barrons and I are the most alike we'll ever be. I hold the essence of him, but not the beast. I've suffered no curse. I've not lived his life. We are more different than you think. I've a mere four years of living, and my future will lead me in different directions. My experiences will shape me into who I become. Barrons and I will never again be as alike as we are in this moment."

I hear truth in his words. Masdann is a newly born version of Barrons, without any of his past. He looks like Barrons and, at the core, shares his essential makeup, but their paths will diverge greatly from here.

"You hold a dangerous power." He could cause enormous damage to an enormous number of people.

"I have neither the desire nor intention of weaving others' dreams. I have more than enough of my own. The Dreaming fascinates me. All possibles exist there. I've pledged my loyalty to you, as both queen and MacKayla Lane. It's programmed into my essence. I could never betray you. It's not possible. There, Barrons and I will never differ. And should you ever have need of me, I will be there."

"Why did you betray Cruce?"

"There is no betraying one such as he," Masdann replies. "There is only putting a rabid dog down. He was the old king all over again, worse. He grew more depraved and greedy with each passing day. I saw what was coming during my sojourns in the Dreaming, the many possible futures, none of them good for anyone but Cruce, and vowed to put a stop to it. I saw what he would do to this world and countless others. I was unable to kill him as I don't possess Barrons's power. I'm not the beast and can never be. That is yet another way you can tell the difference between us. I could only try to glamour myself as his beast, glamour his crimson eyes, and you would see past my glamour. I knew we'd have to switch places to take Cruce down."

I look at Barrons, frowning. "I would have thought you'd despise having, for lack of a better word, a clone."

Masdann laughs. "He nearly killed me when he saw me for the first time."

Barrons murmurs, "Then I realized what a foolish thing Cruce had done, how easily Masdann might be used against him, and that Masdann sought me for precisely that reason."

Masdann snorts. "You saw too much of yourself in me to dislike me."

To me, he says, "I'll keep my distance, my queen, if that makes you more comfortable."

I smile faintly. Once I finish wrapping my brain around this, I can't say I'd mind having two Barronses around sometimes, with different strengths to offer. It sounds to me as if Masdann has his own unique gift of premonition, seeing all possibles in the Dreaming, another tool we might use to protect our world. "Is there truly an Unseelie elixir that bestows immortality without costing emotion and soul?"

Masdann inclines his head, wings lifting, rustling as he resettles them. "There is. I will bring it to you, and return the other items Cruce bid me thieve from Faery. But I would ask something of you, and hope you will hear me out. I've been pondering the future of the Fae and have ideas I would share."

Sighing, I kick out a chair and drop into it.

One day, I'll sleep. Right now, I have a job to do.

I'm MacKayla Lane, High Queen of the Fae.

And I'm open to discussion, counsel, all points of view. We've a world of unique beings, I still have no idea how to sing the walls back up, and I'm beginning to wonder if I should.

Perhaps the split courts, the divide between the realms of Mortal and Fae, the many walls, some fashioned of substance, others of fear, were part of the problem.

To Masdann, I say, "I'm listening."

53

I'll stop the world and melt with you

MAC

THREE DAYS LATER, I'M sitting with Barrons in the Jimmy Durante Club, devouring my second platter of Guinness-battered fish-and-chips as the chanteuse croons about a world that will always welcome lovers as time goes by, bracing myself for my father's death and my work with the Light Court, which I will commence once he passes.

I'm not willing to go to Faery right now. I intend to be holding Daddy's hand when he closes his eyes for the last time.

Once he's no longer with us (I can't think the word "dies," I simply can't) I'll sift to Faery with hundreds of *sidhe*-seers. After meeting with Ixcythe, Azar, and Severina to tell them what I'm going to do, I'll unfreeze the Winter Court subjects, one by one. The *sidhe*-seers will give them a cup from the true Cauldron of Forgetting, which Cruce stole and substituted with a useless replica, followed by a drop of the Unseelie Elixir of Life; then help the newly reborn Fae adjust to the reality of being young, immortal, without baggage, possessing both emotion and a soul, assuming they have one in there somewhere. Then, after freeing the prisoners in Ixcythe's labyrinth, restoring the immortals, and returning the humans to Earth, I'll move to the courts of Spring, Autumn, and Summer and do the same.

The Fae will be a new species; the Tuatha De Danann, as I suspect they once were long ago, although back then they were merely extremely long-lived, not immortal.

I'll never tell the newborn Tuatha De Danann that the Cauldron exists and will destroy it. From this moment forward, there will be no erasing of the past. Each memory the Fae make they must bear and carry forward. It's the memories of our failures, our worst moments and darkest hours that weigh on us and make us try harder, do better.

I suspect Ixcythe, Azar, and Severina will balk. They'll want to keep their memories, because they're power-hungry and damaged, and they'll see it as a way to be more cunning and powerful than their subjects, possessing knowledge others lack.

They *will* drink from the Cauldron of Forgetting if I must chain them to a beam and force it down their throats. Everyone is starting over, no exceptions.

Once the Light Court is restored and newborn, Masdann will bring the Shadow Court to Faery. He says the Unseelie are eager to meet their light brethren. They're only four years old, quite young themselves. They'll meet and mingle and, hopefully, in time, become a tribe.

Despite my grief, and the grief that is yet to come when my father . . . is no longer here . . . I'm looking forward to helping the Fae find their way.

There will soon be eight kingdoms in Faery, where both courts will reside. Dublin of Eternal Night will be used as a vacation spot of sorts—it's too beautiful to destroy, and it's the Unseelies' home—but no one will ever permanently live there again. I want the Unseelie prison unmade, once we make sure no living being remains trapped within.

Christian sifts in and jars me from my reverie. "I heard you're restoring the Fae. How do you plan to govern them?"

I blink at the woman standing next to him and use my True Magic to determine if what I'm seeing is glamour.

It's not.

"Lyryka, is that *you*?" I exclaim.

She nods, smiling.

Half and half, so that's why Cruce hid her away. She's breathtakingly lovely, the finest of both courts. "I hope you're planning to stay," I tell her as I open my arms to draw her into a hug.

She's glowing when she steps back. "For a time, perhaps," she allows. Then she curtsies slightly and adds, "My queen." The curtseying and bowing, the *my queen*s make me uncomfortable but, for now, I suspect the formalities are necessary, not for me, but my subjects. Those changes I make I'll implement slowly.

"A long time, perhaps," Christian growls.

His arm is around her waist, and it's obvious they're lovers. Chemistry sizzles between them. Death and the librarian, I think, amused. But seriously, she's perfect for him, light to his darkness, warmth and bubbling joy to his reserve and seriousness.

He's changed. Strong, centered, self-assured, he's a powerful prince in his prime. When he looks at Barrons, he inclines his head in greeting, the way Barrons does. Barrons cuts him a look of irritation but inclines his head back. "Not my tribe, Highlander," he growls.

Christian laughs then his eyes narrow as he stares behind me, eyes narrowing and darkening. "Och, that fuck did not. Christ, he's going to be even more insufferable now."

I turn to see who Christian is talking about and instantly light up with joy.

"Dani!"

"Mac!"

Dani slips into freeze-frames then she's next to me. And we're hugging, and I'm so happy to see her, I almost can't stand it. "God, we have so much to talk about," I tell her, smiling, squeezing her hand.

"I'm so sorry about your dad," Dani says quietly. "I know how much he means to you."

And her gaze promises me when I lose him, she'll be right next to me, sitting at my bedside while I weep, dragging me out and into the world again, when it's time. The same way we took turns doing after she lost Dancer.

Then Ryodan is standing next to Dani, and I'm so flabbergasted by what I sense, I'm speechless. *That's* what Christian meant. Insufferable, indeed. But that's Ryodan, king in every century.

Stunned, I say to Barrons, "The king's power chose. And it's not you. But the mural—"

"—was choice," Barrons reminds. "I made a different one. It was Christian who gave us the idea. When he transformed fully into Death, the king's power came to him and he rejected it. He suspected whoever wanted it most strongly would get it. I wanted it. If you were to be queen, I would be king. But the king's power had always been watching four contenders, not three. It was hovering around Ryodan for a long time, too."

"I had powerful motivation to be chosen," Ryodan says. "As king, I can travel the stars with Dani. We'll never be separated by the limitations of our forms. When Barrons and I went into the Unseelie prison, we spent the night in the old king's castle, working every dark spell we knew, kicking up a storm of power, to draw the king to us."

"When the king came, I bowed out," Barrons says. "Leaving only two contenders: Ryodan or Cruce."

"The next day, after Barrons left to find you, the king's power chose me," Ryodan says.

Dani says, "Ryodan came to the arena where the Hunters were holding us, to redeem the king's boon and free us."

"But they wouldn't accept it because Dani had already saved herself," Ryodan says, with pride.

"Okay, folks, I know I've missed a lot. Bring me up to speed, baby. What's going on?"

I freeze.

That was *not* my father's voice behind me. It's impossible. He's two levels above me, dying.

My gaze flies to Barrons because I can't turn. I can't face confronting that I'm hallucinating, hearing things.

Barrons murmurs via our bond, *I have no idea how, but your father is standing behind you with your mother, looking healthy and strong, although his left arm is in a sling and his hands are not fully healed. Kat, Sean, and Rae are with them. Breathe, Mac. It may be the child. I sense something unusual about her.*

I turn.

"Daddy," I breathe faintly, feeling as if I might slump to the floor from shock and relief. "But how?" I glance at Rae, who's standing between Kat and Sean, holding their hands. Barrons is rarely wrong. "Did *you* do this?"

She nods, beaming. "I bring greetings from the Spyrssidhe, great queen. They told me your father was poisoned by a magic potion, and I make bad magic things go away."

"Rae's gift is neutralizing dark magic," Kat says quietly.

"She healed me, too," Sean says. "I have no idea when or how, but Cruce bound my power, preventing me from fully completing the transformation to Unseelie prince. Rae sensed the dark magic he'd worked the moment we met and neutralized his spell. She insisted we bring her here today so she might remove the toxin from your father's heart."

Rae frowns up at me. "I'm sorry I couldn't heal him all the way, great queen." She wrinkles her nose. "But he's very badly broken."

"What do you mean?" I ask worriedly

Mom laughs softly. "It's nothing. Rae can feel Jack's arthritis and the pain that lingers in his arms and hands."

"He hurts still," Rae frets.

Dad says to Rae, "Baby, nothing hurts me anymore, thanks to you."

He offers me a one-armed hug, and I finally manage to move. I rush to him and am swallowed in half a great bear hug I thought I'd never get to feel again. I press kisses to his cheek, free an arm, tug my mother into our group embrace.

When finally I extricate myself, I drop to my knees and hug Rae. "I don't know how I can ever thank you."

"Oh, that's easy," she says swiftly. "Restore the Spyrssidhe's privileges at court. They're ever so sad to be banished. They went into hiding 'cause the other fairies went mad. They think you can fix it all and make everything happy again."

I vow, "From this day forward, the Spyrssidhe are no longer banished and hold full rights as Fae. And I will make things happy again. I promise."

"Which brings me back to my original question," Christian says, "How do you plan to govern them?"

I rise and glance around at our small, powerful group. "We all have parts to play. You, Ryodan, Barrons and the Nine, the *sidhe-seers*, Sean, Inspector Jayne—wait, has anyone seen Inspector Jayne?"

"He went into hiding to protect his family," Ryodan tells me.

"Will someone track him down and tell him to come back?" I ask.

"I'll take care of it," Christian tells me.

"Christian, I keep forgetting. Do you think Chloe might consider taking the Unseelie Elixir of Life, given . . . well, you know, Dageus?" I ask.

Tiger-gold eyes flare lucent as he growls, "I think that'll bloody well be a resounding yes."

Ten minutes later, we've pushed together tables, and I'm having lunch with Barrons, my parents, Dani and Ryodan, Christian and Lyryka, Sean, Kat, the tiny wonder that is Rae, who gave me my father back, plus a Hel-Cat (who keeps snagging food from every-one's plate) raising flawlessly stacked Guinnesses to toast what will undoubtedly be a far from perfect future.

I glance around the table, gaze moving slowly from face to face, as I soak up the laughter and savor the unique flavor of testy banter that flows richly between those who would lay down their lives for one another.

This moment is perfect.

And it's all we ever have. This moment, right now.

We're fools if we fail to cram all the living and loving we can possibly do into each and every one.

FIRST EPILOGUE

—— • • • ——

SOME TIME LATER . . .

AZAR

AZAR, PRINCE OF AUTUMN, stood in the winter kingdom, staring at the miles and miles of snowy land, unable to fathom why he felt compelled to come here today.

But he didn't fully fathom many things of late. Everything was new to him.

The Tuatha De Danann had suffered great calamity and loss, the queen had told them. She'd been able to ensure their survival only by restoring them to their earliest forms, with no memory of events that had passed before.

Each of them was now newborn. Beginning life fresh, with no baggage, but for whatever they incurred by their actions from this day forward.

He had no memory of life before the queen restored them, yet there were certain things that stirred in him a powerful emotion. All of the Fae were experiencing it; something the queen called déjà vu—already having seen or been before.

She'd told them regardless of their memory loss, it was not possible to eviscerate the core of one's being and, so long as they possessed emotion, the imprint of love remained. There would be those so deeply ingrained in their hearts, they would one day be drawn together again.

Azar began to walk, wondering what beckoned him in this icy land, so different from his home. He inhabited the noisy, celebratory kingdom of eternal harvest, that sprawled vast and wide beneath buttery dawns and crimson and saffron sunsets, gardens overflowing with mandarin pumpkins, spicy, scarlet apples, and buttery gourds. In the Autumn kingdom all was vivid, with a constant hum of voices and celebration.

Here was a hushed land of few colors, void of gardens, carpeted with snow, stretching beneath a sky so blue it dazzled the eye and towering trees glazed with ice that sparkled as if diamond crusted beneath the brilliant sun.

He found the air here—unlike the temperate harvest clime of Autumn, perpetually smoked by the fires of Samhain—crisp, bold, and invigorating. Here there was no crackle of leaves beneath his boots, only the soft crush of snow.

From time to time, he would stop as he walked to gaze wonderingly at intricate patterns etched in ice on the boughs of trees, marveling at the skill of the artist who'd painted them with such care. And, from time to time, he would pause, perplexed that here was an unexpected grassy knoll, bursting with brightly colored flowers amid the snow.

He walked for time uncounted, reveling in being alive.

You are tabula rasa, the queen had told them. *Each of you is now a book with blank pages. You choose what you write upon them. Choose well. I will only interfere if it seems we are, as a species, about to make the same mistakes again.*

He liked being a blank book that yet held the resonance of those things he once loved. He suspected his fresh start was a gift whose true, exquisite value he might never know. He trusted he would find his way to matters of his heart again.

As he topped a snowy crest in a forest, he drew to an abrupt halt, transfixed, staring into the glade beyond, blood quickening in the way it did whenever he encountered a person or thing that had been important to him, in that time forgotten.

Two princesses stood, their heads close, talking excitedly about plans to continue reshaping the land.

One was golden and bright, the other pale radiance. It was the pale princess, who stood upon a thick carpet of snow blossoms, that took his breath away.

He strode forward to greet them, and they turned, as one, smiling.

He sketched a formal bow. "I'm Azar, prince of Autumn. I bid you good day and bring greetings from my court."

"I'm Severina," the golden princess replied. "Although we are not currently in my kingdom, I bid you welcome to Summer." She glanced from the pale princess to Azar and back again, then back and forth again, eyes widening with delight.

The winter princess was staring at Azar with the same blend of wonder, fascination, and joy he'd inexplicably felt upon seeing her, with a kiss of rose blossoming in her cheeks.

Eyes dancing, Summer gave Winter a quick hug and kiss and said breathlessly, "I'll come back later. Perhaps *much* later. Till tomorrow, then?"

"Tomorrow," the winter princess agreed, with a warm smile. "We'll paint the labyrinth. I don't care much for that place. Perhaps we could replace it with something new?"

Summer said excitedly, "Flowers and fountains, with a small garden house."

"That sounds divine."

After Summer vanished, Winter turned back to Azar and curtsied low. "Greetings, Prince Azar. I bid you welcome to my heart and home." She frowned, looking flustered. "I meant 'hearth' and home," she corrected, blushing. "I'm Ixcythe. And I'm delighted to meet you."

"Ixcythe," Azar echoed her name, savoring the way it felt on his tongue, but there was something . . . something else he would call her, something that felt just right. "I think I shall call you 'Ix.'"

SECOND EPILOGUE

— · • · —

SOME TIME LATER . . .

CHRISTIAN

I STAND IN THE CORRIDOR, gazing down at Lyryka, wanting to say a million things, saying none of them.

It took a long time for me to come around to this moment but eventually I placed aside my selfish desires and arrived.

When first Lyryka mentioned her dream, I consoled myself with the thought that the Silvers in the White Room behind Barrons Books & Baubles were shattered, and there was no way to fulfill it.

But in time, I'd come to understand how important it was to her and I'd begun making inquiries, first of Barrons, who'd refused to tell me one bloody thing about his hundred or so Silvers other than he was sorry I'd ever seen them.

It was Kat who told me where to find what I sought. Here at the abbey, beneath their feet, the entire time.

Today, she escorted us here, and one of the Shedon broke the powerful wards sealing the door.

Now Lyryka and I stand outside the golden hall, and I'm wondering why the bloody hell I ever did such a bloody stupid thing as take it upon myself to find the way to give Lyryka what she wanted, knowing it would only take her away from me.

I smile faintly. I know why I did. I have only to look at her, see the excitement, wonder, and joy in her fascinating eyes to know I'd do it again and again.

Trapped for three quarters of a million years, Lyryka hungers to see the world, live her own stories, bold and free. And she doesn't want company. I can't fault her for that. We all must make our way alone before we're much good at making our way together.

Still. Bloody hell. She's under my skin. My desire for her never wanes. Doesn't matter how many times I've had her in my bed, I'll miss her body next to mine. I'll walk into our bedroom in the morning to find an empty bed, hungering to hear her cranky early-morning grumbles and, later, our endless conversations about anything and everything. My castle will feel so bloody empty without her.

I'll miss flying the skies beside her, soaring the Highlands, listening as she exclaims with delight over the smallest of things.

I'll miss her funny way of seeing life as if it's all one great big epic story. I'll miss her diction, her eclectic choice of words.

I'll never be able to look at a Guinness bottle again. I'll end up shaking it, hoping she's inside.

"Oh," she exclaims, staring up at me, gleaning my depth of emotion, "you *so* like me, Christian."

"I do."

"No, I mean you really, *really* like me."

"What can I say? Duality is my poison." This goodbye is killing me. I hate it. I will not fuck it up for her. *I love you*, I don't say. She's not ready for that. *But, oh, Lyryka, how I love you.*

She beams. "And I've got duality in spades."

"You do. Stay. Just a bit longer. A few more days." Bugger it, I wasn't going to say that. I may be safer not opening my mouth again.

She sobers. "It's never going to get easier, Christian. In fact, the longer I stay, the harder trying to say goodbye will become."

Precisely what I'd be counting on. But I won't say it again, and I won't press.

"I've been waiting for this moment all my life, Christian. Dreaming of it. The choices, the freedom. Just look at all those mirrors. I can choose any one of them. I'm finally, truly free. Thanks to you, Christian. You broke my bottle and shattered my ice and set me free."

I exhale gustily and say urgently for the hundredth time, "The Silvers are dangerous. Remember what I told you about the Hall. Choose quickly, Lyryka. Don't dally. Remember, the image each shows is not where they lead."

"Oh, for heaven's sake, I know all of this. You've told me at least a hundred times."

"Half a dozen, at most."

"You're worried about me."

"And you're delighted about that."

"I am."

"You're naïve."

"I am," she agrees. "And vulnerable and open and kind, and the universe is hard on people like me."

"You're not people."

"I was using that—"

"—I know, in the broadest conceptual sense."

We smile at each other then I growl, "Goddamn it, Lyryka, I'm going to miss you."

"I know," she exclaims, radiant. "It's amazing. I'll be out there in the world, and someone's going to be somewhere else, *missing* me. But they won't summon me or demand my presence or try to hold on to me because they care about me and they want me to be free."

"Utterly, deliriously free. I want you drunk on choices, sloshed on life. I wish you the finest, most heroic adventures beside the grandest of companions. But one day, if you decide to come back . . ."

"One day," she clarifies, "when I *do* come back . . ."

"You might come to me."

"I *will* come to you."

"And I'll be waiting."

"And you will give me all the sex I demand because you'll be so happy to see me," she assures me with complete confidence.

I smile at her and arch a brow. "We'll see."

She arches a brow back. "Oh, we most certainly will."

When she leans in to kiss me, I close my eyes and savor every nuance of it, sear it into my memory, in exquisite detail, to keep me company for however long this woman makes me wait.

Lyryka is worth waiting for.

THIRD EPILOGUE

— • • • —

AND YET MORE TIME LATER . . .

MAC

I STAND ON THE SIDEWALK in front of Barrons Books & Baubles and tip back my head, scrutinizing the elegant, Old World façade of the bookstore, nodding with satisfaction.

I love this place. But something was missing.

I just finished adding a café, which I christened Korrie's Korner, after one of my best friends from high school who loves reading as much as I do. Long ago, we used to dream of opening our own bookstore and café together. I can't wait to tell her about it and hope she'll come to see it. We recently reconnected, and she sounds ready for a change.

I think she'll love Dublin and what I've done with the café I named for her. Korrie's Korner is a place where people can come to have a smashing good cup of coffee and read a book, curled in a window seat or one of dozens of overstuffed armchairs. Perhaps gather before the fire, discussing history, current events, anything and everything, tackling the issues facing our world, finding solutions. With luck, I'll draw the brightest hearts and minds in Dublin and eavesdrop shamelessly. I'm not as busy with the Tuatha De Danaan as I thought I would be. The Fae are doing extremely well governing their kingdoms. And now I have a place in the mortal realm that will connect me to the diversity of humans with whom I share the planet.

The only reason it took me so long to get around to creating Korrie's Korner was I love the way the bookstore looks and couldn't figure out where to put the café that wouldn't detract or seem odd. While I *am* High Queen of the Fae, not everyone knows that, and I don't want to advertise by having people enter a noticeable pocket of reality tucked into a corner. Besides, the spatial disorientation of Barrons Books & Baubles is already extreme enough.

Ergo, I built up.

"Seriously, Ms. Lane?" Barrons says dryly, behind me.

Ms. Lane. Uh-hmm. He doesn't like it. "Who holds the deed?" I cast a teasing smile over my shoulder.

He arches a brow. "Who holds the woman that holds the deed?"

"As if you'd ever stop holding me just because I put a café on the roof of the bookstore," I say, laughing. "It's perfect there. Admit it."

"Your bookstore. My rugs. Humans will traipse en masse through the establishment, across my rugs, to get to your bloody café. Why not place a few tables out front? How will you explain the countless lemurs marauding about the shop to your patrons?"

I snort with laughter. "The lemurs don't maraud, and you know it. They escaped twice. And they haven't tried to leave again since I added the forest and expanded their floor. Rae loves playing with them when she visits. Besides, between you, me, lemurs, and our friends that drop by, good grief, do you really think *lemurs* are what will strike our patrons as odd?"

"There is that."

"I needed more room, and the rooftop really is the best place," I say as we head for the door. "I tucked in an expansion element. Come, I'll show you. I want to know if you think it's too obvious. I plan to offer Barrons Books and Baubles tees, mugs, calendars, and the like, and I saw these really cute heart-shaped pink Post-its that—oh! Speaking of pink, I'm going to add a bakery to the café with fresh baked cakes every day. I also plan to get some of those hand-tooled leather journals made by local crafters, and some framed, local photography. I have so many ideas." I continue prattling about them as we wind through the bookstore, then draw up short realizing not only is Barrons not paying any attention to me, he's texting someone, completely tuning me out. Consternated, I say loudly, "It's not as if I plan to let the patrons tour the sex dungeon, and really, Barrons, given that I got the café and you got a sex dungeon, I think my renovations are a win-win."

His head whips up, phone gets shoved into his pocket, and his dark eyes glitter.

"I thought that might get your attention."

"And where did you say this sex dungeon is?"

"If you'd been paying attention, you'd know. But no, you tuned me out at heart-shaped pink Post-its."

His hands are on my waist, and he pulls me close and I shiver. I always want this man. Never get enough. And yes, I did put a sex dungeon in. *Before* I built the café.

"It's in the basement," I murmur.

"We don't have a basement."

"We do now. Would you care to see it?"

"Can't get there fast enough."

———— • • • ————

Later, tangled in crimson sheets before a crackling fire, I finally broach a topic that's been bothering me for months.

Barrons says when you ask a question, you must be prepared for every possible answer. I've been afraid of the possible answers to this one.

I roll over onto my side, prop my head on a fist, and stare down at him, my dark, powerful beast of a man, stretched naked on his back, arms folded behind his head, eyes closed, and trace my fingers over the curve of his biceps, down his arm, along his jaw. His torso is still tattooed with black and crimson runes from the dark magic he and Ryodan worked that night in the Unseelie king's castle to entice the power near. He hasn't died since. I run my hand over the shapes, across the ripples of his abdomen, then, before I go lower still, remove my hand. Difficult though it is when Barrons is sprawled naked next to me, I need to focus on thoughts. "Barrons, remember the premonition I told you about?"

"The one where the Fae slipped you the Elixir of Life," he murmurs.

"Yes, that one."

"Why are you still thinking about it?"

"Seriously? I did terrible things."

"It seems to me," he says opening his eyes slowly, "the only thing you did wrong in that version of events was not a reflection of you, in any way other than showcasing your hope, optimism, and desire to achieve peace for both species."

"I wiped out humans and trapped the Nine in limbo."

"In that version, you'd been slipped an Elixir without your knowledge that stripped emotion and soul. The king wasn't entirely correct. With chemicals, and external potions, one's core self *can* be eviscerated. Yours was taken against your will—in that version of events within a premonition," he clarifies tightly.

"Are you defending me in a premonition where I turned into a she-bitch from hell?"

"I'll defend you everywhere."

"Okay, forget that one. My point is I had *four* unusual fugue states while I was in the chamber beyond time."

"The other three?"

"They were equally awful. In one, I never made it through the Dark Zone that foggy day I got lost. V'lane intercepted me in the alley a short distance from the bookstore and talked me into trusting him. I saw you but we never meet. I chose him. I left with him."

He growls, "That fuck is dead. I burned what was left of him, poked around in the ashes, and waited to see if anything rose. It didn't. I ate them."

I burst out laughing. "You did *not* eat Cruce's ashes."

"The fuck I didn't. And your other two . . . premonitions?"

"I was Cruce's consort, but he had me trapped in a dream-reality from which I couldn't escape. I could hear you roaring for me, telling me the truth of his lies, demanding I wake, chanting a spell to buy me time to escape."

"And the last?"

"Dad died, and I killed all the Fae and the old earth gods—"

"—speaking of, they need to be your next project."

I sigh. "I know. Back to the fugues." I refuse to be detoured now that I'm ready to deal with it. "In my last vision, my rage was so great, my hunger for revenge so consuming the Unseelie king chose me as his successor, and the moment his power passed into me, it exploded back out, and killed all beings but humans."

"Was I in that one?"

"Yes, but I sifted away from you. I went to see Dad's grave on my way to live among the stars."

"O ye of little faith. Why would you run? Do you still believe there's any incarnation of you I wouldn't want? Wouldn't go after, determined to share a life with, to the ends of space and time itself?"

That was actually a big part of what I was wondering. "I was afraid you would despise me for what I did. For not controlling the power."

"Never. Whatever you become. Whatever you do. I'm here. With you. Wherever, together." He rolls to his side, tugs me into his arms, and slants his mouth, hot and hungry, over mine. When at last we part, I'm glowing and distracted, but I'm a woman on a mission. I need to know.

"So," I continue, "I thought about those four fugue states and came up with four possible explanations."

"We're still talking about this?" he growls.

"We are. One: they were merely dreams, my subconscious fears."

"Undoubtedly the right answer."

"You haven't heard the other three. Hush."

"Did you just hush me?"

"Two: that's merely how subtle the queen's gift of prescience is."

"I'll buy that one. Why are you still using that talented mouth of yours to talk when there are so many other things you might be doing with it?"

"Three: Masdann never owned up to weaving my dreams any more than you own up to most of what you do."

"Now I'm being indicted in this conversation. How did we get here?" He laughs and reaches for me.

I scoot away. "Barrons, what if they weren't premonitions or dreams? What if they were déjà vu? How would I ever know the difference between a foreboding about the future versus a feeling that I've been somewhere before?"

"Why does it matter? The realities you glimpsed are not the reality we're living."

I open my mouth then close it again. Then, steeling my spine, I snap, "Four: every single one of those things happened and, each time, you took me back somehow and gave me a reset and kept doing it until I got things right."

He stares at me a long moment then, "Clearly, you think I possess formidable powers."

It doesn't elude me that he didn't deny it.

"One," he continues swiftly, "you're implying you did things wrong in those other realities. You didn't. You were preyed upon in each. In none of them were you a bad person. You were a good person that was savaged into doing bad things. Two: Mac, why are we still talking about it? We're in the right reality."

"Did you somehow take me back in time to undo wrong realities until we achieved this one?"

He smiles faintly. "How would I know? I would have gone back in time, too, and neither of us would retain memory. So, you see," he says, as he tugs me back into his arms, "it doesn't matter. The only thing that matters is that we're here, now, in a sex dungeon that, I feel compelled to add, is staggeringly inventive. Our world is a fine place to be. In this reality, the only one I judge, you did well. I sat back this time, let you make the calls."

I stare into his inscrutable, dark gaze and realize that's all the answer I'm going to get. In this reality, the only one I can judge, I did well. "Now that I think of it, you were different, Barrons. You let me talk and make all the decisions with the rare exception of growling that whatever I was about to do, I wasn't doing it alone. I kept waiting for you to speak up or do something."

"I see. I did nothing to get us through this latest escapade. That's what you think," he says dryly. "I suppose Masdann did everything."

I wink at him. "Jealous?"

"You try living with a doppelgänger in your world."

"I did."

"Only for a short time. I wanted to despise Masdann. I ended up finding him brilliant, devastatingly attractive, clever, imaginative, talented, lethal in battle, nearly as complete a package as the original."

I laugh. "Still, you must admit, you stood by, remarkably quietly, through most of what happened once I left the chamber."

"What did you expect?"

"For you to do what you always do. Stalk, roar, seize control. Threaten. Handle. Conquer. Perhaps even dictate and expect everyone to rush about, blindly obeying."

"Ah the good old days," he says with a sigh. "I've watched you evolve, Mac. From the day you barged into my shop to the day you left your chamber. This wasn't my proving ground. It was yours. In fairness, it was my proving ground as well. I like threatening, handling, and conquering and excel at it. It would be all too easy for me to keep doing it, and never step out of your way. I want an equal. You are. And you handled things superbly."

"Thank you. Jericho."

"Always. Mac."

Like Dani and Shazam, Barrons and I speak in code. When Dani says, *I see you, Yi-yi*, Shazam knows she's saying she loves him.

Each time I say, *Thank you*, I'm telling him he's my sun, moon, and stars.

And each time Barrons replies, *Always. Mac*, I know what it means.

His "always" is a pledge of love, a promise eternal, and a guarantee that while we may never live happily ever after for very long, we will live. Together. Vibrantly and passionately.

Fire to his ice.

Ice to my fever.

THE END

ACKNOWLEDGMENTS

———— • • ————

In *Kingdom of Shadow and Light*, Mac muses: "Most of the time I feel like I just bumble about and get lucky with the help of my amazing friends. The truth is, nothing I've ever done would have succeeded if I'd been alone."

While this is true about virtually everything in my life, it's especially true about KOSAL—a novel I was afraid I would never write, leaving the Fever series eternally incomplete.

Two years of chronic carbon monoxide exposure from 2015 through early 2017 left me with severe physical and cognitive challenges. The physical: Parkinson's symptoms; adrenal crash/HPA axis dysfunction; lung, vascular, and heart complications. The cognitive: inability to form sentences, locate words in my brain, do basic math, write, find my way home if I left the house.

In addition to physical and cognitive issues, the effect of prolonged exposure on my brain (neurotransmitters and receptors) left me in a state of deep depression and anxiety. That anxiety was exacerbated by the fact that once the exposure stopped, I was told to sit back and wait to see how sick I got as carbon monoxide recovery is an issue of reperfusion. As the oxygen returns to long-starved tissues, it causes cell death, so you actually get briefly better, then worse. And you have no idea how bad it will get. I sat and watched grid after grid of my brain go dark, one physical system after the next fail. As Christian would say: Who thinks this shit up?

Perhaps my most defining moment of the ordeal was when, after trying repeatedly, desperately to write and failing for over eighteen months, I sat on my sofa trying to decide what life was worth—*if* it was worth living—if I could no longer tell stories.

If I became *that* woman, the one with brain damage, who people regarded with pity as I walked by and murmured softly but never softly enough "She used to be a good writer."

If I could no longer support myself, if I never healed.

It was a time of stupefying fear.

A time of intense internal reflection.

A time of enormous gifts.

A time of hope to strengthen me.

Chrisanthi Fekkos: Thank you for the hours of friendship and conversation and the gift of your incandescently healing craniosacral massages that you refused to let me pay for because you knew if I couldn't write, I couldn't make money. And neither of us knew how long it would take me to heal, or even if I would. Thank you for sending light into my body and heart during the darkest night of my soul.

Sara Johnstone Smith: I could write a novel about the many ways you are the wind beneath my broken wings, convincing me I can always heal, gently but firmly keeping me focused ahead not behind, working without compensation until I could pay you again, championing my slightest gains. Thank you for the Chick-fil-A and the laughter and not mentioning the gun while understanding it. I'm sorry I put you through that.

My brother, Brian, for so many things and especially for going to NOLA with me at Booklover's Con, watching me like a hawk, rescuing me when you could see I was about to go down.

My tribe: Nora Luna, Sally Short Blondaiu, Kimberly Mann Cousins, Dawn Frakes Mosely, Nicole Garcia, Andrea Resichmann

Sullivan, Sara Johnstone Smith, Sue Ramjatan, thank you for always having my back, knowing I can't see the predators coming and spotting them for me, for protecting me and loving me and being my people. You are the finest women I know.

A special debt of gratitude to a woman I've never met who had a profound impact on my life through her book *My Stroke of Insight: A Brain Scientist's Personal Journey*: Dr. Jill Bolte Taylor. A Harvard-trained neuroanatomist, she suffered a massive stroke in the left hemisphere of her brain that caused severe physical and cognitive damage. Although her injury was a stroke versus my carbon monoxide poisoning, many of our battles were the same, and I drew strength from her journey. Her story offered assurance that a full recovery from substantial injury could be made. Whenever I felt the feathery, dark tendrils of despair brushing against my brain, I reminded myself what Dr. Taylor went through, how tirelessly she warred to recover, how fully she did, and how long it took. I resolved to do no less. She was my hero, the woman that *did*, proving it was possible for me, too.

My publisher, Random House: I asked and you granted, giving me time to complete my healing, write *Kingdom of Shadow and Light*, and get back on my feet. A thousand times, thank you. KOSAL wouldn't exist without you. (And I'd have lost my house.)

My editor, Shauna Summers: From the moment I delivered *Darkfever* instead of the expected *Night of the Highlander*, you championed Fever and me, and saw the series through from beginning to end. I truly couldn't have done this without you. Your wisdom, insight, guidance, and friendship mean the world to me. You are the epitome of the beautiful way women can support one another.

As always, many, many thanks to my incredible team at Random House: Lexi Batsides, Kara Welsh, Scott Shannon, Matthew Schwartz, Gina Wachtel, Madeleine Kenney, Gina Centrello, Kim Hovey, Scott Biel, Jordan Pace, Allison Schuster, Jennifer Garza, Quinne Rogers, Nancy Delia, Caroline Cunningham. This book, the series, wouldn't exist without you. Thank you for your patience and kindness, for stepping in to help me when I so desperately needed it.

The Moning Maniacs: We are forever connected by the magic of thousands of red threads. Thank you for being the best fans in the universe and waiting so long for KOSAL. Your enthusiasm, energy, excitement, and unwavering belief in me was a lighthouse guiding me to safety over a dark sea. Not getting to throw a con, to see and hug all of you is torture, and I can't wait for the day we're together again! To Selena McKissick, Capri Bolton, and the team of fabulous moderators, thank you for your dedication every day. You deftly navigate the slivers of our online community with kindness and sincerity.

I could fill a book with the things I've learned over the past few years but will distill it to a few.

Life is hard.

It's also beautiful.

We are not what we do for a living.

We are not only the color of our skin or gender or sexual orientation.

We're the love we give and receive, the actions we take when the world is chaotic and hard, what we demand of ourselves, and how we take care of one another in the darkest of times.

Like MacKayla Lane, we transform, if we're lucky and fiercely committed, from innocent, to shattered, to warrior, to wise woman capable of leading and lighting the way for others in need.

This is the end of the Fever series.

Thank you for coming on the journey with me.

Karen

GLOSSARY

— • • • —

PEOPLE

SIDHE-SEERS

SIDHE-SEER (SHEE-SEER): A person on whom Fae magic doesn't work, capable of seeing past the illusions or "glamour" cast by the Fae to the true nature that lies beneath. Some can also see Tabh'rs, hidden portals between realms. Others can sense Seelie and Unseelie objects of power. Each *sidhe*-seer is different, with varying degrees of resistance to the Fae. Some are limited; some are advanced, with multiple "special powers." For thousands of years the *sidhe*-seers protected humans from the Fae that slipped through on pagan feast days when the veils grew thin, to run the Wild Hunt and prey on humans.

MACKAYLA LANE (O'CONNOR): Main character, female, twenty-three, adopted daughter of Jack and Rainey Lane, biological daughter of Isla O'Connor. Blond hair, green eyes, had an idyllic, sheltered childhood in the Deep South. When her biological sister, Alina, was murdered and the Garda swiftly closed the case with no leads,

Mac quit her job bartending and headed for Dublin to search for Alina's killer herself. Shortly after her arrival, she met Jericho Barrons and reluctantly began working with him toward common goals. Among her many skills and talents, Mac can track objects of power created by the Fae, including the ancient, sentient, psychopathic book of magic known as the *Sinsar Dubh*. At the end of *Shadowfever* we learn that twenty years before, when the *Sinsar Dubh* escaped its prison beneath the abbey, it briefly possessed Mac's mother and imprinted a complete copy of itself in the unprotected fetus. Although Mac succeeds in reinterring the dangerous book, her victory is simultaneous with the discovery that there are two copies of it; she *is* one of them and will never be free from the temptation to use her limitless, deadly power. In *Feversong*, Mac vanquishes her inner *Sinsar Dubh* and is free at last. When Aoibheal passes the true Magic of the Fae to her, Mac becomes the High Queen of the Fae.

ALINA LANE (O'CONNOR): Female, deceased, older sister to MacKayla Lane. At twenty-four she went to Dublin to study at Trinity College and discovered she was a *sidhe*-seer. She became the lover of the Lord Master, also known as Darroc, an ex-Fae stripped of his immortality by Queen Aoibheal for attempting to overthrow her reign. Alina was killed by Rowena, who magically forced Dani O'Malley to trap her in an alley with a pair of deadly Unseelie. Although the *Sinsar Dubh* resurrected Alina in *Feverborn*, in *Feversong*, Alina died when Mac sang the Song of Making, as the ancient melody deemed her existence anathema to the natural order of the universe.

DANIELLE "THE MEGA" O'MALLEY: Main character. An enormously gifted, genetically mutated *sidhe*-seer with an extremely high IQ, super strength, speed, and sass. She was abused and manipulated by Rowena from a young age, molded into the old woman's personal assassin, and forced to kill Mac's sister, Alina. Despite the darkness and trauma of her childhood, Dani is eternally optimistic and determined to survive and have her fair share of life plus some. In *Shadowfever*, Mac discovers Dani killed her sister, and the two, once as close as sisters, are now bitterly estranged. In *Iced*, Dani flees Mac and leaps into a Silver, unaware it goes straight to the dangerous Hall of All Days. We learn in *Burned* that, although mere weeks passed on Earth, it took Dani five and a half years to find her way home, and when she returns, she calls herself Jada. In *High Voltage*, Dani becomes a shifter, able to transform into a Hunter.

ROWENA O'REILLY: Grand Mistress of the *sidhe*-seer organization until her death in *Shadowfever*. She governed the six major Irish *sidhe*-seer bloodlines, but rather than training them, she controlled and diminished them. Fiercely power-hungry, manipulative, and narcissistic, she was seduced by the *Sinsar Dubh* into freeing it. She ate Fae flesh to enhance her strength and talent, and kept a lesser Fae locked beneath the abbey. Dabbling in dangerous black arts, she experimented on many of the *sidhe*-seers in her care, most notably Danielle O'Malley. In *Shadowfever* she is possessed by the *Sinsar Dubh* and used to seduce Mac with the illusion of parents she never had, in an effort to get her to turn over the only illusion amulet capable of deceiving even the Unseelie king. Mac sees through the seduction and kills Rowena.

ISLA O'CONNOR: Mac's biological mother. Twenty-some years ago Isla was the leader of the Haven, one of seven trusted advisors to the Grand Mistress in the sacred, innermost circle of *sidhe*-seers at Arlington Abbey. Rowena (the Grand Mistress) wanted her daughter, Kayleigh O'Reilly, to be the Haven leader, and was furious when the women selected Isla instead. Isla was the only member of the Haven who survived the night the *Sinsar Dubh* escaped its prison beneath the abbey. She was briefly possessed by the Dark Book but not turned into a lethal, sadistic killing machine. In the chaos at the abbey, Isla was stabbed and badly injured. Barrons tells Mac he visited Isla's grave five days after she left the abbey, that she was cremated. Barrons says he discovered Isla had only one daughter. He later tells Mac it is conceivable Isla could have been pregnant the one night he saw her and a child might have survived, given proper care after a premature birth. He also says it is conceivable Isla didn't die but lived to bear another child (Mac) and give her up. Barrons theorizes that Isla was spared because the sentient evil of the *Sinsar Dubh* imprinted itself on her unprotected fetus, made a complete second copy of itself inside the unborn Mac, and deliberately released her. It is believed Isla died after having Mac and arranging for her friend Tellie Sullivan to have both her daughters smuggled from Ireland and adopted in the States, forbidden ever to return to Ireland.

Augusta O'Clare: Tellie Sullivan's grandmother. Barrons took Isla O'Connor to her house the night the *Sinsar Dubh* escaped its prison beneath Arlington Abbey more than twenty years ago.

Kayleigh O'Reilly: Rowena's daughter, Nana's granddaughter, best friend of Isla O'Connor. She was killed twenty-some years ago, the night the *Sinsar Dubh* escaped the abbey.

Nana O'Reilly: Rowena's mother, Kayleigh's grandmother. An old woman living alone by the sea, prone to nodding off in the middle of a sentence. She despised Rowena, saw her for what she was, and was at the abbey the night the *Sinsar Dubh* escaped more than twenty years ago. Though many have questioned her, none have ever gotten the full story of what happened that night.

Katarina (Kat) McLaughlin (McLoughlin): The daughter of a notorious crime family in Dublin, her gift is extreme empathy. She feels the pain of the world, all the emotions people work so hard to hide. Considered useless and a complete failure by her family, she was sent to the abbey at a young age, where Rowena manipulated and belittled her until she became afraid of her strengths and impeded by fear. Levelheaded, highly compassionate, with serene gray eyes that mask her constant inner turmoil, she wants desperately to learn to be a good leader and help the other *sidhe*-seers. She turned her back on her family's criminal enterprises to pursue a more scrupulous life. When Rowena was killed, Kat was coerced into becoming the next Grand Mistress, a position she felt completely unfit for. Although imprisoned beneath the abbey, Cruce is still able to project a glamour of himself, and in dreams he seduces Kat nightly, shaming her and making her feel unfit to rule or be loved by her longtime sweetheart, Sean O'Bannion. Kat has a genuinely pure heart and pure motives but lacks the strength, discipline, and belief in herself to lead. In *Burned,* she approached Ryodan and asked him to help her become stronger, more capable of leading. After warning her to be careful what she asked him for, he locked her beneath Chester's in a suite of rooms with the silent Kasteo. In *Feversong,* Kat has given birth to a daughter, Rae, who possesses unique abilities. Kat never divulges the identity of Rae's father.

Jo Brennan: Mid-twenties, petite, with delicate features and short, spiky, dark hair, she descends from one of the six famous Irish bloodlines that can see the Fae (O'Connor, O'Reilly, Brennan, the McLaughlin or McLoughlin, O'Malley, and the Kennedy). Her special talent is an eidetic, or sticky, memory for facts, but unfortunately by her mid-twenties she has so many facts in her head, she can rarely find the ones she needs. She has never been able to perfect a mental filing system. When Kat clandestinely dispatches her to get a job at Chester's so they can spy on the Nine, Jo allows herself to be coerced into taking a waitressing job at the nightclub by the immortal owner, Ryodan, and when he gives her his famous nod, inviting her to his bed, she's unable to resist, even though she knows it's destined for an epic fail. In *Burned,* Jo turns to Lor (who is allegedly Pri-ya at the time and won't remember a thing) after she breaks up with Ryodan to "scrape the taste of him out of her mouth." She learns, too late, that Lor was never Pri-ya, and he has no intention of forgetting any of the graphically sexual things that happened between them, although, frankly, he'd like to be able to. In *Feversong*, Jo was killed by MacKayla Lane, while Mac was possessed by the *Sinsar Dubh*.

PATRONA O'CONNOR: Mac's biological grandmother. Little is known of her to date.

THE NINE

Little is known about them. They are immortals who were long ago cursed to live forever and be reborn every time they die at precisely the same unknown geographic location. They have an alternate beast form that is savage, bloodthirsty, and atavistically superior. It is believed they were originally human from the planet Earth, but that is unconfirmed. There were originally ten, counting Barrons's young son. The names we know that they currently go by are Jericho Barrons, Ryodan, Lor, Kasteo, and Fade. In Burned *we discover one is named Daku. There's a rumor that one of the Nine is a woman.*

JERICHO BARRONS: Main character. He is one of a group of immortals who reside in Dublin, many of them at Chester's nightclub, and is their recognized leader, although Ryodan issues and enforces most of Barrons's orders. Six feet three inches tall, black hair, brown eyes, 245 pounds, date of birth October 31, allegedly thirty-one years old, his middle initial is Z, which stands for Zigor, meaning either "the punished" or "the punisher," depending on dialect. He is adept in magic, a powerful warder, fluent in the druid art of Voice, and an avid collector of antiquities and supercars. He despises words, believes in being judged by one's actions alone. No one knows how long the Nine have been alive, but references seem to indicate in excess of ten thousand years. If Barrons is killed, he is reborn at an unknown location in precisely the same condition as he was the first time he died. Like all of the Nine, Barrons has an animal form, a skin he can don at will or if pushed. He had a son who was also immortal, but at some point in the distant past, shortly after Barrons and his men were cursed to become what they are, the child was brutally tortured and became a permanent, psychotic version of the beast. Barrons kept him caged below his garage while he searched for a way to free him, hence his quest to obtain the most powerful book of magic ever created, the *Sinsar Dubh*. He was seeking a way to end his son's suffering. In *Shadowfever*, Mac helps him lay his son to final rest by using the ancient Hunter, K'Vruck, to kill him.

RYODAN: Main character. Six feet four inches, 235 pounds, lean and cut, with silver eyes and dark hair nearly shaved at the sides, he has a taste for expensive clothing and toys. He has scars on his arms and a large, thick one that runs from his chest up to his jaw. As the owner of Chester's and the brains behind the Nine's business empire, he manages the daily aspects of their existence. Each time the Nine have been visible in the past, he was king, ruler, pagan god, or dictator. Barrons is the silent command behind the Nine; Ryodan is the voice. Barrons is animalistic and primeval, Ryodan is urbane and professional. Highly sexual, he likes sex for breakfast and eats early and often.

LOR: Six feet two inches, 220 pounds, blond, green eyes, with strong Nordic features, he promotes himself as a caveman and likes it that way. He is heavily muscled and scarred. Lor's life is a constant party. He loves music, hot blondes, and likes to chain his women to his bed so he can take his time with them, willing to play virtually any role in bed for sheer love of the sport. Long ago, however, he was called the Bonecrusher, feared and reviled throughout the Old World.

KASTEO: Tall, dark, scarred, and tattooed, with short, dark, nearly shaved hair, he hasn't spoken to anyone in a thousand years. There is a rumor floating around that others of the Nine killed the woman he loved.

FADE: Not much is known about him to date. During events in *Shadowfever*, the *Sinsar Dubh* possessed him briefly and used him to kill Barrons and Ryodan then threaten Mac. He is tall, heavily muscled, and scarred like the rest of the Nine.

FAE

Also known as the Tuatha De Danann or Tuatha De (TUA day dhanna or Tua DAY). An advanced race of otherworldly creatures that possess enormous powers of magic and illusion. After war destroyed their own world, they colonized Earth, settling on the shores of Ireland in a cloud of fog and light. Originally the Fae were united and there were only the Seelie, but the Seelie king left the queen and created his own court when she refused to use the Song of Making to grant his concubine immortality. He became the Unseelie king and created a dark, mirror-image court of Fae castes. While the Seelie are golden, shining, and beautiful, the Unseelie, with the exception of royalty, are dark-haired and dark-skinned, misshapen, hideous abominations with sadistic, insatiable desires. Both Seelie and Unseelie have four royal houses of princes and princesses who are sexually addictive and highly lethal to humans.

Unseelie

UNSEELIE KING: The most ancient of the Fae, no one knows where he came from or when he first appeared. The Seelie don't recall a time the king didn't exist, and despite the court's matriarchal nature, the king predates the queen and is the most complex and powerful of all the Fae—but he lacks a single enormous power that makes him the Seelie queen's lesser: she alone can use the Song of Making, which can call new matter into being. The king can create only from matter that already exists, sculpting galaxies and universes, even on occasion arranging matter so that life springs from it. Countless worlds call him God. His view of the universe is so enormous and complicated by a vision that sees and weighs every detail, every possibility, that his vast intellect is virtually inaccessible. In order to communicate with humans he has to reduce himself into multiple human parts. When he walks in the mortal realm, he does so as one of these human "skins." He never wears the same skin twice after his involvement in a specific mortal episode is through. In *Feversong*, after learning his concubine Aoibheal/Zara left him by choice and wanted nothing to do with him, the king abdicated his power, but refused to choose a successor.

Dreamy-Eyed Guy (aka DEG, *see also* Unseelie King): The Unseelie king is too enormous and complex to exist in human form unless he divides himself into multiple "skins." The Dreamy-Eyed Guy is one of the Unseelie king's many human forms and first appeared in *Darkfever* when Mac was searching a local museum for objects of power. Mac later encounters him at Trinity College in the ancient languages department, where he works with Christian MacKeltar, and frequently thereafter when he takes a job bartending at Chester's after the walls fall. Enigma shrouded in mystery, he imparts cryptic bits of useful information. Mac doesn't know the DEG is a part of the Unseelie king until she and the others are reinterring the *Sinsar Dubh* beneath Arlington Abbey and all of the king's skins arrive to coalesce into a single entity. The Dreamy-Eyed Guy seems to be an exception to the rules governing the Unseelie king's skins and may currently exist independently of the king.

Concubine (originally human, now Fae, *see also* Aoibheal, Seelie Queen, Unseelie King, Cruce): The Unseelie king's mortal lover and unwitting cause of endless war and suffering. When the king fell in love with her, he asked the Seelie queen to use the Song of

Making to make her Fae and immortal, but the queen refused. Incensed, the Seelie king left Faery, established his own icy realm, and became the dark, forbidding Unseelie king. After building his concubine the magnificent shining White Mansion inside the Silvers, where she would never age so long as she didn't leave its labyrinthine walls, he vowed to re-create the Song of Making and spent eons experimenting in his laboratory while his concubine waited. The Unseelie Court was the result of his efforts: dark, ravenous, and lethal, fashioned from an imperfect Song of Making. In *Shadowfever*, the king discovers his concubine isn't dead, as he has believed for over half a million years. Unfortunately, the cup from the Cauldron of Forgetting that Cruce forced upon the concubine destroyed her mind, and she doesn't retain a single memory of the king or their love. It is as if a complete stranger wears her skin. In *Feversong*, the concubine drinks an elixir the king created for her that restores her memory but can't restore her emotion, leaving her a passionless husk of bitterness and resentment at the species that so deeply manipulated her. At long last, she recalls being Zara. The Dreamy-Eyed Guy demands three boons from MacKayla once she's queen. Mac restores Zara's mortality and returns her to her original home world. Given the changes the Song of Making wrought in all the Seelie, it's suspected Zara's emotion has also returned. The Dreamy-Eyed Guy/king have not yet requested the third boon.

CRUCE (Unseelie, but has masqueraded for more than half a million years as the Seelie prince V'lane): Powerful, sifting, lethally sexual Fae, he believes himself to be the last and finest Unseelie prince the king created. Cruce was given special privileges at the Dark Court, working beside his liege to perfect the Song of Making. He was the only Fae ever allowed to enter the White Mansion, so he might carry the king's experimental potions to the concubine while the king continued with his work. Over time, Cruce grew jealous of the king, coveted his concubine and kingdom, and plotted to take it from him. Cruce resented that the king kept his Dark Court secret from the Seelie queen and wanted the Dark and Light Courts to be joined into one, which he then planned to rule himself. He petitioned the king to go to the Seelie Court and present his "children," but the king refused, knowing the queen would only subject his imperfect creations to endless torture and humiliation. Angry that the king would not fight for them, Cruce went to the Seelie queen himself and told her of the Dark Court. Incensed at the king's betrayal and quest for power, which was matriarchal, the queen locked Cruce away in her bower and summoned the king. With the help of the illusion amulets Cruce and the king had created, Cruce wove the glamour that he was the Seelie prince, V'lane. Furious to learn the king had disobeyed her, and jealous of his love for the concubine, the queen summoned Cruce (who was actually her own prince, V'lane) and killed him with the Sword of Light to show the king what she would do to all his abominations. Enraged, the king stormed the Seelie Court with his dark Fae and killed the queen. When he went home to his icy realm, grieving the loss of his trusted and much-loved prince Cruce, he found his concubine was also dead. She'd left him a note saying she'd killed herself to escape what he'd become. Unknown to the king, while he'd fought with the Seelie queen, Cruce slipped back to the White Mansion and gave the concubine another "potion," which was actually a cup stolen from the Cauldron of Forgetting. After erasing her memory, he used the power of the three lesser illusion amulets to convince the king she was dead. He took her away and assumed the role of V'lane, in love with a mortal at the Seelie Court, biding time to usurp the rule of their race, both Light and Dark Courts. As V'lane, he approached MacKayla Lane and was using her to locate the *Sinsar Dubh*. Once he had it, he planned to acquire all the Unseelie king's forbidden dark knowledge, finally kill the concubine who had become the current queen, and, as the only vessel holding both the patriarchal and matriarchal power of their race, become the next, most powerful, Unseelie king ever to rule. At the end of *Shad-*

owfever, when the *Sinsar Dubh* is reinterred beneath the abbey, he reveals himself as Cruce and absorbs all the forbidden magic from the king's Dark Book. But before Cruce can kill the current queen and become the ruler of both the Light and Dark Courts, the Unseelie king imprisons him in a cage of ice beneath Arlington Abbey. In *Burned,* we learn Dani/Jada somehow removed the cuff of Cruce from his arm while he was imprisoned in the cage. Her disruption of the magic holding him weakened the spell. With magic she learned Silverside, she was able to close the doors on the cavernous chamber, and now only those doors hold him. In *Feverborn,* Cruce escapes, and in *Feversong,* he gives Mac his half of the Song of Making so she can save the world from being destroyed by the black holes the Hoar Frost King created in *Iced.*

UNSEELIE PRINCES (AKA THE FOUR HORSEMEN OF THE APOCALYPSE): Highly sexual, insatiable, dark counterparts to the golden Seelie princes. Long blue-black hair, leanly muscled dark-skinned bodies tattooed with brilliant, complicated patterns that rush beneath their skin like kaleidoscopic storm clouds. They wear black torques like liquid darkness around their necks. They have the starved cruelty and arrogance of a human sociopath. There are four royal princes: Kiall, Rath, Cruce, and an unnamed prince slain by Danielle O'Malley in *Dreamfever.* In the way of Fae things, when one royal is killed, another becomes, and Christian MacKeltar is swiftly becoming the next Unseelie prince. Kiall and Rath are killed by Barrons and Ryodan in *Burned.* Currently Sean O'Bannion is the Unseelie prince Famine, Christian MacKeltar is the Unseelie prince Death. The prince Pestilence has not been reborn.

UNSEELIE PRINCESSES: The princesses have not been heard of and were presumed dead until recent events brought to light that one or more were hidden away by the Unseelie king, either in punishment or to contain a power he didn't want loose in the world. At least one of them was locked in the king's library inside the White Mansion until either Dani or Christian MacKeltar freed her. Highly sexual, a powerful sifter, this princess is stunningly beautiful, with long black hair, pale skin, and blue eyes. In *Burned* we learn the Sweeper tinkered with the Unseelie princess(es) and changed her (them) somehow. Unlike the Unseelie princes, who are prone to mindless savagery, the princess is quite rational about her desires, and logically focused on short-term sacrifice for long-term gain. It is unknown what her end goal is, but, as with all Fae, it involves power.

ROYAL HUNTERS: A caste of Unseelie sifters, first introduced in *The Immortal Highlander,* this caste hunts for both the king and the queen, relentlessly tracking their prey. Tall, leathery skinned, with wings, they are feared by all Fae. This caste was created when the ancient Hunters donated part of their essence to the king to use in an attempt to birth more children but the Hunters were offended by what the king created. The Royal Hunters were banished by the original Hunters.

CRIMSON HAG: One of the Unseelie king's earliest creations, Dani O'Malley inadvertently freed this monster from a stoppered bottle at the king's fantastical library inside the White Mansion. Psychopathically driven to complete her unfinished tattered gown of guts, she captures and kills anything in her path, using insectile, lancelike legs to slay her prey and disembowel them. She then perches nearby and knits their entrails into the ragged hem of her bloodred dress. They tend to rot as quickly as they're stitched, necessitating an endless, futile hunt for more. Rumor is, the Hag once held two Unseelie princes captive, killing them over and over for nearly 100,000 years before the Unseelie king stopped her. She reeks of the stench of rotting meat, has matted, blood-drenched hair, an ice-white face with black eye sockets, a thin gash of a mouth, and crimson fangs. Her upper body is lovely and voluptuous, encased in a gruesome corset of bone and sinew. She prefers to abduct Unseelie princes because they are immortal and afford an unending supply of guts, as they regenerate each time she kills them. In *Iced*, she kills Barrons and Ryodan, then captures Christian MacKeltar (the latest Unseelie prince) and carries him off. The Crimson Hag is defeated in *Burned* by Mac, Dani, Barrons, and Ryodan, and Christian is rescued.

FEAR DORCHA: One of the Unseelie king's earliest creations, this seven-foot-tall, gaunt Unseelie wears a dark pin-striped tailcoat suit that is at least a century out of date, and has no face. Beneath an elegant, cobwebbed black top hat is a swirling black tornado with various bits of features that occasionally materialize. Like all the Unseelie, created imperfectly from an imperfect Song of Making, he is pathologically driven to achieve what he lacks—a face and identity—by stealing faces and identities from humans. The Fear Dorcha was once the Unseelie king's personal assassin and traveling companion during his liege's time of madness after the concubine's death. In *Fever Moon*, the Fear Dorcha is defeated by Mac when she steals his top hat, but it is unknown if the Dorcha is actually deceased.

HOAR FROST KING (GH'LUK-RA D'J'HAI) (aka HFK): Villain introduced in *Iced*, responsible for turning Dublin into a frigid, arctic wasteland. This Unseelie is one of the most complex and powerful the king ever created, capable of opening holes in space-time to travel, similar to the Seelie ability to sift but with catastrophic results for the matter it manipulates. The Hoar Frost King is the only Unseelie aware of its fundamental imperfection on a quantum level, and like the king, was attempting to re-create the Song of Making to fix itself by collecting the necessary frequencies, physically removing them from the fabric of reality. Each place the Hoar Frost King fed, it stripped necessary structure from the universe while regurgitating a minute mass of enormous density, like a cat vomiting cosmic bones after eating a quantum bird. Although the HFK was destroyed in *Iced* by Dani, Dancer, and Ryodan, the holes it left in the fabric of the human world can be fixed only with the Song of Making.

GRAY MAN: Tall, monstrous, leprous, capable of sifting, he feeds by stealing beauty from human women. He projects the glamour of a devastatingly attractive human man. He is lethal but prefers his victims left hideously disfigured and alive to suffer. In *Darkfever,* Barrons stabs and kills the Gray Man with Mac's spear.

GRAY WOMAN: The Gray Man's female counterpart, nine feet tall, she projects the glamour of a stunningly beautiful woman and lures human men to their death. Gaunt and emaciated to the point of starvation, her face is long and narrow. Her mouth consumes the entire lower half of her face. She has two rows of sharklike teeth but prefers to feed by caressing her victims, drawing their beauty and vitality out through open sores on her grotesque hands. If she wants to kill in a hurry, she clamps her hands onto human flesh, creating an unbreakable suction. Unlike the Gray Man, she usually quickly kills her victims. In *Shadowfever,* she breaks pattern and preys upon Dani, in retaliation against Mac and Barrons for killing the Gray Man, her lover. Mac makes an unholy pact with her to save Dani.

RHINO-BOYS: Ugly, gray-skinned creatures that resemble rhinoceroses with bumpy, protruding foreheads, barrel-like bodies, stumpy arms and legs, and lipless gashes of mouths with jutting underbites. They are lower-caste Unseelie thugs dispatched primarily as watchdogs and security for high-ranking Fae.

PAPA ROACH (AKA THE ROACH GOD): Made of thousands and thousands of roachlike creatures clambering up on top of one another to form a larger being. The individual bugs feed off human flesh, specifically fat. Consequently, postwall, some women allow them to enter their bodies and live beneath their skin to keep them slim, a symbiotic liposuction. Papa Roach, the collective, is purplish-brown, about four feet tall with thick legs, a half dozen arms, and a head the size of a walnut. It jiggles like gelatin when it moves as its countless individual parts shift minutely to remain coalesced. It has a thin-lipped beaklike mouth and round, lidless eyes.

SHADES: One of the lowest castes, they started out barely sentient but have been evolving since they were freed from their Unseelie prison. They thrive in darkness, can't bear direct light, and hunt at night or in dark places. They steal life in the same manner the Gray Man steals beauty, draining their victims with vampiric swiftness, leaving behind a pile of clothing and a husk of dehydrated human matter. They consume every living thing in their path from the leaves on trees to the worms in the soil.

Seelie

AOIBHEAL, THE SEELIE QUEEN (*see also* Concubine): Fae queen, the last in a long line of queens with an unusual empathy for humans. In *Shadowfever*, it is revealed the queen was once human herself and is the Unseelie king's long-lost concubine and soul mate, Zara. Over half a million years ago the Unseelie prince Cruce drugged her with a cup stolen from the Cauldron of Forgetting, erased her memory, and abducted her, staging it so the Unseelie king believed she was dead. Masquerading as the Seelie prince V'lane, Cruce hid her in the one place he knew the king of the Unseelie would never go—the Seelie Court. Prolonged time in Faery transformed Aoibheal, and she became what the king had desperately desired her to be: Fae and immortal. She is now the latest in a long line of Seelie queens. Tragically, the original Seelie queen was killed by the Unseelie king before she was able to pass on the Song of Making, the most powerful and beautiful of all Fae magic. Without it, the Seelie have changed. In *Burned*, the Unseelie king took the concubine to the White Mansion and imprisoned her inside the boudoir they once shared, in an effort to restore her memory. In *Feversong*, Aoibheal/Zara regains her memory but not emotion and, disgusted at the endless abuse by the Fae, abdicates power to MacKayla Lane, who, later, returns Zara to a mortal state, as she no longer wants to be immortal.

DARROC, LORD MASTER (Seelie turned human): Once Fae and trusted advisor to Aoibheal, he was set up by Cruce and banished from Faery for treason. At the Seelie Court, Adam Black (in the novel *The Immortal Highlander*) was given the choice to have Darroc killed or turned mortal as punishment for trying to free the Unseelie and overthrow the queen. Adam chose to have him turned mortal, believing he would quickly die as a human, sparking the succession of events that culminates in *Faefever* when Darroc destroys the walls between the worlds of man and Fae, setting the long-imprisoned Unseelie free. Once in the mortal realm, Darroc learned to eat Unseelie flesh to achieve power and caught wind of the *Sinsar Dubh*'s existence in the mortal realm. When Alina Lane came to Dublin, Darroc discovered she was a *sidhe*-seer with many talents and, like her sister, Mac, could sense and track the *Sinsar Dubh*. He began by using her but fell in love with her. After Alina's death, Darroc learned of Mac and attempted to use her as well, applying various methods of coercion, including abducting her parents. Once Mac believed Barrons was dead, she teamed up with Darroc, determined to find the *Sinsar Dubh* herself and use it to bring Barrons back. Darroc was killed in *Shadowfever* by K'Vruck, allegedly at the direction of the *Sinsar Dubh*, when the Hunter popped his head like a grape.

SEELIE PRINCES: There were once four princes and four princesses of the royal *sidhe*. The Seelie princesses have not been seen for a long time and are presumed dead. V'lane was killed long ago, Velvet (not his real name) is recently deceased, R'jan currently aspires to be king, and Adam Black is now human. Highly sexual, golden-haired (except for Adam, who assumed a darker glamour), with iridescent eyes and golden skin, they are extremely powerful sifters, capable of sustaining nearly impenetrable glamour, and they affect the climate with their pleasure or displeasure. Currently there are only two Seelie princes alive: Azar, prince of the Autumn Kingdom, and Inspector Jayne (once human, now Fae), who is prince of the Spring Kingdom.

V'LANE: Seelie prince, queen of the Fae's high consort, extremely sexual and erotic. The real V'lane was killed by his own queen when Cruce switched faces and places with him via glamour. Cruce has been masquerading as V'lane ever since, hiding in plain sight.

VELVET: Lesser royalty, cousin to R'jan. He was introduced in *Shadowfever* and killed by Ryodan in *Iced.*

DREE'LIA: Frequent consort of Velvet; was present when the *Sinsar Dubh* was reinterred beneath the abbey.

R'JAN: Seelie prince who would be king. Tall, blond, with the velvety gold skin of a light Fae, he makes his debut in *Iced* when he announces his claim on the Fae throne.

ADAM BLACK: Immortal prince of the D'Jai House and favored consort of the Seelie queen, banished from Faery and made mortal as punishment for one of his countless interferences with the human realm. Has been called the *sin siriche dubh,* or blackest Fae, however undeserved. Rumor holds that Adam was not always Fae, although that has not been substantiated. In *The Immortal Highlander* he is exiled among mortals, falls in love with Gabrielle O'Callaghan, a *sidhe*-seer from Cincinnati, Ohio, and chooses to remain human to stay with her. He refuses to get involved in the current war between man and Fae, as he is fed up with the endless manipulation, seduction, and drama. With Gabrielle, he has a highly gifted and unusual daughter to protect.

THE KELTAR

An ancient bloodline of Highlanders chosen by Queen Aoibheal and trained in druidry to uphold the Compact between the races of man and Fae. Brilliant, gifted in physics and engineering, they live near Inverness and guard a circle of standing stones called Ban Drochaid (the White Bridge), which was used for time travel until the Keltar breached one of their many oaths to the queen and she closed the circle of stones to other times and dimensions. Current Keltar druids are Christopher, Christian, Cian, Dageus, and Drustan.

Druid: In pre-Christian Celtic society, a druid presided over divine worship, legislative and judicial matters, philosophy, and the education of elite youth to their order. Druids were believed to be privy to the secrets of the gods, including issues pertaining to the manipulation of physical matter, space, and even time. The old Irish "drui" means magician, wizard, diviner.

CHRISTOPHER MACKELTAR: Modern-day laird of the Keltar clan, father of Christian MacKeltar.

CHRISTIAN MACKELTAR (turned Unseelie prince): Handsome Scotsman, dark hair, tall, muscular body, and killer smile, he masqueraded as a student at Trinity College, working in the ancient languages department, but was really stationed there by his uncles to keep an eye on Jericho Barrons. Trained as a druid by his clan, he participated in a ritual at Ban Drochaid on Samhain meant to reinforce the walls between the worlds of man and Fae. Unfortunately, the ceremony went badly wrong, leaving Christian and Barrons trapped in the Silvers. When Mac later finds Christian in the Hall of All Days, she feeds him Unseelie flesh to save his life, unwittingly sparking the chain of events that begins to turn the sexy Highlander into an Unseelie prince. He loses himself for a time in madness and fixates on the innocence of Dani O'Malley while losing his humanity. In *Iced*, he sacrifices himself to the Crimson Hag to distract her from killing the *sidhe*-seers, determined to spare Dani from having to choose between saving the abbey or the world, then is staked to the side of a cliff above a hellish grotto to be killed over and over again. In *Burned*, Christian is rescued from the cliff by Mac, Barrons, Ryodan, Jada, Drustan, and Dageus, but Dageus sacrifices himself to save Christian in the process.

CIAN MACKELTAR (*Spell of the Highlander*): Highlander from the twelfth century, he traveled through time to the present day, and is married to Jessica St. James. Cian was imprisoned for one thousand years in one of the Silvers by a vengeful sorcerer. Freed, he now lives with the other Keltar in current-day Scotland.

DAGEUS MACKELTAR (*The Dark Highlander*): Keltar druid from the sixteenth century who traveled through time to the present day, married to Chloe Zanders. He is still inhabited (to an unknown degree) by the souls/knowledge of thirteen dead Draghar, ancient druids who used black sorcery, but has concealed all knowledge of this from his clan. With long black hair nearly to his waist, dark skin, and gold eyes, he is the sexiest and most sexual of the Keltar. In *Burned*, we learn that although he gave his life to save Christian, Ryodan brought him back and is keeping him in a dungeon beneath Chester's.

DRUSTAN MACKELTAR (*Kiss of the Highlander*): Twin brother of Dageus MacKeltar, he also traveled through time to the present day, and is married to Gwen Cassidy. Tall, dark, with long brown hair and silver eyes, he is the ultimate chivalrous knight and would sacrifice himself for the greater good if necessary.

HUMANS

JACK AND RAINEY LANE: Mac and Alina's parents. In *Darkfever,* Mac discovers they are not her biological parents. She and Alina were adopted, and part of the custody agreement was a promise that the girls never be allowed to return to the country of their birth. Jack is a strapping, handsome man, an attorney with a strong sense of ethics. Rainey is a compassionate blond woman who was unable to bear children of her own. She's a steel magnolia, strong yet fragile.

DANCER: Six feet four inches, he has dark, wavy hair and gorgeous aqua eyes. Very mature, intellectually gifted seventeen-year-old who was home-schooled and graduated from college by sixteen with a double major in physics and engineering. Fascinated by physics, he speaks multiple languages and has traveled extensively with wealthy, humanitarian parents. His father is an ambassador, his mother a doctor. He was alone in Dublin, considering Trinity College for grad school, when the walls between realms fell, and has survived by his wits. He is an inventor and can often think circles around most people, including Dani. He seems unruffled by Barrons, Ryodan, and his men. Dani met Dancer near the end of *Shadowfever* (when he gave her a bracelet, the first gift from a guy she liked) and they became inseparable. In *Iced,* Dancer made it clear he has feelings for her. Dancer was the only person Dani feels like she can be herself with: young, a little geeky, a lot brainy. Both he and Dani moved around frequently, never staying in one place too long. They had many hideouts around the city, aboveground and belowground. Dani worried about him because he doesn't have any superpowers. In *Feversong,* Dani finally admitted to her feelings for Dancer, but he had a congenital heart defect and died after they became lovers.

FIONA ASHETON: Beautiful woman in her early fifties who originally managed Barrons Books & Baubles and was deeply in (unrequited) love with Jericho Barrons. Fiendishly jealous of Barrons's interest in MacKayla, she tried to kill Mac by letting Shades (lethal Unseelie) into the bookstore while Mac was sleeping. Barrons exiled her for it, and Fiona then became Derek O'Bannion's lover, began eating Unseelie, and was briefly possessed by the *Sinsar Dubh*, which skinned her from head to toe but left her alive. Due to the amount of Fae flesh Fiona had eaten, she could no longer be killed by human means and was trapped in a mutilated body, in constant agony. Eventually she begged Mac to use her Fae spear and end her suffering. Fiona died in the White Mansion when she flung herself through the ancient Silver used as a doorway between the concubine and the Unseelie king's bedchambers—which kills anyone who enters it except for the king and concubine—but not before trying to kill Mac one last time.

ROARK (ROCKY) O'BANNION: Black Irish Catholic mobster with Saudi ancestry and the compact, powerful body of a heavyweight champion boxer, which he is. Born in a Dublin controlled by two feuding Irish crime families—the Hallorans and O'Kierneys— Roark O'Bannion fought his way to the top in the ring, but it wasn't enough for the ambitious champ; he hungered for more. When Rocky was twenty-eight years old, the Halloran and O'Kierney linchpins were killed along with every son, grandson, and pregnant woman in their families. Twenty-seven people died that night, gunned down, blown up, poisoned, knifed, or strangled. Dublin had never seen anything like it. A group of flawlessly choreographed killers had closed in all over the city, at restaurants, homes, hotels, and clubs, and struck simultaneously. The next day, when a suddenly wealthy Rocky O'Bannion, champion boxer and many a young boy's idol, retired from the ring to take control of various businesses in and around Dublin previously run by the Hallorans and O'Kierneys, he was hailed by the working-class poor as a hero, despite the fresh and obvious blood on his hands and the rough pack of ex-boxers and thugs he brought with him. O'Bannion was devoutly religious and collected sacred artifacts. Mac stole the Spear of Destiny (aka the Spear of Longinus that pierced Christ's side) from him to protect herself, as it is one of two weapons that can kill the immortal Fae. Later, in *Darkfever*, Barrons killed O'Bannion to keep Mac safe from him and his henchmen, but it's not the end of the O'Bannions gunning for Mac.

Derek O'Bannion: Rocky's younger brother, Derek began snooping around Mac and the bookstore after Rocky is murdered, as his brother's car was found behind the bookstore. He became lovers with Fiona Asheton, was ultimately possessed by the *Sinsar Dubh*, and attacked Mac. He was killed by the *Sinsar Dubh* in *Bloodfever*.

Sean O'Bannion: Rocky O'Bannion's cousin and Katarina McLaughlin's childhood sweetheart and adult lover. After the Hallorans and the O'Kierneys were killed by Rocky, the O'Bannions controlled the city for nearly a decade, until the McLaughlins began usurping their turf. Both Sean and Kat despised the family business and refused to participate. The two crime families sought to unite the business with a marriage between them, but when nearly all the McLaughlins were killed after the walls crashed, Katarina and Sean finally felt free. But chaos reigns in a world where humans struggle to obtain simple necessities, and Sean suddenly finds himself part of the black market, competing with Ryodan and the Fae to fairly distribute the supply of food and valuable resources. Kat is devastated to see him doing the wrong things for all the right reasons and it puts a serious strain on their relationship. Sean becomes the Unseelie prince Famine.

Mallucé (aka John Johnstone, Jr.): The geeky son of billionaire parents until he killed them for their fortune and reinvented himself as the steampunk vampire Mallucé. In *Darkfever*, he teamed up with Darroc, the Lord Master, who taught him to eat Unseelie flesh for the strength and enormous sexual stamina and appetite it confers. He was wounded in battle by Mac's Spear of Destiny. Because he'd been eating Unseelie, the lethal prick of the Fae blade caused parts of him to die, killing flesh but not his body, trapping him in a half-rotted, agonizing shell of a body. He appeared to Mac as the Grim Reaper in *Bloodfever*, and after psychologically tormenting her, abducted and held her prisoner in a hellish grotto beneath the Burren in Ireland, where he tortured and nearly killed her. Barrons killed him and saved Mac by feeding her Unseelie flesh, changing her forever.

THE GUARDIANS: Originally Dublin's police force, the Gardaí, under the command of Inspector Jayne. They eat Unseelie to obtain heightened strength, speed, and acuity, and hunt all Fae. They've learned to use iron bullets to temporarily wound them and iron bars to contain them. Most Fae can be significantly weakened by iron. If applied properly, iron can prevent a Fae from being able to sift.

INSPECTOR O'DUFFY: Original Garda on Alina Lane's murder case, brother-in-law to Inspector Jayne. He was killed in *Bloodfever*, his throat slit while holding a scrap of paper with Mac's name and address on it. It is currently unknown who killed him.

INSPECTOR JAYNE: Garda who took over Alina Lane's murder case after Inspector O'Duffy, Jayne's brother-in-law, is killed. Big, raw-boned Irishman who looks like Liam Neeson, he tails Mac and generally complicates her life. Initially, he's more interested in what happened to O'Duffy than solving Alina's case, but Mac treats him to Unseelie-laced tea and opens his eyes to what's going on in their city and world. Jayne joins the fight against the Fae and transforms the Gardaí into the New Guardians, a ruthless army of ex-policemen who eat Unseelie, battle Fae, and protect humans. Jayne is a good man in a hard position. Although he and his men can capture the Fae, they can't kill them without either Mac's or Dani's weapon. In *Iced,* Jayne earns Dani's eternal wrath by stealing her sword when she's too injured to fight back. Ultimately, Jayne becomes the Seelie prince of Spring.

CHARACTERS OF UNKNOWN GENUS

K'Vruck: Allegedly the most ancient of the Unseelie caste of Royal Hunters—although it is not substantiated that he is truly Unseelie. He was once the Unseelie king's favored companion and "steed" as he traveled worlds on its great black wings. Enormous as a small skyscraper, vaguely resembling a dragon, it's coal black, leathery, and icy, with eyes like huge orange furnaces. When it flies, it churns black frosty flakes in the air and liquid ice streams in its wake. It has a special affinity for Mac and appears to her at odd moments as it senses the king inside her (via the *Sinsar Dubh*). When K'Vruck kills, it is the ultimate death, extinguishing life so completely it's forever erased from the karmic cycle. To be K'Vrucked is to be removed completely from existence as if you've never been, no trace, no residue. Mac used K'Vruck to free Barrons's son. K'Vruck is the only being (known so far) capable of killing the immortal Nine.

Shazam: The last remaining Hel-Cat in existence, selected by the Hunters to become one of them. Shazam shifts into the feminine Hunter, Y'rill.

Sweeper: A collector of powerful, broken things, it resembles a giant trash heap of metal cogs and gears, first encountered by the Unseelie king shortly after he lost his concubine and descended into a period of madness and grief. The Sweeper traveled with him for a time, studying him, or perhaps seeing if he, too, could be collected and tinkered with. According to the Unseelie king, it fancies itself a god.

Y'RILL: The Hunter (original form is Shazam) who chooses Dani O'Malley to be her "child."

ZEWs: Acronym for zombie-eating wraiths, so named by Dani O'Malley. Hulking anorexic vulturelike creatures, they are five to six feet tall, with gaunt, hunched bodies and heavily cowled faces. They appear to be wearing cobwebbed black robes but it is actually their skin. They have exposed bone at their sleeves and pale smudges inside their cowls. In *Burned*, Mac catches a glimpse of metal where their faces should be but doesn't get a good look.

PLACES

ARLINGTON ABBEY: An ancient stone abbey located nearly two hours from Dublin, situated on a thousand acres of prime farmland. The mystically fortified abbey houses an order of *sidhe*-seers gathered from six bloodlines of Irish women born with the ability to see the Fae and their realms. The abbey was built in the seventh century and is completely self-sustaining, with multiple artesian wells, livestock, and gardens. According to historical records, the land occupied by the abbey was previously a church, and before that a sacred circle of stones, and long before that a fairy shian, or mound. *Sidhe*-seer legend suggests the Unseelie king himself spawned their order, mixing his blood with that of six Irish houses, to create protectors for the one thing he should never have made—the *Sinsar Dubh*.

ASHFORD, GEORGIA: MacKayla Lane's small, rural hometown in the Deep South.

BARRONS BOOKS & BAUBLES: Located on the outskirts of Temple Bar in Dublin, Barrons Books & Baubles is an Old World bookstore previously owned by Jericho Barrons, now owned by Mac-

Kayla Lane. It shares design characteristics with the Lello Bookstore in Portugal, but is somewhat more elegant and refined. Due to the location of a large Sifting Silver in the study on the first floor, the bookstore's dimensions can shift from as few as four stories to as many as seven, and rooms on the upper levels often reposition themselves. It is where MacKayla Lane calls home.

BARRONS'S GARAGE: Located directly behind Barrons Books & Baubles, it houses a collection of expensive cars. Far beneath it, accessible only through the heavily warded Silver in the bookstore, are Jericho Barrons's living quarters.

THE BRICKYARD: The bar in Ashford, Georgia, where MacKayla Lane bartended before she came to Dublin.

CHESTER'S NIGHTCLUB: An enormous underground club of chrome and glass located at 939 Rêvemal Street. Chester's is owned by one of Barrons's associates, Ryodan. The upper levels are open to the public; the lower levels contain the Nine's residences and their private clubs. Since the walls between man and Fae fell, Chester's has become the hot spot in Dublin for Fae and humans to mingle.

DARK ZONE: An area that has been taken over by the Shades, deadly Unseelie that suck the life from humans, leaving only a husk of skin and indigestible matter such as eyeglasses, wallets, and medical implants. During the day it looks like an everyday abandoned, run-down neighborhood. Once night falls it's a death trap. The largest known Dark Zone in Dublin is adjacent to Barrons Books & Baubles and is nearly twenty by thirteen city blocks.

FAERY: A general term encompassing the many realms of the Fae.

HALL OF ALL DAYS: The "airport terminal" of the Sifting Silvers where one can choose which mirror to enter to travel to other worlds and realms. Fashioned of gold from floor to ceiling, the endless corridor is lined with billions of mirrors that are portals to alternate universes and times, and it exudes a chilling spatial-temporal distortion that makes a visitor feel utterly inconsequential. Time isn't linear in the hall, it's malleable and slippery, and a visitor can get permanently lost in memories that never were and dreams of futures that will never be. One moment you feel terrifyingly alone, the next as if an endless chain of paper-doll versions of oneself is unfolding sideways, holding cutout construction-paper hands with thousands of different feet in thousands of different worlds, all at the same time. Compounding the many dangers of the hall, when the Silvers were corrupted by Cruce's curse (intended to bar entry to the Unseelie king), the mirrors were altered, and now the image they present is no longer a guarantee of what's on the other side. A lush rain forest may lead to a parched, cracked desert, a tropical oasis to a world of ice, but one can't count on total opposites either.

THE RIVER LIFFEY: The river that divides Dublin into south and north sections, and supplies most of Dublin's water.

TEMPLE BAR DISTRICT: An area in Dublin also known simply as "Temple Bar," in which the Temple Bar Pub is located, along with an endless selection of boisterous drinking establishments including the famed Oliver St. John Gogarty, the Quays Bar, the Foggy Dew, the Brazen Head, Buskers, the Purty Kitchen, the Auld Dubliner, and so on. On the south bank of the River Liffey, Temple Bar (the district) sprawls for blocks, and has two meeting squares that used to be overflowing with tourists and partiers. Countless street musicians, great restaurants and shops, local bands, and raucous stag and hen parties made Temple Bar the *craic*-filled center of the city.

TEMPLE BAR PUB: A quaint, famous pub named after Sir William Temple, who once lived there. Founded in 1840, it squats bright red and cozy, draped with string lights, at the corner of Temple Bar

Street and Temple Lane, and rambles from garden to alcove to main room. The famous pub boasts a first-rate whisky collection, a beer garden for smoking, legendary Dublin Bay oysters, perfectly stacked Guinness, terrific atmosphere, and the finest traditional Irish music in the city.

TRINITY COLLEGE: Founded in 1592, located on College Green, and recognized as one of the finest universities in the world, it houses a library that contains more than 4.5 million printed volumes including spectacular works such as the *Book of Kells*. It's ranked in the world's top one hundred universities for physics and mathematics, with state-of-the-art laboratories and equipment. Dancer does much of his research on the now abandoned college campus.

UNSEELIE PRISON: Located in the Unseelie king's realm, close to his fortress of black ice, the prison once held all Unseelie captives for more than half a million years in a stark, arctic prison of ice. When the walls between man and Faery were destroyed by Darroc (a banished Seelie prince with a vendetta against the Seelie queen), all the Unseelie were freed to invade the human realms.

THE WHITE MANSION: Located inside the Silvers, the house that the Unseelie king built for his beloved concubine. Enormous, ever-changing, the mansion has many halls and rooms that rearrange themselves at will.

THINGS

AMULET: Also called the One True Amulet. *See* The Four Unseelie Hallows.

AMULETS, THE THREE LESSER: Amulets created prior to the One True Amulet, these objects are capable of weaving and sustaining nearly impenetrable illusion when used together. Currently in the possession of Cruce.

COMPACT: Agreement negotiated between Queen Aoibheal and the MacKeltar clan (Keltar means "hidden barrier or mantle") long ago to keep the realms of mankind and Fae separate. The Seelie queen taught the MacKeltar clan to tithe and perform rituals that would reinforce the walls that were compromised when the original queen used a portion of them to create the Unseelie prison.

CRIMSON RUNES: This enormously powerful and complex magic formed the foundation of the walls of the Unseelie prison and is offered by the *Sinsar Dubh* to MacKayla on several occasions to use to protect herself. All Fae fear them. When the walls between man and Fae began to weaken long ago, the Seelie queen tapped into the prison walls, siphoning some of their power, which she used to reinforce the boundaries between worlds . . . thus dangerously weakening the prison walls. It was at that time the first Unseelie began to escape. The more one struggles against the crimson runes, the stronger they grow, feeding off the energy expended in the victim's effort to escape. MacKayla used them in *Shadowfever* to seal the *Sinsar Dubh* shut until Cruce, posing as V'lane, persuaded her to remove them. The beast form of Jericho Barrons eats these runes and seems to consider them a delicacy.

CUFF OF CRUCE: A cuff made of silver and gold, set with bloodred stones; an ancient Fae relic that protects the wearer against all Fae and many other creatures. Cruce claims he made it, not the king, and that he gave it to the king as a gift to give his lover. According to Cruce, its powers were dual: it not only protected the concubine from threats, but allowed her to summon him by merely touching it, thinking of the king, and wishing for his presence.

DOLMEN: A single-chamber megalithic tomb constructed of three or more upright stones supporting a large, flat, horizontal capstone. Dolmens are common in Ireland, especially around the Burren and Connemara. The Lord Master used a dolmen in a ritual of dark magic to open a doorway between realms and bring through Unseelie.

THE DREAMING: It's where all hopes, fantasies, illusions, and nightmares of sentient beings come to be or go to rest, whichever you prefer to believe. No one knows where the Dreaming came from or who created it. It is far more ancient even than the Fae. Since Cruce cursed the Silvers and the Hall of All Days was corrupted, the Dreaming can be accessed via the hall, though with enormous difficulty.

ELIXIR OF LIFE: Both the Seelie queen and Unseelie king have a version of this powerful potion. The Seelie queen's version can make a human immortal (though it will not bestow the grace and power of being Fae). It is currently unknown what the king's version does, but it's reasonable to expect that, as the imperfect song used to fashion his court, it is also flawed in some way.

THE FOUR STONES: Chiseled from the blue-black walls of the Unseelie prison, these four stones have the ability to contain the *Sinsar Dubh* in place if positioned properly, rendering its power inert, allowing it to be transported safely. The stones contain the Book's magic and immobilize it completely, preventing it from being able to possess the person transporting it. They are capable of immobilizing it in any form, including MacKayla Lane, as she has the Book inside her. They are etched with ancient runes and react with many other Fae objects of power. When united, they sing a lesser Song of Making. Not nearly as powerful as the crimson runes, they can contain only the *Sinsar Dubh*.

GLAMOUR: Illusion cast by the Fae to camouflage their true appearance. The more powerful the Fae, the more difficult it is to penetrate its disguise. Average humans see only what the Fae want them to see and are subtly repelled from bumping into or brushing against it by a small perimeter of spatial distortion that is part of the Fae glamour.

THE HALLOWS: Eight ancient artifacts created by the Fae possessing enormous power. There are four Seelie and four Unseelie Hallows.

The Four Seelie Hallows

THE SPEAR OF LUISNE: Also known as the Spear of Luin, Spear of Longinus, Spear of Destiny, the Flaming Spear, it is one of two Hallows capable of killing Fae. Currently in the possession of MacKayla Lane.

THE SWORD OF LUGH: Also known as the Sword of Light, the second Hallow capable of killing Fae. Currently in the possession of Danielle O'Malley.

THE CAULDRON: Also called the Cauldron of Forgetting. The Fae are subject to a type of madness that sets in at advanced years. They drink from the Cauldron to erase all memory and begin fresh. None but the Scribe, Cruce, and the Unseelie king, who have never drunk from the Cauldron, know the true history of their race. Currently located at the Seelie Court. Cruce stole a cup from the Cauldron of Forgetting and tricked the concubine/Aoibheal into drinking it, thereby erasing all memory of the king and her life before the moment the cup touched her lips.

THE STONE: Little is known of this Seelie Hallow.

The Four Unseelie Hallows

THE AMULET: Created by the Unseelie king for his concubine so that she could manipulate reality as well as a Fae. Fashioned of gold, silver, sapphires, and onyx, the gilt "cage" of the amulet houses an enormous clear stone of unknown composition. It can be used by a person of epic will to impact and reshape perception. The list of past owners is legendary, including Merlin, Boudicca, Joan of Arc, Charlemagne, and Napoleon. This amulet is capable of weaving an illusion that will deceive even the Unseelie king. In *Shadowfever*, MacKayla Lane used it to defeat the *Sinsar Dubh*. Currently stored in Barrons's lair beneath the garage, locked away for safekeeping.

THE SILVERS: An elaborate network of mirrors created by the Unseelie king, once used as the primary method of Fae travel between realms. The central hub for the Silvers is the Hall of All Days, an infinite gilded corridor where time is not linear, filled with mirrors of assorted shapes and sizes that are portals to other worlds, places, and times. Before Cruce cursed the Silvers, whenever a traveler stepped through a mirror at a perimeter location, he was instantly translated to the hall, where he could then choose a new destination from the images the mirrors displayed. After Cruce cursed the Silvers, the mirrors in the hall were compromised and no longer accurately display their true destinations. It's highly dangerous to travel within the Silvers.

THE BOOK (See also *Sinsar Dubh;* she-suh DOO): A fragment of the Unseelie king himself, a sentient, psychopathic book of enormous, dark magic created when the king tried to expel the corrupt arts with which he'd tampered, trying to re-create the Song of Making. The Book was originally a nonsentient, spelled object, but in the way of the Fae it evolved and over time became sentient, living, conscious. When it did, like all Unseelie created via an imperfect song, it was obsessed by a desire to complete itself, to obtain a corporeal body for its consciousness, to become like others of its kind. It usually presents itself in one of three forms: an innocuous hardcover book; a thick, gilded, magnificent ancient tome with runes and locks; or a monstrous amorphous beast. It temporarily achieves corporeality by possessing humans, but the human host rejects it and the body self-destructs quickly. The *Sinsar Dubh* usually toys with its hosts, uses them to vent its sadistic rage, then kills them and jumps to a new body (or jumps to a new body and uses it to kill them). The closest it has ever come to obtaining a body was by imprinting a full copy of itself in Mac as an unformed fetus while it possessed her mother. Since the *Sinsar Dubh*'s presence has been inside Mac from the earliest stages of her life, her body chemistry doesn't sense it as an intruder and reject it. She can survive its possession without it destroying her. Still, the original *Sinsar Dubh* craves a body of its own and for Mac to embrace her copy so that it will finally be flesh and blood and have a mate.

The Box: Little is known of this Unseelie Hallow. Legend says the Unseelie king created it for his concubine.

The Haven: High Council and advisors to the Grand Mistress of the abbey, made up of the seven most talented, powerful *sidhe*-seers. Twenty years ago it was led by Mac's mother, Isla O'Connor, but the Haven got wind of Rowena tampering with black arts and suspected she'd been seduced by the *Sinsar Dubh,* which was locked away beneath the abbey in a heavily warded cavern. They discovered she'd been entering the forbidden chamber, talking with it. They formed a second, secret Haven to monitor Rowena's activities, which included Rowena's own daughter and Isla's best friend, Kayleigh. The Haven was right: Rowena had been corrupted and ultimately freed the *Sinsar Dubh.* It is unknown who carried it from the abbey the night the Book escaped or where it was for the next two decades.

IFP: Interdimensional Fairy Pothole, created when the walls between man and Faery fell and chunks of reality fragmented. They exist also within the network of Silvers, the result of Cruce's curse. Translucent, funnel-shaped, with narrow bases and wide tops, they are difficult to see and drift unless tethered. There is no way to determine what type of environment exists inside one until you've stepped through, extreme climate excepted.

IRON: "Fe" on the periodic table, painful to Fae. Iron bars can contain nonsifting Fae. Properly spelled iron can constrain a sifting Fae to a degree. Iron cannot kill a Fae.

MACHALO: Invented by MacKayla Lane, a bike helmet with LED lights affixed to it. Designed to protect the wearer from the vampiric Shades by casting a halo of light all around the body.

NULL: A *sidhe*-seer with the power to freeze a Fae with the touch of his or her hands (MacKayla Lane has this talent). While frozen, a nulled Fae is completely powerless, but the higher and more powerful the caste of Fae, the shorter the length of time it stays immobilized. It can still see, hear, and think while frozen, making it very dangerous to be in its vicinity when the Fae is unfrozen.

POSTE HASTE, INC.: A bicycling courier service headquartered in Dublin that is actually the Order of *Sidhe*-Seers. It was founded by Rowena, who established an international branch of PHI in countries all over the world to stay apprised of all developments globally.

PRI-YA: A human who is sexually addicted to and enslaved by the Fae. The royal castes of Fae are so sexual and erotic that sex with them is addictive and destructive to the human mind. It creates a painful, debilitating, insatiable need in a human. The royal castes can, if they choose, diminish their impact during sex and make it merely stupendous. But if they don't, it overloads human senses and turns the human into a sex addict, incapable of thought or speech, capable only of serving the sexual pleasures of whomever is their master. Since the walls fell, many humans have been turned Pri-ya, and society is trying to deal with these wrecked humans in a way that doesn't involve incarcerating them in padded cells, in mindless misery.

SHAMROCK: This slightly misshapen three-leaf clover is the ancient symbol of the *sidhe*-seers, who are charged with the mission to See, Serve, and Protect mankind from the Fae. In *Bloodfever*, Rowena shares the history of the emblem with Mac: "Before it was the clover of Saint Patrick's trinity, it was ours. It's the emblem of our order. It's the symbol our ancient sisters used to carve on their doors and dye into banners millennia ago when they moved to a new village. It was our way of letting the inhabitants know who we were and what we were there to do. When people saw our sign, they declared a time of great feasting and celebrated for a fortnight. They welcomed us with gifts of their finest food, wine, and men. They held tournaments to compete to bed us. It is not a clover at all, but a vow. You see how these two leaves make a sideways figure eight, like a horizontal Möbius strip? They are two S's, one right side up, one upside down, ends meeting. The third leaf and stem is an upright P. The first S is for See, the second for Serve, the P for Protect. The shamrock itself is the symbol of Eire, the great Ireland. The Möbius strip is our pledge of guardianship eternal. We are the *sidhe*-seers and we watch over mankind. We protect them from the Old Ones. We stand between this world and all the others."

SIFTING: Fae method of travel. The higher ranking, most powerful Fae are able to translocate from place to place at the speed of thought. Once they could travel through time as well as place, but Aoibheal stripped that power from them for repeated offenses.

SINSAR DUBH (**AKA THE BOOK**): Originally designed as an ensorcelled tome, it was intended to be the inert repository or dumping ground for all the Unseelie king's arcane knowledge of a flawed, toxic Song of Making. It was with this knowledge he created the Unseelie Court and castes. The Book contains an enormous amount of dangerous magic that can create and destroy worlds. Like the king, its power is nearly limitless. Unfortunately, as with all Fae things, the Book, drenched with magic, changed and evolved until it achieved full sentience. No longer a mere book, it is a homicidal, psychopathic, starved, and power-hungry being. Like the rest of the imperfect Unseelie, it wants to finish or perfect itself, to attain that which it perceives it lacks: in this case, the perfect host body. When the king realized the Book had become sentient, he created a prison for it and made the *sidhe*-seers—some say by tampering with their bloodline, lending a bit of his own—to guard it and keep it from ever escaping. The king realized that rather than eradicating the dangerous magic, he'd managed only to create a copy of it. Much like the king, the *Sinsar Dubh* found a way to create a copy of itself and planted it inside an unborn fetus, MacKayla Lane. There are currently two *Sinsar Dubh*s: one that Cruce absorbed (or became possessed by), and the copy inside MacKayla Lane that she refuses to open. As long as she never voluntarily seeks or takes a single spell from it, it can't take her over and she won't be possessed. If, however, she uses it for any reason, she will be obliterated by the psychopathic villain trapped inside it, forever silenced. With the long-starved and imprisoned *Sinsar Dubh* free, life for humans will become Hell on Earth. Unfortunately, the Book is highly charismatic, brilliant, and seductive, and has observed humanity long enough to exploit human weaknesses like a maestro.

SONG OF MAKING: The greatest power in the universe, this song can create life from nothing. All life stems from it. It was originally known by the first Seelie queen, but she rarely used it because, as with all great magic, it demands a great price. It was to be passed from queen to queen, to be used only when absolutely necessary to protect and sustain life. To hear this song is to experience Heaven on Earth, to know the how, when, and why of our existence, and simultaneously have no need to know it at all. The melody is allegedly so beautiful, transformative, and pure that if one who harbors evil in his heart hears it, he will be charred to ash where he stands.

UNSEELIE FLESH: Eating Unseelie flesh endows an average human with enormous strength, power, and sensory acuity; it heightens sexual pleasure and stamina; and is highly addictive. It also lifts the veil between worlds and permits a human to see past the glamour worn by the Fae, to see their actual forms. Before the walls fell, all Fae concealed themselves with glamour. After the walls fell, they didn't care, but now Fae are beginning to conceal themselves again, as humans have learned that the common element iron is useful in injuring and imprisoning them.

VOICE: A druid art or skill that compels the person it's being used on to precisely obey the letter of whatever command is issued. Dageus, Drustan, and Cian MacKeltar are fluent in it. Jericho Barrons taught Darroc (for a price) and also trained MacKayla Lane to use and withstand it. Teacher and apprentice become immune to each other and can no longer be compelled.

WARD: A powerful magic known to druids, sorcerers, *sidhe*-seers, and Fae. There are many categories, including but not limited to Earth, Air, Fire, Stone, and Metal wards. Barrons is adept at placing wards, more so than any of the Nine besides Daku.

WECARE: An organization founded after the walls between man and Fae fell, using food, supplies, and safety as a lure to draw followers. Rainey Lane works with them and sees only the good in the organization, possibly because it's the only place she can harness resources to rebuild Dublin and run her Green-Up group. Someone in WeCare authors the *Dublin Daily,* a local newspaper to compete with the *Dani Daily;* whoever does it dislikes Dani a great deal and is always ragging on her. Not much is known about this group. They lost some of their power when three major players began raiding them and stockpiling supplies.

ABOUT THE AUTHOR

KAREN MARIE MONING is the #1 *New York Times* best-selling author of the Fever series, featuring MacKayla Lane, and the award-winning Highlander series. She has a bachelor's degree in society and law from Purdue University.

karenmoning.com
Facebook.com/KarenMarieMoningfan
Twitter: @KarenMMoning

ABOUT THE TYPE

This book was set in Caslon, a typeface first designed in 1722 by William Caslon (1692–1766). Its widespread use by most English printers in the early eighteenth century soon supplanted the Dutch typefaces that had formerly prevailed. The roman is considered a "workhorse" typeface due to its pleasant, open appearance, while the italic is exceedingly decorative.